As a child, **Fiona Harper** was constantly teased for two things: having her nose in a book and living in a dream world. Things haven't changed much since then, but at least she's found a career that puts her runaway imagination to use!

Fiona loves dancing, so clear the floor if you're ever at a party with her, and her current creative craze (one of a long list!) is jewellery making. She loves good books, good films and good food, especially anything cinnamon-flavoured, and she can *always* find room in her diet for chocolate or champagne!

Fiona loves to hear from readers and you can contact her through fiona@fionaharper.com or find her on her Facebook page (Fiona Harper Romance Author) or tweet her! (@ FiHarperAuthor)

Make my Wish Come True

FIONA HARPER

MILLS & BOON

Mills & Boon, an imprint of Harlequin (UK) Limited,
Eton House, 18-24 Paradise Road, Richmond, Surrey TW9 1SR

© Fiona Harper 2013

ISBN: 978 0 263 91029 2

097-1113

Printed and bound by
CPI Group (UK) Ltd, Croydon, CR0 4YY

ACKNOWLEDGEMENTS

Thank you to both Anna Boatman and Anna Baggaley, who are both brilliant editors and lovely to work with. To all the team at Harlequin UK, for giving me the chance to write the kind of books I've always dreamed of writing. Also, to my very first editor at Harlequin, Kim Young. I know I wouldn't be taking the next step in my career if it hadn't been for her support and belief in me. I'd also like to say a big thank you to my amazing agent, Lizzy Kremer.

I'd especially like to thank Daisy Cummins for allowing me to pick her brains on the work of an assistant director and for the invaluable insider information on the film industry. I'd also like to say a cheeky thank-you to my sister, Kirsteen, my step-sisters, Justine and Alexandra, and to both my daughters, for helping to give me plenty of insight into the complicated, wonderful, exasperating, but ultimately inspiring, world of sisterhood. I love you all, and I couldn't have written this book without you.

For my go-to girls—
Donna and Barbara, and Heidi and Daisy

&

PROLOGUE

Christmas 1981

Juliet sat on the brown velour sofa, her arms folded across her chest, and watched her sister play amidst the wreckage of wrapping paper and discarded curling ribbon. Gemma's fair curls bounced as she chatted away to her new dolly and brushed its hair. Juliet glanced at her digital calculator, still in its packaging, sitting beside her on the sofa and felt a little bit sick.

That doll had been on *her* Christmas wish list, not Gemma's. Mummy must have got mixed up somehow. But Daddy said Mummy was a bit sad at the moment, and it made her do strange things.

Gemma stopped brushing the doll's hair and looked up. 'When's dinner?' she asked. 'I'm hungry.'

Juliet looked at the clock on the mantelpiece. It said ten past four. She was hungry too. Christmas lunch should have been hours ago. She wanted to go and ask Daddy, but last time she'd ventured into the kitchen he'd been hunched over the table, crying softly.

'Soon,' she told Gemma, trying to smile.

Her sister nodded and returned to fussing with her doll. Juliet just sat there, feeling even sicker.

After a few moments, Gemma stood up and picked up the doll. 'I'm going to go and show Mummy what I've done with Georgina's hair,' she said.

Juliet jumped off the sofa and stood in the doorway. This is what she'd been dreading. 'Not right now,' she told Gemma softly. 'Mummy had to go out for a bit.'

Gemma's eyebrows lifted in surprise, but she didn't question her older sister's words. That was because she was five. Juliet was nine and she was a big enough girl to know the truth. Daddy had said so. He'd also said Gemma was too little, that she wouldn't understand, and that it was Juliet's job to make sure she didn't find out.

A sudden image of her mother running from the house, raw stuffing still clinging to her fingers, then jumping into the car and driving away left Juliet feeling breathless and shaky, but Gemma glanced back up at her, eyes so large and trusting, and she covered it all over with a smile.

'Is she coming back soon?' her sister asked, only half-interested in Juliet's answer as she started twisting the doll's hair, attempting her own five-year-old version of a plait.

Juliet kept smiling, even though it felt like her insides were being sucked into a big dark hole.

'Yes,' she said, and blinked back the moisture that had gathered in the corner of her eyes.

She bent down a little bit so she was on Gemma's level. 'If you want, I'll show you how to plait Georgina's hair properly, and then you can show Mummy when she comes home.'

Gemma threw her arms round Juliet's neck and squeezed her hard. 'You're such a good big sister, Juliet! I love you.'

People liked Gemma the best because she was cute and 'bubbly'. Juliet didn't know exactly what that meant, but she suspected it meant not shy and nervous, like she was. Sometimes she wished Gemma was different, but right now she understood why people liked it when her little sister directed all that enthusiastic affection at them.

She *was* a good big sister, wasn't she? And she would keep on being a good big sister, the best she could be.

She sat down cross-legged on the carpet and Gemma sank down beside her. Juliet took the doll and with a frown of concentration began to braid its hair. 'Here,' she said, 'this is how you do it ...'

And once she'd shown Gemma, she let her have a go too. And while her sister chatted and plaited, her chubby little fingers almost tying themselves in knots, Juliet glanced towards the living-room door.

Maybe while Gemma was busy she ought to go and see if Daddy needed help cooking the dinner. Somebody had to do it. And she didn't know if Mummy was ever coming back.

&

CHAPTER ONE

Juliet stopped and let the shoppers flow round her as she reached into her handbag and pulled out her Christmas note-book. She got a rush of warmth, of comfort, every time she picked it up, and this occasion was no different. She smiled as she looked at the pretty botanical print of poinsettia on the cover.

Other people had Christmas wish lists, but Juliet didn't go in for wishing much these days. Wishing didn't get you anywhere. If things were going to be perfect, you needed to plan, make lists, research. Juliet was very keen on making Christmas perfect, and this book was her road map, her shining beacon in the midst of all the festive chaos. It was diary, organiser, address book and To Do list all rolled into one, and once November came around it hardly left her side. She flipped it open and quickly found the page with today's shopping list, marked with a colourful sticky tag.

Ah, yes.

Glacé cherries for the Rudolph cupcakes she'd promised to make for the Christmas Fayre, cinnamon sticks and cloves for mulling apple juice after the church carol service, two more rolls of Sellotape and a metre of red velvet ribbon.

She slid her book carefully back into her bag and began to

dart through the Christmas shoppers with nimble ease, spotting gaps before they properly appeared, judging who was going to keep moving and who was going to stop and marvel at the pretty Christmas lights.

And marvel they should. Juliet was very proud of her hometown, and Tunbridge Wells was at its prettiest this time of year. No wonder so many of the supermarket chains and department stores filmed their big-budget Christmas adverts here every October. The Pantiles was the location of choice – one of the town's oldest streets with its Victorian and Georgian buildings, its little shops nestling beneath the two-hundred-year-old colonnade. White lights hung between the white pillars and twisted round the branches of the trees that ran down the centre of the paved street, and every shop window was immaculately decorated with greenery and tempting Christmas fare. The scent of mulled wine and roasting chestnuts drifted from the traders in the market.

But Juliet really didn't have time to stop and stare, to marvel or smell anything this afternoon. Her Christmas notebook was calling to her from inside her bag, tugging at her consciousness, reminding her of all the unticked boxes on her To Do list that were waiting hungrily to be filled.

She glanced at the old-fashioned clock mounted above one of the boutiques. Ten past two, and she had to be at the boys' school by three twenty. Once she'd got her shopping, she needed to post a parcel for her elderly neighbour and then she'd just about have enough time to dash to the butchers and order the turkey.

That lovely plump bird was the linchpin to Christmas dinner. Crossing off that item would start a chain reaction throughout her To Do list, leaving it awash with little ticks. The thought made her slightly giddy. However, she was distracted from the image of all of those satisfied little boxes by strains of 'All I Want for Christmas Is You' belting out from inside her handbag.

Gemma?

Juliet stopped walking and rummaged for her mobile.

Not Gemma.

Just St Martin's primary, sending out an all-parent alert that head lice were rife in the school again. Great. With four heads to check she'd be spending the whole evening with a nit comb in her hand. A complete time suck. Just what she needed at the moment.

She closed the message and searched the display for a hint of any other new communication, but nothing flashed, nothing beeped. No new icons had appeared. She tucked the phone back inside her bag, angrier at her sister than she'd already had been. What had she expected?

Oh, she knew what Gemma's working day was like, how difficult it was to make or receive personal calls, that she often only got a few seconds to reply to texts late at night. She bragged about it often enough when she made one of her 'flying visits' home.

No, that was being unkind.

Gemma didn't really brag. It was just the way she told her stories about working on film sets, meeting exciting people, visiting exotic locations …Well, it was probably hard not to let it sound as if you were the kind of person who was much more interesting than the average suburban housewife.

The last time she'd seen Gemma had been at the bank

holiday barbecue in August. Juliet had finally managed to corner her and ask her to pull her weight this Christmas. Much to her surprise, Gemma had agreed, but now there was total radio silence. Once again, Gemma was AWOL when anything family-related was on the cards.

The whole situation was starting to give Juliet a horrible sinking feeling. With the promise of extra help, she might have gone a bit overboard once the Christmas preparations had got underway. Now it wasn't just a case of *wanting* her sister to display some sisterly loyalty; she might actually have to rely on her, and that was a very scary thought.

No need to panic yet, though. It was still only the first Friday in December and Gemma was due back in just over a week. She could manage until then. But maybe she'd send her sister another little reminder, just to make sure she didn't forget there were things they needed to discuss …

She stared at her phone. What she really wanted to ask was why Gemma did everything she could to stay away from her family, even at Christmas, but she feared that it might only make Gemma run away faster and harder. Juliet exhaled slowly. Now was not the time to confront that issue, so instead she just fired off a jaunty little text – no demands, no pressure – and then she slid her phone back into her bag and started walking in the direction of the post office.

She'd only gone a dozen steps when her phone rang a second time. Now *this* was probably Gemma. When you wanted her she was nowhere to be found, and when you gave up waiting and carried on without her, suddenly she'd appear and throw all your careful plans into chaos. Typical.

'Yes?' she said, perhaps a little too sharply.

'Mrs Taylor?'

The voice was low and rich, with the timbre of authority to it. Definitely not Gemma.

'Yes?' she said again, trying to sound more like an upstanding citizen than a fishwife.

'This is PC Graham from Tunbridge Wells police station.'

Oh, God! Was everyone all right? The kids! Had there been an accident with the twins? Or had Violet bunked off with some of those new friends she'd started hanging around with? And she couldn't even begin to imagine what kind of scrape too-independent-for-her-own good Polly might have got herself into.

She couldn't seem to speak. Couldn't seem to ask the police officer any of that. She just made a tight little croaking noise that he must have taken as an invitation to carry on.

'It's regarding Sylvia Wade … She's your great-aunt, I believe?'

Juliet cleared her throat and forced down her panic. Somebody needed her. This was no time to get all hysterical.

'Can you tell me what's happened? Is she hurt?'

'Don't worry, she's … fine.' She heard the officer take a deep breath. 'Fighting fit, actually,' he added with a wry hint to his tone. 'I just think you need to get down to the Leisure Centre as soon as you can.'

*

Gemma rapped on the trailer door – loud enough to be heard, but not so firmly it might be interpreted as a demand. As she waited the icy wind cut into her cheeks and her knuckles froze into a fist. Glamorous job? Hah! Don't make her laugh. She pulled the hood of her waterproof closer round her face and got ready to smile brightly.

He wouldn't open the door himself, of course. Too used to having a faceless someone to do it for him.

She knocked a second time and her phone buzzed in her pocket. She ignored it. Even if it was the director, ranting and raving about the whereabouts of his A-list actor, answering it would only slow her down.

It seemed an age before she heard a muffled 'Yeah?' from the other side of the trailer door. If she'd gone by tone of voice alone, she'd have guessed he was soaking up the sun on a Caribbean beach, not freezing to death on the fringes of Western Ireland in December.

A wall of heat hit her when she stepped inside. No wonder he sounded so relaxed. The temperature in here really was verging on tropical. It was certainly warm enough for the six-foot hunk of blond gorgeousness she'd come looking for to only be dressed in a faded T-shirt and a pair of shorts as he lounged on a sofa further down the trailer. She closed the door behind her and instantly started to sweat in her layers of thermals and assorted woolly things.

'Hey, Gemma,' he said, and smiled, revealing his far too white teeth. For some reason she found all that symmetry slightly irritating.

Even more irritating was the state of his undress. He was supposed to be wearing the dark garb the wardrobe department had carefully selected to suggest a tortured hero on the verge of saving the world. However, she let none of her annoyance bleed through to her tone of voice. 'They're ready for you on set now, Toby.' Her face was a mask of calm as she re-jigged times and schedules in the back of her head.

If she could hurry him along, they might not lose any filming time before the light went. She'd had to change the call sheet for the following day three times already. The last batch of A4 sheets sat ready and waiting in her makeshift office and she really didn't want to dump them and start all over again.

She glanced around. Where was the girl from wardrobe? She'd seen her come in here not half an hour ago, and she could have sworn she hadn't seen her leave. 'Has Caitlin gone to fetch something from the truck?' she asked innocently.

Toby just smirked and his eyes darted towards the back of the trailer where the bedroom was situated. 'Something like that.'

Gemma's stomach sank and she visualised dropping her call sheets into the waste-paper basket one by one, calling Tobias Thornton, action star and sex god, every name under the sun as she did so.

As great as her job was, she occasionally wished she didn't work in the film industry. It spoilt all the fantasy. When this film came out, her friends would make her go and see it with them so she could tell them all the gossip and inside secrets, but while they sat in the dark and sighed at Toby's drop-dead smile and killer abs, all she'd be thinking about was how many times she'd come close to wiping that smile off his face with her clipboard.

What she wouldn't give for a real hero, the kind of man these actors pretended to be, but never were. The problem was that she always chose men who *seemed* dynamic and exciting, but eventually turned out to be a little ... well, flaky.

There was a thud from somewhere near the bedroom and the wardrobe assistant emerged, holding a pair of dark trousers. 'Oh, hi ...' she said airily. Too airily for the blotchy blush creeping up her neck. 'I was just ... you know ... doing some emergency repairs on Toby's leathers.' She shot him a nervous look and giggled.

That *could* have explained Toby's trouserless state and the slight delay, but Gemma doubted it. Caitlin's hair was all mussed up and her sweater was on inside out.

She said nothing. She didn't care what they got up to – although she'd thought Cait had a bit more sense. All she cared about was getting one hot film star back into his leathers and onto a speeding motorbike.

'All fixed now?' she asked, checking her watch yet again.

Caitlin nodded.

'Great. Then perhaps you could help Toby *into* his clothes, so we can get going?' She hadn't been able to help that little inflection. Too tempting. But to take any sting out of the comment, she teamed it up with her best Second Assistant Director smile. Her secret weapon.

Toby and Caitlin exchanged guilty glances and then he ran a hand through his hair, looking just the tiniest bit sheepish.

Job done. In one smooth move she'd let them know she wasn't a pushover, but that she also wasn't going to get her knickers in a twist about it – as long as Toby was out of that trailer door in full costume in the next five minutes, of course.

The wry smile he gave her said: *Message received and understood.*

She smiled back, a real one this time, and pulled her hood up over her hair, only to discover that in the heat of the trailer her curls had frizzed to twice their usual volume. Fabulous. She jammed her hood over the fluff and headed for the door, bracing herself, and then she was out into the driving wind, clutching her coat closed as she trudged across the car park of the Victorian hunting lodge they were using as their base. She didn't even take a moment to drink in the rugged scenery: the choppy, grey lough and the ancient rugged mountain that towered over it. She *did* use the opportunity to mutter a few choice words into the wind, words concerning toddler-brained actors, weather that seemed to have a personal vendetta against her and anything else that came to mind.

The warmth of Toby's trailer had made coming back out into the freezing cold even worse, which didn't improve her mood much. It also sparked a longing within her.

She wished she really was lazing on a palm-fringed beach. The urge to jump on a plane and do just that when this shoot was finished was becoming irresistible.

It had been a long job, maybe that was it. She really deserved a quiet, relaxing Christmas when this was all over, before she jumped on another plane to another far-flung location and it started all over again. She sighed. That sunlounger on a Caribbean beach was practically calling her name.

If only she hadn't caved in to Juliet's nagging and told her she'd spend Christmas at hers. Juliet had gone on and on about Christmas the last time Gemma had seen her and Gemma had eventually just blurted something out to keep her quiet.

It had all been Juliet's next-door neighbour's fault. If he hadn't picked a fight with her, she'd have never had *three* G&Ts, and then she might have been able to talk her way out of it. At the very least she might have been able to remember exactly what Juliet had said to her. The only thing to do now was to play along and pick up the details piece by piece. Juliet was sure to give her chapter and verse at some point, anyway. Probably in the form of a laminated sheet with idiot-proof instructions.

But that wasn't something she was going to worry about at this precise moment. It was time to get one up-himself action star onto the set. She signalled for the luxury four-wheel drive that was ready and waiting, puffs of smoke rhythmically pumping out of its exhaust. Toby emerged from his trailer as it pulled near and ten seconds later the car was speeding away up the drive. When it had disappeared from view, Gemma smiled to herself. Now *that* was why she earned her lovely fat pay cheque.

She pulled her phone out of her pocket and called through to a rather harried First AD to let him know that their star was on his way. Fabulous. Time to go and start dishing out those call sheets …

Her phone had just hit the bottom of her pocket when it buzzed at her again.

What now? She hoped desperately that they weren't going to tell her it had started raining again and that she'd be back on A-list babysitting duty within ten minutes. But when she stared at the caller ID she realised it wasn't either of those options.

I know you must be terribly busy rubbing shoulders with Brad Pitt or whoever, but I really need to talk to you about Christmas. ;-) Call me. Jx

The cute little winky face didn't fool Gemma one bit. She could hear the silent screaming that had gone on while her sister had composed her breezy little message. She stared at it as the screen dimmed from bright to half-lit. She knew she needed to talk to Juliet about Christmas. She'd known it for about a fortnight now. But …

The image of a gently swaying palm tree over golden sand and a cocktail big enough to house goldfish flitted across her mind.

She sighed.

She wasn't in the mood to talk about gingerbread recipes ad nauseam or debate whether to have turkey or goose for the big day. She also wasn't in the mood to deal with thinly veiled comments on how she lived her life, how often she phoned or if she'd remembered to ask about the kids' school reports. If she responded now she'd only come across as stressed and defensive. Which she was.

Later. She'd talk to Juliet later. When she'd finished work. When she had more time.

When she'd had a couple of gin and tonics, maybe.

CHAPTER TWO

Twenty minutes later Juliet found herself standing outside the ball pit in the local leisure centre's soft-play area. She closed her eyes and opened them again, not quite able to believe what she was seeing. There was Great-aunt Sylvia, sitting in the middle of the thousands of brightly coloured plastic balls, looking grim. Apart from her aunt, herself and two uniformed officers, the play area was almost deserted. A few cross-looking mothers were hurrying their children into their coats and shoes and tutting about having to cut short their afternoon's activities.

'She won't come out, no matter what we say,' the petite female officer told Juliet. 'She keeps asking for Mary.'

Juliet nodded. Well, no luck there. Her mother had been dead for almost five years. She stepped into the ball pond and waded towards her aunt. 'Hello, Aunt Sylvia … These nice police officers are wondering if you'd like to come out of here now.'

Aunt Sylvia shot a withering look at the two uniformed people looking on. 'I don't like the look of that girl. Eyes are too close together. She'll get up to no good when she grows up, you mark my words!'

Juliet stared at her great-aunt helplessly. Somewhere deep

inside she wanted to weep – for the indignity of the situation the old woman was in now, for who she'd become and who she'd forgotten she'd once been – but Juliet didn't do crying. Not in public, at least. And especially not when everyone else was expecting her to make everything right again.

She held out her hand. 'It's time to go home now, Aunt Sylvia. Come on …'

Her aunt's head snapped round as she stopped glaring at the female police officer and transferred her attention to Juliet. 'Mary!' she exclaimed.

Juliet gave her a weak smile. She supposed that in her aunt's dementia-riddled mind, the boundaries between mother and daughter had somehow blurred. And the older she got, the more she saw her mother's face staring back in the mirror at her. Same brown eyes, same long nose and high cheekbones. Not exactly pretty, but with enough good bone structure that she'd never be plain, either. But in the last few months the grooves in her forehead had grown deeper and her eyes had become more hooded. Her age – and her divorce – were showing up there now.

Sylvia crossed her arms. 'These people put me in here and won't let me get out again,' she said. 'That's why I said they had to fetch you. I knew you'd come and sort it all out! You always were such a good girl …'

'I'm not Mary,' she said soothingly. 'It's Juliet. Mary's daughter.'

A flicker of confusion passed across the old woman's features. Juliet inched a little closer, but her aunt, suddenly wary and now doubting the identification of her visitor, just backed away.

Juliet sighed. *If you can't beat 'em, join 'em.* She lowered herself, jiggling slightly to push the balls out of the way, until her bottom made contact with the slippery plastic padded floor.

Aunt Sylvia suddenly smiled. 'Oh, yes! I remember ...' She stared out across the sea of bright plastic for a moment, her lips in a slight curve, lost in a memory that Juliet suspected might evaporate before she managed to vocalise it.

But then she muttered, 'Lively little thing, Mary's daughter. She looked like an angel with those big blue eyes and white-blonde curls.'

Something inside Juliet sank. After all the hours spent with her great-aunt over the last couple of months ...

She'd been blonder when she'd been little, but her hair had always been straight with a wavy kink. She'd never been blessed with the wispy ringlets her aunt was describing. It wasn't this sister that Sylvia was remembering.

Her aunt blinked and turned to her again. 'You know her, you say? Mary's little girl?'

Juliet opened her mouth to explain it all patiently again, but closed it before any sound emerged. What was the point? 'Yes, I know her,' she replied wearily.

Sylvia smiled back. 'Did she send you to me? She's been away for such a long time.'

Gemma hadn't seen Aunt Sylvia since last Easter, and the old woman could really do with regular visits from people she knew and remembered. Not that Juliet's twice-weekly sessions seemed to be helping much. Back in the summer Sylvia had nearly always called her by name, even if there had been a handful of days when she'd smiled and nodded blankly, then referred to her as 'that nice young girl'. But as the days had become shorter and greyer, her great-aunt had grown more and more confused, as if her memory was seeping away with the sunlight. Now she only knew who Juliet was one visit in four, and even then her recollection was patchy, fading in and out, like a badly tuned radio.

'No, Gemma didn't send me,' she told her aunt. 'But she'll be home for Christmas this year, so you'll see her then.'

'Oh, good! Do you think she'll want a sweetie when she gets here? Little girls like sweeties.' Aunt Sylvia plunged her hands into the plastic balls beside her, not seeming to register the noisy rattling that echoed through the hangar-like building. She pulled her handbag out and rested it on her lap, then rummaged inside before proudly producing a small object, which she held carefully between thumb and forefinger. Juliet thought it might once have been a boiled sweet, but the lint and other old-lady gunk from the bottom of the bag had disguised it almost completely.

'Here it is! Do you think she'd like it?'

Juliet thought of Gemma, how everything was so effortless for her, how she breezed in and out of everyone's lives without a care in the world, and she found herself saying, 'Yes. I think she'd like it very much. Why don't you save it for her?'

Juliet had never really considered herself as having a naughty side, but she got a strange warm feeling when she thought of Gemma having not only to suck, but to swallow, the furry little ball of sugar when Juliet dragged her along for her next visit. Because drag Juliet would.

Sylvia dropped the sweet into a clean cotton handkerchief and placed it carefully back in the corner of her bag. Juliet wondered if it would have grown by the next time she saw it, like a strange kind of handbag snowball, rolling around in the fluff and debris.

'It's time to go home now,' she repeated when her aunt closed her handbag and looked back up at her. Aunt Sylvia stared at her blankly for a second then held out a hand for Juliet to grasp hold of. She supported her aunt while she got to her feet, and then guided her back across the floor of the ball pond and helped her over the padded step that led to the main floor of the soft-play area.

The two police officers breathed out a sigh of relief and offered to take them back to Greenacres, the nursing home that really shouldn't have lost Aunt Sylvia in the first place. Juliet was most cross about that. It wasn't as if they didn't charge enough.

The offer of a lift for Aunt Sylvia was tempting, but Juliet reckoned they'd get further if she just took the old lady back herself. She was used to Juliet's car and was possibly less likely to get confused and distressed all over again if someone she knew – or almost knew – drove her.

Juliet checked her watch and felt her neck muscles tighten. Ten to three. She only just had enough time to take her aunt back to Greenacres, have a firm word with someone in charge, then race to St Martin's to pick up her youngest three children.

They were just reaching her car, parked a little oddly in front of the leisure centre, when Juliet pulled up short.

The turkey!

Oh, well. There was nothing for it now. She was just going to have to cram that into her already packed schedule for tomorrow.

It doesn't matter, she told herself. *It's fine. You can handle it. You're good at organising and multi-tasking and getting things done.*

Even so, once she'd checked her aunt was strapped in securely, then started up her car and made the ten-minute drive back to the nursing home, the empty row of boxes in her Christmas notebook began to haunt her.

*

Juliet drummed her fingers on the steering wheel and checked the clock on her car dashboard for the umpteenth time.

'Ow!' a small voice from behind her said.

She glanced in the rear-view mirror to see what her youngest three children were up to. 'Polly, leave your brother alone.'

Polly stared back at her and pushed her glasses up on the bridge of her nose, the picture of ten-year-old innocence. 'I didn't do anything he didn't deserve.' Ten-going-on-forty, that was.

Juliet unclipped her seatbelt and turned to face her daughter, who was wedged between her two younger brothers in their booster seats. 'I've told you before, Polly, you can't just rule over your brothers with a rod of iron because you're older than them.'

Polly looked unimpressed. 'Someone's got to.' She flicked a haughty look at Josh, who was obviously the accused in this situation. 'These children are positively feral, Mother.'

Juliet didn't have time to argue with a ten-year-old about her parenting skills, so she turned to Josh. 'What did you do?'

'Nothing!'

She looked at Polly, knowing her daughter would be only to happy to testify against him.

'He keeps moving his leg over onto my bit of the seat, and I'm compressed enough as it is. I did warn him I'd make him move it if he did it again.'

Well, she couldn't fault Polly's logic, but she could hardly let her daughter police the rest of the family's behaviour – they'd all be locked up and sentenced to torture within the week if that were the case. Even Juliet. 'If the boys give you trouble, you're supposed to come to me about it,' she told Polly. 'Understand?'

Polly rolled her eyes, but eventually gave her a reluctant nod.

When Juliet turned back round to face forwards again, she noticed the clock on the dashboard. It was already three forty. Where in the world was Violet? She pulled her phone out of her coat pocket and sent another short and to-the-point text to her daughter, warning her that the taxi service was leaving in exactly three minutes, and that if she wasn't here by then she'd have to get two buses home instead.

Just as she was turning the key in the ignition to start up the car, the door opened and Violet flopped into the passenger seat with a sigh. She was smiling, looking completely unconcerned that she'd kept the rest of them waiting.

She laughed, shaking her head. 'You'll never guess what Abby just said—'

Juliet turned the key and revved the car. 'We've all been sitting here in the cold waiting for you, and you *know* the boys have swimming tonight!'

Violet's warm, open expression closed down and she scowled back at her mother. 'I'm not *that* late! God, Mum! And I was helping Kiera find her scarf, so it wasn't my fault anyway.'

Juliet shook her head, clipped her belt back up and winced at the sound of crunching gears as she put her car into reverse.

Not my fault … Now where had she heard that before? Violet was turning into a mini version of Gemma.

As she drove she could see Violet out of the corner of her eye, hunched in the passenger seat, arms folded and scowling. The atmosphere wasn't improved by the start of a squabble in the back seat, either, as Polly accused Josh of leaving his arm two millimetres further into her space than it should have been, and then Jake jumped in to defend his brother and deliberately drew Polly's fire by invading her space from the other side.

'Stop that!' Juliet yelled. 'Jake, you just kicked me in the back! Now, the three of you calm down and behave yourselves.'

And then she turned to her eldest daughter. They needed to have a little chat about her attitude, or else she'd turn out just like her aunt, causing mayhem for everyone else then refusing to take responsibility for it, but she realised she was now approaching a mini roundabout that always got clogged up at that time of day. 'We'll talk about this later, Vi,' she said, glancing quickly in both directions. 'But you've got to learn to express your opinions without being rude, because I won't have you talking to me like—'

Unfortunately, the fight in the back seat erupted again at that moment and a deft kick in the back of her seat from Jake caused her to pitch forward. Her foot slipped off the clutch as she was crossing the roundabout and the car growled then stalled as it straddled the little white hump.

The car to her right slammed on its brakes and the driver leaned on his horn. Juliet's heart pounded and her arms shook. The man was using his hands in the most creative of ways and she could lip-read enough of his tirade to know he thought she was a middle-class bitch who shouldn't be allowed to operate a vehicle.

A stalled car in the middle of the junction meant that traffic backed up in all four directions. Horns blared. Drivers swore. All four of Juliet's children started to scream and shout at each other, letting each other know, without holding back on the toilet-related insults, just whose fault it was.

Juliet found she couldn't move. She was just frozen, fingers clenched around the steering wheel. She couldn't even remember which pedal to press or what to do next to get the car started again. But the noise – the engines, the horns, the bickering children – was burrowing into her skull in a way she just couldn't bear.

'Will you just *shut up*!' she bellowed at the top of her

lungs, surprising herself with the volume, hearing the croak as her voice broke when she reached maximum decibels.

Outside the car the commotion continued, but inside everything went still and quiet. Violet, Polly, Josh and Jake stared at their mother open-mouthed.

She could feel the echo of her words pulsing around inside her head and it scared her slightly. She didn't shout like that. Ever. And she certainly didn't lose her temper with her children, not to this degree, anyway. Of course, she disciplined – she'd read countless books on how to do it properly – but she never just screamed at the kids. Right from when they were babies she'd always feared the kind of woman who did that was also the kind of woman who dragged toddlers down the street with their arms half out of their sockets or walloped them in the middle of supermarkets.

She'd had a feeling that things were a little off-kilter for weeks now, but she'd just put it down to the idea of Christmas looming ahead of her. As much as she loved the season, it would now be forever associated with the departure of the man she'd planned to spend her life with. If your husband choosing Boxing Day to announce your marriage was over didn't leave a stain on a celebration, then she didn't know what did.

Still, Juliet was good with stains, knew all the tricks and tips to get them to vanish. With the right amount of determination, you'd hardly ever know they'd been there once she'd finished with them. This one would be no different. She'd just have to try harder.

She became aware of quiet breathing beside her and in the back of the car. Silence verging on the miraculous. For the first time in years all four kids had shut up at the same time. She needed to reward them for that, didn't she? Positive reinforcement.

'Thank you,' she said quietly, and if she'd been able to feel anything in the numbness of the after-shock of her outburst, she'd have been pleased at how calm and rational she sounded.

'Mum …?' a shaky voice said from beside her. 'Are you okay?'

Juliet took some air in and held it. There was nothing left now. Not the dizzying frustration, not the clawing sense of racing towards a goal that got ever further away. Not even the fear that Violet would turn out to be exactly like Gemma and push her away for ever. Just nothing. It was wonderful.

'Yes,' she said, letting the breath out again. 'Everything's fine.'

The ability to not only think but also drive returned, so she started the engine, yanked the car into gear and without making eye contact with any of the drivers giving her withering looks she carried on her journey to the swimming pool.

&

CHAPTER THREE

The kids were still a bit subdued over tea that evening, but once they'd all tidied their plates away and headed off in their individual directions the sounds of normality began to creep back into Juliet's household – the stomp of Violet's feet on the stairs, an argument breaking out on the landing, the tinny cacophony of a cartoon show somewhere on a television …

'Your dad's going to be here at seven thirty,' Juliet yelled up the stairs. 'Make sure you have your stuff together by then.'

And, miraculously, they did. By the time Greg rang the doorbell four overnight bags were lined up in the hall and four children were in various stages of getting their winter coats on.

Greg looked tense when she opened the door. 'Are they ready?'

Juliet nodded. It was odd, her standing here and him standing there. She hadn't quite got over the shock of it each time he arrived to pick up the kids for his allotted weekend. She still wasn't really sure what had gone wrong between them. They'd thought themselves the perfect couple, and this their perfect house, and then their four perfect children had come along and they'd been so happy … But now she could see how smug they'd been in the middle of all that perfection, how complacent.

She hadn't seen it coming. Not in the slightest.

It was as if on her rigidly maintained To Do list she'd forgotten to reserve a tick box for 'prepare for the disintegrating of your life and a painful divorce'. How stupid of her. She was never normally that disorganised.

'Can I open the car, Dad?' Josh said, pushing past Juliet's legs and reaching for the key in his father's hand.

'No, I want to!' Jake said, trying to nudge his brother out of the way.

Greg handed the key over to Josh. 'Josh can open the car up now and you can lock it when we get there,' he told Jake. Both boys ran off in the direction of the drive. At least Violet and Polly stopped to give their mother a kiss on the cheek before they went out the door.

She ran after them, hugged them to her, one under each arm, and gave them a proper kiss. 'Love you,' she said, squeezing them, 'and I'm sorry about earlier on.'

Violet shrugged.

Polly gave her an unblinking stare. 'You know, as shock tactics go, it was really rather good.'

Juliet couldn't help but smile. She ran after the boys and kissed them as she helped strap them into their booster seats in the back of Greg's car.

When the doors were closed, the kids effectively sound-proofed from their conversation, Greg looked at her across the top of the car.

'You look tired, Juliet,' he said as he knocked on the window and signalled for Josh to return his keys. 'Maybe you should try to chill out a little instead of doing the whole Christmas rigmarole this year?'

The smile immediately dropped from Juliet's face. Oh, he sounded so polite and reasonable. So polite and reasonable she wanted to knock his block off. He still thought he had a say about how she behaved, or could comment on how she looked? Seriously? He'd given up that right when he'd moved out and moved on.

And there was nothing wrong with wanting to make Christmas a happy time, when nothing went wrong and everything was perfect. Greg's surprise exit had put a blight on the festivities two years ago and last Christmas had been their first one living apart, the poor kids ferried from pillar to post and feeling very unsettled, so Juliet was determined this year should be extra special, especially as their father was being totally selfish about the whole thing.

'Goodbye, Greg,' she said through teeth so tightly clenched her jaw was starting to hurt, and then she bent and smiled brightly and waved to their children in the car. They didn't need to know their mother and father were arguing again.

She kept it up as he shook his head and climbed into the driver's seat and pulled away, but the effort of keeping that smile in place as they pulled out of the drive started to make her head pound. Once the Mercedes had rounded the hedge and joined the traffic on the road outside, she let it all out in a most colourful and unladylike word, the sort of thing she'd trained herself out of saying when the kids had been small, and then she hugged her arms around her to stave off the cold and marched back into her empty house in her slippers.

Maybe it wouldn't be so galling if Greg hadn't found it so easy to move on. They'd split, he'd grieved and now he had a new girlfriend. Easy as that. Sometimes Juliet wished she could find someone else, just so she could show him she wasn't lagging behind, that he had no reason to pity her.

As she stalked into the kitchen and reached inside the fridge for a bottle of Pinot Grigio, she spotted her phone lying innocent and silent on the kitchen counter and her thoughts turned from one self-absorbed family member to another.

She kept eyeing her mobile while she emptied a generous amount of wine into a wine glass and took a large slug. And then she flexed her texting fingers.

*

When Gemma eventually fell into bed she didn't even bother to put her pyjamas on. She just stripped down to her T-shirt and crawled under the covers. She picked her phone up off the bedside table and squinted at it. Two twenty-five. She had to be up in – what? – three hours? It was positively inhuman.

She flumped back heavily onto the soft down pillows and stared at the ceiling as tiredness rolled over her, but instead of sinking beneath those glorious waves, she was tossed and turned on them, feeling the pull of gravity on her eyelids but not quite able to surrender to unconsciousness.

Grunting, she reached for her phone and swiped the

screen to wake it up. As usual, this was the only time she'd had all day to check her messages. The little badge on the app told her there were five waiting. It wouldn't take a genius to guess who at least one of them was from. Her eyes rolled back in her head as she stared at the screen, promising a reprieve, but then, rather annoyingly, they refocused themselves again.

It had been the day from hell. Toby Thornton had had one of his legendary meltdowns and Gemma hadn't even had the time to eat, let alone sit down in the last twenty-four hours. It was her job to sort things out again, to charm their star into setting foot on set again, and it was taking every last ounce of her resources to make that happen. Millions of dollars were at stake. She didn't have time to indulge Juliet's petty moans about the right kind of ivy or whether they should have a red or gold theme for the Christmas table settings.

She couldn't deal with her sister now. She needed a bit of down time first, so she decided to check Facebook instead.

Cute cats who couldn't spell … Sick-making chain-posts about how wonderful women friends were … Her cousin Shelley's dog dressed in a party hat … Yada, yada, yada.

But then Gemma stopped scrolling and blinked. Holding her breath, she went back up and had a proper look at the photo in her timeline.

It was Michael. Damn, he looked good. Even though it had been seven months since they'd split, she still felt a little jolt go through her.

He'd look even better if he wasn't wrapped around some trollop with glossy brown hair and a wide smile. Well, not *wrapped around* wrapped around. He was hugging her from the back, his arms draped over her shoulders like he was a preppy cardigan. Their cheeks were pressed together and they were laughing at the camera.

Cow.

Even though she knew she shouldn't, she tapped his profile picture to visit his timeline. Big mistake. If she'd thought she'd felt terrible when she'd climbed into bed, she felt even worse now his status had smugly morphed from 'in a relationship with Allie Cameron' to 'engaged to Allie Cameron'.

She felt sick. Her thumb was shaky on the home button as she hid the picture and closed the app without looking at it again. Suddenly she wasn't sleepy in the least. Michael had been different from all the others. Perfect, she'd thought. He was supposed to have been the one that lasted.

Ugh. Well, she might as well get all the crap over with at once …

Without waiting to talk herself out of it, she checked her messages. As predicted, there was one from Juliet.

> *Gemma! Will you PLEASE reply to my texts! I know you don't realise it, but you're being very selfish. I need to talk to you. SOON. Call me! J x*

She stared at her phone, unable to produce a noise from her open mouth. Who did Juliet think she was? Honestly! It wasn't as if she was just lounging around doing nothing all day. There was a reason she hadn't had time to text back. It was called having a job, having a life. Just because Juliet didn't have one and decided to cram her days full with fussy little craft activities and gourmet cooking, it didn't mean she could pass judgement on anyone who didn't want to do the same.

But that was typical Juliet. If you weren't doing things her way, you were doing them wrong. And it had always been like that, no matter how hard Gemma had tried.

No wonder the people she worked with felt more like family than her own sister did. Not the actors, of course. They were a law unto themselves. But the rest of the crew. For a few months at a time they'd live together, eat together, share everything. It felt more like home than sitting on Juliet's pristine sofa trying not to drop biscuit crumbs. At least film people knew how to work as a team, and they needed and respected her contribution.

She lay still and stared at the ceiling. Why? Why was she putting herself through this? And the more she thought about it, the more she wondered if spending Christmas with her sister was a good idea after all. Goodwill to all mankind? Hah! The way she was feeling right now, Juliet might end Christmas night in a body bag.

&

CHAPTER FOUR

It was so quiet in the house that Juliet was tempted to slump into an armchair with a bottle of wine and not get up again. The only thing that stopped her was a good, hard look at the kitchen clock. It was only ten past three on Saturday afternoon. She'd resisted the urge to do that kind of thing after Greg had left and she certainly wasn't going to do it now. Besides, she had too much to do. The clotted cream fudge the kids were giving out as teacher presents this year wouldn't make itself.

She was just measuring out the golden syrup when she became aware of a dull electronic hum in a nearby garden. She listened to its comforting droning while she boiled the mixture, then whisked it until it began to crystallise, but as she poured it into the pan to cool she frowned.

The mower had started off as a muffled hum, but now it sounded as if it was much closer, almost as if it was right outside her kitchen window. She walked over to the other side of the room, wiping her hands on her apron, to look out over her back garden.

The next second she was running outside, wooden spoon still in her hand.

'Will! What on earth do you think you're doing?' she shouted.

Her next-door neighbour just looked up then kept walking the mower along her lawn. 'I think I'm cutting your grass,' he said, totally deadpan.

Juliet's mouth opened and closed. She put her hands on her hips and frowned. Eventually she said, 'I was going to get around to that myself, you know.'

'Do you want me to stop?' he yelled over the noise of the engine.

She frowned even harder. She knew he would if she asked him to, but the thought of having to add one more job to her schedule made her shoulders sag. He was almost two-thirds of the way through now, anyway. It would be silly to ask him to stop, but it didn't sit comfortably with her to let him do it for nothing, so she went back inside and returned a few minutes later with two brightly patterned bone-china mugs of tea and held one aloft. He nodded but didn't come and collect it until he'd dealt with the extra tough grass round the bottom of her lone apple tree.

She sipped her tea and watched him over the rim of her mug as he switched the mower off and jogged lightly up her long, thin garden to join her. She blushed as he approached.

She'd always considered him a nice-looking man. He was tall and sporty looking, with chestnut-brown hair and eyes that she thought of as warm, even though she couldn't remember the precise colour. He was younger than her by a couple of years, but she never got the feeling he was taking pity on the middle-aged woman next door. Besides, she didn't look too bad for a woman who'd just hit forty. She took good care of herself, dressed nicely.

'Thanks,' Will said as he took the mug from her and gave her one of his rare but rather captivating smiles.

They both stood and looked at Juliet's freshly mown garden. 'Actually, it's me that needs to thank you. I've been meaning to do that for weeks.'

He shrugged. 'I was doing my garden anyway ...'

'I know. I could hear you while I was in the kitchen making fudge for the kids' teacher presents. It just took me a while to work out the rumble of the mower had moved closer and was in *my* garden instead of yours.'

His eyebrows lifted. 'Fudge? That sounds very labour-intensive.'

She sighed and shook her head. 'I've always done something home-made. It started off when Violet was little and Greg was just starting the business. It was the cheap option back then, and somehow it's just become a tradition.'

His eyelids lowered a little, as if he was studying her. Juliet resisted the urge to fidget. It was always so difficult to tell what Will was thinking.

'Traditions like that aren't carved in stone, you know. You can change them any time you want. Wouldn't it be quicker to just run down to the supermarket and pick up a bottle?'

'I suppose so ... but the teachers get so much wine and chocolate this time of year, I just wanted to give them something special.' Her expression softened and her lips curved. 'And I don't want to be accused of contributing to the alcoholism of primary school teachers ...'

'But contributing to their obesity is okay?'

'Shut up,' she said, and laughed softly.

He turned to study the garden as he drank his tea. She'd thought, when they first met, that maybe there was a little flicker of something between them. She'd quickly eradicated it, of course, since she'd still been married to Greg and Will had been tied up with a serious girlfriend. And then after Greg had left she just hadn't been in any shape to think about men at all – unless abject hatred was involved. She looked across at him, frowning as he stared at a patch of clumpy grass near the greenhouse, and wondered if she was going to have to tell him not to get the strimmer out, but then he turned to her and spoke first.

'If you don't mind me saying, Juliet, you look like you've had one hell of a week.'

'Thanks!' she said in mock outrage. Will didn't always say a lot, but when he did, he definitely didn't mince his words. He wasn't wrong, though. She sighed and held out her hand for his empty mug. 'Come in for another one of those when you're finished and I'll tell you all about it. I even have fudge cooling in the pan …'

Wills ears pricked up. She knew he had a fondness sweet things, and she could always make another batch for the kids' teachers.

'It's a deal,' he said, and smiled again, more gently this time, and something at the bottom of Juliet's stomach quivered.

She held her breath and nodded. And then she took the mugs into the kitchen and closed the door without looking back.

She didn't know if she liked that quiver.

It wasn't an altogether unpleasant sensation, but it wasn't an altogether comfortable one, either.

*

Twenty minutes later Will appeared in her kitchen and sat down on one of the mismatched chairs she'd paid an inordinate amount of money for in a second-hand furniture shop down the high street. The sextet of chairs now surrounding her heavy oak kitchen table said *quirky, eclectic, free-spirited…* Which was the look she'd been going for. Even if she did feel a bit of a fake when she sat in them sometimes.

He looked all fresh and windblown and she felt her stomach do that weird thing again. She'd been with Greg so long that she'd all but forgotten what the first flush of attraction felt like. Was this it? Or was it just her IBS flaring up again? She really couldn't say.

'Please tell me there really is fudge,' he said, looking at the tray still cooling on the kitchen counter.

She picked it up and placed it into the centre of the kitchen table, but it went too quiet as he watched her cut it into neat squares and suddenly she felt very self-conscious under his gaze. 'More tea?' she asked a little too loudly, and prised a generous helping of clotted cream fudge onto a plate.

Will shook his head. 'I think I've already drunk a gallon this afternoon.'

Juliet frowned as she divided one of the fudge squares in two and popped it on a plate for herself. 'It's a bit rich to eat on its own.' She scanned the kitchen, looking for something else to offer him, and her gaze came to rest on a bottle sitting near the hob, one she'd opened for the casserole she'd made yesterday. She grabbed the red wine and plonked it down on the kitchen table with a thud.

Will's eyebrows raised.

'You're right,' she said, sighing. 'It has been one hell of a week.'

She peeked out of the window. Although it was just after four, the sun was close to setting. It was practically evening. Not too early for a civilised glass of wine with a friend.

He didn't exactly smile, but his eyes warmed, so she fetched a couple of glasses from the cabinet and poured them both a modest amount. It didn't take long to fill him in on the whole story of Aunt Sylvia's great escape the day before. Somehow her glass emptied and she found herself reaching for the bottle and dishing out more wine – a more generous helping this time. It seemed a shame to leave a tiny bit in the bottom of the bottle.

When she was halfway through it, she started to wonder about the wisdom of too much Merlot with only half a square of fudge to line one's stomach, especially as Will had listened so sympathetically to her tale of woe that she just kept talking.

'It seems so quiet at the weekends when the kids are at Greg's,' she said, her shoulders slumping a little. 'I know I moan that they drive me insane when they're here, but it's even worse when they're gone.' She sighed. 'Oh, well. I suppose at least I've got them all to myself for Christmas this year.'

Will, who'd been not-so-surreptitiously reaching for

another piece of fudge, looked at her. 'I thought you said Greg and the new girlfriend were supposed to be coming here for a united family Christmas?'

She shook her head. And then nodded. 'Well, I offered, but apparently Anoushka made plans that were just too good to pass up. A once-in-a-lifetime opportunity that came through her job, Greg said.' She hated the tinge of bitterness that had crept into her tone. 'They're going to Bali, or somewhere like that. Escaping the Christmas madness.'

Will looked puzzled. 'That doesn't sound like the Greg I know.'

Juliet shrugged. It didn't sound like the Greg she knew either. He hadn't been like that when they'd been married. She'd have loved it if he'd wanted to drop everything just to be with her, or if he'd whisked her off on an exotic holiday. But work and commitments had always come first with Greg. And she'd understood that. Supported it, even. But he'd changed the moment he'd met flipping Anoushka, and for some reason that really cheesed her off.

She shook her head and took another large slug of wine. 'She's the love of his life, apparently. At least, that's the only explanation he gave me when I called him on it.'

Without warning her eyes filled with moisture. She quickly looked down at the table and worked her eyelashes hard, trying to get it to evaporate. After a few seconds a warm hand covered hers. She took in a shuddering breath then peered at Will through the long fringe that had fallen over her face when she'd bowed her head.

His expression might have seemed neutral to a stranger, but Juliet glimpsed the understanding in his eyes. 'I know it's hard …'

She nodded. After a few seconds she slid her hand from underneath his and curled her fingers round the stem of her wine glass. She knew he knew.

'It's just that once you have a ring on your finger, you think you've earned the right to be the love of someone's life. I mean, if they didn't feel that way, why would they marry you in the first place?' This was a question she'd asked herself a thousand times since Greg's surprise exit, and a thousand times more since he'd met the fabulous Anoushka.

'I wouldn't mind …' Now the confessions had started spilling out of her she couldn't seem to stop. 'But she's not the trophy wife upgrade, is she? I think I could have coped with that better, because Greg was always fussy about appearances, and I know I'm hurtling into middle age …'

Will gave her a look that might have said *Stop it!* but she ignored him.

'But she's two months older than me. She's shorter and at least a dress size bigger. She's not Juliet mark two, the sleeker, faster model. She's just … different.'

Not her.

Maybe that's why Greg had never once told her she was the love of his life. Not that she'd realised his omission until far, far too late.

'More fool him, then,' Will said firmly, but Juliet couldn't read his expression. It wasn't a possessive kind of look, more a *I'm sticking up for my friend* kind of look. What had the hand thing been about, then? Did he like her? And did she want him to? Oh, she was so confused!

She didn't want to be 'back on the market' again. It was too nerve-racking. The Juliet who used to date and go dancing and knew how to talk to men who weren't her husband seemed like a creature from a parallel universe.

'Did you feel this way when Samantha left?' she asked.

'If you mean, did I understand my significant other running off then hooking up with an older, fatter woman, then no.'

Juliet couldn't help but laugh. This was what she liked about Will. He always made her feel better. His presence was … comforting.

He gave her a wry smile. 'Did I second-guess myself for months afterwards? Yes. I know Sam and I weren't together anywhere close to the amount of time you were with Greg, but it does get better. You just need to give yourself time, Juliet.'

Time. How unfortunate that time was a commodity in short supply in her life at the moment. Juggling kids and home had been hard enough when there'd been another adult around. Doing it on her own now there was a part-time job and a senile aunt thrown into the mix was nigh on impossible. Will was right, though. She needed time.

Oh, not just the days and weeks and months ticking past, although that had helped. She didn't even really want Greg back any more. She just didn't want to be jealous of what he had now. If life was fair, it would be her who was having a passionate affair, while her ex moped around his empty house regretting what he'd so carelessly thrown away.

A snuffle of laughter almost escaped. Yeah, right. Passionate affair? Who in their right mind would want one of those with her?

'It gets so complicated, doesn't it?' she said thoughtfully, and then, just to see how Will would respond to the probe, she threw in another question. 'And have you had enough time? Have you moved on?'

Will thought for a moment, and then he nodded. 'I think I have.'

Which led to something else she wanted to know. 'So why haven't I seen a steady parade of attractive women beating down your door?'

'Well, there hasn't been any actual *door beating* as such, but I've been on a few dates.'

Oh. She hadn't expected him to say that. 'Anyone nice?' she asked nonchalantly and twisted the stem of her wine glass in her fingers.

He sighed. 'That's not the problem.'

She glanced up at him. 'Then what is?'

He shook his head gently. 'I just always seem to go for the wrong type …'

'What does that mean?'

'There have been a few girls I've been out with that have sparked my interest, but I let it fizzle out after a few dinners. The ones I want to see again always end up reminding me of Sam.'

'Really?'

'I don't mean looks-wise, I mean personality-wise…' He

lifted one shoulder then let it drop again. 'Even when I try not to, I end up asking out someone who turns out to be just like her – free-spirited, unpredictable.'

'Exciting, you mean,' Juliet said, feeling her stomach sink. There it was again, that phrase. *Free-spirited*. It seemed that was what men wanted, even when they didn't want to want it.

Will held her gaze. 'Unreliable.'

She found she couldn't look away. 'And you don't want that?'

'No,' he said softly. 'I'm ready to stay in one place, put down some roots. That's why I bought that big old house next door in the first place.'

'Probably shouldn't have made the big old marriage proposal to go with it without finding out if she wanted that too.'

That's when Sam had run. And, unlike Greg, who'd at least had the decency to have a conversation with her before he'd left, Sam had just upped and gone, packed her bags and disappeared, leaving only a short and unsatisfactory note.

A flicker of discomfort crossed Will's features. She began to apologise, but he shook his head and dismissed the words before they'd left her mouth. This was why she didn't drink much, and especially not on an empty stomach; she always ended up saying things she regretted later.

'You're right,' he said. 'And that's why I'm not in the market for another relationship like that – another woman like that. I'm looking for someone sensible, grounded. Someone who understands the concepts of home and family.'

Those words could have been instantly forgettable, if not

for the way he was looking at her. Brown. His eyes were brown. Her pulse skipped again and she held her breath.

Something new appeared in Will's expression. Something that looked suspiciously like a question.

In an instant, Juliet was out of her seat and clearing away wine glasses and fussing with fudge pans. *Why?* she asked herself, as she placed the empty wine bottle in the glass recycling. *Why couldn't you have just stayed still and looked back at the good-looking man who seems to like you? Why did you have to scurry away like Polly's scared hamster?*

Even now she couldn't stop her busyness. It seemed to be her default position when anything uncomfortable happened. Eventually, she managed to slow herself down enough to *not* put on a pair of rubber gloves and start the washing-up. Instead she turned to look at Will, who was pushing his chair back and reaching for the jacket that was half-dangling on the floor.

'Sorry,' she whispered.

His mouth didn't move from the straight line it was set in, but somehow she felt as if he was giving her the slightest of smiles. 'For what?'

For not being ready, she wanted to say, but all she did was swallow.

Will gave her an infinitesimal tilt of the head. 'The fudge was fabulous, by the way ...'

'Thanks,' she said weakly as he disappeared through the back door. She heard him collect the mower and wrestle it back into his own garden, and when everything was silent outside once more she sat back down at her kitchen table and finished the entire pan of fudge off on her own.

&

CHAPTER FIVE

Gemma stopped her car outside Juliet's house, engine still running, but didn't pull onto the drive. She sat there for a few moments, staring at the neatly-clipped evergreen hedge.

This was stupid. She was a grown woman in her thirties, but every time she approached Juliet's front door the same thing happened: the years peeled away and suddenly she felt like a little kid who was merely something to be tolerated, a problem to be managed.

She drew in a long breath and blew it out again. This was no big deal. Just Juliet. She handled tougher situations on a daily basis at work.

Don't care. It doesn't matter what she thinks of you.

She pulled down the sun visor in her sports car and checked her reflection in the mirror. Apart from a couple of blonde ringlets, only her eyes were visible. As she stared at herself they transformed from round and wide like Bambi's to apathetic and hooded like Garbo's.

Good. She was ready.

Visiting one's relations shouldn't really involve goals and manoeuvres and tactical planning, but Gemma had learned the hard way that going in and dealing with Juliet without a battle plan was like going to war with a water pistol. The plan for today: a flying visit. She would swoop in, deliver the kids' Christmas presents, chat for as long as she absolutely had to, then exit by fourteen hundred hours. It should be a piece of cake.

She took a deep breath and let it out again before edging her car onto the noisy gravel drive. She was sure Juliet had resisted paving, not only because she liked the old-fashioned look of the little stones, but because no one could approach her domain without her knowledge.

The place looked gorgeous, as it always did at Christmas. The steep gables and red brick of Juliet's Victorian house suited the season so well. Plain white fairy lights were wound round a tree in the front garden and the struts of the covered porch. An evergreen wreath, complete with pine cones, silver jingle bells and a big red velvet bow graced the glossy black front door with its stained-glass panels, and the lights of a Christmas tree twinkled tantalisingly through the leaded windows of the living room. No doubt, half a forest's worth of greenery would be inside, tastefully draped on fire-places and wound round the banisters.

Gemma turned off the engine, got out of the car then went round to the boot to retrieve the two big bags of presents she'd bought for her nieces and nephews. When she'd been shopping for them she'd felt warm and fuzzy – generous – but now the overflowing bags just seemed a little bit much, as if she was trying to make up for something.

Which she was. Not that Juliet knew that yet, of course.

As she closed the boot, Juliet opened the front door and stood waiting for her on the front step. She smiled – albeit thinly – and wrapped her arms across her middle to stave off the chill of the December afternoon. Gemma wished she could experience a little lift of joy at their reunion, but her stomach began a downward journey, like a lift travelling all the way to the basement.

'Hi!' she said, walking towards Juliet, her own smile feeling just as brittle and fake. She avoided a full hug, using her laden-down arms as an excuse, and just leaned in to kiss Juliet's cheek.

There was a stampede of feet once she got into the hall and three small forms came racing towards her and flung their arms around her hips and legs and middle, emitting squeals of, 'Auntie Gemma!' 'Here, let me take those,' Juliet said, and began to relieve Gemma of her bags before she'd even given an answer.

'Hey, Josh …' Gemma said a little breathlessly. 'You're squeezing a little hard, mate.'

He looked up at her, still squeezing. He was surprisingly strong for someone that small. 'I'm Jake. That's Josh,' he said, and the other twin just giggled and started squeezing just as hard.

'Whoever you are, cut it out!' she yelled. 'Or I'll put those Christmas presents back in the car and take them back home.'

That did the trick. Both boys released her and stood watching her hopefully, faces a picture of angelic innocence.

Juliet shook her head. 'You know the rule, boys. No presents until Christmas morning.' And she disappeared upstairs with the parcels, much to the very vocal disappointment of the twins. With no brightly wrapped incentive to keep them hugging her, the smaller ones ran off again, leaving the way open for their older sister.

Polly was staring at her in a most unnerving fashion. Gemma smiled at her.

'You sent me a card that said "Happy Birthday Groovy Eight Year Old",' Polly said in an accusing tone. 'I'm ten.'

Whoops. To be honest, Polly was lucky she'd got one at all. Gemma wasn't very good at that sort of thing. 'Sorry,' she said with a big smile, 'but you're growing up so fast I can hardly keep track! Look at you!'

Thankfully, Polly seemed appeased by that answer. 'You can make it up to me next year,' she said matter-of-factly.

Gemma smiled and gave her a kiss. 'I promise I'll get you one with a big eleven on it.'

Polly just blinked. 'I was thinking more in terms of cash. And notes are better than coins.'

Gemma bit back a giggle. She'd got her old man's wheeler-dealer instincts, this one. But she remembered how galling it was to be thought younger than you were at that age, especially when you were the younger sister, always straining to catch up to your older sibling and never getting any closer. She pulled a ten-pound note out her pocket. 'Why don't I start now?' she said in a whisper. 'But don't tell the others.'

'Don't tell the others what?' a voice said from the top of the stairs.

Gemma spun round. 'Violet!' She waited while her eldest niece descended the stairs then scooped her into a hug. She didn't always get it right with the little ones, but she and Vi got on like a house on fire. She pulled back and took a good look at her niece. 'Nice outfit, and I would kill for those legs!'

Violet was wearing a Fearless Vampire Killers T-shirt and skinny jeans that looked sprayed on.

'I'd kill for a pair of those shoes,' she said, indicating Gemma's bright red suede heels, 'but Mum won't let me.'

'You'll have to forgive her,' she said, glancing up, 'she's too old to remember what having fun is like.'

'But you're old too!' Violet protested. 'And you know how to have fun.'

'Thanks … I think,' Gemma said, laughing softly, and then she leaned closer. 'Has that cute boy you mentioned in your last email asked you out yet?'

Violet blushed and shook her head. She started to answer, but Juliet appeared on the landing at that moment, so they just shared a conspiratorial smile.

Juliet frowned as she came back down the stairs and Gemma could feel her sister's disapproval radiating stronger with every step. She knew Juliet and Violet had been going through a bit of a bumpy patch – didn't all fifteen-year-olds do that with their mothers? – but she couldn't really help it if Vi saw her as the cool auntie she could talk to about stuff.

When Juliet reached the hall she smiled sweetly and said, 'It's really lovely to see you after such a long time.' But Gemma heard the reproach beneath her words, as only a sibling could. That was the way Juliet did things. Nothing showed on the surface; all the negative stuff simmered unhealthily underneath. Gemma couldn't stand all that passive-aggressive business.

'Lovely to see you too,' she said, smiling back and wishing Juliet's perfect shell would crack just once, just to see if she was really human.

'Tea?' Juliet asked, and led the way through to the kitchen.

Gemma nodded, but braced herself while Juliet filled the kettle. In her experience, her sister always asked the most dangerous questions while doing mundane tasks.

And here it came …

'It's very early for you to be bringing the kids' Christmas presents,' Juliet said as she flicked off the tap and placed the kettle on its stand.

Translation? *How have you managed to deliver actual presents more than a week before the day, instead of sending guilt-inflated gift cards that arrive in the first week of January?*

Gemma tried to ignore it. She wasn't as heartless as Juliet made her sound. She nearly always worked right up until Christmas Eve and then dashed off on her annual Christmas holiday – the only proper break she had all year, because she always seemed to be working in the summer. And the kids never complained about having plenty of money to spend on iTunes or in the toy shop.

She shrugged. 'Just trying to be a bit more organised this year. How's Aunt Sylvia?' she added, attempting to deflect the conversation elsewhere. She'd tell Juliet the real reason for delivering the presents at some point. But later. After she'd had a chance to soften her up a little.

A slow, slightly un-Juliet-like smile lifted the corners of her mouth. Almost a naughty smile – except that couldn't be. Because, Gemma knew that if she and Juliet had been born on the same day, her sister would have been the good twin and she would have been the evil one.

She decided to probe what that strange little smile was all about. 'What's up? Is something the matter with Aunt Sylvia?'

Juliet picked up the kettle and poured boiling water into a waiting teapot. 'Oh, she's about the same as she has been for the last few months. Actually, I thought we could pay her a visit this afternoon. Violet's going to mind the little ones for a couple of hours.'

Gemma glanced at the clock in dismay. *A couple of hours?*

So much for a flying visit.

*

Juliet led the way into the day room at Greenacres and pulled out one of the high-backed armchairs so Gemma could sit opposite their great-aunt. As much as the thought of that fluffy sweet waiting patiently for Gemma in the depths of Aunt Sylvia's handbag tickled her, she had more serious reasons for insisting Gemma came here this afternoon.

She wanted her sister to see just how far their great-aunt had deteriorated, hoping – in vain, maybe – that it'd prompt Gemma into spending more time with her family. It wouldn't be long before Sylvia forgot them both completely.

'Hello, Aunt Sylvia,' Juliet said, watching closely as Gemma lowered herself into the chair. She then pulled one round for herself. 'Look who's here!'

Sylvia blinked and looked at her new visitor. 'Gemma!' she exclaimed and pressed her wrinkly fingers over her mouth while her eyes shone.

'Hi, Auntie Syl,' Gemma said. 'Long time no see.'

'Too long,' Sylvia said sharply, but then smiled again. 'Never mind. You're here now – that's all that matters.' She turned to look at Juliet. 'Hello.'

'Hello.'

Sylvia's brow wrinkled slightly.

Her aunt stared blankly at her for a few seconds before returning her attention back to Gemma. 'Oh,' she said suddenly, 'I just remembered! I've been saving something special for you.' She reached down beside her chair for her handbag and rummaged inside for a few seconds before dropping something small into Gemma's hand.

It was the punchline Juliet had been anticipating for more than a week, but now the moment had arrived, she really didn't feel much like laughing.

Of course Sylvia would remember Gemma. Everybody did. It was Juliet who was turning shades of grey, disappearing quietly into the wallpaper of her humdrum life.

Gemma was looking at the object in her palm, a bemused expression on her face. Juliet held out her hand to take it from her. She knew where the bin was and Gemma didn't. 'Here, let me …' She began to rise, but then Gemma dropped the item into her waiting hand and she discovered it was neither sticky nor fluffy. In fact, it was slightly heavy and the tiniest bit cold. Delicate. She looked down at her palm and found a gold and diamond ring sparkling there.

'I couldn't possibly …' Gemma was saying.

Juliet dropped the ring back into Gemma's hand then stood up and backed away.

Her grandmother's engagement ring – the one she'd left to Sylvia on strict instructions that their eldest granddaughter would get it when they were both gone.

Despite the protestations, Aunt Sylvia pressed Gemma's fingers closed around the three diamonds in their rose gold setting. 'No, you have it. It would look better on a pretty thing like you than on my bony old fingers.'

Gemma's eyebrows raised slightly, but she didn't look shocked, or guilty, Juliet realised. Didn't she know?

Of course she didn't know. That would involve being present for family events and listening to what other people said, and neither of those things were Gemma's strong suit. Juliet scowled as Gemma kissed their great-aunt and slid the ring into her pocket. 'Thank you, Auntie Syl. This means a lot to me.'

And she said it with such a sweet sincerity that Juliet wanted to scream. In fact, she must have made a muffled noise of some sort, because Sylvia turned to look at her again. 'Didn't you say you were going to get the tea, dear?'

'Uh …' Juliet's mouth refused to work properly. She swallowed and tried again. 'I just …'

She had to get away, get out of here. Otherwise she was going to create a scene. And Juliet never created scenes. Even when Greg had left she'd only let big silent tears fall down her face as she'd watched him climb into his car, slam the door and drive away.

She looked towards the day-room door, and then, without deciding to, she was walking. Out of the room, down the corridor and into the small kitchenette that the nurses used to make their tea. Juliet was here so often that they let her use it whenever she visited. She stared at the dull white cabinet in front of her. She knew the teabags were inside, but she didn't reach out and open the door.

She felt something rising inside her chest, something bitter and dark. This was no bubble of naughty laughter at a fluffy sweet. It was cold, tasting of emptiness. It scared her so much that she squashed it down again, closed her eyes and concentrated on making it disappear.

When she thought she'd finally regained control, she opened the cupboard door, retrieved the cheerful Union Jack teabag tin someone had saved after the Jubilee and made tea for three.

What else could she do?

Helping was what Juliet did. And if people only half-remembered her when she did that, she'd probably disappear completely if she stopped.

*

Gemma glanced across at Juliet as they drove back to her house from the nursing home.

'What's up with you?'

Juliet's face was a picture of calm, but she was clutching the steering wheel so hard the tendons were standing out on the backs of her hands. She flicked the indicator and sailed round a corner at an even speed. 'Nothing.'

Gemma could let this drop. That's what Juliet obviously wanted her to do. And it was the option she usually chose.

There was enough tension between the two of them without adding more issues into the mix, but today – because she was feeling a little guilty maybe – she decided to press on. 'Well, it's obviously not nothing, because you've got a face like a smacked fish.'

Beautifully done, Gemma. You waded in nice and gentle-like.

And then she just kept going: 'You wanted the ring, didn't you?'

She regretted that comment the moment it left her mouth. Why had she said that? Why? She'd told herself she was going to tread round the subject carefully, give Juliet the opportunity to tell her herself. She'd guessed that her sister's mood had something to do with Gran's ring, because she'd been behaving almost normally up until that point.

'No,' Juliet said, but the serene mask was slipping. Her jaw was tense and she glared at the oncoming traffic as she waited to turn right at a junction.

'Yes, you did. It's just the kind of old-fashioned stuff you go all gooey over.'

Juliet suddenly swerved into the kerb and stopped, yanking the handbrake on before turning to look at Gemma. 'It's not about the ring! Not about the diamonds and gold, anyway …' She shook her head and let out an exasperated sigh. 'It's about … Oh, forget it. You wouldn't understand.'

'I'm not a little kid any more, Juliet. You could try to give me the *chance* to understand, but you never do. So tell me … What is it that is so wonderfully complex that my poor little brain could never hope to grasp?'

Juliet kept her eyes on the road ahead, and when she spoke

her voice was heavy. 'I just wanted someone to think about me first for once, that's all. I'm tired of being second best.' She thought for a moment. 'No, it's not quite that … I'm tired of being the warm-up act.'

Gemma turned to look at her, nose wrinkled. 'Huh?'

'It's the story of my life,' Juliet said bitterly. 'Take Greg – I feel like I was one he settled for until the real love of his life came along. I was keeping bloody Anoushka's seat warm, basically.'

If Gemma didn't know any better, she'd have thought *Bloody Anoushka* was the woman's full name, because Juliet never called her anything else these days.

When she spoke again, her voice had taken on a grim tone. 'And then there's you …'

Gemma instantly rose to her own defence. 'What did I do?'

Juliet looked over her shoulder, indicated, released the handbrake and started driving towards home again. 'Don't pretend to know you weren't the favourite. Once you arrived Mum and Dad just doted on you and I just seemed to fade into the background, like I was the one they practised on until they were ready for you.'

Gemma's mouth dropped open. How could Juliet believe such things? Didn't she know that all their mother had talked about when Gemma had visited was how lovely Juliet's wedding had been, and what a good cook she was, how adorable her children were and why didn't Gemma find a nice man like Greg instead of wasting her time with all those losers?

Her stomach dived. Oh, hell.

If that was what Juliet believed, no wonder there was always a whiff of resentment in the air when they got together. Unfortunately, it was probably going to take another decade for them to unravel that issue, and Gemma had more pressing matters on her mind, like stopping a fully-fledged Juliet meltdown when she let slip what she'd been avoiding bringing up all afternoon.

First things first … She racked her brain to find a way to bring the conversation onto a happier note. She really needed Juliet to be feeling warm and forgiving when she broke the news.

'I think you should have the ring,' she said, nodding to herself. 'After all, you're the eldest. It makes sense.'

Juliet carried on driving, but at the same time she seemed to go very still, and Gemma suddenly realised that maybe she was the last one to catch on to who the ring had been intended for all along.

'I meant it when I said it wasn't about a couple of diamonds,' Juliet said. 'Anyway, it's Aunt Sylvia's ring now. She can give it to whoever she wants.'

Gemma frowned. 'She did seem a little bit mixed up today …'

Juliet let out a weary sigh. 'It's more than that, Gemma! You'd know that if you were around more. I visit twice a week, and only a handful of times since October has she remembered who I was.'

'Don't be daft!' Aunt Sylvia couldn't possibly be that bad. At least, Gemma didn't want to believe things had deteriorated so badly. Surely that couldn't happen to the spunky old lady who'd always seemed so sharp, who'd always been able to beat her at rummy, no matter how hard she'd tried? 'Of course she remembers you,' she told Juliet. 'She just has a bit of a problem with names now and again.'

'You're fooling yourself, seeing things from your own unique, Gemma-centred perspective as always,' Juliet replied, regaining some of her usual self-righteous air. 'Whether you want to admit it or not, she's gone downhill very fast, and that's just another reason why I really, *really* need your help this Christmas.'

Gemma's eyes widened. On any other day she'd have been stupidly pleased to hear Juliet say something like that, but today that was the last thing she wanted to hear. All she was going to do now was prove Juliet right about her once again.

She swallowed. Oh, hell. She had to tell her. Couldn't put it off any longer. She owed Juliet that at least.

So, as her sister pulled into her driveway and turned off the car engine, she blurted out the secret she'd been keeping all afternoon.

&

CHAPTER SIX

'I can't believe you!' Juliet yelled, as she crashed through the front door and marched down the corridor. She wasn't sure exactly where she was going, she just needed to keep striding. When she reached the study she turned round and headed back in Gemma's direction, meeting her in the hall. 'You're jetting off to the Caribbean for Christmas and leaving me here on my own? *Again?*'

Her sister's mouth opened and closed but no words came out.

'Bloody St Lucia, as well!' Juliet screamed. 'Rub it in, why don't you?'

She became aware of four pairs of eyes watching her from the living-room doorway, let out a shriek of frustration and strode off in the direction of the kitchen. Probably not a good idea. There were heavy things in there. And knives.

Gemma was either stupid enough or foolhardy enough to follow.

'I'm sorry,' Gemma said, her eyes looking large and moist and sorrowful. Juliet felt a tug of sympathy down in her gut, but she stamped on it. It wouldn't work, not this time.

She sucked in a breath through her teeth, held it for a second and blew it out again. 'You promised! I'm behind with the preparations, because every time I try to tick something off my list, something unexpected crops up. I've hardly got enough time to sleep before Christmas Day as it is – and that's when I thought you were going to be around to help!'

'Juliet, you make the whole thing such hard work. And that's not what Christmas is about. It's not called a *holiday* for nothing, you know. Why don't you have a quiet Christmas, just you and the kids, and leave all the fuss for another year?'

Her sister really had no clue, had she? It was too late for that.

'Aside from the kids – who have been behaving like monsters, by the way – I've arranged with the home for Aunt Sylvia to spend the day with us, Doris Waterman always comes because all her children now live in America, and then there's a couple of au pairs who go to our church, and the last-minute additions of Uncle Tony and his new girlfriend.'

Gemma frowned. 'Which one's Uncle Tony?'

'*Gemma!* You're missing the point! I would never have invited so many if I'd thought you weren't going to be here to help me.'

Juliet slumped down into a chair and laid her head on the kitchen table. Her right temple had started to throb right about the time Gemma had announced she had tickets to fly to St Lucia on the eighteenth and she was worried something was going to burst if she didn't try to calm down a bit.

She felt like crying. Really crying. Not that eye-fanning,

tissue-dabbing kind of crying, but the kind of sobbing that made one sound like a demented baboon and produced lots of snot.

Gemma swore softly, and Juliet heard the sound of a kitchen chair scraping on the flagstones before the rustle of fabric confirmed that her sister had joined her at the kitchen table. 'I didn't realise …'

Juliet lifted her head and stared at her sister. 'You never do realise, that's the problem.' It was high time Gemma took responsibility for her actions. Juliet wasn't going to let her off the hook because she'd mumbled out an apology and made puppy-dog eyes. 'Why would you do such a thing?'

'I don't know!' Gemma wailed. 'It was a spur-of-the-moment kind of thing! You sent me that snotty text and then there was a situation at work, and—'

'Spare me,' Juliet said drily. 'We all know how wonderful your job is and how it's so much more important than anyone else's. It must be such a hard life sucking up to movie stars all day long. Boo hoo.'

Gemma glared at her. 'There's a lot more to it than that! I don't just float around batting my eyelashes, you know. I'm one of the most sought-after Second ADs in the business.'

'Oh, yes. Sorry. I forgot to bow down and worship at the Temple of Gemma! I do beg your pardon.'

A hardness appeared in her sister's expression that Juliet had never seen before. 'I think I preferred it when you let it all fester away inside, kept neatly in place with a ten-foot pole stuck up your bum,' she informed her.

Juliet stood up and walked over to the window. 'Well,

you're the one who pulled it out,' she said in a superior tone. 'It's not my fault if you don't like the stink.'

*

There was that. Gemma couldn't deny that she was the one who'd unleashed this no-holds-barred version of her sister. The phrase *be careful what you wish for* came to mind, but she'd never been one for listening to advice. Especially her own.

It had just been a moment of impulsive madness at the end of a really long shoot, when all her mental energy had been used up and the only thing left floating around in her head were those tropical paradise fantasies she'd been indulging in for weeks. And then Juliet's sniping text had arrived and it had just sent Gemma over the edge.

'Why would you promise something like this and then go back on it?' Juliet wailed.

To be honest, the gin had pretty much wiped that conversation from her memory banks. She couldn't actually recall *promising* anything. 'I always say I'll be around for Christmas,' she muttered, 'and I never am.'

Juliet almost laughed at that. 'And that's supposed to make it better?'

Gemma shook her head. The second the words had left her mouth she'd realised how lame they sounded. But before she'd spoiled everything with the impulsive click on a holiday advert at the top of her web browser she really had been intending to spend Christmas in Tunbridge Wells with Juliet, not that her sister would ever believe that now.

I'm sorry,' she said, really meaning it. 'I promise I'll come next year, stay a month if I have to.' Why did she do these things? Sometimes she really needed to think before she reacted, especially when Juliet was involved.

Juliet folded her arms and looked at her. 'If you *have* to …?'

Okay, that hadn't come out right. 'I meant, if you need me.'

The haughty look on her sister's face told her she needed Gemma about as much as she needed a hole in the head. The realisation hit Gemma like a bullet to the chest. No wonder she avoided coming here. Juliet wasn't interested in creating some balance in their relationship, and this … This was just another point-scoring exercise, with Gemma cast as the loser right from the outset.

Well, this time Gemma had some ammunition of her own to throw. 'You know why I stay away? You really want to know?'

'Enlighten me, o wise one …'

That sarcastic, supercilious tone Juliet often used on her, and only her, got right up her nose. 'Because even if I do the right thing, I do it the wrong way. Even if I try, I haven't tried hard enough. It's exhausting being your sister! I can't be the person you want me to be, because the person you want me to be is *you*! I'm not you, Juliet. And, guess what, I don't want to be!'

Uh-oh. Maybe she'd gone a little too far with that one, because Juliet went very, very pink in the face and she seemed to be struggling to form a coherent sentence. Gemma's eyes widened as Juliet marched right up to her and poked one beautifully French-polished nail in her chest.

'Well, maybe I wish I could be as selfish as you are! Maybe I wish *I* could bugger off to the Caribbean and leave Christmas to someone else for once. God knows, I deserve it!'

As Gemma stared back at Juliet, her brain and mouth empty of words, she realised how much older her sister looked. How much more tired. There were new lines round her eyes and her highlights hadn't been touched up in months. She hadn't noticed earlier, because Juliet always looked so polished, and she supposed she always expected her to be that way, but looking at her now was like looking at one of those paintings made of dots – from a distance it all looked so put together and pretty, but close up it was a bit of a mess.

This wasn't just some usual Juliet rant about family responsibility. Something was wrong. Something was really wrong. And it looked as if it had been building up for months and no one – not even Juliet – had noticed it.

Gemma had never really believed in bolts of inspiration from on high, but that's what happened to her in the following seconds. A blinding moment of clarity.

'Maybe you should,' she said.

'Maybe I should *what*?'

She looked Juliet straight in the eye. 'Bugger off and leave Christmas to someone else for once.'

Juliet stared at her. 'What on earth are you talking about?'

'You're right,' Gemma said, standing up and meeting her

sister at eye level. 'You always have to do it. Maybe it's time someone took over.'

Juliet's mouth twitched and Gemma couldn't tell if she was going to laugh or cry. 'And how – excepting angelic intervention – would that happen?' she said, with more than a touch of desperation in her tone.

'Take my plane tickets and go to St Lucia for a fortnight.'

*

Juliet stared at her sister. 'Have you had an aneurysm or something? I can't just drop everything, leave my kids behind and flit off to the Caribbean for a fortnight.'

Gemma stared right back at her. 'Yes, you can.'

She shook her head. 'No.' And then she shook it some more. 'That's the kind of thing *you* do, Gemma. It's not me. I can't. And what would I do about Christmas? I've already invited everyone! I can't cancel on them less than a fortnight before the big day. Who'll cook the dinner and everything?'

'I will,' Gemma said, looking deadly serious. 'We'll swap. You can have my Christmas and I'll do yours.'

That's when Juliet began to laugh. And not just tittering giggles; she threw her head back and bellowed her amusement out until her lungs were sore and her eyes were streaming. The kids, who'd very sensibly been hiding out in the living room since the two sisters' return, came running to see what all the hilarity was about. When Juliet opened her eyes, she found them all standing in the kitchen staring at her. Violet, in particular, looked a little worried.

She was clutching on to Polly, who wasn't fazed at all, just curious. The boys were young enough to join in and laugh along with her, without really knowing what the joke was about.

She took a steadying breath and smiled at them.

'What's up, Mum?' Vi said, her expression watchful.

Juliet sighed. 'Nothing. Auntie Gemma just said something really, really funny, that's all.'

'It wasn't a joke,' Gemma mumbled.

A little hiccup of laughter escaped from Juliet's lips. 'I know.'

Gemma put her hands on her hips. 'I could cook Christmas dinner!'

The expression on her face reminded Juliet of when Gemma had been around two and Juliet seven, and Gemma had refused to wear nappies any more because her big sister didn't. As always, she'd got her way, and, as always, everyone else had been clearing up the messes for weeks afterwards.

'It requires not only cooking skills, but organisation and strategic planning,' Juliet warned. 'You can't just get up in the morning and wing it, you know.'

Her sister glowered at her. 'You have no idea what I do all day when I'm at work, do you? Logistics is my thing. It's what I do best.'

Juliet did her hardest not to start laughing again. And failed.

The younger kids wandered off now the fun was over and it looked like another spat was brewing. Only Violet stayed to hear the whole thing out. 'Why are you talking about Auntie Gemma cooking Christmas dinner?' she asked. 'You're not going away, are you?'

That sobered Juliet up pretty quick. 'No, darling. I'm not.' She'd thought Vi had been the least upset of all her children when she'd had to break the news they weren't going to be seeing their father over the Christmas holidays, but maybe she'd allowed herself to be fooled by a bit of teenage bravado. She walked over and hugged her eldest, and Violet even let her. 'Gemma just made a joke about me going on her beach holiday and her staying here to look after you all. It wasn't anything serious.'

Gemma huffed out a breath. 'I said it wasn't a joke! I was trying to be nice.'

'You *are* nice, Auntie Gemma,' Vi said, peeling one arm away from her mother and inviting her aunt to hug her from the other side. Gemma rolled her eyes, but she didn't turn her niece down. So Juliet and Gemma stayed like that for a few moments, joined by a fifteen-year-old and almost touching, but as soon as Violet released them, she and Juliet retreated to opposite corners of the kitchen, eyeing each other like boxers in a ring.

Juliet kept staring at Gemma, but used a soothing voice on her daughter. 'Can you go and check what the boys are up to, Vi? It's gone awfully quiet, and that usually means trouble.'

Violet looked nervously between her aunt and her mother, then left to check on her brothers.

Gemma lifted her chin. 'I meant what I said. The offer still stands.'

Juliet shook her head. It felt heavy on her shoulders. 'I

know you did,' she said wearily, 'and that's the saddest thing of all. Because if you really knew me, if you really understood one tiny thing about me, you'd know that I'd *never* abandon my kids at Christmas.'

&

CHAPTER SEVEN

Juliet woke up with her face stuck to something smooth and flat. And moist. She poked a finger at the edge of her mouth and discovered she'd been drooling. She blinked a couple of times and tried to make sense of her surroundings. The hard thing beneath her cheek was the kitchen table. The overhead light was on and its harsh glare made her want to close her eyes again, but she pushed her body up with her hands so she was sitting up straight and looked around. A heap of satiny fabric and tinsel lay strewn on the table in front of her.

Oh, yes. Polly's angel costume.

The last thing she remembered was rubbing her eyes and telling herself just another ten minutes and then she'd crawl upstairs to bed, set the alarm for five thirty and then get up and finish it off in the morning.

She twisted her head to look at the clock on the wall. Ten past two. She moved her jaw, loosening it a little. She was exhausted, but that was hardly surprising. She'd always been pleased all of her children had wanted music lessons, but now she was starting to wonder if it had been such a good idea. Not only was there the inevitable ferrying of her brood to and from those lessons, but Christmas brought a flurry of

rehearsals, dress rehearsals and finally the ear-splitting per-
formances themselves.

And then there was the baking, the standing behind trestle
tables and handing out glasses of wine poured from boxes
that she always seemed to get roped into. She was on the
PTA of both her children's schools, and they didn't even
bother asking if she was going to organise the refreshments
each year any more. They just assumed she'd take charge,
pull together a rota of willing – and not-so-willing – helpers,
wave a magic wand and, hey presto, wine and mince pies,
orange squash and Santa-shaped cookies would appear from
nowhere.

She linked her hands, straightened her arms above her
head and stretched to loosen out the kinks in her spine,
before yawning wide and long, and then she stared at the
mass of half-finished angel costume on the table in front of
her.

She just needed to finish tacking the tinsel round the hem,
then make a halo out of a mangled coat hanger and more
sparkly stuff and it'd be done. Of course, it should have
been finished weeks ago, all ready to go, and it would have
been – if she'd known about it. But at teatime, while stuffing
her face with pasta and home-made tomato sauce, Polly had
enquired loudly where her angel costume was.

'What angel costume?' Juliet had replied, her heart racing
and an icy sensation washing over her.

'The one for the carol concert,' Polly had said and turned
her attention to twirling tagliatelle round her fork. 'Miss
Barker gave us all a slip to take home with what we had to
wear.'

Juliet stopped washing up and raced to where Polly had thrown her book bag in the hall when she'd come in from school. A quick search revealed two reading books, a host of drawings, an empty crisp packet and a pair of dirty socks. No slip. 'There's nothing there, Polls!' she yelled and marched back into the kitchen, bag in hand as proof.

Polly had shrugged and slurped the last tail of pasta up into her mouth with a smack. 'Oh,' she said, totally unfazed. 'It must still be in the drawer under my desk. Sorry. But I need to be an angel when I sing my solo at the concert tomorrow.'

Juliet had closed her eyes and counted to ten. And then twenty. When, oh when, would these schools learn that giving kids slips of paper to hand to their parents was a disaster waiting to happen? She really wanted to yell at someone, but she clenched her teeth and swallowed the feeling.

'Never mind,' she'd said, not as calmly as she'd have liked. 'It's fine. I'm sure we can do something with a pillowcase and a bit of tinsel.'

That was when her daughter's ever-cool demeanour cracked. She stared back at Juliet in horror. 'A *pillowcase*?'

Juliet nodded. 'That's all I can do at the last minute. The shops are shut and Violet has the dress rehearsal for her dance thing tonight.'

Polly's eyes filled and her bottom lip wobbled while the edges of her mouth pulled down and out. She'd always made a strange rectangular shape like that when she cried, ever since she was a baby. Greg had always joked it made her look like a pillar box, but Juliet wasn't finding it very funny as fat tears rolled down Polly's cheeks and plopped onto her plate.

'B – but Tegan has a Disney dress and Arabella's grandma made her one from scratch, with real feathers on the wings and everything!'

Juliet crouched down by Polly's chair and put her arm round her, ignoring the twins as they loudly and enthusiastically mimicked their sister's wailing. 'I'll make it look really good, I promise. We'll use the fancy pillowcases from the guest bedroom, the ones with frills on them.'

Polly crossed her arms and shook her head. 'No. It won't do! That's not what I wanted. I need it to be perfect!'

That's when Juliet had lost her only barely reined-in temper. Result? One tense-shouldered mother hunched over a sewing machine, and one tearful child who'd needed a few extra cuddles at bedtime. In the end she'd remembered the bridesmaid's dress that Violet had worn for Greg's sister's wedding. Puff sleeves, a sash and full skirt in off-white silk. A few additions here and there and it would be wonderful.

She leaned back in her chair and pressed her hand over her mouth as she let out yet another gigantic yawn, then she pushed the chair away and sloped out of the kitchen and up the stairs to bed.

The alarm went off far too early the following morning, but Juliet didn't have the time, or the energy, to argue with it. After dropping the kids off at their respective schools, she headed out of town to one of the nearby retail parks. Both boys wanted this year's must-have toy – an action figure that did all sort of things Juliet couldn't even remember, and didn't really want to – but the Internet company she'd ordered them from had emailed her to say they only had one left in stock.

None of the other big websites could promise to deliver it before Christmas, if they even had it in stock at all, and the companies that did 'click and collect' were all showing it was sold out on their websites. How could she give one boy their dream present and not the other? But she knew that many of those big retailers didn't allow you to reserve on the website if there were only a couple left in store. Her only hope was to try any place that might stock it and hope they still had one left on the shelf that wasn't showing up for reservation on the website.

She was there early enough to find a parking space and jump out, check Toy World, discover they didn't have any but the branch in Maidstone might have, and jump back in her car within fifteen minutes. By the time she got to Maidstone, however, it was a different story. When she'd scoured the shelves, trying to see if one was stuck at the back or hidden behind something else in the wrong spot, and had come up empty, she queued up at customer services. Of course, the store only had one member of staff on duty, an unusually spotty and slow-witted junior who needed to ask his supervisor to do everything for him. Probably even wipe his nose.

She was second in the queue when she heard the woman in front of her ask exactly the same question she was going to ask, and receive a weary no, so when her turn came she and the junior sales assistant just stared at each other and then she mumbled, 'Never mind,' and walked out of the shop.

By the time she got to Bluewater she'd almost lost the will to live. Inside the shopping centre was Juliet's definition of hell. The wide walkways were crammed with people jostling each other, the queues at the cash tills in every shop seemed to snake for miles and the jaunty music pumping from the speakers in the ceiling was making her want to pick up something sharp and attack someone with it. Seriously, if she heard 'Happy Holidays' one more time she was going to scream!

Both toy shops she trudged to had felt-tip-written signs pinned on the inside of the windows, firmly warning customers they were out of stock of Robotron Xtreme, and in a haze of disappointment, she wandered into John Lewis and sought to soothe herself with the sight of all those desirable home furnishings. And it worked. Enough for her mind to clear and realise they had a toy department on the top floor, anyway.

She quickly ran to an escalator and marched up it and onto the next one. She was marching through the pink and girly toy section when she pulled up short. There, stuffed among the Barbies and Hello Kittys was the holy grail – Robotron Xtreme! Obviously dumped in the wrong department by someone who'd changed their mind.

She silently prayed blessings on that fickle soul as she lunged for it and hugged it to her chest with both arms. She wasn't about to let it go, even if rugby-tackled.

Once the toy was paid for and in a bag, she was heading back to the car, but the euphoria she'd felt at the moment of sale started to drain away. By the time she was driving back towards Tunbridge Wells she felt as if she was in trance. A quick check of the clock on the dashboard revealed that she didn't have time to go home, so she sped straight to the boys' and Polly's school, hid the present in the boot before she picked them up, then headed off to fetch Vi.

The twins were even more ear-splittingly energetic than usual on the drive over, and then she remembered it had been the class party that day and, despite each parent providing both a healthy and a 'treat' donation for the food, she suspected her boys had consumed nothing but E-numbers and the poor teacher would now be faced with disposing of multiple pots of cherry tomatoes and trays of rapidly curling brown-bread sandwiches.

'I'm hungry,' Josh whined.

'Me too,' his brother added.

'I'm going to cook tea as soon as we get in …' Lord, forgive her – dubious frozen casserole from the back of the freezer. 'So you'll just have to wait until then.'

She was as good as her word, too. Within twenty minutes of walking through the front door, she was dishing up tough-looking meat, slicing chunks off a home-made loaf to go with it and calling the kids to the table. Vi, Polly and Josh appeared, but Jake was nowhere to be seen.

'Where's your brother?' she asked all of them, but directing most of her attention to Violet, who she was attempting to train up as her second-in-command.

Violet looked heavenwards and crossed her arms. 'How should I know? I try to steer clear of the runts as much as possible.'

Juliet didn't have time to lecture her daughter on her attitude to her brothers at the moment; Polly had to be at the parish church by six thirty to get ready for the carol concert, which started at seven fifteen. And she'd also said she'd try to pop in to her neighbours' mulled wine and mince pie evening once the younger ones were safely tucked up in bed. Since she'd only be a few doors away, she'd bribed Violet to babysit for the evening. She even considered the tenner her daughter had wangled out of her for doing it a bargain. When was the last time she'd put on a nice dress and talked to adults about adult things?

And Will was going to be there. She half-wanted to see if that twinge of something she wasn't quite ready to name happened again. Not that she knew what she'd do about it if it did.

She discovered Jake behind the sofa in the living room, surrounded by bits of gold foil. It didn't take more than a couple of seconds to work out that her hungry little man had raided the Christmas tree for the Belgian chocolate decorations she'd hung there earlier in the week and now was regretting it thoroughly. He looked up at her with big eyes, his complexion grey.

Oh, no!

Juliet knew that look. She picked her son up under the arms as he clamped his hand across his mouth and mumbled, 'I don't feel very well.'

Thankfully, they had a downstairs toilet. Not so thankfully, they only made it as far as the hall before the inevitable happened. The sound of regurgitated party food and liquid chocolate hitting the flagstone floor was not pleasant. Juliet swallowed her revulsion down and just kept running.

When the worst of it was over, she called Violet to keep an

eye on him, then returned to the hall with a mop, bucket and disinfectant to clear up the mess. It was only then that she realised that the tiles had not been the only casualty of Jake's greediness. Polly's angel costume had been draped across the chair in the entrance way, and while it had been covered in dry-cleaner's plastic, the hem had been peeping out of the bottom. Streaks of pinky brown sick were now congealing on the tacked-on tinsel.

Forgetting about the floor, she grabbed the dress and ran to the utility room with it. The only thing to do was to rip all the hard work she'd done last night off the watermarked silk before it stained. Perhaps a strand of clean tinsel tied around the waist would add the extra sparkle it needed now the hemline was plain?

There was a wail behind her from the entrance to the utility room, and she turned to find her youngest daughter there, tears streaming down her face. Juliet left the dress and pulled Polly into a firm hug. 'It's okay,' she said calmly, even though she could feel her internal thermostat rising, even though voices inside her head were screaming about the time ticking away, the hall floor and the grey-looking child hunched over the toilet in the room next door. 'I'm going to fix it, and it'll be just as pretty, you wait and see. Now go and eat your dinner.'

Polly nodded tearfully and trotted off back to the kitchen. Juliet stared at the dress, her head pounding. What had she thought she could do to rescue it? Something to do with tinsel, but she couldn't remember what. It didn't matter, anyway, because she didn't have time for that now.

She rushed next door and checked on Jake, who was looking a bit sorry for himself but hadn't been sick again. Hope-fully, now he'd let the pressure off his overloaded stomach, he'd be okay. She was pretty sure this was the result of too much chocolate, not the dreaded sickness bug that had been going around school.

'How are you feeling?' she asked him, crouching down beside him and rubbing his back.

'Bit better,' he said mournfully.

She wiped his face and gently led him upstairs to brush his teeth, then brought him back downstairs and tucked him up on the sofa with a bucket next to him. Yes, her lovely upholstery was in danger there, but it was quicker to get to him if he needed her.

'You just call me if you need me,' she told him. 'I'll be right back. I've just got to go and check on Polly's dress.'

The next fifteen minutes were spent running between Jake, the other children eating dinner in the kitchen and the utility room, to see if the sick stains were showing on the dress now the adornments had been removed. On one pass through the living room she stole a replacement strand of silver tinsel for Polly's costume, then ran upstairs. She wouldn't be needing her little black dress any more, but maybe she could smarten up what she had on for the carol concert. Higher heels and her silver cardigan ought to do it.

When she came back downstairs she went to find Violet. 'You can be in charge while I run Polly to the church,' she told her.

Violet crossed her arms. 'I'm not clearing up if he's sick.'

'Fine,' Juliet said, manhandling Polly out of her summer

rain mac and into her winter coat – honestly, when would that child ever learn to dress for the appropriate season? 'Then make sure he stays on the sofa and throws up in the bucket.'

Violet made a face and stomped off. Juliet grabbed the angel dress and her warmly wrapped-up child and headed for the car. She calculated she just about had time to drop Polly off, run back home to do her make-up – which would have to be a refreshing of what she already had on – brush her hair, find a pair of heels and then she could dash back to the church for the service, dragging Josh with her to give Violet some peace to look after Jake. And if he was looking perkier when she got back, maybe she'd pop into Mike and Sarah's just to say Merry Christmas and drop off the nice bottle of wine she'd bought them. Surely one glass of mulled wine and twenty minutes of adult conversation wouldn't be too much to ask?

She sat in the carol service, mentally rejigging her To Do list as children sang and recited poems and stumbled their way through Bible readings. She paused while Polly sang her solo, of course, but went straight back to thinking about Christmas cake and stocking fillers right afterwards, and all the while the tinny carols she'd heard in a thousand shops for the past month kept running round inside her head, so loud they threatened to drown out the Angel Gabriel on stage, announcing the birth of the Messiah in a manger made out of corrugated cardboard and hamster bedding.

She left the church feeling slightly, very slightly, less stressed about the rest of the evening. If she hadn't been looking forward to being just Juliet for a while instead of a busy mum of four, she might have been tempted to climb into bed with a good book, but this was her one invite to do something this year where she wasn't helping or serving – partly because of a packed timetable, but partly because invitations hadn't been as forthcoming recently. Old friends weren't quite sure what to do with her now she and Greg had split up.

Once Polly and Josh were back at home and brushing their teeth before bed, and Jake had been checked on and Violet mollified, Juliet ran upstairs to swipe some more lipstick across her drying lips and refresh her mascara. She let her hair out of her ponytail and brushed it quickly. She was just poking diamond studs into her ear holes when Violet knocked on her door.

'What's up?' Juliet asked, squinting at her reflection in her dressing-table mirror. Had the lighting in here got worse, or was she starting to need glasses?

'Abby's invited me to a party and I want to know if I can go.'

Juliet pressed her lips together as she forced the stud through the soft flesh of her earlobe. She wasn't keen on that girl. Abby had been caught bunking off school once and always seemed to have a crowd of boys hanging round her. 'Will her parents be home?'

'I think so.'

Juliet turned to look at her daughter. 'Think so isn't good enough. I need to know for certain. Get me her mother's mobile number and I'll talk to her about it.'

Violet reacted as if her mother had asked her to hold hands with her while walking down the high street. 'You're so embarrassing! No one else's parents do that!'

Juliet decided not to fight that point now. 'When is it?'

Violet played with the door handle and looked at her sock-clad feet. 'Christmas Eve,' she said quietly.

Juliet spun round, dropping the second stud on the carpet as she did so. 'Christmas Eve! But you know that's our special family night!'

Violet shrugged.

Juliet turned and crouched down, running her hand across the carpet in search of her lost earring. 'We'll talk about this later, Violet. Right now I haven't got the time.'

There was a loud huff from the other side of the room. 'That means no … you always say we'll talk about it later when you're going to say no! God, Mum …! I'm not a baby any more. I can go out with my friends if I want to. And I want to …' She paused for dramatic effect. 'Much more than playing stupid games with Miss Know-It-All and the runts!'

'Violet!' Juliet's reply was terse but not explosive; even so, she felt the rage beginning to boil inside her, making her stomach quiver and her fingertips itchy. 'I do *not* have time for this now!'

Violet flounced from the room, and Juliet continued to hunt for her lost earring, all the while feeling like a pressure cooker just about to blow. Eventually she gave up searching, yanked the first earring out and threw it on her dressing table, then shoved her feet in the first pair of heels she found in her wardrobe and clomped downstairs to say goodnight to the kids.

She was met at the bottom of the stairs by Jake, trailing the blanket she'd covered him with, puffing his cheeks out and trying to keep his mouth closed. The way his eyes were popping was slightly alarming.

She kept her voice low, soothing. 'Jake…where's the bucket, sweetie?'

He just shook his head and she saw the panic in his eyes.

'Jake,' she screamed, forgetting all about low and soothing, '*where's the bucket*?'

Half a second after that the bucket was a moot point and Juliet was trying not to look at her shoes.

&

CHAPTER EIGHT

Juliet tried to work out what to do first – comfort Jake, clean up the hall for a second time or shout 'Ewww' about the slightly warm and squishy stuff that was seeping into her left shoe. She opted for the former and hugged her snivelling six-year-old to her, never minding what else was transferring itself onto her best black trousers.

She guided him upstairs, stood him in the bath and washed him down, and she was just tucking him into bed when the phone rang. She ignored it.

But then the distant cry came from downstairs. 'Mum! It's for you!'

Not wanting to yell so close to her poorly son, Juliet stuck her head out of the twins' bedroom door before she yelled back her answer. 'Tell them to call back later! I'm busy with your brother.'

Violet's clumping steps came closer and then Juliet could see her face as she rounded the corner in the staircase. Instead of looking mildly put-upon, as she usually did when required to answer the phone, she was wide-eyed. 'It's a policeman,' she said quietly. 'He says he needs to talk to you.'

Juliet motioned for her eldest to go and keep an eye on

one of her youngest and took the handset from Violet as she passed her on the landing.

'Hello ...?' she said, as she stared down over the banisters at the ugly-looking puddle in the middle of her otherwise pristine entrance hall. Twice in one day. That had to be some kind of record.

'Mrs Taylor?'

Juliet's stomach dropped. She knew that voice, and she was having a horrible sense of déjà vu. 'What has she done this time?'

There was a weary sigh and then PC Graham asked if she could come and talk to her great-aunt. Apparently, she had installed herself on the back seat of a bus and wasn't inclined to get off again. She'd got on earlier in the afternoon and had been riding the 281 round its route ever since and was now loudly complaining about the lack of a tour guide.

Juliet closed her eyes and shook her head. That pressure-cooker feeling was back, so bad her ears were threatening to pop. 'I can't ...' she mumbled weakly. 'I just can't ...'

She couldn't do any of this. Not any more. It was all too much – the driving, the organising, the chasing round after everyone and never having any time for herself.

'It would really help if you could—'

'I can't!' she said louder. Didn't the man understand English? 'I'm on my own and I have a sick child and I just ... can't.' And then she pressed the button to hang up the phone.

She stared at the handset for a couple of moments, and then she walked into her bedroom and shoved it under the stack of pillows and cushions she always arranged nicely at the head of the bed. It might have made a noise under there, but she couldn't tell if it was a call coming in or the ringing in her ears.

She felt like an inflatable raft on a deep and churning river that was desperately trying to stay above the surface as it headed for the rapids. All she could do was cling on and hope she survived the ride. But instead of the sound of roaring water in her ears, all she could hear was 'Happy Holidays.'

It was coming.

She could feel it coming.

Juliet picked up the nearest pillow, buried her face in it and screamed for all she was worth.

*

Violet stood in the doorway of Juliet's bedroom, biting her lip.

Juliet began to shake. It started deep down and reverberated through her limbs. She hadn't been aware of it, but she'd sunk to the floor and now her top half was draped over the edge of the bed, her legs crumpled beneath her. She steadied herself by placing a hand on the mattress and pushed herself to her feet.

It hadn't been easy to keep a lid on it all before, but it had been do-able. However, since that chat – that argument – with Gemma a couple of days ago, she was starting to think she was losing her mind. From the look on Violet's face, her daughter was starting to think so too.

Get a grip, Juliet. You can't have that. You will *not* turn into your mother. You will not pile all the things on this sweet girl that she piled on you.

She pulled oxygen into her lungs as best she could, considering her ribs felt as if they were being squeezed in a vice and she was finding it strangely difficult to breathe properly. 'Is Jake okay? He hasn't been sick again, has he?' Her voice was high and soft, much like Violet's, actually. Much like her own when she'd been that age.

Violet shook her head. 'He says he's feeling better now it's out. He wants to watch TV.'

Juliet shrugged. 'Okay.'

Violet frowned. 'But you always say no TV before bed-time.'

She just kept on staring at Violet, too weary to even say she didn't care about that rule tonight.

Violet stepped forward. 'Are you okay, Mum?'

Juliet pressed the fingers of one hand against her forehead and rubbed gently. Was she all right? She really didn't know. She swallowed. 'Um … I think I'm just a bit stressed, actually. I'm not feeling … not feeling very well. I think I'll give the party a miss and just go to bed early.'

She looked longingly at the bed. She'd love to dive in it now, but there were children to be reassured and a puddle of sick to be cleared up still. She fancied she could catch a whiff of it, even up here in the bedroom.

She inhaled through her nose and out through her mouth, just as she learned at Pilates, and then she turned to face Violet. 'Why don't we all snuggle up on the sofa and watch a movie together? It's been ages since we've done something like that.'

Some of the fear left Violet's eyes and she nodded. And then she smiled gently. 'I'll go and get the others rounded up.' Then she walked over to Juliet and flung her arms round her. 'I'll even clear up the sick, if you like?'

A tear slid down Juliet's cheek and she squeezed her daughter back. 'No, it's fine,' she whispered, 'I'll do that. You go and ask the others what they want to watch – and try and let it not turn into World War Three, okay?'

She nodded and walked towards the door, but glancing back repeatedly as Juliet swiped the single tear away with the end of her sleeve. Violet took one last look at the threshold before she disappeared down the stairs.

Juliet picked up the pillow, faintly smeared with nude lipstick, and peeled the slip off of it.

Just for a moment, she'd been staring at herself instead of Violet – overwhelmed, but trying to take on grown-up responsibilities to ease her mother's load – and it had scared her more than even the screaming had.

*

She was woken by the sound of her sons pounding the life out of each other on the landing. She stumbled out of bed, her hair standing up on one side and told them to put a sock in it. Both boys froze and smiled innocently at her. From the way Jake had his brother in a headlock, she guessed he was fighting fit again.

She felt strangely light and strangely empty, as if something had stopped pushing her down, but at the same time she just couldn't settle to anything. She kept wandering into

rooms and forgetting why she'd gone in there. She didn't
even look in her Christmas notebook once. In the end, partly
because she'd noticed the mismatching pillowcase she'd got
out the evening before, she decided to change the rest of her
bed linen. There was something about the smell and feel of
clean sheets that made one feel as if everything was going to
be all right.

As she was stripping the duvet cover she became aware
of a presence in the doorway. She turned to find Violet
there again. Was her daughter checking up on her? Had
their roles somehow become reversed? Because it shouldn't
be that way, it really shouldn't. She knew that from experience.

She smiled at Violet, a bright, sunny smile that she mostly
had to fake, but she wanted her to know that everything was
back to normal. No more outbursts. No more screaming. She
didn't even think she had the energy in her to do it this morning, anyway.

Violet studied her, but when she spoke, the question that
came out of her mouth was a bit of a surprise. 'Mum …What
Auntie Gemma said about going on holiday wasn't a joke,
was it?'

Juliet tried to think up a breezy denial, but her head was
empty. 'No, it wasn't a joke …'

Violet nodded thoughtfully. 'We didn't think it was.'

We?

But Juliet couldn't think about that at the moment. She
needed to reassure her daughter. 'Auntie Gemma might not
have meant it to be a joke, but it might as well have been.'
She opened her arms and walked towards her daughter. 'I

wouldn't do it to you, sweetie. I wouldn't go away and leave you at Christmas. I just couldn't.'

Juliet folded her arms around her daughter and breathed in her scent.

'Don't take this the wrong way, Mum,' Violet mumbled into her shoulder, 'but maybe you should.'

Juliet pulled sharply back and stared at her. 'What do you mean?'

Vi looked up at the ceiling and shifted awkwardly. 'You're not happy.'

Tears sprang with force to the backs of Juliet's eyes. 'Of course I'm happy! I've got you … and Polly … and the boys. What more could I want?'

Violet looked back at her and one side of her mouth tipped up in a rueful smile. 'If you're anything like me, you might want a boyfriend.'

Juliet shook her head. She knew it had been two years and she really should want a boyfriend, but she wasn't sure she did. Even her maybe-it-is, maybe-it-isn't relationship with her next-door neighbour was enough to freak her out. 'There's more to life than boyfriends,' she told Violet.

Vi gave her a one-shouldered shrug. She looked less than convinced by her mother's pronouncement, and it made Juliet smile. Oh, to be that young and that carefree again – when the only thing you stressed about was whether the boy you liked liked you back. She'd forgotten life could be that simple.

'But you miss Dad, don't you?'

Juliet sat on the edge of the bed and patted the spot beside her. Violet joined her.

'I did at first,' she said, 'but now I think maybe I just miss having someone to share things with.'

Violet looked surprised at that admission. 'But you've been so unhappy since he left. I thought you'd get better after a bit – and sometimes you are – but then you get all stressed and just start shouting at us.'

Juliet's mouth dropped open. 'Do I?'

Violet nodded. 'And it's been worse since the Christmas decorations went up in town.'

Juliet pressed her palm against her forehead, as if she could ward off the growing tension there. She had felt more frazzled since the Christmas preparations had been added to her already hectic workload, but she hadn't realised she'd been taking it out on the kids. 'I'm sorry,' she whispered, and willed herself not to cry. The one thing she thought she was actually good at – being a mother – she was actually failing at too.

'Mum … ?'

'Yes?'

Violet took at deep breath. 'I think you're tired. That's why you're cross all the time. And when I get moody, you always tell me to go and relax, to do something I love, like listen to my favourite music or read a book. I know I stomp off and moan when you tell me that … but it works.'

Juliet nodded and gave her daughter a damp smile. She knew it worked. 'What are you trying to say, darling?'

A look of unusual determination passed across her daughter's features. 'I'm trying to say that you should do the swap.'

The *swap*? Gemma's ridiculous idea?

'I think you should go on Auntie Gemma's holiday.'

Juliet started shaking her head softly. 'I can't leave all of you at Christmas … What kind of parent would I be?'

Violet swallowed. 'The kind of parent who's stressed and unhappy and who doesn't usually have time to sit and watch a movie with us, because she's too busy sewing angel wings onto pillowcases and making fudge to make our teachers fat.'

The words were like a slap in the face.

But not a spiteful slap. A wake-up slap. Juliet suddenly saw herself through her children's eyes and what she saw she didn't like very much. She'd thought she'd been sidestepping her mother's mistakes, but maybe she was just making awful ones of her own.

She did it all for her kids. But was it worth it if the mother they got in return was a cross old bag who didn't have time for them any more? She took hold of Violet's hand. 'I know you'd understand if I went away for Christmas darling, because you're old enough, but Polly … and the boys …'

'Oh, they understand,' Violet said, very matter-of-factly. 'We had a family meeting and I was the one sent up here to break the news.'

Juliet closed her eyes and ran her tongue over her bottom lip, then she opened her eyelids again and stared at her daughter. 'You had a family meeting?'

Violet nodded. She tugged on her mother's hand. 'Come on … You can see for yourself.'

Feeling as if she'd wandered into some strange universe, and half-expecting to see a white rabbit with a watch bobb-

ing along the landing, Juliet followed her daughter down the
stairs and into the living room where the other three children
were sitting in a row on the sofa, their legs out straight in
front of them where they were too short to reach the floor.

'Is this true?' she asked them, taking in their serious
faces. 'Do you think I should swap Christmases with Auntie
Gemma?'

The boys nodded violently and Polly crossed her arms
and gave her one of her ten-going-on-forty stares. 'Face it,
Mother,' she said. 'We love you, but you're a total nightmare
to live with at the moment. You've got to learn to chillax.'

Violet handed her the phone, wearing a determined
expression. 'You need to call Auntie Gemma.'

&

CHAPTER NINE

The expression on Will's face was almost comical. His frown deepened. 'Say that again?'

Juliet wasn't surprised he hadn't understood the first time. It had come out in a bit of a rush. She cleared her throat and tried again. 'I wondered if you could keep an eye on things for me over the next few weeks. Like I said, I'm going away for Christmas. To St Lucia. And I'm leaving tomorrow.'

He blinked. 'Ok-ay ...'

'Don't you believe me?'

Will opened his front door wide and motioned for her to come inside. She rebalanced the tin of brownies she'd brought as a bribe and walked past him into the hallway. Will's house didn't have the perfectly executed interior design plan that hers had, but she liked it anyway. Compared to her home, it was a little sparse on things like cushions and ornaments and wall hangings, but there was plenty of brown leather and warm colours. Despite its masculine feel, it was cosy.

He led her into the kitchen, put the kettle on, then leaned back against the kitchen counter and regarded her carefully. 'Is everything okay?'

Juliet nodded, even though last night's pillow-screaming

incident might have suggested otherwise. 'I just need a break.'

The understanding warmth that filled his eyes made her relax a little. 'Yes. You do.'

And he seemed to be satisfied with her explanation, because he turned and made her a cup of coffee. 'So you want me to keep an eye on the place?'

Juliet accepted the mug from him, then shifted her weight onto her other foot. 'I was … uh … thinking more along the lines of keeping an eye on the kids.'

Will's eyes widened and he put his coffee down on the counter. 'You mean you're leaving them on their—'

'No, of course not! I wouldn't leave them on their own!'

'Then, who—'

'My sister's coming to look after them.'

Will's expression instantly took on a cynical edge. 'Ah.'

'Exactly,' Juliet said. 'I'd rather they were all still alive by Boxing Day.'

Will nodded. 'I'm not sure your sister is going to listen to anything I have to say. She thinks I'm a know-it-all moron with a stick shoved up his bum. She told me so in those exact words once.'

Juliet sighed. That *was* one of Gemma's 'go to' insults. She seemed to bestow that label on anyone who didn't approach life in her own haphazard manner. 'And that's exactly why I need your steadying influence,' she said, and deliberately opened the polka-dot cake tin and let the warm, chocolatey smell waft out of the tin. 'Please …?'

Defeat was written all over Will's face as he swallowed hard and his eyes fixed on the brownies. Juliet stifled a smile. If ever there was a guy who proved the old proverb about food being the route to a man's heart is true, it was this one.

'You realise that, by your silence, you've just agreed that I've got an uncomfortably large piece of wood up my backside?' But he still reached out and took a brownie.

Juliet shrugged. 'She says the same thing about me. You're in good company.'

Will's eyes crinkled at the edges. 'You know I'll do anything to help, but …' He bit into the brownie and shook his head a little while he chewed. When he'd swallowed he said, 'I don't know … This just doesn't seem like you, rushing off to God knows where at hardly a moment's notice.' He stopped eating and looked at her thoughtfully. 'I know you need to move on after Greg … but don't change too much, Juliet.'

She nodded, even though she wasn't sure exactly what she was agreeing to. *Something* in her life needed to change, that was for sure, before her kids asked her to stay away six months of the year because she was so ratty. For the next couple of weeks her location and the scenery would change, but after that? Who knew?

*

Gemma breathed in as she knocked on Juliet's door. When her sister opened it they greeted each other as normal. In other words, it was artificial and awkward, but that was hardly surprising after the way they'd left things last time they'd seen each other.

Gemma had known when Juliet had called her that she hadn't been comfortable agreeing to the swap. That irritated her. Why was it so hard for Juliet to accept anything from her? Was she really that much of a loser?

They went into the kitchen and Juliet made a cup of tea for them both. The kids were still at school and the silence seemed to echo in the large kitchen, the hand of the over-sized clock above the Aga ripping through the seconds. Juliet took a sip of tea and looked at Gemma over the top of her mug.

'Thank you for doing this,' she said, but her voice was tight and strained.

Gemma nodded. They hadn't exactly reached a truce, but it seemed they'd both decided to holster their hatchets for the moment. Well, maybe she could use that to her advantage. For years she'd trailed round after Juliet, always the weaker half of the equation, always the mess creator rather than the mess cleaner-upper, and now it was her chance to tip the scales in the other direction. She discovered she was quite looking forward to it.

There was one thing she needed to clear up, though, before Juliet flitted off to sunnier climes and put her out of her mind.

'You're wrong about what you said the other day,' she said. 'I never was the favourite. That's just not true.'

Juliet's brows shot up, as if to say: *Really? You want to go there?*

Yes, Gemma did want to go there. It was time Juliet started listening to what she had to say, instead of instantly dismissing it as trivial. She nodded.

Juliet looked her straight in the eye. 'Then who got to go to university and who had to stay at home?'

Gemma blinked. Wow. That was – what? – more than fifteen years ago, and she was still smarting about it? This was not where she'd expected this conversation to go. 'That wasn't my fault and you know it. If Dad hadn't died …'

She turned to look out of the kitchen window, her eyeballs stinging.

Juliet had just finished her A levels when he'd had the heart attack. Mum had fallen apart. Months after the funeral she still hadn't been able to drag herself out of bed in the mornings, hadn't stopped sobbing every day. Juliet had taken over doing everything – the cooking, the food shopping, making sure her younger sister had new school uniform when she needed it.

Gemma had never told anyone, but she'd dreaded the weekend in October when Juliet had been due to leave for Leicester University to do a course in textile design, but that weekend had come and gone and Juliet hadn't gone anywhere. And then she didn't go the next weekend, or the next. Neither of them had talked about it. Gemma had been too scared. She'd only just turned fourteen and she'd had no clue what she was going to do with her mother if Juliet left.

Months later she'd overheard them talking about it. 'Next year,' Juliet had said, and their mother had nodded listlessly.

But it had taken two clueless teenagers more than a year to work out that their only remaining parent wasn't just grieving heavily, that there was something more serious, something more permanent, going on. They'd got her to go to the doctor eventually, and he'd prescribed antidepressants and had suggested counselling – which she had to wait nine months for – and another year had slipped by without Juliet packing her bags and heading north. The awful thing was, Gemma couldn't even remember if she'd noticed at the time whether Juliet hadn't gone, whether she'd ended up taking her sister's steadying presence for granted.

*

Juliet handed Gemma a flowery notebook with as much solemnity as if it were Holy Scripture. 'Everything is in there,' she said. 'The To Do list, phone numbers and addresses of the butcher, the organic grocer, the recipe for mum's famous stuffing—'

Gemma snatched the book out of her hands and clutched it to her chest, hoping that breaking Juliet's physical contact with it might prevent the verbal assault she knew was coming. 'Got it. It's all in here. I'll protect it with my life,' she said. And the way she was intending keep it safe was to put it in the kitchen drawer and not look at it again. Seriously, her job involved organising a million things and balancing multiple fragile egos every day. She was sure she could handle four kids, a long-lost uncle, two old ladies and a turkey.

Juliet scrunched her immaculately plucked eyebrows together, gaze still locked on the book like a tractor beam. 'And don't forget that there are still a few stocking presents to buy for the twins and Polly, and that Violet has organised a shopping trip to Bluewater with her friends on the twenty-second. You just need to go back onto the M25 and get off at junction two for the—'

Gemma held up the book, effectively cutting her off. Now it was in her hands, she could wield its magic powers. Perhaps it could help Juliet to stop stressing so she could get her out of the house and off to the airport. 'I won't forget,' She said, tapping the book with her fingernail. 'It's all in here, remember?'

Juliet nodded. Then she opened her mouth and closed it again, frowning. Gemma knew she wanted to keep spouting instructions, but she could hardly argue with her own divine commandments, could she?

'Is that the doorbell I hear?' Gemma smiled and headed for the hallway, even though the only sound she'd heard in the previous seconds was the screaming in her sister's brain as control was wrenched from her clutches. 'That must be your lift to the airport.'

She carried on with the charade, flinging the door open wide and looking hopefully down the path, fully prepared to joke about faulty hearing at her age, but she came face-to-face with Mr Stick Up His Butt from next door.

'Oh, it's you.'

His eyebrows rose maybe a millimetre. 'Lovely to see you again too, Gemma.'

They stared at each other and then she stepped back and allowed him access. Juliet had told her that Will had offered to give her a lift to Gatwick. She should have known he'd turn up early. He and her sister were made from the same stuff.

Juliet grinned at him and stopped fussing with her matching suitcases, which were lined up in the hall in height order. Gemma realised she hadn't seen her sister smile that way in a long time. 'Thanks so much for this,' she gushed.

'You know you really didn't have to. I could have got a taxi.'

Will shrugged. 'It's what friends do.'

Gemma resisted the urge to snort gently. As far as she could tell, Juliet and Will had been 'friends' since not long after Greg had moved out. If they were lucky, one of them might make a move sometime before the end of the century.

Not her kind of approach to romance at all. She liked a man who knew what he wanted and wasn't afraid to say so. And if he wanted her, so much the better. None of this dancing around, pretending to be friends when you really wanted something else. Still … Whatever floated their boats. It was nothing to do with her.

As Will took the large case out to his waiting car, Juliet leaned in close and said in a low voice, 'I've asked him to … you know … lend a helping hand if you need it.'

Gemma squeezed back, but when they pulled apart to look at each other she said, 'I'm not an eighteen-year-old left alone at home for the first time, Juliet. And I don't need some accountant babysitting me—'

'He's an architect.'

'Whatever,' she muttered. She really didn't care what Will Truman did for a living and it didn't make any difference to the point she was trying to make. But she must have sounded more dismissive than she'd intended, because Juliet looked a little hurt as they disentangled themselves. The superior, very *Juliet* look was back. 'It's just that doing Christmas is such hard work. A big responsibility.'

Gemma nodded, trying to look as serious as possible. This was not the time to start another fight.

Juliet looked at her. 'I know you think I make a production of it …'

Ah. Busted.

'… but the kids love our little traditions, and it's important this year, especially as neither Greg nor I are going to be around …'

She paused and glanced over to Will's car, then looked longingly inside the house. Gemma had the feeling that Juliet was on the verge of wrenching her luggage from her willing chauffeur and putting it all back in the hallway. It was just as well Juliet had said her goodbyes to the kids before they'd packed them all off to school, otherwise Gemma reckoned she'd have had a hard time getting her sister out of the house. Talk about being stuck in your own rut.

But no way was this holiday going to waste. Gemma had paid good money for it, and it was too late to cancel or change details. Also, her kids had been right: Juliet needed this. And Gemma needed to do it for her.

'You're going,' Gemma told her sister firmly and nudged her out of the door and onto the front step.

Juliet grabbed hold of her arm – a little dramatic for her, maybe – pinching the sleeve of her cardigan up in her fist. 'Promise me you'll try to do as much of it as you can,' she said, looking more than a little desperate. 'Not for me. For them. These little traditions … Keeping them going will make it seem like I haven't abandoned them.'

Gemma swallowed. 'Okay. I promise.'

Only then did Juliet start to relax. She kissed Gemma on the cheek then headed off to where Will was holding the passenger door open for her. She waved as she passed him her holdall and got in.

Mr Stick Up His Butt also gave Gemma a little sarcastic salute. She fixed a cheesy grin on her face, just to let him know there was no way he was going to win that game, and waved back. She kept it up until they disappeared out onto the main road and then she went back inside the house.

&

CHAPTER TEN

Juliet walked off the plane and down the steps onto the tarmac of Hewanorra International airport. Her eyes were gritty and her legs were stiff, despite the Premium Economy seat her sister had booked. During the approach, they'd flown down the western edge of the island and she'd sat with her nose pressed to the porthole-like window, her mouth slightly open as a mountainous, volcanic island revealed itself beneath the puffy white clouds that clustered over and around it.

All journey she'd had a fidgety sensation in her stomach, and she hadn't been sure if what she was feeling was excitement or nerves, but now she'd actually set foot on the ground she felt disconnected from reality, and half-expected to be woken from a dream to find herself back in Tunbridge Wells, refereeing a fight between her children.

She stumbled along after the other passengers, hardly noticing the time spent in the immigration line, or the wait for her cases at the carousel. And then she was out of the cool air of the small terminal and scanning the crowd for her name on a rectangle of cardboard. She finally saw it, held up by a man of about fifty, wearing casual long shorts, a short-sleeved shirt and a wide smile.

'Welcome to paradise,' he said in his lilting accent, and reached to take her cases for her. She let him, forgetting all the usual checks and questions she'd have normally asked to make sure he wasn't a con man about to run off with her belongings. 'I'm Bradford, and I'll be your driver this afternoon.'

She climbed in the back of his smart, four-wheel drive and welcomed the moment he closed the door and the air conditioning kicked in. Bradford informed her it would take more than an hour to reach her resort, up on the northern end of the island, and settled into giving her an intermittent running commentary on anything he thought she might find interesting, from identifying the different fruit trees lining the road to the names of towns and fishing villages along the coast.

Juliet listened with interest, her eyes glued to the scenery outside the tinted window of the car. She suddenly realised how entrenched in her own life she'd become, almost believing that there was nothing beyond chilly, middle-class English suburbia. That was all she thought about these days. She'd forgotten there was a big wide world out there, one that her sister travelled with envying regularity.

She hardly saw another flat piece of terrain after she left the airport. As the journey continued they climbed higher and higher, along a road that took them through a pass in the mountains to the other side of the island. There were deep valleys and steep hills and the abundant vegetation seemed to be waging a war to fill every available space, even the places that humankind had conquered and occupied. She'd thought Kent was green and pleasant, but this … this was something else.

Lush, green foliage was everywhere. Mangoes hung over the edges of the roads in their thousands, as well as cashews, breadfruit and dates. There were palms of every size, every shape, some squat and wide, some tall and skinny, some with yellow coconuts huddling underneath the umbrella of frilly branches for shade. And bananas … Bananas were everywhere.

The houses were just as fascinating, most painted in colours such as cobalt, canary, mint or watermelon. Most were typical Caribbean style with shallow, tiled roofs and balconies. They perched on the steep terrain attached to the ground at one end, but lifted on pillars where the land fell away beneath them.

There were a few grand houses with stone balustrades and large gardens, but most were compact and had a higgledy-piggledy look about them. Many dwellings were little more than concrete shells or sheds, sometimes patched with corrugated iron. She was surprised more weren't in tatters, given the tales Bradford had to tell about the last hurricane to hit the island, and how it had caused massive mudslides and was responsible for the large sections nibbled out of the road they were travelling on.

She looked nervously up at the searing blue sky dotted with clouds. 'There aren't any hurricanes forecast for Christmas, are there?'

Bradford just laughed. 'No, ma'am, you're safe. The rainy season is from June to November.'

Juliet slumped back against the comfy seats and exhaled.

Normally she wouldn't have to ask these kinds of questions, feeling stupid and unsophisticated. Normally she researched a place intensively before picking it as a holiday destination, and then she carried on doing her homework, right down to every type of room offered by every hotel she was interested in – which had the best views and whether there were balconies, air conditioning, Wi-Fi …

She realised she didn't know anything about the place Gemma had booked, except its name: Pelican's Reach. A cold feeling shot through her as she considered that her sister might never have given up her backpacking ways and that she might be spending the next fortnight in a tin hut on the sand.

Eventually Bradford turned off the main road onto a narrow track that headed through some shallow hills – well, shallow compared to the volcanic peaks in the centre of the island. After a short drive, they pulled up at a whitewashed gatehouse and were waved through after Bradford and the security guards had exchanged enquiries about each other's families.

They continued down over the lip of a hill into what seemed like a perfect and exclusive little village. No hulking hotel blocks here, only low structures. The larger ones looked like plantation houses and different-sized villas were clustered in groups on a steep hillside overlooking a secluded bay.

Bradford parked in front of a large building and helped her out of the car. Bellboys rushed to collect her luggage and a uniformed hotel employee welcomed her to Pelican's Reach, then took her into a reception area with terracotta tiled floors and high ceilings with whirring fans. She was led to one of the many groups of dark wood and wicker sofas with pristine white cushions.

A woman appeared beside her. 'Hello, Mrs Taylor, my name is Cordelia and I'm your personal ambassador. I'm here to help you with anything you need during your stay.' She paused to smile and carried on. 'Let's get you checked in first, then the shuttle can take your bags to your villa. Would you like a rum punch while you're waiting?'

Juliet nodded and perched on the edge of one of the sofas, still peering around.

This was definitely *not* a tin hut.

Juliet wasn't quite sure whether to be relieved that Gemma had obviously acquired a taste for luxury in her old age, or affronted that she'd booked this place for herself, fully intending to leave her sister to the purgatory of the family Christmas at home.

Someone appeared with a squat glass filled with cubes of ice and a dusky pink cocktail. She sipped it tentatively, not really being one for rum, but the sweetness of the fruit juice and a hint of spices in the ice-cold liquid meant it went down rather well. Too well, maybe. By the time Cordelia had returned with her room key her glass was practically empty.

'You're in one of our premium villas,' the woman told her. 'They're set just a little way away from the main resort, in their own private bay.'

Juliet glanced at her suitcases, still sitting near the reception desk. 'I hope it's not a long walk.' The clock above the reception desk said it was five forty in Pelican's Reach, which meant it was closer to ten back home, and Juliet

wasn't sure she had the energy to leave the reception building, let alone trek to her villa.

Cordelia smiled brightly at her. 'Don't you worry about
walking, Mrs Taylor. Peter here is going to take you to your
room.'

A lad who didn't seem much older than Violet appeared
and ushered her back outside. Bradford's car was gone and
in its place something that looked like a bigger, sleeker version of a golf cart. Her driver indicated she should sit next to
him and then they were off through the resort, down narrow
brick-paved paths.

They left the main hotel buildings behind, which occupied
the flatter area near the beach, and headed up the hillside.
The shuttle climbed a short hill that took them past the end
of the main beach and onto a road that ran above a little cove
on the same bay. Here, only a handful of villas were dotted
near the edge of a low cliff.

Peter stopped the buggy at the penultimate villa on the
track. Juliet climbed out and stared at it. Was this all for her?
All she'd been expecting was a hotel room. She must have
really underestimated how much Gemma got paid to do that
job of hers.

Peter insisted on escorting her through the small garden
that led to the front door of her villa. She wandered behind
him up a path fringed with beautiful shrubs, and when he
reached the door he ushered her inside with a grand arm gesture.

She didn't notice when her driver left, because all she
could do when she walked inside was stand and stare. Outside vibrant colours were everywhere, intensified by the

bright overhead sun into almost painful richness, but in here it was an oasis of white.

She was standing in a vaulted bedroom, the pale painted beams and slats of the ceiling showing. Neutral tiles covered the floor and wispy curtains billowed slightly at the windows, disturbed by the artificial breeze purring from an air-conditioning unit. The furniture was simple and stylish, all white wicker and wood. Dominating it all was a four-poster bed draped in mosquito nets, the only concession to colour some stone-coloured cushions nestling against the puffy pillows and a matching runner at the bottom of the light quilt.

The room was big enough to also house a comfy-looking white sofa and coffee table, and a writing desk up against the wall. Behind her was a walk-in wardrobe and a door through which she could spy spacious en-suite bathroom. But it was the windows she couldn't a tear her eyes from. They ran from floor to ceiling with arches at the top, and in the central arch was a pair of French windows leading out onto a balcony with a criss-crossed railing.

She didn't make a decision to unfasten the catch and walk outside, she just did it. The sun was lower in the sky now, but still golden and warm. She guessed that sunset was still maybe an hour or two away. She walked forward, rested her palms on the railing and stared out at the view below her. Underneath the balcony was a terrace fringed with low tropical vegetation, and beyond that she could see the pale yellow sand of the small cove.

If she looked to her right – northward, she guessed – the small headland she'd passed over blocked part of the view of the main resort, but beyond she could see the land as it flattened out towards the shore, seeming to sharpen to a point where the curving beach jutted into the ocean. A lone tree swayed in the breeze at the end of the long strip of sand.

She realised that she'd been holding her breath for the longest time. Not just the few minutes that she'd been exploring her villa, but for months. Maybe even years. It was as if she'd been hanging onto it because she'd never had the proper time or room to expel it, and she did it now, letting it all out in one long, satisfying sigh.

And when she was finished, she stood completely still, just breathing in and out and listening to the birds and insects singing their different yet harmonious songs and feeling the soft tease of the salty breeze on her skin.

Juliet wasn't sure if she believed in love any more, not after the way things had turned out with Greg, but if she ever could consider falling in love again, she thought Pelican's Reach would be the top of her list.

*

When Juliet wandered back inside she found her cases had been delivered, so she set about unpacking them, stuffing T-shirts into drawers and throwing sandals into the walk-in wardrobe. More than once as she emptied a case she looked longingly at the four-poster, with its dreamy nets hanging down. She'd dearly love to sink face first into all that gorgeous white bedding, but she knew she really should try to stay awake as long as possible to beat the jet lag.

Yawning, she reached into the front pocket of her suitcase. Her hands closed around some unfamiliar items, so she pulled them out to get a proper look.

Two bikinis! One crimson and plain, the other ruffled with turquoise polka dots. Upon closer inspection of the same pocket, she found a note and a small, flat box wrapped in Christmas paper. She placed the present on the bedside table and unfolded the scrap of paper, which looked as if it had been hastily torn from a spiral-bound notebook.

> *J, Since I'm not going to be getting the use out of these, I thought you should. And don't open the present until Christmas Day. That's an order! G x*

She held the red bikini up by the shoulder straps – what there was of it! – and her eyes popped open wide. Really? At her age! She didn't think so.

Okay, it wasn't obscenely skimpy, but it certainly wasn't the sort of thing she'd ever had the courage to wear. The polka-dot one gave a little more coverage, thank goodness. She thought of the plain black one-piece she'd only just put in the chest of drawers and swiftly stuffed both bikinis back into the pocket and zipped it up tight. The present she tucked into the drawer of her bedside table.

Right. Everything done. The only thing left was to get the empty cases out of sight and into the wardrobe. When that was done she walked back into the bedroom, hardly daring to look in the direction of the four-poster. The best thing she could do was get out of here before she succumbed to the temptation of that comfy-looking mattress.

That decided, she stripped off her travel clothes and

replaced them with a floral sundress and flip-flops, then she picked up her floppy hat and sunglasses and headed off to explore the rest of her villa.

Downstairs was a sitting room, decorated in the same style as the room above, and beyond that a terrace with a plunge pool. At one end of the wooden railing that surrounded the terrace was a small white gate, and beyond it she discovered wooden stairs leading down onto the small private beach. The sand there was unblemished by human footprints and she kicked off her flip-flops and sank her toes into the silky grains, sighing.

When had she last stood on a beach and allowed the sand to pool between her toes? She was usually chasing after one of her kids, trying to prevent them from destroying other people's sand castles or attempting cross-channel swims.

However, sighing soon turned to another kind of sound, as she realised the sand was far too hot to stand on and still keep all the required layers of skin on her feet. She ran the couple of dozen steps to the shore, where frothy waves licked the shimmering pale sand and let the cool water sooth her slightly scorched soles.

The water was delicious, warm and pleasant after only a couple of seconds of acclimatisation. Keeping to the surf-moistened part of the beach, she started to walk towards the tiny headland that separated her little patch of Pelican's Reach from the main part of the resort. When she got to the rocks at the far end, she discovered she could skirt the headland, keeping almost completely to the sand. With no plan in mind other than to stave off sleep by keeping moving, she wandered the full length of the main beach, until she reached a rocky breakwater. It curled around the ocean-facing part of the beach like a protective arm, preventing the harsher surf at the bay's edge from stealing the sand back into the sea it had come from.

She stood there for a few moments, watching the waves crash against the other side of the rocks, then turned and headed back towards the busier, central part of the beach. It was the tail end of the day now, and not many sunbathers draped themselves across the wooden sunloungers that were spaced evenly along the sand. There were a couple of bodies still in the water and a handful more with their eyes closed or reading books. She passed a small thatched bar under a couple of palm trees but carried on, heading for Pelican Joe's, the main bar that spilled onto the beach in stepped terraces full of tables and chairs.

The bar area wasn't busy yet, but a few couples and families arrived and staked claim to favourite tables while a plethora of bar staff smiled and mixed cocktails in every colour of the rainbow. She wandered over to the polished granite bar and picked up a menu. The choice was dizzying. Cocktails for every mood and taste and occasion. The back page listed the virgin cocktails for kids and she smiled, thinking how Violet would have loved ordering one of those and how she would have sat primly on one of the bar stools, pretending she was very grown up as she sipped it through a straw.

Juliet drew in a sharp breath and held it.

No. She couldn't think of them yet. Not so soon after leaving. Not while the separation from them was still so raw. If she let Violet and Polly, Jake and Josh into her thoughts too much at the moment she'd end up sinking into a snivel-ling heap right here in front of the bar. She was too tired to cope with the homesickness that was threatening to come in waves.

But Juliet was very good at keeping going when a collapse or breakdown threatened, so she drew herself taller, let out the air she'd been holding and picked up the menu again. When the barman asked her what she wanted she couldn't settle on a cocktail, so she ordered a dry white wine, just as she would have done at home, and added a bar snack to go with it. She found a small, empty table at the far edge of one of the sprawling terraces and sipped her drink and ate her mango chicken while watching the sun go down.

As she sat there half-dazed with tiredness the bar filled up around her. Some people settled down to eat from the sim-ple menu, others came for a drink and headed off to one of the other restaurants on the resort. Even though Pelican Joe's was busy, it was peaceful. No bad behaviour, no shouting or whining kids. It was as if the atmosphere of this laid-back little island had seeped into everyone who'd been here for more than a few hours.

Juliet tried to join them, sitting still, noting not just the tangerine and pink of the sunset, but the lemon sky and the grey clouds above it, but somehow she felt out of sync with everyone around her, as if she was a metronome ticking too fast while everyone else marched to a slower beat.

She realised that all of the people she could see were very well turned out. She'd been used to being one of the school mums who was always nicely dressed back in Tunbridge Wells, but these people were in a different league. They lounged around the five-star resort hardly noticing its understated luxury, as if they were used to it all the time. That in itself was enough to frighten her off from striking up a conversation with someone, even if she'd been awake enough to make sensible small talk.

But the other reason she wasn't more sociable was that she noticed she was the only person sitting on her own. Now it was getting later, families disappeared and suddenly the bar was filled with couples. Everywhere she looked, people were holding hands and sneaking meaningful looks at each other across the table.

And, just like that, paradise became slightly depressing.

She got up and walked away from her table, leaving the last bit of her glass of wine undrunk, and headed to the reception area, where she ordered a shuttle to take her back to her villa. All the while on the short ride there she tried to hush the thoughts whispering at the fringes of her mind. This was the holiday of a lifetime, and she was going to make sure she made the most of it, have fun! That's what Gemma would do. The last thing she wanted was to leave her lonely and sad life behind, only to discover she was lonely and sad here as well.

Even her stylish villa seemed too empty when she stepped inside.

This was what she'd longed for, wasn't it? Time. Space. Room to breathe. Precious commodities in her life. But now they were within her reach she felt like a pauper who had been made a millionaire and hadn't the first clue how to spend her riches.

She walked towards the French windows, not bothering

with turning a lamp on as she went, and stepped outside onto the balcony. At least out here she had the rough song of the crickets and the other night animals to keep her company.

Had she been this lonely back in Tunbridge Wells?

Probably.

But maybe her busy life served more than a purpose than to drive her crazy. Maybe she even invested in the craziness a little. Because she wasn't sure she liked what came creeping in when it all stopped.

The night air was still warm enough for her not to need a cardigan and a gentle breeze blew off the sea, lifting only the wispiest tendrils of hair from her face. She tipped her head back and marvelled at the stars. Light pollution in her town had fooled her into thinking they were finite in number, countable – if she'd had the time or the patience to take on the task. But here there were so many she could hardly make out the individual constellations.

It goes on forever, she thought, *and I'm such a tiny, tiny part of it. So why does it feel like the whole thing will come crashing down if I even pause for a second?*

Her eyes slowly accustomed to the darkness, and she began to pick out the individual shrubs in the dark blur of vegetation at the edge of terrace. After studying sky and sea and sand, she turned her attention to what was right and left of her balcony. Her villa was the fourth in a row of five. The first one, nearest the resort, had a few lights on, but the next two were dark, giving no indication if they were inhabited or not. She twisted to look at the one on the other side. Light spilled from the bedroom onto the balcony and she suddenly realised she wasn't the only one enjoying the cool night breeze and the blinking stars.

The other villa was maybe only twenty feet away, but Juliet was hidden in the darkness and she felt no embarrassment at studying her neighbour.

He was tall and lean, resting his elbows on the railing of the balcony, a squat glass tumbler of either whisky or dark rum in his hand. Dressed in pale khaki trousers and a linen shirt, he looked totally at ease, as if he'd always belonged here, even though his European features and short dark hair indicated he probably wasn't a native St Lucian.

He took a sip from his glass then returned to watching the sea.

He was early thirties, she guessed, with strong symmetrical features and cheekbones to make a girl weep. If there was any imperfection in him at all, it was maybe his nose was a little too long, a little too straight.

She stood there watching him for maybe ten minutes. Partly because of the forgotten warmth raising the hairs on her arms and turning her breathing shallow, but partly because, even though he had no idea she was there, just knowing another human was nearby made her feel less alone.

Of course, his beautiful girlfriend would probably wander out and join him shortly, steal a sip from his glass and press a kiss to his neck. Juliet waited for her to arrive, subconsciously realising it would give her permission to stop looking. It would allow her to go back inside, collapse onto her vast four-poster bed and sleep for a week.

But the goddess who belonged to this god never came.

Maybe she was already asleep, sprawled in her bed after glorious lovemaking. Maybe she was waiting for him in a tub full of bubbles. Juliet hoped the goddess wouldn't mind if she borrowed him for just a bit. All she wanted was his proximity; she wouldn't be stupid enough to ask for anything more.

She let out a breath and looked away. This was ridiculous, the sort of thing Violet probably did when she spotted a lad she liked.

She leaned on the railing, letting the rough wood against her forearms remind her of what was real and what was not. She resisted looking at him for as long as she could, but eventually she turned her head for one last glance before heading back inside.

That was when she found him mirroring her, looking back at her from his balcony, an expression of slight amusement on his features. If his profile had been gorgeous, face on he looked even better.

She held her breath, not quite sure if he could see her, or if he was just taking in the scenery. And if he was aware of her presence, what should she do? Had he known she'd been watching him? Was it too late to save face by giving him a neighbourly wave?

As if he could hear the thoughts racing through her mind, he tilted his head, then lifted his glass and saluted her with it.

Juliet flushed and fled back inside her darkened villa.

&

CHAPTER ELEVEN

So, this is what being Juliet feels like, Gemma thought, as she opened her eyes the next morning. She was sleeping in Juliet's bed, living in Juliet's house, eating Juliet's food and looking after Juliet's kids. It was like being in an alien world, albeit a stylish, neutral-toned alien world that wouldn't look out of place between the pages of *Fabulous Homes* magazine. Everything felt elegant, organised and maybe a little too perfect.

She rolled over and turned on the light. She'd been going to look at the clock, but the first thing she noticed was the picture on Juliet's bedside table. It was a snap of their family – Mum, Dad and the two girls – taken on a holiday in Devon when Gemma had been about ten.

She had always loved that photo. All of them together, grinning at the camera with their arms round each other. She smiled back at the frame sleepily and yawned. However, as Gemma continued to stare groggily at the picture she noticed something she hadn't seen before. There was a sadness behind Juliet's sunny smile that set her apart from the others, even though she was in the centre of the shot, leaning in between Mum and Dad from behind.

Odd. Gemma had always thought marrying Greg had had

something to do with the stressy, uptight woman her sister had become, but the seeds of it were here in this picture, years before she'd even met him. It shouldn't be like that. They'd had such a happy childhood. Idyllic, almost.

She closed her eyes and yawned again, too tired to dissect that thought now, then focused on the clock.

Yuck. Six thirty. She was used to getting up at the crack of dawn, but she hadn't anticipated just how much willpower it would take to drag herself out of bed this morning. Without the adrenalin rush working on set brought, sliding her feet out from under the warm duvet until they hit the floor seemed like an impossible task. And it didn't help that Juliet had the most comfortable bed in the history of beds.

Still, she needn't have worried. The twins decided to help her by barging into the room at full pelt and launching themselves on top of her. While they bounced up and down, one of them with his knee in a very sensitive place, she thought she might have heard the word *breakfast* amongst the chatter.

She pushed back the hair from her face and tried to focus on one twin. Either one. She didn't care which. 'You're hungry?'

The boys bounced harder. Lovely.

'Okay, okay …' She tried to move and got an elbow in her face for her efforts. '*Boys!*'

The bouncing stopped.

Gemma took a moment to absorb the fact she'd sounded just like Juliet, then she sat up. 'Go and get your school uniforms on and I'll be down in five minutes to make your breakfast, okay?'

Jake and Josh just looked at her.

'And you'd better hurry up, or the only choice on the menu will be porridge.'

The boys glanced at each other, communicated telepathically, then dashed out of the room, giggling. Gemma flopped back onto the mattress and stared at the ceiling. If this was how Juliet's days started, no wonder she was in such a bad mood most of the time. Oh well, this had to be easier than cajoling truculent movie stars. She'd never been able to get Tobias Thornton to do anything by just threatening him with porridge. Not that she actually knew how to cook porridge from scratch. But the boys didn't need to know that, did they?

This bed really was wonderfully comfy …

The next thing Gemma knew was that she'd been startled awake by a child's face pressing virtually nose to nose with her own. She let out a scream, which didn't seem to faze Polly at all. She tipped her head to one side and studied her aunt carefully. 'Are you hungover?' she asked in that sweet little lisping voice of hers. 'I can make you a cup of tea if you are.'

Gemma pulled the covers up over her face. 'No, I am not hungover!' she said through the Laura Ashley duvet cover.

'Okay,' she heard Polly say, but the child didn't seem very convinced.

Gemma pulled the duvet back down again and stared at her niece. 'All I had to drink last night was half a gallon of Diet Coke, just like you.'

Polly blinked. 'Do you still want that cup of tea, or not?'

'Not. I think I'd better make it myself, seeing as you're hardly tall enough to see over the kitchen worktop.'

Polly shrugged. 'Whatever … And FYI, you might want to brush your teeth. Your breath is a little … you know.' And she waved a hand in front of her nose before skipping out of the room, humming 'Rudolph the Red Nosed Reindeer'.

Gemma didn't know whether to laugh or scream.

Oh, my God! A little Juliet-in-training. Heaven help us all!

Still, she'd been called worse by much less intelligent people, so she batted Polly's wince-making honesty out of her mind and concentrated on getting out of bed, slinging on a robe and heading downstairs to see what the twins were up to.

She found them sitting at the kitchen table, looking expectant, knives and forks in hands.

'Mummy makes us pancakes every morning,' Jake said.

'With maple syrup and honey and sugar and strawberries …' his brother chimed in.

Gemma was just about to say she knew how to *order* pancakes, when Violet trailed in, munching half a slice of toast.

'Don't believe a word the runts say. Pancakes are for special occasions only. Weekday breakfasts are strictly cereal with chopped fruit.'

'Nice try, boys,' Gemma told them, grinning, and then she rummaged through the larder for something to pour in a bowl for them. *That* she could manage.

After a minute searching she popped her head out and

looked at Violet, who was leaning against the kitchen counter reading a magazine. 'Where are the kids' cereals? All I can find in here is Juliet's high-fibre stuff.'

Violet lowered the magazine a fraction and raised her eyebrows.

Yikes. This *was* the kids' cereal. She pulled a box out and gathered a couple of tubs from the shelf on the opposite side of the larder. 'How about Shreddies with chopped banana and sprinkles?' she said as she re-entered the kitchen.

From the cheer she received, you'd have thought she'd offered them a trip to Disneyland. She dumped the cereal and cake decorations in the middle of the table, got a bottle of milk from the fridge and plonked a bowl down in front of each boy. 'You do the cereal and sprinkles,' she said, 'I'll do the banana.'

Yes, the kitchen looked like a mini-tornado had whipped through it when the kids had finished eating, but she got them out the door and into the car on time. Violet navigated to the grammar school, then Polly took over and directed her back to St Martin's Primary. Gemma could have done without the comments on other people's driving from her ten-year-old human satnav, but at least she got them to the playground on time. The sense of satisfaction she got waving them off as their teacher rang the bell and marched them into school was every bit as warming as sending a movie star off to set.

And instead of having to race around all day like she did when she was at work, she could attack the day's chores at a leisurely pace. No need to check Juliet's little flowery book, because it was blatantly obvious what her next task was.

First stop: the supermarket. Seriously, these kids needed a little excitement in their diet!

In fact, if things went as well as they had done the last twenty-four hours, she wasn't going to need Juliet's twee little notebook at all. She didn't know what she'd been worried about. So far it had all been easy peasy.

*

Juliet woke at one a.m. and then again at two. At two thirty she punched her pillow and let out a frustrated growl. Stupid jet lag.

She rolled over and stared at the mosquito netting above her bed, only just able to make out the soft gauze in the darkness. The horrible empty feeling tried to creep up on her again, but she refused to let it near. She also pushed away thought of her kids, stopped herself wondering what they were doing now and if they'd got to school on time.

If she let herself go down that path, she'd just spend the whole day in bed feeling miserable, and it was because of them she was doing this, remember? It was practically her duty to stop moping and enjoy herself, so that when she got back home they'd have a happy and refreshed mother to start the New Year with. The trick would be to keep herself busy so she didn't get maudlin.

So she reached over, turned on the bedside light and picked up one of the paperbacks she'd brought with her. By four she'd decided she didn't have enough brain cells functioning to keep track of a complicated thriller and resorted to reading the hotel information folder from cover to cover. By six o'clock she had her day planned out – meals, snacks, time at the beach, a trip to the spa –everything. She wrote it all down in a pocket notebook and tucked it into her beach bag. No reason why she couldn't turn her plans for the perfect Christmas into the perfect Christmas holiday, was there?

It seemed like an age before the main restaurant opened for breakfast. Not that she was sure she was hungry. Her body clock was all over the place, but at least it was something to do.

Outside it was gloriously sunny. What else had she expected? She decided not to call for a shuttle, so after packing her beach bag she slung a cotton jersey sundress on over her swimming costume and headed down the steps into the cove. She'd walk round, just as she had done the night before.

At her feet sank into the sand, she couldn't resist a little glance at the villa next door. No sign of life. Part of her had half expected to see him still standing at the balcony railing, calmly watching her.

Stupid, really. *Nice fantasy, Juliet, but he's much too good-looking and much too young for you. If you couldn't even keep the interest of your average-looking suburban husband, why would such a man even notice you exist?*

Only he had. Noticed her.

In a very small way. It hadn't been a phantom he'd raised his glass to the night before. Not that she was going to read anything much into that. It had just been a friendly gesture, nothing more.

She sighed as she crossed the rocks and headed for the

centre of the resort. The beach was virtually deserted, the only sign of life a couple of determined swimmers and a handful of hotel staff who were raking the beach into perfection, removing any pebbles and clumps of seaweed that had been audacious enough to cling on to the sand as the tide had retreated.

Beyond Pelican Joe's bar was a large swimming pool surrounded by hibiscus trees. It too was deserted, save for the little robot attached to a hose that was scuttling around on the bottom, dealing with all the rubbish. She felt a strange affinity for that little machine. It was in the most beautiful place in the world, but it never noticed, because it always had its head down, doing its job, cleaning up after other people.

Once breakfast was over she headed for the beach. She was sure that with judicious application of sunscreen and carefully timed sunbathing sessions she could turn something approaching an attractive colour before she went home. What better proof of the perfect holiday than the perfect tan?

She walked to the far end of the beach, lay face up on a lounger for twenty minutes, then face down for another twenty, then dragged her lounger under the small, waxy-leafed tree so she could carry on with her thriller.

The day sped past. She swam in two of the pools, ate a beach barbecue for lunch, then went back to her air-conditioned room for an afternoon nap before sunbathing on her private beach and then showering before dinner. She tried to get in the waterside restaurant that specialised in seafood, but it was fully booked and she ended up back at Pelican Joe's eating mango chicken again.

When she got back to her villa she poured herself a gin and tonic from the well-stocked bar in her living room and went to sit at the little table on the covered section of her terrace, feeling too self-conscious to wander out onto her balcony again. From her position she could glance over at the neighbouring villa in relative secrecy.

He was there again, drink in hand. This time, sitting on a chair with his feet propped on the balcony railing. The outside light was on and he was reading a battered paperback in its dull glow while giant moths danced around the glass casing. She sneaked a look every now and then, trying to make it seem as if she was just taking in the scenery.

After about quarter of an hour, he said something in a language she didn't recognise. Italian or Spanish she guessed, but she wasn't sure.

Even though he hadn't shouted, his question shattered the silence. She'd been staring at the rising moon, and she jumped in her chair and whipped her head round. She'd assumed he was talking to the goddess, somewhere in the bedroom, but he wasn't looking back inside his villa. He was looking at her.

She felt a blush climbing up her neck and was glad the darkness camouflaged it. 'I'm sorry …' she answered, her voice sounding squeaky, '*Je ne comprends pas.*' She was pretty sure he wasn't French, but that was the only language she'd learned at school, so that was the language that came out on autopilot.

He nodded. 'I was asking if you would like a drink,' he said in the most sexily accented English she'd ever heard, and raised his empty glass.

Italian. He sounded Italian.

'I need a …' he paused while he searched for the right word 'refill … and wondered if you did also.'

Juliet shook her head and then realised he probably couldn't see her fully from where he was. She stood up and took a step out from under the cover of the balcony's edge and lifted up her half-full glass.

'No. I'm good,' she replied, and mentally smacked herself for saying so. 'Still some left. And I'm tired …' She did an exaggerated yawn to demonstrate the point, and instantly wanted to curl up and die of embarrassment. 'Jet lag,' she added, not that the explanation would help her regain any of her dignity. He must think she was a right nutter – an eccentric English lady on holiday on her own.

He lifted his glass and gave her that little nod again. 'Then I wish you sweet dreams.'

Juliet nodded nonchalantly and tried not to melt as he turned and headed back through the French doors and into his softly lit bedroom.

&

CHAPTER TWELVE

As Gemma walked into Juliet's kitchen she was greeted by a rowdy and enthusiastic cheer. All four kids were sitting expectantly round the table, waiting for their evening meal – something Juliet always had said she had to threaten death or injury to get them to do. She placed a stack of takeaway pizza boxes in the centre of the table and stood back, out of range of the feeding frenzy.

They were still just tucking into their first slices when the doorbell rang. She jogged back to the hall, purse in hand, suspecting the collection of coins she'd dumped in the delivery driver's waiting palm maybe hadn't added up to quite the right amount. She *had* let the twins count it …

But when she opened the door she discovered that the tall, dark shape behind the stained-glass panels wasn't a motorcycle-helmeted youth. It was someone altogether much less welcome.

'Can I help you?' she asked, keeping the door mostly closed and casually blocking the space with her body.

Will Truman stared back at her. 'Can I step inside for a second?'

Gemma didn't move. So it had started already, and Juliet had only been gone just over twenty-four hours. 'Look, I know what you told my sister, but I've got this covered. And I promise, if I need your help, I'll yell.'

A total lie, of course.

He knew it too, from the way his eyes narrowed. Odd. When she'd seen him standing there on the front step she'd had a fleeting thought that she'd put her usual magic to work and charm him off the doorstep and back into his own house. But here they were, barely a minute later, and all she'd succeeded in doing was getting the man's back up.

'It's not that,' he said, giving her a serious look. 'I wanted to talk to you about Juliet.'

Gemma stiffened. 'What about my sister?' She wasn't about to offer romantic advice to this man. Poor Juliet had ditched one boring, high-maintenance husband; she didn't need a second.

A flash of honest concern crossed his features and, damn, if Gemma didn't feel it tugging deep down inside. She was so used to dealing with fully grown male toddlers or total philanderers that she'd almost forgotten the male species was capable of more noble emotional states.

'Is she really as okay as she says she is?'

Gemma opened her mouth to say of course she was, but she realised she was hardly qualified to make that judgement, especially as she and Juliet had only been in the same room as each other for a few hours in the last couple of months. The truth was she was worried about Juliet too, and Mr Uptight here probably had information she needed, seeing the amount of time he spent sniffing around her.

She opened the door wide and stepped back to let him inside, and was just debating whether to make him talk right there, or take him into the sitting room, when an almighty crash came from the kitchen. They both raced down the corridor, Will slightly in front, which irked her.

They arrived to find Josh and Jake fighting over a piece of cheesy garlic bread. It seemed Jake had lunged across the table and knocked his chair over in the effort to wrest the prize for his brother's sticky fingers. Will righted the chair while Gemma separated the warring factions. She then rummaged under the tower of cardboard pizza boxes for a smaller one and flipped the lid open, revealing a second order of garlic bread. She slapped it down on the table between them.

'Sit! Eat! And I don't want a fight about who's having the squashed piece and who's having the new bit. You can have half each.' She ripped the mangled piece of garlic bread in two and dropped half on each boy's plate.

Hang on. *Plates?* When had they made it out of the cupboard? Juliet must have the kids trained better than she thought. She'd just slung some kitchen roll in their general direction and let them get on with it.

Will glanced around the kitchen table. 'Where's Violet?'

Gemma watched his eagle-eyed sweep of the room, saw the furrowing of his brow. He'd come to talk to her about Juliet? Hah! Give her a break. He was just checking up on her.

'Violet?' she said innocently, and pretended to think hard. 'Oh, yes. The big one. I know I saw her somewhere recently …'

Will opened his mouth, but she barrelled on.

'Oh, I remember!' she added with a sarcastic little smile. 'Last night when I dropped her off at that strip club.'

His expression of concern hardened into something else.

Gemma exhaled forcefully. 'Well, you kind of asked for that. What kind of moron do you think I am?'

Polly, who was halfway through a slice of pepperoni, put her hand up in the air.

'Don't answer that,' Gemma said grimly, and Polly let her arm drop, looking slightly disappointed.

One of the boys obviously thought this was a fun game, because his arm shot up in the air too. She was pretty sure it was Jake.

'Didn't you hear what I just said to your sister?' Gemma asked.

He blinked at her. 'I have a different question.'

'And that would be …?'

'What's a strip club?'

'Maybe we should have this conversation somewhere more private,' Will suggested.

Gemma hated him for being right. She nodded towards the conservatory, which was joined onto the kitchen by double doors. It was far enough away to afford them a little privacy, but close enough for them to intervene should the Garlic Bread Wars resume. They walked to the end of the tiled room and stood by the French doors that led onto the garden.

'Violet's at a friend's,' she said, raising her eyebrows. 'Okay? This isn't camp X-ray, you know. The kids are allowed to have a social life.'

'Well, I'm sure you know this, but … Juliet always makes

Violet tell her how long she is going to be and how she's getting home.'

Gemma gave him a tight smile. 'All arranged.'

Or it would be, when she'd managed to shove this pain in the neck out of the door and text Violet. She glanced back towards the hallway. 'Didn't you say you had something to ask me?'

Will's exhaled. 'The truth is I'm worried about Juliet. This whole holiday idea is most unlike her. There isn't something you're not telling me, is there? She's not ill or anything like that?'

Gemma wanted to tell him it was none of his damn business, but the look in his eyes stopped her. Okay, maybe he had been checking up on her, just a little bit, but when was the last time she'd seen anyone that concerned about her sister? Juliet had been teetering on the edge of something. Why hadn't she realised before it had all reached boiling point?

Maybe because you were too busy drawing up battle plans and trying to get away as quickly as possible.

She swallowed. She felt terrible about that, especially now she realised it should have been her, not Will, asking these questions about Juliet, and that maybe she should have been asking them a long time ago.

She ran a hand through her hair. 'I think she's just a bit stressed. And I'd booked a trip for myself, so when I realised that maybe she needed the break more than I did I suggested she went instead.'

His brows lowered as he studied her face. 'Yes, she told me that.'

What? He didn't think she could be that altruistic? Just what had Juliet been saying about her to him?

'Nothing much more to say,' she said calmly. 'I'm sure she'll still be fine after a couple of weeks' rest.'

'I hope you're right,' he said, not looking much happier than when he'd first knocked on the door.

Ugh. He was one of those men, wasn't he? The kind with a knight-in-shining-armour complex, and Juliet was his current damsel in distress and had to be protected from big, old, ugly dragon Gemma. Which meant he was going to be in her hair for the next fortnight whether she wanted him to be or not. Fabulous.

And, as if he'd read her mind, he said, 'I'll be back at the weekend to see if you need anything,' then started striding towards the front door.

Gemma trotted after him. 'That's really not necessary, you know. In fact, now you've seen that I'm not a serial killer and the kids are surviving, I'd appreciate it if you didn't keep sticking your nose in.'

He didn't say anything until they got to the hall, but he turned to look at her as he walked out the door. 'Listen, I know we don't get on that well ...'

Understatement of the year!

'... but I made Juliet a promise. I know she had a packed schedule and was concerned it was all too much to juggle. All I'm offering is a bit of neighbourly help.'

Gemma smiled sweetly at Will, remembering belatedly that charming people was what she did best. 'Thanks but no thanks,' she said, then shut the door in his face while he was still opening his mouth to argue back. Infuriating man! She didn't need him stepping into her sister's place while she was away.

She just turned to march back into the kitchen when the doorbell rang again. She wrenched the front door open and yelled, 'What now?' before she'd even seen who was standing there.

It wasn't Will, but the pizza delivery driver. He held out a handful of small change. 'There seems to be a bit of a problem with your payment …'

*

Whose great idea had it been to go Christmas shopping on the last Saturday before Christmas with four kids in tow? Not only that, but they'd waited until the afternoon, when the whole of South East England seem to have converged on Tunbridge Wells.

Oh yes, Gemma thought sarcastically to herself, it had been *her* wonderful idea.

Well, not so much an idea as Plan B. Plan A had been get out nice and early to beat the crowds, but Plan A had gone by the wayside when she'd overslept and hadn't tumbled out of bed until after eleven.

She'd only been living Juliet's life for three days now and already she was exhausted. Christmas holiday? Hah! She'd come straight off the film set to *this*. She thought her job was demanding, but at least she could blow off steam at the end of a day, take a break now and then, but this was relentless. And, as cute as the kids were, this was all very hands-on, not much time to be 'fun Auntie Gemma'. There was the cooking and the driving and – oh, my God! – the washing. Not to mention the nose wiping, now the twins had got the sniffles. Her only saving grace was that they were old enough to wipe *other* bits themselves.

She bustled down the pedestrianised shopping area, a twin in each hand, Polly leading the way and providing a running commentary on the local history of the area, and Violet lagging behind, messing around on her mobile phone. There was obviously some kind of teenage crisis going on, because Violet had been fairly helpful with the little ones until she'd got a message for her friend Abby, and since then they'd been texting back and forth in a frenzy.

They just had two more shops to visit and then they'd be finished. According to Polly, Christmas dinner would be a total disaster if they didn't get the right kind of Christmas crackers, and she knew exactly which ones Juliet had had her eye on. Ones with *nice* presents inside.

'This one! This one!' Polly said, jumping up and down and attempting to drag Gemma into one of the more upmarket gift shops. 'Mummy liked the silver ones with the red holly berries on them and she said I could keep the berries afterwards, if I wanted to.'

Gemma was tempted to ask what use Polly could have for a couple of dozen plastic holly berries, but she was afraid to ask. She realised there were a lot of things she was afraid to ask Polly.

She didn't see what all the fuss was about herself. Half the fun of cheap supermarket crackers was in the awful jokes and making fun of the tacky plastic prizes. Who needed a luxury cracker hat, for goodness' sake? Everyone was still going to rip them off after five minutes, no matter how nice the paper was. But she supposed she'd promised Juliet that she'd try and do Christmas her way, and that irritating man from next door must be rubbing off on her with all his 'I made a promise' stuff, because she couldn't quite bring herself to say 'stuff it' to the whole thing and wing it.

One thing that gave a small sense of satisfaction was that she hadn't resorted to carrying Juliet's notebook around with her like a talisman. Apart from a quick peek to check what was needed for Christmas dinner, she hadn't looked at it at all. Thankfully, Juliet had been very organised about the food. There was a row of thick black ticks down the page, indicating that all the shopping had been done already. The only thing left to get was cranberry sauce.

Apart from that, Gemma didn't think she needed the notebook. The kids were pretty good at telling her what they were up to, and she'd managed to get all the last-minute things Juliet had rattled off to her before she'd shoved her sister out the door to the airport. She had everything under control.

The shops weren't shutting for another hour, so they wandered up to the cheaper end of the town and Gemma decided to go to the Pound Shop after seeing a display in the window. Not only did she buy the tackiest box of crackers she could find – who says they couldn't have both? – but she splashed out on some colourful fairy lights for the kids' bedrooms. All those tasteful white lights at Juliet's house were doing her head in.

She let her nieces and nephews choose what they wanted. Jake had a string of snowmen, Josh had lights in the shape of Rudolph noses. Polly opted for snowflakes, adamant she was sticking to her mother's colour scheme. Gemma shrugged and thought, What the heck? At least they were a pretty shape. Violet chose multicoloured stars. It would be good for the kids to be able to show a little bit of their own personality in their bedrooms, to develop their own Christmas style.

As they were leaving the shop Polly piped up, 'What time is our nativity rehearsal?'

Gemma stopped dead. The twins were taken by surprise and didn't stop moving as quickly as she did, thereby yanking her shoulders out of her sockets, and Violet, who'd been head down and texting, bumped into the back of her.

'What nativity rehearsal?'

Gemma knew all about the nativity play at church. Polly and the boys hadn't stopped talking about it, but this was the first time she'd heard anything about a rehearsal! Much to Gemma's astonishment, Polly reached into the handbag she'd insisted bringing with her and pulled out her own Christmas notebook. She flicked past the opening pages and prodded an entry with a finger.

'Ah! Here it is ... "Nativity rehearsal: four thirty p.m.".

Gemma fumbled for her phone, letting go of Jake's hand as she did so, and giving him a firm look to let him know that if he even thought about running off, he'd be reindeer food, and checked the time on its display. Three forty-five already!

She grabbed Jake's hand again did a one-eighty and headed off back towards the car park. The cranberry sauce would have to wait. 'We won't be too late if we leave now,' she told the children as she hurried them along. 'We'll go straight there.'

'But we haven't got our things!' Polly said in a shrill voice. 'And it's a dress rehearsal. We have to have our costumes!'

Gemma tried to explain that the Sunday School leader would probably prefer to have the three of them there without their costumes than not have them there at all, but Polly really didn't want to listen. She just got more and more upset until she went pink in the face and burst into tears.

While she'd been hurrying the children along, Gemma had concocted a plan to have a quiet gingerbread latte in the coffee shop next door to the church while they rehearsed, but she couldn't quite stand the sight of Polly's pink and crumpled face.

'Okay, okay…' she said soothingly. 'How about this: I'll drop you off at the rehearsal then race home, get the costumes and bring them back? You should have them for the second half, at the very least.'

Polly nodded tearfully as she climbed into the back seat of the car, but Gemma could tell that her niece found this idea only slightly less devastating than the first option. She was going to have to drive really fast to get back to the church on time, but what other option did she have?

Once she'd dropped the kids off at the church, she did a quick U-turn in the middle of the road, ignoring the beeping horns, and raced off in the direction of Juliet's house. Thankfully, the costumes were just where Polly had said they would be – on the back of the utility-room door – but as Gemma ran back through the kitchen she spotted Juliet's notebook sitting innocently on the counter. She was starting to hate its prissy flowery cover, its neat, small handwriting.

If you'd paid attention to me, it seemed to say, *you'd have avoided all that hassle this afternoon. If you'd looked at my lists and colour-coded diagrams, you wouldn't have made such a mess of things.*

It was starting to sound a lot like its author.

Gemma glowered at it as she walked past. 'You're nothing special,' she said out loud. 'There was a minor hiccup, but it all got sorted out in the end.'

Think what you like, the book replied. *But we both know it's just going to snowball from now on in. If you don't follow me to the letter, Christmas will be a disaster, and Juliet will never, ever trust you with anything again.*

It was at that point that Gemma picked up the book, threw it in the bread bin, clamping the lid firmly on top, and dashed out of the house, slamming the door behind her.

&

CHAPTER THIRTEEN

W hen the smaller ones were finally in bed Gemma trudged downstairs, feeling like a balloon that had no air left in it. She found Violet in the living room, flicking through the channels with the sound turned off. Gemma half sat, half dropped onto the other end of Juliet's big squashy sofa.

'Nothing good on?' she asked. 'We could always watch a DVD.'

Violet just scowled harder. 'Don't really care.'

Gemma sat and watched her niece jab at the button on the remote. She was pretty sure Violet wasn't paying attention to the channel guide at the bottom of the screen. When they'd gone through the movie channels and into the sports, she decided enough was enough. She knew that look. She'd worn it often enough herself.

'Boy trouble, huh?'

Violet's whole body sagged and she pouted. Gemma relaxed back into her corner of the sofa, pulling her legs up underneath herself. 'You can talk to me about it, if you like – strictly confidential. There's not much I don't know about bad dating situations.' Someone might as well learn from her mistakes, because she never seemed to.

Violet turned her attention back to the TV, but put the

remote down. On the screen, an ice hockey match played out in silence.

'There's a boy I like …'

Gemma nodded. Yep. That was pretty much where the trouble started. 'Does he like you back?'

Violet's mouth pulled down in one corner and she shrugged. 'I thought so … I thought he was on the verge of asking me out, but then this other girl in my year' – she made a face that left Gemma in no doubt as to what sort of girl Violet thought she was – 'she started flirting with him.'

'And he flirted back? You think he likes her?'

Another shrug. 'I didn't see him flirting, just talking to her, and we're still texting each other, it's just …' Violet wrenched her eyes away from the screen, where a hockey player was getting crunched up against the perspex shield that surrounded the rink. 'My friend Abby is having a party the day after tomorrow, and he's going and she's going …'

Gemma made a knowing face. 'You think if she pushes, something might happen between them?'

Violet nodded.

'Well, you'll just have to make sure you keep him mono-polised for the evening.'

Her niece let out a heartfelt sigh.

'You're not invited?'

Violet perked up. 'Oh, I'm invited – and I asked Mum if I could go, but she didn't get around to giving me an answer before she left. She said we'd "talk about it later".'

Uh-oh. In Juliet-speak, that meant: *I'll say no later, but*

*keep you hanging on for a bit, just because I don't want to
be seen to be mean right from the outset.*

'Why didn't she want you to go?'

Violet pulled her legs up onto the sofa and sat
cross-legged, almost mirroring her aunt's pose. 'It's this
whole Christmas Eve thing … It's supposed to be a family
games night, but it's always a disaster. The boys are too
young, and get bored if we choose anything too interesting,
and Polly has a meltdown if she doesn't win, and I … well,
I'd just rather do something less sad.'

Ah, family games night. That was a legacy from their parents. Juliet had always loved setting up all the board games,
being banker at Monopoly. It had been fun. Well, the start
of the evening had been fun. Juliet had always got more and
more tense as the evenings had worn on.

When she was a bit older, Gemma had realised this was
because every now and then their father would employ a
sophisticated method of signalling to suggest that maybe
Juliet didn't always collect rent from Gemma when she
landed on her. She'd been totally oblivious to the fact until
she'd overheard an argument in the hallway one year and
Juliet had stomped off to bed, saying it wasn't fair and
Gemma always got everything easy because she was the
youngest. It had been hard to enjoy their Christmas Eve sessions after that. Gemma had always been wondering if she
was really having the run of luck she thought she was having, or whether everyone was letting her do well because
they didn't think she was capable of winning on her own.
That tended to tarnish any victories a little.

She could understand why Violet wasn't keen on the idea

now, especially with such a big age gap between her and the twins. She thought about what her niece had said for a moment. 'I could still play games with the little ones if they wanted, but maybe we can talk about you going to this party … with conditions,' she added quickly.

Violet almost bounced off the sofa. 'Really?'

'We'll talk about it,' Gemma said, and when she saw Violet's smile start to slide, she said, 'and I mean a proper discussion. Okay?'

Violet grinned and nodded. 'Thank you, Auntie Gemma! This is going to be the best Christmas ever!'

Gemma grinned back. She was quite pleased about the *best Christmas ever* comment. Who said she couldn't 'do' Christmas? Yes, things were a little busy, but she had everything under control, no matter what that fussy little notebook tried to tell her. And maybe doing a Juliet Christmas with a little bit of a Gemma spice thrown into the mix wasn't so bad after all.

Violet picked up the remote and took the television off mute. 'How about a film?'

Gemma smiled. 'You know me … I love films.'

'Great,' Violet said, pulling up the TV guide. 'I saw that *Before Dawn* is on one of the film channels in about ten minutes. I love Tobias Thornton, don't you? He is *so* yummy!'

Gemma wasn't quite sure she was ready to hear that kind of thing from her teenage niece. It sounded as out of place as if Polly had said it. Also, she wasn't sure she could take a couple of hours of watching that peacock of a man strut around the screen – not so soon after her last job.

'How about *Love Actually* instead?' she said. 'I feel like something Christmassy, and there's nothing much festive about a mutiny on a nuclear submarine.'

She looked at Violet, hoping she'd take the bait. It was either that or resist the urge to put a cushion over her head all evening.

'Okay,' Vi said eventually, 'but I'm not watching the bit with the naked people. It's gross.'

Gemma just smiled and handed Violet her cushion.

*

Gemma rushed into the day room of Greenacres nursing home and searched out the silvery head of her great-aunt. She found Sylvia sitting near the window, just as she'd been last time. Gemma plopped into the chair opposite her and gasped a quick, 'Hi, Auntie Syl!'

'You're late,' Sylvia said, frowning. 'You usually come at two and it's two thirty almost.'

Gemma took a moment to catch her breath. 'Sorry,' she said, and tried to explain about the kids' activities. The way her day had panned out, her aunt was lucky she'd made it here at all. First, there'd been the nativity at Juliet's church, and all the mingling and coffee-drinking after the service, while trying to drag the kids away, and then the boys had a Boys' Brigade Christmas party from one to three, while Polly had a play date a short drive away from one thirty to three thirty, which had left Gemma a window of about an hour and a quarter to speed to the nursing home and squeeze in a visit with Aunt Sylvia.

She wasn't sure how much of her explanation went in, but her aunt nodded and stopped scowling at her, so she must have caught some of it.

'Actually, it's Juliet who usually comes to visit you on a Sunday.'

Sylvia's brow wrinkled, increasing the line count there by at least a thousand.

'My sister,' Gemma explained. Normally, she'd have been tempted to make a joke, say something like, *You know, the one with the slightly constipated expression* ..., but she didn't. Somehow, it just wasn't that funny any more.

She pulled a little bottle of lily of the valley hand cream out of her bag. 'Here ... This is from her.'

While leafing through Juliet's book the previous evening, keeping half an eye on Colin Firth as he chatted up the Portuguese girl, Gemma had found a little list at the back of Juliet's notebook. 'Things to take Aunt Sylvia.' It seemed that Juliet always brought a little present with her on a Sunday – some nice biscuits, or some moisturiser or some flowers – little things that their aunt would like, even though she'd probably forget where they'd come from or who'd given them to her. Gemma had seen the hand cream sitting on the kitchen counter and had guessed it might be the one on Juliet's list.

'Oh, you are a good girl!' Sylvia said warmly, as she accepted the bottle. 'It's my favourite. How did you know?'

'It's from Juliet,' Gemma said again, not quite sure if she was sad or angry about repeating herself, although she wasn't angry at Sylvia, only the disease that was nibbling little pieces of her away.

It was hard work talking to her aunt, Gemma discovered. Sometimes Sylvia was completely lucid and could talk about a subject for five or ten minutes without tripping up at all, but just as Gemma would get into the swing of things and forget that there was anything wrong, the conversation would either take an unexpected turn or just become nonsensical. It required a few agile mental acrobatics to keep up sometimes.

But when they'd visited a couple of weeks ago, Juliet had seemed patient and understanding, even when Sylvia had given Gemma the family heirloom that she now realised had always been earmarked for her.

Gemma had always thought that Juliet had sat on high, judging her, but now another view of their relationship was slowly creeping up on her. Juliet was generous with her time, her energy, her support, but she set very high standards for herself, and punished herself if she failed to meet them. While her notebook might look pretty and benign, all that order, the empty boxes demanding to be ticked, the plans waiting to be executed … It could all seem a little over-whelming and threatening. Juliet might judge Gemma, but she judged herself twice as hard.

'You've drifted off,' Sylvia said, tapping Gemma's knee with a bony finger. 'I thought that was supposed to be my job.'

Gemma jerked back into reality and found her aunt smiling at her, a little twinkle in her eye. *This* was the Aunt Sylvia she remembered, quick-minded and witty, and she was going to make the most of it while she put in an appearance. 'How about a game of rummy?' she asked, and Sylvia's smile grew wider.

'I'll go and get some cards,' Gemma said, and went to hunt for a pack in the stack of board games on a shelf on the other side of the room. When she returned, Sylvia delved into her handbag.

'I've just remembered,' she said cheerfully, 'that I've got something for you in here.'

Gemma smiled. 'It's not another ring, is it?'

Sylvia shook her head then produced something small and furry-looking with a flourish. 'No. It's a sweetie!'

&

CHAPTER FOURTEEN

Juliet checked her watch. She'd bought a cheapish digital one she could wear in the water and was using the timer to calculate her sunbathing sessions. She seemed to have been lying on this sunlounger for an age, but the beeper had yet to go off.

Really? Still ten minutes of her thirty-minute session to go? Time really dragged here in St Lucia, whether you wanted it to or not.

She sat up and studied the other people on the beach. They looked totally in the swing of things. There were a couple of people who hadn't moved on their sunloungers all morning. If they were still in the same flopped-out positions after lunch, she might have to alert someone to go and check they were still breathing.

While the thought of having something interesting to do gave her a little surge of excitement, she couldn't help feeling a bit jealous of those boneless sunbathers, even if they were going to end up with the skin tone of an elephant.

She checked her watch again. Eight minutes left.

With a snort she collapsed back onto her lounger and closed her eyes. Surely relaxing wasn't supposed to be this difficult? Honestly, she'd been here four days now and while everyone else ambled, Juliet strode. Where everyone else drifted lazily in the pool, she did laps. And she'd tried all sorts of activities to wear herself out and get rid of some of this nervous energy – tennis, aqua aerobics, yoga – but nothing seemed to work. How could she have the perfect relaxing holiday, if she couldn't relax perfectly? It was most frustrating.

When her beeper went, and not before, she gathered up her belongings and headed off to the dive shack. It was four o'clock and time for her snorkelling session. She'd done it once before in Majorca with Greg. He'd dashed off and left her struggling with a pair of flippers that hadn't wanted to stay on her feet. As a result, she'd spent more time trying to get them to stay put than watching any actual fish.

The man at the shack stored her bag and kitted her out with a mask and snorkel in the right size and showed her how to fit it properly. She gave the flippers back to him, saying she'd rather do without, thanks. Other guests began to arrive too. The small boat took twelve on each session and the places started to fill up. Most people had booked, but a few stragglers came along to fill up the couple of empty slots.

The last person to arrive was someone she hadn't antici-pated. She didn't know why. It wasn't as if she'd decided the Italian from the villa next door was a vampire or anything, but somehow she just hadn't expected to see him in the day-light.

She tried to look unconcerned as he strolled up in a pair of swimming shorts and not much else. *Crikey*. She'd thought abs like that were only for the kind of men Gemma was always bragging about working with, men who had hours every day to work out with personal trainers; she hadn't realised real men could be made of the same stuff.

Juliet had never really thought herself the kind of woman who went a bit gooey over some male muscle. She considered herself above that. She liked wit and intelligence, that kind of thing. But as she stood trying not to look at her new next-door neighbour's taut thighs and shoulders she discovered they reduced her to marshmallow as effectively as the next female.

She was also very glad she'd decided to put on a long T-shirt over the polka-dot bikini she'd dared to wear for the first time today. She hadn't been going to, but her one-piece had been leaving nasty strap lines and was threatening to spoil her perfect tan-in-progress. He probably wouldn't even look her way, but if he did, she didn't want to feel all wobbly-bellied next to all that rock-hard perfection.

But then he did. Look her way.

And it wasn't just her belly that felt wobbly. Her knees joined in too.

He frowned slightly, and after a second he gave her a little nod and a smile. Juliet tried to smile back, but she found a tic in her left cheek was stopping it being a symmetrical affair. She must look slightly demented! And how on earth had he recognised her after a handful of shadowy greetings in the dark?

She'd seen him again the last two nights, and sensed that going out onto her balcony, acknowledging his presence before disappearing inside again, was becoming a ritual they both expected. She was probably just imagining things.

'Good afternoon,' he said in that beautiful voice of his. 'We are neighbours, yes?'

Juliet nodded – her only avenue of communication, as her tongue seemed to have doubled to twice its usual size. That would explain her current state of speechlessness and the overwhelming urge to drool.

He waved his hand towards the bit of ocean they were about to head off into and his mask swung from his fingertips. 'Have you done this before?'

She shook her head, then realised she really ought to make an effort to speak. He was going to think her simple otherwise. 'Yes … I mean, no. I mean … I tried it once but didn't really …' She trailed off. This was not the right time to be giving the poor man her life story. He was only being polite.

He gave her a smile that only lifted one corner of his mouth. It was possibly the sexiest thing she'd ever seen.

And then it was time to get in the boat. Juliet was all hot and flustered and the boat driver had to tell her twice where to sit. Thankfully – maybe – the Italian ended up at the front end of the boat, while she sat in the stern, and it gave her a chance to regulate her breathing. That sort of thing was important while you were snorkelling, wasn't it? Now was really not the time to forget how.

Once all the passengers were aboard, the driver and other crew member made sure everyone was ready then the small speedboat motored slowly away from the wooden dock and headed north, round the headland that marked the end of the main beach and into another, smaller bay. They picked up speed once they were out of the shallows. The wind blew Juliet's ponytail back and each time the hull of the fibreglass boat smacked against the waves every bone in her body jarred. She gripped onto her seat and tried to look relaxed.

Thankfully, it was only a five-minute trip to the snorkelling spot. There wasn't much of a beach in this cove, just low cliffs with large boulders at the bottom, and the water was so clear she could see that the ocean floor fell away fairly steeply from the land at first, before flattening further out into a blanket of pale sand.

There was a frenzy of activity while shoes were discarded, masks fixed in place, T-shirts removed. Juliet kept hers on. Some of the others, including the Italian, exited the boat by tipping over backwards, like she'd seen people do when scuba-diving on television, but Juliet and a couple of the other novices chose to use the ladder at the back of the boat.

Even though the sun was lower and less fierce than it had been earlier in the day, the water was heavenly. Cool, but not too cold. She wedged the rubber mouth piece of her snorkel behind her lips, took a deep breath, and stuck her face under the water.

Wow.

There were little silver fish with dark stripes that ran from head to tail, swimming in shoals that danced with the underwater tide, sometimes flowing with it, sometimes coquettishly turning en masse and then shooting away. She saw a strange, long, ugly fish with blue spots and one that flapped along the sandy floor. And there were others with yellow and black stripes that kept to the shallows. She was even lucky enough to spot a tiny, delicate seahorse bobbing close to a lump of coral that resembled a giant underwater brain.

There was a tap on her shoulder, and Juliet found one

of the instructors beside her. She lifted her head out of the water to see what he wanted, but he shook his head and stuck his face back in again. She copied. He pointed to a shoal of iridescent squid darting in and out of the larger rocks, changing direction every few seconds, and it was so beautiful that Juliet almost forgot to breathe through her snorkel.

She grinned at the instructor, did a thumbs-up sign, and went off to explore further. The group didn't stay together the whole time, but spread out across the small bay. Every now and then there'd be a shout and they'd all gather to see something unusual – a bright fish or some coral or a fat starfish – and then they'd all drift apart again, letting their curiosity choose their path.

She lost all sense of time, allowing the currents to take her where they would, trying to remember all the different kinds of fish she'd seen so she could find out what they were when she was back on dry land. Out of the corner of her eye she thought she saw a flash. The squid again? She really hoped so. The forty-five-minute session must be up soon, and she would love one last look before they headed back to the resort. She kicked and headed off in the direction of where she thought she'd seen the shoal, but it was difficult to tell. The water was a little murkier here and it was harder to see properly.

And then she looked down and realised *why* the water was murkier here. The bottom was incredibly close, not far beneath her feet if she let them dangle down, and instead of smooth sand there were only jagged-looking rocks and mounds of razor-sharp coral. Juliet lifted her head out of the water and realised she could only just see the boat. She must have drifted a lot further than she'd thought.

Don't panic, she told herself. They wouldn't have brought the group here if it was properly dangerous. She put her face back in the water so she could see what her legs were doing and kicked harder, aiming to propel herself away from the rocks and out into deeper water. It worked. For about five seconds. And then the swell just pushed her back to where she'd started. Her heart began to pound.

She started kicking in earnest, keeping moving, backing away from the rocks so she could tell how close she was, but it was hard to get enough power behind her leg movements, because she had to keep them small enough to save her feet from hitting the coral and boulders only centimetres away. She made a little progress, then lifted her head out of the water and tried to wave at someone, but they were all getting back into the boat and everyone's attention was fixed there and not on the shore.

She was getting tired now. A quick check of her watch revealed they'd been out almost an hour. The wake of another larger speedboat, which had powered through the bay a minute or two before, joined with a particularly large wave and Juliet let out a little gurgle of a scream as she found herself rushing towards the rocks again.

But then a strong arm gripped her around the waist and pulled her backwards. She coughed and spluttered, having swallowed a little seawater when she'd opened her mouth to scream, but she joined the instructor in kicking to propel them both away from the shallows.

It was only when her heart rate subsided and she stopped

frantically churning the water up with her legs that she looked down and realised the strong muscled limbs in the water beside her own weren't the dark skin of the instructor's, but a lovely shade of Mediterranean gold.

*

'Let's see what they look like,' Gemma said as she plugged Polly's snowflake fairy lights into the wall. Finally, they'd had some time to set them up and they'd spent the last ten minutes winding them through the bars at the head of her Victorian-style bed frame.

Polly dashed across the room to flick the main light switch off then jumped back on her bed and stared at the plastic snowflakes, looking much more like a ten-year-old than she usually did. There was something about her wide eyes and barely held breath that grabbed Gemma somewhere deep down inside. She clambered onto the bed behind Polly and scooted in close so they could witness the turning-on ceremony together. Polly instinctively leaned back into her.

'Turn them on!' Josh called from the doorway, jumping up and down in time with his brother. Polly had insisted they try her lights out first, and she'd allowed the boys to act as audience, even if she hadn't yet consented to them crossing the threshold into her territory.

'Go on, Polls,' Gemma whispered into her ear, finding the contact of the small, warm body against hers strangely comforting.

Polly took a deep breath then reached for the little switch near the base of the lights.

For a moment the snowflakes glittered, shadows danced, and the whole room was flooded with a bluish light, transforming it into a snowy grotto. Both boys gasped and Polly, still transfixed by the lights, reached for Gemma's arm and squeezed.

But then the flickering grew stronger, there was a popping sound and it went dark again. In fact, *everything* went dark. Including the landing light and the glowing red display of Polly's digital alarm clock.

The boys screamed, then ran across the room and dived onto Gemma and Polly on the bed, much to Polly's displeasure. From somewhere along the landing, she heard Violet shout, 'Hey! Who turned off the Wi-Fi?'

Oh, crap.

This was what you got for buying fairy lights from the pound shop, she supposed.

'We're not allowed to say that word, Auntie Gemma,' Polly said beside her, but her voice was thin and shaky.

'What word?' Gemma asked, scrunching up her forehead. Why on earth wouldn't Juliet let them say 'Wi-Fi'?

'Crap,' Jake said helpfully, more than a hint of a giggle in his tone.

Uh-oh. She'd said that out loud?

'Poop, then,' she said, correcting herself, and the twins fell about laughing, making the mattress bounce.

Gemma sighed. 'I don't suppose anyone knows where the fuse box is, do they?'

Polly clutched her harder and Gemma could feel her shaking her head against her arm. 'I don't like the dark,' she whispered. 'It's too big.' Gemma could feel the little girl quivering against her, so she wrapped her arm around her and held her firmly, surprised by the rush of warmth and determination that surged through her.

'Who's got a torch in their room?' Gemma asked cheerfully, careful not to sound worried herself in case it made Polly worse.

'We have!' the boys said in unison, and started to climb off the bed.

'Hang on!' Gemma shouted. 'I think I'd better go with you.' There was no telling what danger these two could get themselves into in a darkened house.

Polly held on tighter. 'Don't leave me,' she whimpered.

Gemma rubbed her back. 'I won't, but you'll have to come with us. Can you be brave and do that for me?'

Polly shook her head. 'I want to stay here.'

Gemma's eyes were getting used to the dark a bit now, and she looked between the boys, who were on the verge of making a break for freedom, and Polly, who was doing her best to cement herself to the bed. 'If we don't move, we can't turn the lights back on,' she told Polly. 'It'll be okay.'

Gemma didn't wait for an answer, guessing the more time Polly had to think about it, the more she'd freak herself out. She stood up, intending to offer her niece her hand, but Polly clung on to her like a large and rather heavy baby monkey, and she had no option but to carry her. Gemma ignored the extra weight and led the boys along the landing to their bedroom, where after much searching and almost as much silliness they eventually produced three torches.

'Why don't you let Polly have one?' she asked the boys. 'You two can share and I'll take the third.'

'I don't want that one,' Polly said, rebuffing the first offering and sounding much more like her usual self. 'It's Thomas the Tank Engine and I hate Thomas the Tank Engine.'

'Here,' Gemma said, thrusting the colourful but plain torch in Polly's direction. 'The boys can have Lightning McQueen and I'll have Thomas.' Honestly, she really didn't care what the stupid thing looked like, as long as it worked.

'Violet?' she called as they emerged from the boys' bedroom.

Violet appeared with her mobile phone held up, using its dull glow to light her path. Gemma discovered she was also ignorant to the location of the fuse box. Oh well, there was only one thing for it, then.

'We're going to have to go downstairs and find the place to turn the lights back on,' she told them. Polly began to cry. And she was starting to become such a dead weight that Gemma didn't think they'd make it down the stairs without the pair of them toppling over and reaching the bottom in a heap.

Come on, Gemma! You're usually good with last-minute hiccups and complications. Think!

'I know,' she said brightly, letting Polly slither to the floor. 'Why don't we have a treasure hunt? It'll be fun in the dark.'

'What's the treasure?' Polly said sulkily, never one to miss picking up on the holes in a plan.

Gemma racked her brains. 'How about we raid the tin of Quality Street as a reward after we find the fuse box?'

The boys cheered. Even Violet smiled. Polly looked less than convinced.

'And I'll tell you what,' Gemma said, crouching down and looking her niece in the eye. 'Every good expedition needs a leader, someone to be chief explorer and keep everyone else in line. Do you think you can do that for me?'

The boys groaned, but Polly stood up straighter, set her jaw and nodded.

'Okay, then,' Gemma said, and she made them join hands in a Taylor family crocodile. 'Let's go and have an adventure!'

*

Juliet almost choked on seawater all over again. It was *him.* The Italian!

They were far enough away from the rocks now for the current to have eased. She stopped kicking.

The plan had been to wriggle free, turn round and give a breezy word of thanks, then make her way back to the boat, but she discovered that being held against a firm physique as the water lapped round them was something she was not in a hurry to get away from.

He must have noticed she'd stopped swimming, because he stopped too. She held her breath as he loosened his hold on her and twisted her round to face him.

'Are you okay?'

She felt herself redden, and it had nothing to do with the power of the sun. 'Yes … I'm fine … It was just the current was a little strong over there and I was getting tired.'

He frowned. 'When we were getting back into the boat, I realised you were missing.' He nodded in the direction of the speedboat. 'It was not good for them to let you wander so far away, especially if you are not a strong swimmer.'

'Oh, I *am* a strong swimmer,' she interjected, then frowned also. That had been a long time ago. When had she had the chance to do any serious swimming in the last decade? Even if they made it to a bit of water as a family, she'd always had a toddler or a fledgling swimmer to take care of. There hadn't been any time to swim properly herself. 'At least, I used to be.'

They fell silent, just treading water, and Juliet realised his hands were still at her waist, holding her lightly but firmly, and their faces were only inches apart. Water dripped down his forehead and his lashes were dark and spiky.

'Thank you,' she sputtered. 'I don't think I was in any real trouble, but it would have taken me a lot longer to break free of the current.'

He smiled at her, and Juliet did her best not to impersonate the jellyfish swimming beneath them. '*Prego.*'

She smiled back. 'We'd better be getting back to the boat …'

He nodded and they set off swimming in tandem. He was obviously the stronger swimmer – how could he not be with all those tightly bunched shoulder muscles? – but he only pulled ahead slightly, and she guessed he was being chivalrous by keeping pace with her.

When they reached the speedboat, he motioned for her to go up the ladder first. She opened her mouth to refuse, realising he'd have a rather unflattering view of her cellulite, but guessed he wasn't going to stop being a gentleman now. There was nothing for it but to grit her teeth and hope her baggy beach T-shirt covered the worst of it. How embarrassing.

She flopped down onto one of the hard fibreglass seats and pulled her mask and snorkel off. When her rescuer joined them, he slid into the empty space next to her. They were the last two back on the boat, and the rest of the party was regarding them with interest. A couple of the younger women gave Juliet snooty looks.

When the driver started up the engine, she turned to sit straight on her seat, to keep the wind from hitting her in the face, and found the Italian looking at her.

'I saved your life,' he said, a hint of amusement glowing in his eyes. 'Now you are indebted to me.'

If she'd been ten years younger she'd probably have told him to take a hike, but since she wasn't she just laughed. 'No need to be so melodramatic,' she said, pushing a stray bit of hair out of her eyes. 'I was hardly in mortal danger, so I don't think I owe you quite that much.'

One eyebrow twitched up. 'Then what *do* you owe me?'

Juliet could hardly believe she was having this conversation. If it had been anyone else, she'd have believed he was flirting with her, but since he was … well, him … she just put it down to neighbourly concern. Either that or he was a con man out to trick a lonely woman out of her travellers' cheques. Since he'd been so gallant earlier on, she could hardly believe that was the case.

And this was fun. She realised she hadn't spoken to many people in the last few days. Not proper conversations. Rich people liked to keep themselves to themselves, it seemed. She bit her lip and considered his question, even though she didn't think for a moment he'd been truly serious. 'I think I owe you a drink,' she finally said. 'I'm sure there must be an appropriately named cocktail on the menu I could thank you with. I'm sure I saw one called The Big Blue, or perhaps a Sea Breeze?'

He laughed. 'Almost every cocktail that bar serves up is pink. Hardly a man's drink.'

She kept her mouth closed but chuckled in the back of her throat. 'I didn't think you'd be the kind of bloke who'd find his masculinity threatened by a bit of grenadine syrup.'

He shrugged. 'Maybe this … *bloke* … would prefer a Piton beer?'

This time she laughed properly, partly because the way he copied her word made it sound exotic and charming, but partly because they both knew this was an all-inclusive resort, that this was a game they were playing, and there would probably be no beer, or even a garish pink cocktail.

But then he held out a hand, his expression mock-serious, and she found she couldn't refuse it. She placed her hand in his and they shook on it. 'It's a deal.'

When she attempted to gently slide her hand away he held onto it. 'Marco Capello,' he said, looking straight into her eyes and raising his brow in a question.

'Juliet Taylor,' she managed to stutter.

And then, before she realised what he was doing, he lifted her hand, pressed his lips gently to the back of it then let it go. Juliet clasped it in her other hand, not knowing quite what to do with it now it was her own again. Further down the boat one of the blondes who'd had her eye on Marco sniffed and crossed her arms.

&

CHAPTER FIFTEEN

'I'm hungry.'

'I'm bored.'

You're whiny, Gemma wanted to say to the twins, who were moaning at her in stereo. They'd been searching for more than forty minutes and she still hadn't been able to locate Juliet's fuse box. For a woman who sorted her spice rack into alphabetical order it was most disorganised, verging on the inconsiderate, in fact.

The kids had enjoyed the 'adventure' at first, but after a while Polly had got too bossy and the boys had lost interest and Violet kept sloping off and having to be called back again. In the end, Gemma lit a couple of Juliet's Christmas candles in the living room, put them high up on the mantelpiece and told the little ones they could have their 'treasure'. Once the tin of Quality Street had been opened all she could hear was the rustling of sweet wrappers and the odd squabble about who was going to have the fudgy ones.

While they had chocolate to occupy them, and Violet to keep watch, Gemma continued the search on her own. Although she'd looked in the kitchen twice, she decided to return there. It was the most logical place after the hall and under-stairs cupboard, which they'd already peered into it three times.

The kitchen was at the other end of the ground floor from the living room, so it got much quieter as Gemma moved away from where the kids were scoffing chocolate. She heard a creak as she neared the kitchen door and froze instinctively, the hairs on the back of her neck standing to attention. Her heart began to thud a little harder.

Don't be stupid, she told herself. *It's an old house. They make all sorts of funny noises. You're only noticing it because it's so quiet with all the electrical stuff turned off.*

Still, she crept into the kitchen in her socks, not making much noise and keeping her breathing light and shallow. When she got a few steps inside the door, she stopped and listened.

Silence. Except for the ticking of Juliet's over-sized kitchen clock.

She was just starting to smile at herself, to press a hand to her chest and shake her head, when a shadow passed across the conservatory. A chill skittered through her. She peered into the darkness, trying to work out if it was just a trick of the light, but then the shadow moved again, coming closer, solidifying into something very much like a tall, hefty man, dressed in dark clothing. He also had a torch in his hand.

Gemma had always thought she'd have the good sense to run as fast as she could in the opposite direction if something like this happened to her, but she found herself thinking of the four unwitting children at the other end of the corridor, of how she was the only thing between them and this ... shape.

She wasn't really sure what happened next. She must have dashed forward, because she ended up on the other side of the kitchen, and there was shouting and banging. He was closer too, grabbing onto her, sounding angry, and since he was a good six inches taller than her, she decided she had to take the only avenue open to her – she lifted the chunky Thomas the Tank Engine torch above her head and clocked him over the head with it.

Time, which had been racing along at breakneck speed, slowed then. Too much, maybe. Because it seemed to take takes for her to bring her arm down again, and the yelp of pain that escaped his lips seemed muffled and distorted.

He was clutching his head, groaning softly.

Good. He'd deserved that. And he'd get more if he didn't scarper quick-smart.

She was about to back away, to stretch for the phone on the nearby kitchen counter, when he reached out and grabbed her arm. As he did so, Gemma got a whiff of woodsy aftershave that reminded her of someone …

'I'm calling the police!' they both shouted at each other.

And then, '*What?*'

Gemma slowly lifted her torch and shone it in his face.

Uh-oh.

This wasn't some faceless shape, or even an axe-wielding maniac. It was Juliet's next-door neighbour, and he had a nasty egg-shaped lump on his temple.

'What are you doing in here?' she shouted, her voice quavering and shrill. 'You scared me half to death!'

'And what are you doing messing around in a dark house?' he yelled back. 'I saw the lights out and the torches swinging around inside and thought you were being burgled!'

That made perfect sense, really. But Gemma wasn't in the mood for hearing perfect sense. She was all full of adrenalin and pent-up fear and she needed to unleash it on someone. 'And why in bloody hell would you think that?'

Will closed his eyes and rubbed his head. 'Because there were a whole string of burglaries in this area last Christmas – you know, someone sneaking in and stealing all the presents from underneath the tree.'

'Oh.' Gemma diverted the torch beam so it wasn't shining straight into his eyes. 'I didn't know that.' And then she frowned. 'If you thought we were being burgled, why didn't you just call the police?'

Will opened his eyes and looked at her, blinking in the light of the torch. 'Because I wasn't sure, so I thought I'd just come round and check, and then I found the conservatory door unlocked …'

Ah. That must have been the boys after they'd been playing in the garden before teatime. She'd meant to check that.

He gave a weary look. 'So why *are* you messing around in the dark with torches?'

Gemma shrugged. 'Fuses blew. And I can't find the box.'

At that moment, Josh came running into the kitchen, waving one of the other torches around. 'Auntie Gemma, Auntie Gemma, can I be chief 'splorer now? Cos I want to go to the North Pole and find Santa.' Then he noticed Will standing there and his eyes went large and round.

'Never mind him,' Gemma said, gripping Josh by the shoulders and turning him one-eighty. 'It's just the ugly troll from under the bridge next door, and I've already beaten him up.'

Will snorted.

'You just go and tell Polly that it's your turn to be chief explorer for a bit, and that she can be in charge of the treasure chest instead.' Somehow, Gemma didn't think Polly would mind swapping to the role of ultimate power: control over all the available chocolate in the house.

'Kay!' Josh said and sprinted from the room.

'Careful! You might –'

There was a crash from the hallway.

'–bump into something,' Gemma finished lamely.

Now Josh was gone, it just left her and Will staring at each other.

'Explorers?' he said, eyebrows raised.

Gemma sighed. 'Polly was scared when the lights went off and giving her something to do helped take her mind off it, and the boys were much more helpful when we pretended we were looking for buried treasure than if we'd been looking for a fuse box.'

Much to her surprise, instead of making some sarcastic comment about 'messing around', he nodded. As he moved, the light shone on the side of his head. That lump looked rather angry.

'Sorry, about your head,' she said. 'I thought you were some deranged attacker.'

Will let out a huff of dry laughter. 'Is that better or worse than a troll? And what was it you hit me with anyway?'

Gemma waggled her torch. 'Good old Thomas,' she muttered.

Will frowned. 'What is it made of? Cast iron?'

She tried to stop herself smiling. 'Worse. It's been designed to survive six-year-old boys. I reckon if there was a nuclear war, the only things left behind would be the cockroaches and this torch.'

Will laughed again, but properly this time, and the sound totally surprised Gemma. She didn't think she'd ever heard him do it before, and it was warm and rich, not the business-man's chuckle she'd expected from him.

'I can't decide if you were being very stupid or very brave,' he finally said.

'I can't decide that either,' she said, ignoring the warm feeling creeping up from her knees.

He'd called her brave.

And, because she was totally unused to Will Truman thinking, let alone saying, anything complimentary about her she cleared her throat and changed the subject. 'I don't suppose you know where Juliet's fuse box is, do you? Your houses are really similar and they might be in the same place.'

He was looking at her in the oddest way. It was quite unnerving. As if she was someone he'd never met before. Or maybe it was the same way you looked at someone who had a particularly hairy wart on their nose. Both options unsettled her.

'Well, do you?'

He blinked and shook his head slightly. 'Under the stairs? That's where mine is.'

'Nope.'

Will frowned and headed off in the direction of hall, holding his torch in his fist, like he was on a cop show. Gemma rolled her eyes and followed him. 'You don't believe me?' she said, as he stared at the door to the under-stairs cupboard. 'Check for yourself.'

That was where trolls belonged, anyway. Under bridges, or stairs, or stuff like that.

Will glanced back at her over his shoulder, then opened the door and ducked inside. Gemma, not about to be put in her place, bundled in behind him.

'See?' she said, shining Thomas around. 'Nothing here.'

They both stared into the gloom.

'What about behind that unit?' Will asked, flashing his torch at a rough set of shelves stacked with cleaning materials and half-used cans of paint, with a neat row of wellington boots – arranged in size order, of course – underneath.

It was a little further inside the cupboard. Will moved towards it, but Gemma ducked in front of him. She'd been searching for this fuse box for almost an hour now. If anyone was going to save the day it would be her.

Anyway, she was shorter than Will and it was easier for her to stand where the cupboard height was reduced by the underside of the stairs. She grabbed one end of the shelving unit and started to wiggle it away from the wall. Will quickly followed suit and it was only a couple of seconds before he was able to shine his torch down the back.

Nothing. Just a patch of wall with some really ugly old wallpaper on it.

They swore in unison, which made her laugh.

She turned to look up at him and found him smiling down at her. She swallowed and looked away.

Okay. That had been a weird little moment. Maybe it was time to get out of here. The paint fumes were obviously getting to her.

She stepped round the shelving unit, which was now protruding from the wall at an angle, and discovered the remaining space had shrunk, meaning she was practically pressed up against him. She should have recognised that aftershave. He always wore the same one.

She'd still been wearing half a smile, but now her cheek muscles relaxed and she closed her mouth, just looked up at him with her eyes wide. He was looking back at her, much the same kind of shock on his features as well. The temperature in the cupboard rose by at least three degrees.

Look away, she told herself. *You're the wrong sister. This shouldn't be happening. He likes Juliet. Sweet, kind, sensible Juliet. Not you. You're the anti-Juliet.*

She tried to tell her legs to move, or her arms – any bit of her, really – but nothing worked. It was all rather worrying. All she could do was look at the angles of his face, thrown into relief by the torch light, and try to remember to breathe.

The seconds thudded by, neither of them moving. His gaze dropped to her lips. Her parted lips.

Gemma held her breath. And as she was asking herself just when she'd started noticing the kind of aftershave Will Truman wore, the lights came back on.

*

They walked off the boat together. Marco jumped out first then offered his hand to Juliet as the small craft knocked against the dock. He also stopped to help all the ladies out of the boat. In a strange way it made Juliet feel less nervous. The other women certainly seemed very pleased about it too.

Once they'd picked up the bags they'd stowed at the dive shack, Marco turned to her. 'Come. I find snorkelling very thirsty work.'

Juliet's eyes widened. 'You mean *now*?'

Marco shrugged and gave her that sexy half-grin again. 'What other time is there?'

That sounded like the kind of thing Gemma would say.

'Oh … okay …' She glanced down at her ratty hair and her sodden T-shirt, which had only been partially dried by the wind and late-afternoon sun on the ride back. 'Let me get changed and I'll meet you at Pelican Joe's.' Thankfully, as always, her beach bag was fully kitted out and there was a large restroom near the main pool where there'd be space to change.

She gave herself a long, hard look in the mirror after she'd put on a sundress and was running a comb through her hair. He was just being friendly, that had to be it. Because there was no way he could be interested in this slightly wrinkly, salty-haired creature with the last tinges of sunburn on her cheeks and nose.

What Juliet wouldn't give for her sister's easy manner right now. She only knew how to make people like her by doing things, being the one they relied on, but Marco didn't want a waitress or a housekeeper. He wanted an exciting companion for drinks, and she was supposed to be it. She searched her features, noticing just a touch of desperation in her expression.

She had to share some of Gemma's DNA, hidden away deep down inside, didn't she? She hoped so. Because tonight she was going to have to squeeze it out of its hiding place and put it to work.

When she returned to the bar, she found him looking very relaxed as he sat on a tall stool, one foot on the footrest, the other on the floor. He still had his swimming shorts on, but had added a short-sleeved shirt. His hair was still a little damp and she noticed that half the eyes in the place were on him. The female half, of course.

She sat down next to him. 'Are you really only going to have a beer?'

He nodded. 'And are you sure that is all your life is worth?'

She knew she ought to joke about showering him in diamonds or pledging him her eternal soul or something but, if you took her kids out of the equation, a beer would pretty much sum up what her life was worth at the moment. What did she contribute to the world really? Some seriously good chutney on occasion, but that was it.

She frowned. It all seemed so blindingly obvious to her now, yet back home she'd always felt that everything she filled her notebook with was so terribly important, and it wasn't, was it?

Marco leaned closer to catch her attention. 'You look very serious. Deciding what to have?'

'Nope. I've decided a beer is very appropriate, so I'm going to join you.'

When the bartender had served them up two bottles of the local brew, Marco gestured towards an empty table on one of the terraces. 'Shall we?'

Juliet shrugged. This whole afternoon was getting increasingly more surreal. 'Why not?'

He tipped his head to one side and looked at her.

'What?' she said, putting a hand up to check her rapidly frizzing hair.

He shook his head and made a very Italian gesture with his hands. 'You are an intriguing woman, Juliet Taylor.'

'Thank you,' she said, because he'd meant it as a compliment – at least, she hoped he had. How was he to know that Gemma was the special one in the family, the one who shone, the one who everybody wanted to be with, and that Juliet was only ever destined to walk in her shadow? She smiled to herself, thinking how different it would have been if Gemma really had been here instead of her. She wouldn't have been trading pleasantries and trying to think up small talk. She'd probably be ripping his clothes off behind a palm tree somewhere.

But Gemma isn't here, is she? You are.

She rapped that scary thought on the knuckles and told it to get a grip on itself.

So, small talk it was … She peppered Marco with questions about himself, hardly giving him time to sip his beer before it went warm. She discovered he was the youngest of five siblings, that he lived on the shores of Lake Garda where his family owned a chain of restaurants, that he was a travel writer and liked the fact he was always moving from place to place. He liked watersports – especially windsurfing – and no one could make pasta like his *Nonna*.

She tried to keep him talking, revealing as few details

about her own life as she could. Fessing up to being an anal-retentive suburban housewife didn't sound nearly so interesting. If only she had Gemma's tales to tell. It would make her sound so much more interesting …

But then Marco kept asking questions, and it was most difficult to bat them away the longer he went on. Why couldn't he be like most men and just talk about himself all night, for goodness' sake?

'You are a woman of mystery,' he said, waving at a passing member of staff for a second round. 'Here I have told you much about my life, and I still know so little about you.'

She forgot about not making that unattractive snorting sound. 'Hardly!'

He nodded. 'I thought so the first night I saw you staring from your balcony, looking so …'

'Jet-lagged?' she suggested, not really joking, although Marco seemed to take it that way.

'No. So … I don't know the right word. Not lonely, but …' He shrugged. 'Forgive my English.'

'Oh, my goodness! Please don't apologise for your English – it's excellent. And if you apologise for your English, I am really going to have to apologise for my Italian, which is limited to flavours of ice cream and asking where the toilet is. It's all I can remember from the CDs I bought when we went to Rome for a weekend once …'

'We …?' he asked. 'Is there a man in your life I should know about?'

She shook her head. 'No. Not any more.'

'You are divorced?'

'Yes.'

He looked intently at her. 'Maybe that explains the sadness I thought I saw in you that first night.'

Juliet went very still and quickly transferred her gaze to the beer bottle in front of her. How had he seen that? Sometimes, when she let herself, she did feel very sad. Not that she even liked admitting that to herself. It seemed so … ungrateful. Even before her marriage had ended she'd felt that way sometimes, but Greg had never noticed, not even when he'd lived with her day in day out, and this man had touched upon the truth within seconds of first seeing her. How had he read her that well?

And no wonder she'd been sad. She'd known that Greg had been getting more and more distant, but the harder she'd tried to be the kind of wife he wanted, the more he'd slipped away from her. If that kind of frustrating existence didn't encourage sadness, she didn't know what did.

'I'm sorry the marriage is over,' she finally said, 'but that's all. I don't want him back.'

'Then what do you want?'

Marco grinned at her, and she found herself smiling too. He was very charming. She thought for a moment. What did she want? She really didn't know. She'd given up wishing for things a long time ago.

She thought about Gemma, and what she would want from Pelican's Reach, and she said, 'To have fun. What else?'

He seemed to like her answer because his smile grew wider. 'Then let us toast to your ex-husband,' he said, 'for he is a very stupid and very generous man.'

Stupid Juliet got. 'Generous?' she asked.

Marco waved a hand to encompass the luxurious resort they were in, but Juliet didn't really want to talk about how she'd ended up here. It would lead to too many difficult questions.

'I thought Rome was beautiful,' she said, trying to veer the subject onto something more neutral. She'd gone with Greg on a business conference, but he'd spent most of his time schmoozing important clients while she'd been left on her own. At least she'd got to see lots of the city. 'I did all the touristy things – the Trevi Fountain, the Sistine Chapel, the Colosseum …'

Marco sat back as a waiter replaced their empty bottles for full ones. Just as well Piton beer didn't seem to be knock-your-socks off strong. 'See? Once again we have started to talk about you, and you have changed the subject quite nicely.'

She had, hadn't she? Not by design. Just because talking about Rome had been much more interesting than talking about Juliet Taylor from Tunbridge Wells. Marco fitted in here. He had the right clothes, the air of entitlement, the easy nonchalance. She knew it was stupid, but she didn't want to admit to this man how ordinary she was.

'You have to tell me something about you,' he said, noticing her hesitation and leaning forward a little. 'I don't even know what your profession is. Or maybe you just flit from exotic location to exotic location, driving men insane by avoiding their questions?'

Juliet stared at him for a couple of seconds. 'Why are you so interested in me?'

He put his bottle down, leaned back in his chair and

looked at her carefully. 'Why is it surprising that someone should be?'

Good question, she thought, with a shiver. And another one she really didn't want to answer, but she was enjoying having someone to talk to, and she couldn't keep evading him all evening in this way. The truth was going to have to come out some time, and it looked like it had to be now. Pity, because for the first time in years she felt as if someone was actually looking at her, noticing her, and she hadn't had to bake a cake or sew anything to get them to do it.

Her heart sank as she opened her mouth and said, 'You wanted to know what I did for a living …?'

He nodded.

Juliet had never believed those cartoons where some poor soul was tormented with an angel on one shoulder and a devil on the other, but she could have sworn she felt a sharp stab on her left deltoid as she opened her mouth to tell him she was a mother of four with a part-time job in a craft shop.

Go on …

Instead of what she planned, she heard herself saying, 'Actually, I work in film.'

She couldn't believe she'd said that! Why? Why had she done that? She hadn't even been thinking of Gemma at that moment, but somehow the lie had slipped out of her mouth as easy as butter off a hot knife.

'Doing what?'

She swallowed. She should tell him the truth. Now.

'An assistant director.' She held her breath for a moment, sure a lightning bolt was going to sizzle its way through the thatched roof of Pelican Joe's and fry her right in her seat, but nothing happened.

'You must have some interesting stories to tell.'

Juliet nodded. She had plenty of stories. Problem was they were all Gemma's.

He drained the last of his beer. 'Would you care to share a few of them with me while we dine? I'm hungry and we Italians don't like to eat alone. It's against our religion.'

Juliet clamped her jaw together to stop her mouth from dropping open. Had Marco actually just asked her to have dinner with him? And what did that mean? Did he just want a little company or did it signal something more? She was so unused to reading signals from the opposite sex that she just didn't know.

But she also knew she'd do anything not to sit at a table for one yet again and watch everyone else talk and laugh their way through dinner.

He must have noticed her hesitation, because he said, 'Unless you have other plans ...?'

She shook her head. 'No.'

He stood up. '*Bene*. How about the waterside restaurant? I hear the crab is very good there.'

She half-rose, but didn't go all the way. 'They always seem to be fully booked.'

Marco smiled. 'We are only two. I am sure they can find us a little space.' He said it with such confidence that she started to believe him, even though the girl she'd spoken to earlier had been most adamant.

But then she thought of something else. 'But don't you ...? I mean, isn't anyone ... um ... going to join you?'

He did that unaffected little shrug that she was starting to realise was his trademark. 'No. I came alone to Pelican's Reach. My trip here was rather … last minute.'

'Tell me about it,' Juliet muttered.

He laughed. 'I thought we had already established that I have told you enough. It is your turn to talk.'

She sighed. Why had she pretended she was Gemma, for heaven's sake? Now she was going to have to keep this up all the way through dinner. Maybe even for the next week or so. She wasn't sure she had that much 'mystery' in her!

But at the same time, the idea was intensely appealing. When was the last time anyone had been interested in anything she had to say, other than, 'Yes, of course I can help …' or 'dinner's ready!'?

Other than Will, of course. God, she'd almost forgotten all about him. Good old Will.

And then she looked up into Marco's brown eyes and his confident yet expectant expression. He was still waiting for an answer. 'Okay,' she said hesitantly. 'But I can't spill the beans too much. Confidentiality agreements and what have you …'

And look how the lies kept coming! She had no idea she had a hidden talent for deception. Although, maybe this was one skill she might not choose to cultivate once she got back home. Not if she wanted to keep looking her kids in the eye.

Marco nodded, buying her answer completely. Maybe, just maybe, she could pull this off.

And maybe she was a little more like her sister than she'd ever realised.

&

CHAPTER SIXTEEN

'What are you doing in the cupboard?'

Gemma had been kind of … stuck … looking at Will, and she now whipped her head round to see Violet poking her head through the cupboard door. 'Looking for the fuse box,' she replied weakly. For some reason it sounded like an excuse, rather than the truth.

'You found it?' Will asked, and he moved, turning so his arm brushed hers. Gemma would have stepped away, but there wasn't any room and all she'd have done is tangle herself up in the ironing board. 'Where was it?'

Violet backed out of the cupboard, giving them room to follow. Gemma made sure Will had plenty of space to go first and then squidged herself out past the hoover and the shelf unit.

'The boys wanted to play Snap, so I went rummaging for the cards in the cupboard next to the chimney breast. And while I was moving the board games around to look for the deck, I spotted a grey metal box with a big red switch, so I flipped it.'

'You've saved the day!' Gemma said, beaming at Violet, but inside she felt as if she was slowly deflating. Why wasn't she ecstatic? She hadn't *wanted* to stay in the dark, had she?

She glanced across at Will, but he was avoiding eye contact, and she couldn't decide if that was a good thing or a bad thing. Good, probably.

'How long's the power been out?' Will asked, directing the question more at Violet than at her.

Violet just shrugged.

'Over an hour,' Gemma said. 'Why?'

'You might want to check the freezer, then,' he suggested. 'See how the food's doing.'

Flip. She hadn't even thought of that. However, she needed to get the turkey out in the morning anyway. This would have just given it a little bit of a head start. She turned off the Thomas torch and left it on the hall table, then made her way back to the kitchen. A quick rummage through the freezer revealed nothing, so she checked the fridge, although she was sure she'd have noticed a giant plucked bird in there before now.

Nada.

She sighed and opened the freezer door again. Was nothing going to be simple today? She started pulling packets and plastic tubs out of the freezer, checking each one as she went, but all she succeeded in doing was numbing her hands. If there was a turkey in there, it was playing hide-and-seek.

'Problem?'

She jumped at the sound of Will's voice. How long had he been standing there? She'd assumed he'd gone back home. Bit by bit, she started stuffing icy containers back into the freezer. 'I can't seem to find the dratted turkey, but I know it's here somewhere.'

Will picked up a packet of frozen peas from the kitchen

counter and handed it to her. She took it from him and shoved it in a space. Juliet probably had the whole space arranged by ingredient and pot size. She was going to kill Gemma when she got back and saw the frozen mayhem. Will handed her another item, and they worked silently like that until everything was back inside.

When they'd finished, she closed the freezer door and stuck her hands under her armpits in an attempt to warm them up a bit.

'Vi, does your mum still have that extra little freezer in the garage? I can't find where she's put the turkey.'

Violet shook her head. 'She got rid of it when she and Dad bought the big fridge a few years ago, said she didn't need it any more.'

'Are you sure?' Gemma said, starting to feel a little desperate. It was Christmas Eve tomorrow and not being able to find the turkey was a pretty pressing matter.

'Totally sure,' Violet said, nodding. 'She gave it away to one of my friends' mums. And, anyway, Mum wouldn't put it in the freezer. She always gets one fresh from the butcher.'

Uh-oh. Gemma had a nasty feeling about this.

'But I don't understand,' she said. 'It's right there in the notebook …' She reached into the bread bin and retrieved it, ignoring Will and Violet's surprised looks, and flipped over to the relevant page. 'Look! A row of big black ticks on the Christmas food page …' She trailed off and pressed her fingers lightly over her mouth.

Will stepped forward. 'What?'

Gemma shook her head. It was all starting to make sense

now, but she could hardly let herself believe it. *Thick* black ticks. She should have noticed before. Juliet's ticks were neat and small, hardly overshooting the boundaries of the little boxes, and these were heavy and clumsy.

Still clutching the notebook, she jogged to the living room, where Polly was refereeing a game of Snap between Jake and Josh.

'I'm not going to get cross …' Gemma said. Not yet, anyway. '… but has anyone been messing around with this?' And she held the book up for them all to see.

Jake and Polly looked up innocently at her and shook their heads. Josh carried on slapping cards down on the pile.

'Josh?'

He froze, card half-peeled off the top of his pack.

'*Josh?*'

He slowly lifted his head.

'Was it you?' she asked, trying to keep her voice steady.

He looked at her with those big eyes and nodded, and Gemma felt a shockwave of Juliet-type panic reverberate through her.

'What did you do?'

Josh swallowed. 'I was helping,' he explained in a quiet voice. 'Mummy ticks something in her book every day, but Mummy wasn't here, so I decided to do it for her.'

Gemma held her breath and closed her eyes. 'Violet?' she asked without opening them. 'Could you take Polly and the boys upstairs and supervise while they get ready for bed. I'll be up shortly to do stories.' And she stood very still while the children stood up and followed their older sister out the door. When it had slammed behind them – Polly only knew one way to close a door – she opened her eyes and looked at Will, who hadn't moved from where she'd last seen him.

'Oh, God …' she whimpered. 'I think I want to die.'

Will gave her an *aren't you being a tad dramatic* kind of look.

Well, maybe she was. But she had good reason!

Those ticks, those thick black ticks? They were all the way down the food preparation pages in Juliet's notebook. *All the way down*. That meant Josh had ticked everything and Juliet had ticked nothing.

'I don't have any food for Christmas lunch,' she said quietly. 'Nothing. Not even a blasted jar of cranberry sauce. And Juliet has invited half of Tunbridge Wells.'

Including Will. She'd seen his name on the guest list, but neither of them had seen fit to mention that yet.

'You've still got one day,' Will said, but the expression on his face said he thought that wasn't enough. Gemma was inclined to agree. It took Juliet *months* to get ready for Christmas. How was she going to do it in just one day? She didn't even know where to start.

And then she noticed the notebook in her hands.

You might not, but I do, it seemed to whisper. *Everything you need is inside me.*

She was tempted to throw it across the room, but she didn't. The darn notebook was her only hope. She shuddered and put it down beside the sofa. She'd look at it later, once she'd calmed down from the evening's already hectic events.

She looked back at Will, who'd been standing there the

whole time watching her, a strange expression on his face. 'That's a lot of shopping to do tomorrow,' he said.

'Thanks, Einstein. Didn't realise that.'

Ah, the look on his face now was much more the one she was used to.

'And you're never going to fit you, four kids and enough Christmas groceries for half of Tunbridge Wells into that tiny car of yours.'

He had a point there. And Juliet's car wasn't much bigger. Even if it had been, she wasn't insured to drive it. She glared back at Will. 'Thanks for pointing that out. It was really helpful.'

He gave her an exasperated look. 'I mentioned it because I was going to offer to drive you. My car's almost twice the size.'

Gemma thought of the Audi she'd seen sitting in Will's driveway. 'It's okay,' she said, tipping her chin up. 'I can manage.'

Will stared at her for a moment, and then he shook his head. 'You are *just* like your sister,' he muttered and picked up the torch he'd left on the mantelpiece and headed down the corridor.

'No I'm not!' Gemma shouted after him. 'And where are you going? The front door's that way.'

He glanced at her over his shoulder as she trotted along behind him. 'I'll go out the way I came in, check the lock on that door. Juliet said something a while ago about it not shutting right.' They turned the corner into the kitchen and he nodded towards the French doors at the end of the conservatory. 'You can lock it behind me and I'll try it from outside.'

Gemma wanted to tell him to get lost, but that was actually a very good idea, especially if what he'd said about burglars was true.

'And if you want to prove to me you're nothing like Juliet, you'll accept my offer of help,' he added as they reached the doors and he turned to face her.

Gemma didn't say anything for a few seconds, caught between admitting he was right and her own stubbornness. She folded her arms. 'Why are you so intent on helping me? What's in it for you?'

He looked rather offended at her question, but instead of yelling at her – which would have been much more satis-fying – he said in a low and even tone, 'I'm not intent on helping *you*. I made Juliet a promise and I'm trying to keep it, that's all. It's important to her that Christmas Day goes well.'

She found she couldn't argue with that, either, damn the man! It was an effort to make her lips form the words, but eventually she crossed her arms tighter across her front and said, 'Fine. Okay. I accept.'

Will nodded, looking just about as pleased as she did. 'Great. The supermarket opens at six a.m. tomorrow.' He must have seen the look on her face, because he added, 'If you want to get everything you need, you're going to have to get there before the shop is stripped clean. I'll pick you up at five forty-five.'

His words echoed round her head. Five forty-five… *a.m.?*

She nodded, not quite able to articulate anything while she was still working out how to get herself and four kids out the house at that ungodly time of day. It didn't help that she saw the hint of a smirk on his lips as he stepped through the conservatory door and closed it behind him.

Locking him out while staring through the glass into his face was stupidly pleasing. She gave him one of her 'secret weapon' smiles, just to show him it didn't bother her at all, accepting his help ... being like Juliet ...

Blooming busybody. Well, by tomorrow lunchtime she'd have everything she needed, then he could disappear off, feeling smug that he'd kept his promise to her sister, and she could have a nice family Christmas with the kids. He'd have done his bit and she wouldn't have to see him again for the rest of the festive period.

From the expression on Will's face as he turned and walked away, she reckoned she wasn't the only one who'd be pleased about that.

*

When Juliet and Marco got to the waterside restaurant, the same girl she'd spoken to earlier was guarding the entrance. She gave Juliet a cursory up-and-down look then turned and smiled warmly at Marco.

'How can I help you, sir?' she asked, tilting her head in an appealing manner.

Marco smiled back at her, accepting her adoration. 'A table for two.'

Instead of dismissing him promptly, as she had done Juliet, the girl made a rueful face. 'I'm sorry, sir. We're fully booked.'

Well, Juliet had warned him. She shifted her weight on the back foot and prepared to turn away. Marco leaned in, took the girl's hand and looked straight into her eyes. 'I'm sure there must be something you can do for us …'

And Juliet listened as he worked his spell on the woman. As he talked she smiled, she blushed, and then she flipped the page in the book in front of her. She looked around then leaned forward and spoke in a whisper. 'Well, if you promise me you won't take too long with your meals, I might be able to squeeze you in before another party arrives.'

And then she summoned a waiter to lead them through the packed restaurant, right out onto a deck overhanging the sea. Most of the area was shaded by a pergola, dripping with tropical creepers, and fat light bulbs were strung in ropes between posts. There were a couple of tables with reserved signs on them, and the waiter sat them at the one squashed into an awkward corner. Marco frowned, and when the waiter left he simply got up and sat at another table, one where tiny white starbursts of jasmine trailed from the pergola above, and put the reserved sign on the table they'd just left.

Juliet looked at him incredulously. 'Can you do that?'

Marco just shrugged. 'I think I just did — this table…'.

She couldn't argue with him about that. It was right on the very edge of the deck, the water lapping musically against the posts underneath them, and if they turned to look out over the water they had an uninterrupted view of what was promising to be a glorious sunset.

Once they'd ordered their starters, Marco handed his

menu back to the waiter and looked at Juliet. 'So … I have one thing to ask you, *Giulietta*.'

She liked it when he said her name that way, stretching out the first syllable and curling his tongue around the rest. Instead of sounding full of straight and upright letters – i's dotted, t's crossed – her name sounded alluring and enticing. Not like her at all.

'Ask away.'

His eyes crinkled most appealingly as he smiled back at her. 'What is a beautiful woman doing alone on such a beautiful island?'

At first, Juliet almost turned her head to see which beautiful woman he was talking about, but then she realised he was talking about her. She blushed and reminded herself that he was Italian, and that Italians flirted. He probably couldn't help himself. It didn't mean anything. Even so, she had the oddest urge to excuse herself and scurry away, past the other tables, past the restrooms and off into the night.

God, Juliet. When did you become such a coward?

She forced her bottom to stay glued to the very comfy seat. 'It happened by accident, really.'

He smiled, keeping his lips together, as if he was charmed by what she was saying, and Juliet couldn't help but smile back as the shaky feeling started to subside.

'Are you telling me that you didn't *mean* to get on a plane to St Lucia, but you ended up here anyway?'

She shook her head, laughing softly. 'Nothing that exciting, unfortunately. My sister initially booked this holiday …' She trailed off, unable to finish her sentence, realising that she couldn't tell the whole truth, because that would expose her earlier lie. Maybe just enough of the truth would do. 'At the last minute she had … family commitments … to attend to and couldn't come.' *Her* family commitments, but she didn't say that. 'So she suggested I take the holiday instead.'

Marco stopped smiling he looked genuinely surprised. 'Then you have a very generous sister! I would not do the same for one of my brothers.'

Juliet grabbed a lifeline he'd thrown her, took the opportunity to change the subject and deflect the attention away from herself. 'And what about you? Surely a man who spends his whole year travelling wants to be home for Christmas? Why are you here on your own?'

He looked back at her, more serious than she'd ever seen him before. 'Families,' he said, sighing slightly, 'they are complicated, no?'

'No,' Juliet said, and then with feeling, 'yes, definitely. I know mine is, but why is yours?'

He gave a little half-shrug and looked at his wine glass. 'My father disapproves of my career choice.'

'I'd have thought your parents would be proud of you. You have the sort of fabulous and exciting job lots of people dream about.'

The edges of his mouth pulled down and he looked back at her. 'My father does not think so. He wanted me to join the family restaurant business and has not forgiven me for not doing so. According to him, I do not work, I just "drift around", using it as an excuse to stay away.'

Juliet took a hasty sip of wine. How many times had she accused Gemma of something very similar? She looked across the table at Marco. She'd only known him for a few hours, but already she could sense a restlessness in him. Working in a restaurant, staying put, wasn't for him. He needed the chance to spread his wings in order to be happy.

Just like Gemma always had. But, unlike Gemma, she found she wasn't irritated with him for being that way. In fact, she found the hint of unpredictability about him thrilling.

'Well, I think you have to do what makes you happy,' she told him, even though she was aware she didn't follow her own advice. 'Are you good at what you do?'

He seemed taken aback at her question, and it was a few seconds before he replied, a frown drawing his dark brows together, 'Very.'

Juliet nodded, and leaned back a little as the waiter delivered her marinated squid. When he had disappeared again Marco asked, 'What about your family problems? Aren't you and your generous sister close?'

That wasn't an easy question to answer. Mostly because she'd stepped into Gemma's shoes for the evening and was trying to work out who to answer as. She decided that since she'd had a couple of glasses of wine and was a novice at this 'faking it' lark, it would probably be better to stick to one story rather than try to mix the two. She was just going to have to keep the lie going and, strangely, she liked the idea of taking a holiday from not just her life but herself for a bit.

'Gemma is almost five years older than me. By all accounts, she was a bit of a surprise to our parents – they hadn't planned on having children so young. But they got the hang of it … eventually. So much so, they decided they wanted more, only it took a rather long time for the next baby to come along.'

He picked up his knife and fork and began eating his langoustine. The sun was dipping low now, bathing one side of his face in pinky-golden light. 'If your parents waited a long time for you, you must have been much loved.'

Juliet pressed her lips together and considered her answer. She remembered how overjoyed her parents had been during her mother's pregnancy, how excited they'd been to bring Gemma home from the hospital. 'Yes. Very loved,' she said quietly. 'But maybe my parents went a little bit overboard … Maybe they forgot they already had a daughter who needed their attention too.'

Marco nodded. 'I am also the youngest. I understand. This causes problems with your sister, even now?'

She sighed. 'More than ever, it seems.'

He gave a knowing nod. 'She is jealous.'

'No,' Juliet said, maybe a little too quickly and a little too loudly. She calmed herself down. 'No. Not jealous, it's just …' She didn't know what she was. And it was hard to talk about herself this way, as if she was outside looking in. 'It's just that I'm the one who always gets all the attention. I'm naturally more outgoing, and she is quiet … sensible. She just gets on with things.'

Ugh, she sounded so boring when she described herself like that.

He put his elbows on the table and rested his chin on his fist. 'And do you *try* to steal all the attention?'

Much to her own surprise, Juliet shook her head. 'No. It just seems to happen that way. I don't know why.' The answer had come deep out of her subconscious, but suddenly she knew it was true. Gemma didn't try to upstage her; she just always did.

She wasn't sure if that realisation made her happy or sad. Yes, she was pleased Gemma wasn't that heartless, but it didn't feel good to know she could be so effortlessly eclipsed, either.

'It is the same with me and my brothers,' he said. 'But they do not understand that. It makes family gatherings … difficult.'

Juliet nodded, a cold feeling growing in her stomach. 'And that's why you're here at Christmas on your own, isn't it? Because staying away is easier.'

He sat up straight and laughed, as if shaking the uncomfortable feeling away. Their conversation had got a little too serious. The mischievous glimmer returned to his eyes. 'And the weather is better and the women are not my sisters, who nag me to help them in the kitchen.'

She laughed. Yes, she could see that. She didn't think Marco was a very domesticated kind of guy.

'I'll bet you were naughty as a child,' she said, smiling.

He smiled properly then. 'Just a little. My brothers used to say I stole toys from them when I was little.'

'And when you were older?'

He smiled at her, no guilt in his expression. 'They accused me of stealing their girlfriends.'

She laughed, not sure whether to take him seriously or not. After that their conversation returned to more shallow things. Juliet got it now. He was just a little bit lonely, like her. He'd wanted someone easy and non-demanding to talk to. Part of her deflated at that knowledge, yet part of her breathed a sigh of relief.

When they'd finished eating they left the restaurant together and headed back to the main reception building in search of a shuttle. However, there was a bit of a crowd and Juliet changed direction. 'This way,' she said, 'we might be able to wander along the beach if the tide is low enough.'

She led him through the reception building, past the main pool and down the steps onto the beach, kicking her sandals off and hooking them over her fingertips as they reached the sand. Then they moved away from the lights of the bar and headed off across the beach.

It was dark, but not totally black. The lights spilling from the balconies of the villas above them made sure of that. And when they reached the edge of the beach she was pleased to see that although the tide wasn't at its lowest ebb it was still possible to pass into their cove with a little clambering. Marco led the way, turning to check back on her progress every few steps, but the rocks were large and smooth for the most part and Juliet did just fine.

At least she did until she stood on one that wobbled, one that was balancing on top of two others. Marco's hand shot out instantly and his fingers wrapped around her wrist. But he didn't rush in and rescue her, just gave her the support needed so she could find her own equilibrium. When the rock had stilled, she looked across at him. His eyes glinted in the darkness. Neither of them moved.

She could hear her heartbeat above the sound of the waves lapping at the bottom of the rocks. His fingers felt warm against her cool wrist and a tiny static charge travelled up her arm, lifting the hairs as it went. She suddenly felt very young, very unsure of what to do next.

Marco tugged her gently, pulling her towards him, and he moved his hand so their palms touched, skin sliding past skin until his fingers meshed with hers. She breathed in and forgot what came next. Oxygen? Who cared about oxygen?

She felt him move, and expected him to close the distance between them, but he started travelling forwards again, holding her hand loosely, letting her know he was hers to lean on should she need him again.

Don't be stupid, Juliet. He wasn't going to kiss you. He doesn't look at you that way. And if you can't cope with a little attention from safe, steady, dependable Will, how on earth do you think you'd cope if this man actually was interested in you? You'd be running so fast in the other direction you'd have made Barbados by morning.

When they reached the sand in their tiny cove, he let her fingers drop. They walked in silence to the wooden steps that led up to Juliet's terrace and he turned to face her. She wondered if he would repeat his invitation of the other evening, offer her a nightcap, but he didn't. He merely stepped in and kissed her cheek lightly.

'*Buona sera, Giulietta,*' he whispered, and he watched her as she walked back up the stairs to her villa.

&

CHAPTER SEVENTEEN

Gemma squinted at her shopping list, hastily copied from Juliet's notebook onto the back of an envelope. It was so early in the morning that one of her eyes was refusing to focus, which didn't bode well for a successful shopping trip. There was a crowd of at least fifty people, revving their shopping trolleys, outside the supermarket doors, waiting for a member of staff to come along with a key to unlock them.

She had a twin in each hand and as a slightly petrified-looking employee approached the doors, she crouched down to talk to both of them. 'What are you looking for first?' she asked them.

'Oranges!' Josh shouted, bouncing a little.

'Oranges!' Jake yelled too.

'No, sweetie,' Gemma said slowly. 'Josh is getting oranges and you are getting …?'

Jake looked blankly at her.

'Brussels sprouts,' she reminded him, and when he didn't look any more clued in, she added, 'They look like baby cabbages.'

He nodded slowly, his eyes wide.

'And remember … first one to come back to the trolley with their item wins a prize!'

He cheered up at that. In fact, he and Josh were jumping up and down so much she had to pull them closer to her before they knocked a little old lady off her feet. 'Sorry,' Gemma said, smiling, as the woman glared at them over her shoulder.

'Prizes?' Will said beside her. 'Where are you going to get those from?'

Gemma would have pegged Will for one of those awful people who actually liked getting up at the crack of dawn, but his mood didn't seem to be any better than hers on this frosty morning.

'I'll find something,' she muttered darkly. The one thing she'd learned in the last twenty-four hours was that with a bit of imagination and the promise of chocolate, she could convince these kids to do almost anything.

At that moment the doors opened. The supermarket employee ran in the opposite direction as soon as he'd got the key out of the mechanism, and as the automatic doors slid apart, as welcoming as a crocodile's yawn, the crowd surged forward. The little granny in front ran over at least three people's feet with her trolley in an effort to get in first.

Gemma made sure she had a good grip on each of the twins, checked that Polly was holding safely onto Will, then joined the stampede. Violet had been allowed to stay at home. There wasn't room in Will's car for six of them and she'd promised to do her share by tidying the house while they were gone.

Gemma found just what she needed right at the front of the shop – cut-price chocolate advent calendars, she swept two up and dropped them in the seat at the front of the trolley. Every time a child returned from a search-and-rescue mission to get something on the list, she popped something from a random door and rewarded them with it. Genius. Take that, Will Truman!

The next twenty minutes were chaos. Jake came back with broccoli, asparagus and then a giant cabbage before Gemma realised the reason he couldn't find Brussels sprouts was because there weren't any; they were all sold out. She gave him a chocolate for trying anyway. You couldn't fault the kid's enthusiasm, even if he was a bit hazy on his vegetable identification.

Things were going really well until they reached the meat and poultry aisle. Will had been wheeling the trolley – with lane guidance and hazard detection, courtesy of Polly – and the boys had enjoyed darting in between the shoppers for their next bit of supermarket treasure. Gemma had been leading the way out in front, grabbing things on the list as she scoured the shelves, but now they all stood in front of row after row of empty shelves and stared.

No turkeys. Not even one.

'There aren't even any chickens,' she wailed, turning to look at the kids. 'What are we going to do? We can't eat a Christmas dinner of just veggies!'

The boys pulled a face, and maybe it was that suggestion that caused Josh to focus a little harder on the problem in hand. 'I can see one!' he said, peering into the bottom shelf of the chiller cabinet.

'Where?' Gemma said breathlessly, crouching low to look where he was pointing. Sure enough, stuffed to the back corner of the shelf and out of view of anyone over the height of three feet was a lone cellophane-wrapped chicken. She lurched for it and clutched it to her chest. 'Got you, you beauty,' she exclaimed loudly.

When she stood up again Will was looking at her, eyebrows raised. She had been talking to a chicken, after all. She ignored him and placed it in the trolley. 'How many have you got coming?' he asked. 'I know it's a large one, but it says it's only going to feed six to eight.'

Gemma stopped smiling and leaned over the edge of the trolley to have a look at the packaging. Blast. He was right. And for some reason she wanted it to be his fault that the chicken was a bit on the skinny side too.

'We need more protein,' she said, putting her hands on her hips and looking around. 'Aha!' She marched up to the section with processed meats and picked four packets of chipolatas and a few of streaky bacon off the shelf. 'We'll just have to bulk up with these. Everybody loves bacon-wrapped sausages!'

She looked round the group. They all looked back at her and, as one, they nodded. 'That's settled then,' she said, regaining her smile. She was starting to get the same kind of adrenalin rush she got when things went crazy on set and that only made her feel even more buoyant. When she was in 'the zone' there wasn't a problem that man or god could throw at her that she couldn't solve.

The rest of the shopping trip was a bit of a blur. She found buy-one-get-one-free party bites and bought a whole stack, then topped the trolley up with crisps, nuts and fizzy drinks. Her plan was simple: fill everyone up with canapés, carbonated drinks and alternative meat sources and they might not notice there wasn't a lot of bird on their plates come dinner time.

Will didn't say much, just wheeled the trolley round after her, looking slightly bemused, as she dashed in and out of the crowds finding the remaining items on her list. She got quite used to him being there, a steadying presence to return to after she'd flown off on a mad whim or dived for something she knew could add a bit of variety or excitement to the menu.

When they finally were loading the copious amount of plastic bags into the boot of Will's car, she couldn't help feeling just a little bit pleased with herself.

'Right, kids! Back in the car,' she yelled, clapping her gloved hands together, but Polly and the twins weren't paying attention. They were staring longingly at the signs for the temporary ice rink that had been set up in the park across the road.

'I want to go skating,' Josh whined.

And once the wish had been made vocal, both Jake and Polly chimed in.

Gemma shook her head, looking at the boot full of Christmas food. 'We can't,' she told them. 'We've got to get this food home.'

'*Please,* Auntie Gemma,' Jake said, and he looked up at her with big puppy-dog eyes. 'Just half an hour? Mummy said she'd take us this year, because she was too busy last year—'

'And the year before that,' Polly interjected, then looked pityingly at her brother. 'But you're too young to remember that.' She turned to look at Gemma. 'I had some skating lessons for my birthday two years ago and I've never got to try the things I learned since then.'

She sounded very matter-of-fact, and her expression seemed as don't-carish as normal, but Gemma couldn't miss the longing there in her eyes. She looked across to Will. 'It's your car,' she said to him. 'Your time we're wasting … I think it's your call.'

He narrowed his eyes a little. What? Did he think she'd just passed the buck? It wasn't that at all. It really would have been thoughtless of her to agree to it without checking with him first. She was trying to do the responsible thing.

He looked over at the signs and beyond, where they could just see the gleaming white of the ice through the shrubs at the park's edge, and sighed. 'Why not? It's cold enough for the food not to spoil if we leave it in the car for a bit.'

All three children burst into rapturous cheers and bounded over to him. Polly even threw her arms around his middle and squeezed tight, closing her eyes. Will looked a little taken aback at first, but then he smiled and ruffled her hair with his hand.

Ten minutes later they were standing at the edge of the rink. Gemma couldn't help grinning. A German Christmas market had been set up round the perimeter of the rink and the delicious smells of gingerbread biscuits and glühwein drifted across the ice towards her, riding on the tinny notes of the Christmas pop songs pumped from hidden speakers.

Polly glided effortlessly onto the ice. She wobbled a little bit as she turned to face them but soon skated off at a steady pace and gained more confidence. The boys bounded onto the ice and instantly found themselves on their bottoms. Jake just laughed but Josh started to cry loudly.

'I thought I said "wait for me",' Gemma said, gripping onto the edge and pulling herself onto the ice. She helped Jake up and directed him to hold on to the barrier while she dealt with his brother. After a quick cuddle and a kiss through his puffy coat sleeve for his sore elbow he was fine again. She managed to get him to his feet, but he lost his balance almost straight away and made a grab for both the edge and Gemma simultaneously. The wall surrounding the edge of the rink stayed steady. Gemma didn't.

It started out as just a shudder, but then just kept getting bigger as it rippled through her. Her arms shot out and she desperately tried to get her legs to go in the same direction. They didn't cooperate. A sudden gust as one of the more experienced skaters whizzed past was all it took to destroy any hope of balance. She trembled and then wobbled and then the ice was coming closer and closer until—

'Oof!' She hit something with her face. Something hard and solid and…*warm*?

Something very much like Will Truman.

Her hands shot out and she gripped onto his arms for support as she attempted to unpeel her face from his chest. It would have been doable if her legs hadn't insisted on travelling backwards and away from her. Firm hands came round her shoulders and steadied her.

'I haven't done this in a while,' she mumbled against his coat.

'No kidding,' was the dry response, but she could hear him smiling.

She managed to dig the toes of her skates into the ice and get some traction, which allowed her to bring her legs back under her body, and then she prised herself away from his warm body and looked up into his face.

There was a tell-tale residual warmth in his eyes. 'You okay to stand on your own?'

She nodded, discovering that skating and talking and being quite this close to Will wasn't a combination she could handle. Thankfully, he saved her from being mute for the rest of the skating session by gently setting her upright. The ability to make words returned.

'That was hairy,' she said, laughing nervously, but before she could thank him, Polly had swooped in behind her.

'Come on, Auntie Gemma. I'll show you how to do it!' And she took hold of her hand and started pulling her along the ice. Gemma's lack of skating skills meant she couldn't really argue.

It took all her concentration to stay upright at first, just keeping her focus on her feet and letting Polly worry about where the other skaters were, but after a few circuits she found she was starting to manage on her own. She glanced up, looking for the twins, and spotted them on the other side of the rink with Will. He was teaching them how to put one foot in front of the other without ending up in a heap, and no matter how many times the boys overstretched their skating limits and hit the ice, he picked them up again and carried on.

The ice was cold and solid beneath Gemma's skates, but

something inside her started to melt. That took a special kind of patience, that did, teaching two tearaway six-year-olds to skate, and they weren't even his kids.

She shook herself. Now was not the time to start getting all … whatever … about Juliet's next-door neighbour. She needed to concentrate on her feet, before she started heading face first towards the ice again, and this time no one was around to catch her.

But that soft, slightly gooey feeling lasted all the way through the skating session and through the drive home afterwards. The fact he insisted on unloading the groceries and taking them into the house with her didn't help. She wasn't sure whether to be disappointed or relieved when he finally said his goodbyes and headed back next door.

As Gemma put the shopping away she started to notice a worrying lack of difference in her surroundings. Where the hell had Violet got to? She was supposed to have sorted out all the breakfast mess and hoovered the downstairs by now.

'Violet?' she yelled.

Moments later her niece sloped into the room, still punching buttons on her mobile phone. 'Yeah …' she mumbled, her full attention on the screen.

'You promised you were going to tidy up,' Gemma said, frowning, but at least the gooey feeling was being nibbled away by her growing irritation.

Violet just shrugged. 'I'll get round to it.'

Gemma nabbed her phone out of her hand and replaced it with a bag of groceries. 'Yes, you will. Starting now.'

Vi rolled her eyes, but she didn't argue. Gemma carried on emptying plastic bags and stuffing items into either the

larder or the fridge, but when she picked up the penultimate
bag she had a surprise – a Chinese feast for one and a bottle
of nice red wine.

She didn't remember buying those. It seemed someone
had inadvertently brought their shopping into the wrong
house.

After giving Violet strict instructions to get cracking with
the hoover when she'd finished putting things in the freezer,
Gemma nipped out the front door and made her way next
door and rang the bell.

Will frowned when he saw her standing there. 'I think
some of your stuff got mixed up with ours,' she said.

'Oh,' he said, looking surprised. 'Thanks.'

She handed the bag over, and they stood there, looking
awkwardly at each other for a few seconds. 'I'm sorry we
hijacked your Christmas Eve,' she said. 'Thank you. For the
lift to the supermarket, the skating … everything.'

And she meant it. She was used to being around men who
loved themselves so much they always thought everything
should be done for them, rather than the kind who were
capable and focused and … nice.

He hadn't said anything back yet, and when she looked
more closely she discovered he was regarding her with a
wary expression. 'What?' she said.

'You said thank you.'

'And …?'

'And I'm just waiting for the punchline.'

'There isn't one,' she said, not rising to the bait, taking the
higher road, all that kind of stuff. 'Not this time anyway.'

'Then you're welcome,' he said softly.

'Okay … Well, I'll just be off then … Bye.'

'Goodbye, Gemma,' he said and put his hand on the door.

Why wasn't he closing it? He was letting all the cold air in.

Oh.

It was because she was standing in the way.

She quickly shuffled off his front step and walked backwards up his drive. 'No more dramas for the next twenty-four hours,' she said. 'I promise.' And then she turned and jogged next door without looking back.

&

CHAPTER EIGHTEEN

When Juliet woke up the next morning, she lay still and stared at the ceiling through the draping mosquito net. She thought about reaching for her book, yet her arm never seemed to make it off the duvet. It was still very early – just before six – but she had to get up soon, because she was due to take a catamaran cruise down the western side of the island, with various stop-offs to see the most popular tourist destinations.

This day couldn't feel less like Christmas Eve if it tried. Usually the twenty-fourth was a day of panic, of last-minute shopping, preparation, racing against the clock and then crashing into bed some time after midnight.

She got up and started to pack everything she'd need into a beach bag. However, when she opened her chest of drawers to pull out her sensible black one-piece, the red bikini winked at her. It would be much cooler than the costume in this humidity …

Without stopping to talk herself out of it, she yanked the tiny red top and bottoms out of the drawer and put them on. She could always cover up with a T-shirt when she went swimming.

When she got to the dock, a dozen or so Pelican's Reach

guests were already waiting to board their craft. It was a gleaming twin-hulled boat, with a large cabin and a covered seating area at the back.

As the deckhands yelled to each other and untied ropes, Juliet stood at the back of the boat and did a little three-sixty-degree turn, scanning the area with her hand over her eyes to stop herself squinting. She'd wondered if she'd see Marco this morning, but it was only just eight o'clock and she guessed he must be a night owl, because she'd never seen him at breakfast. Come to think of it, she'd never seen him before late afternoon.

But, just as the catamaran was about to cast off, he came running up the dock and leapt on board. Juliet was sitting in the stern and her heart did a little flip as he caught her eye, looked pleasantly surprised, then sat down next to her, grinning.

'I didn't know you were coming on this,' she said, clutching her bag on her lap.

'Neither did I until ten minutes ago,' he said, and pushed his sunglasses on top of his head. 'But I saw the flyer and I thought, why not?' His smile faded a little. 'Do you mind? I promise I am not following you.'

Juliet laughed. More from the idea of a man like him following her around than anything else. Even Greg hadn't done that in the early days. 'No, I don't mind. It will be nice to have someone I know to talk to.' Most of the rest of the passengers were couples or families; she'd been getting ready to feel like the proverbial gooseberry again.

'*Bene*,' he said, then clapped his hands and stood up. 'What are we doing sitting back here? Come. It is better up the front end of the boat.' And he took her hand and led her up past the cockpit to the area between the twin hulls in front of the mast, and sat down on the fibreglass deck, his legs resting on the string net that made up the front portion of the bow.

They got underway almost immediately, and once the sails were up – although Juliet guessed it wasn't that windy, because the engine was still on – they spent the next hour sailing down the island's west coast. The breeze was delicious. She rested back on her hands, tipped her head back to the sun and closed her eyes. Heaven.

Marco didn't stay with her the whole time, but she didn't mind that – she had no claim on him. He'd get curious and look over the side of the boat, or go and ask one of the crew what a town on the shore was called, or strike up conversation with one of the other groups of tourists. He was like Gemma, she realised, in that he found it easy to talk to anyone about anything, even if he only had the flimsiest grip on the subject matter. People felt comfortable around him. Before they were halfway to their first destination, he'd charmed all the women and was buddies with the men.

Juliet just sat on deck, content to be half aware of his comings and goings. He always came back to her and shared a story, either from someone he'd just talked to or from sailing escapades on Lake Garda, where it seemed almost every child learned to sail as soon as they could toddle.

When they'd been sailing for about an hour, he held out his hand for hers and tugged her to standing. 'Come, Juliet. You cannot see this for the first time sitting down.'

Juliet had been staring out to sea, wondering if she could

catch a glimpse of Martinique off to the north, and when she turned she gasped out loud. They'd come far enough down the coast now to have a spectacular view of the Pitons, the twin volcanic mountains that St Lucia was famous for, rising like sharp points from the sea. She'd had a fuzzy view of them from the aeroplane, but from this angle, with all of the haze of the day swept away by the fresh salty air, they were stunning.

She stayed at the bow, drinking it all in, as the catamaran rounded the headland into a wide bay. The old capital of Soufriere lay scattered before them across low-lying hills, with the mountains as a dramatic backdrop.

The passengers loaded into a convoy of minibuses and headed up into the rainforest for a gondola ride through the trees. The little craft were hardly more than metal frames with wooden seats and a wooden floor, and they glided silently through the trees on a thick metal cable held aloft by sturdy pylons. She wasn't a huge fan of heights, but she was okay if she had something solid to hold onto and the bars of the gondola were thick and well-welded, and she found she didn't mind the experience at all.

They were sitting at the back of the group of eight. There was Marco and Juliet, a young couple who looked like they might be on their honeymoon, two girls in their twenties and a father and a daughter. One guide, Davidson, whom Juliet had been chatting to, sat at the back of the gondola and the other was right at the front, pointing out the different trees and plants and giving a running commentary.

It was cooler here up in the mountains and so peaceful, even though the air was filled with the songs of unseen birds and the calls of insects and tree frogs. When they finished their slow ascent and crested the top of the ridge she held her breath. The gondola stayed there for a moment, swinging gently, so people could take photos.

The whole north-west end of St Lucia was spread out before them. Rolling hills packed with tropical plants, one after the other, until she could see a smudge of yellow through the haze near the coast and then the bright, deep blue of the sea beyond. She was almost sad when the craft began moving again, meaning they were near their halfway point and it would be time to get off and do a short trek before getting back into the gondola and making the return journey back to the base.

But when they disembarked, instead of the few moments to enjoy the cool mountain air and the sounds of the forest, they were all herded into a group and their guides started looking them up and down. Then they produced tackle and harnesses from a small hut on the flat concrete expanse that marked the gondola station. Someone shoved a helmet into Juliet's hands. She turned to Marco, puzzled, but he just shrugged.

Davidson was busy helping the young girl into a harness. Juliet tapped him on the shoulder. 'Excuse me?'

He finished what he was doing and turned round, completely unruffled. 'Yep?'

Juliet thrust the collection of tackle she had in her hands at him. 'What's all this for? The gondola trip back can't be any more dangerous than the trip up, can it?'

'It isn't,' Davidson replied, smiling, and Juliet began to relax a little. 'This is for the zip lining.'

Juliet almost dropped her tackle. 'I beg your pardon?'

'Zip-line-ing,' Davidson said slowly, as if she didn't understand English.

Juliet's jaw moved up and down a few times before any words spilled out. 'But I'm not booked for zip lining. I'm booked for the gondola ride and that's it. The lady at the hotel said so.'

Davidson just shrugged. 'Looks like you're booked up for zip lining now.'

Juliet tried to press the tangle of straps and clips into his hands. 'No, really. I'll just go back down on one of the other ones.'

Davidson laughed gently. 'We were in the last one.' He nodded to where the gondola had come to rest only minutes before. The stand was empty.

'When's … when's …?' Her voice was all scratchy and high. She tried again. 'When's it coming back?'

The guide sighed and looked at her sympathetically. 'It's not. There's only one way down this mountain now.'

Her stomach rolled and she clutched the harness to her midriff. She glanced nervously at the rest of the group who were already halfway into their gear.

'It's perfectly safe,' Davidson assured her.

Juliet nodded blankly, but all she could think about was the waiver she'd signed before getting in the gondola, the one that said she understood that if death or injury were to occur she accepted responsibility for her actions. She'd thought at the time it was a little OTT for what was basically a mini version of a cable car, but everyone knew what health and safety regulations could be like …

She swallowed. 'There's really no other way?'

Davidson's mouth pulled down at the corners and he shook his head. 'Sorry, but we're going to do a short training run before we start the main thing. You'll see. It'll be cool.'

The next few minutes were a haze as Davidson strapped her into her harness. It was made of two pieces – one that went over her shoulders and a bit that wrapped round her bottom and thighs – and they were held together with a couple of massive clips. When she tried to walk, she looked like a cowboy, but she didn't care. She was strapped up tight, held together, and somehow that made her feel slightly less afraid.

And then her hard hat was on and she was walking to the platform that led to a low, short wire over a shallow incline. Juliet concentrated hard on everything Davidson had to say, but she felt as if her memory was a great dark sponge, soaking everything up and refusing to let anything out again.

Marco was in his element, volunteering to go first and whooping as he sped down the line. Juliet couldn't even watch. He waved and grinned at her when he got to the other platform, but she kept shaking her head every time the line was free again, until it was just her and the girl left.

She gathered she must be American, because her father, who had been one of the first to go, was now yelling things like 'You can do it, honey!' and 'Just suck it up!' from the other platform. But it was obvious the girl was frozen with terror. Much like her, really. However, Juliet forgot that for a moment. She wanted to zip down that line and go and make that oaf *suck it up*. Didn't he realise how scared the poor kid was?

She put on her best brave face – just as well she was an expert at it – and turned to the girl. 'Listen,' she said, 'I'll admit that I'm just as scared as you are about doing this, and I'm older, heavier and creakier, but I reckon if I can do it you can too.'

The girl's eyes just widened and she gripped the rail tighter.

'I'm Juliet. What's your name?'

'Amy,' the girl said shakily.

'Well, Amy, I have a daughter a bit older than you, and she did something like this a couple of years ago. She told me she was terrified at first, but really loved it after the first line, and it's all very safe. Look at how many clips and safety wires there are!'

'Too right!' Davidson said from beside them.

A brainwave hit Juliet. 'Listen, why don't I go first – and if I don't scream, you'll know it's not so bad, and that you'll be fine too. Okay?'

After a moment's hesitation, Amy nodded, and Juliet's stomach dived. Look what she'd just talked herself into!

As Davidson led her forward and clipped her onto the double wires, adding in a safety line for good measure, she fought the urge to whimper. *Oh, God, please don't let me end up as a tangle of flesh and bones halfway down a mountain somewhere.* Her kids needed her. This couldn't be it. She visualised them all, lounging round at home, fighting over the last of the candy canes on the Christmas tree and her heart rate calmed a little. But her knees wobbled as she stood on the edge of the platform and her jaw muscle went into spasm.

Davidson, who'd been nothing but a typical laid-back St Lucian up until then, looked her straight in the eye and spoke firmly to her. 'You're going, Juliet.'

It wasn't a question.

She tried to dig the toes of her trainers into the rough wood of the platform, but he gave her a gentle shove, and suddenly the only thing that was stopping her plummeting twenty feet into a lush carpet of greenery was a couple of thin wires and some fabric straps. She clamped down on her jaw, glad she couldn't even find the breath to scream as she hurtled down the wire, the words *death or injury* rushing through her brain.

*

Violet was out at her party, dropped off safely with her mobile phone in her handbag and a lift home arranged with one of the other girls' mums, and Polly and the boys were in bed. All Gemma had to do now was wait, and she filled the time by finishing off wrapping some of the small bits for the kids' stockings. The only problem was that Juliet had run out of sticky tape.

She rummaged through the kitchen drawers, and when she came up empty she resorted to raiding the kids' craft box. No tape. But she did find a Pritt Stick, and went to work welding the presents closed with it as best she could.

When that was done, and stockings filled and ready, she retreated to the living room with a glass of wine, turned off all the lights bar the ones from the Christmas tree and switched on just in time to catch *The Holiday* on the TV, and while Kate Winslet and Cameron Diaz swapped lives and fell in love, Gemma leafed through Juliet's Christmas notebook.

She sighed, picked up a pen and added a light row of ticks next to Josh's thick black ones. It felt odd writing in Juliet's book, as if she was trespassing somehow. After she'd done that, she flicked through a couple of pages, and then a couple more. It was slightly addictive. Maybe because, between the lines, squashed in with the calendar items in a packed schedule, underneath the tick boxes and threaded the whole way through, was a fascinating insight into her sister.

Boy, did Juliet know how to pay attention to details. She noted down tiny little things other people probably wouldn't bother with, like adjustments in cooking times to make a dish perfect, or her guests' culinary preferences so she was sure not to serve them up something they didn't like. But there were other things too, more worrying things, like pages of designs for table settings, some scribbled out crossly, and each drawing was just a tiny tweak different from the last. And the fact that every minute of every day was tightly scheduled with no time for fun or relaxing or anything nice.

And Juliet did this year after year, if the row of neat notebooks on the bookshelf in the study were to be believed. The more Gemma dug into the notebook, the more one word rang round her head. *Why?* She just didn't understand what drove her sister, in this, and in life in general, but this time of year seemed to be the focal point of all her energy, the time when all her sister's little neuroses reached fever pitch.

Gemma remembered Christmas at home when she was a child as being wonderful – happy and relaxed. Juliet had recreated many of their mother's recipes and traditions, so why didn't her version of Christmas feel the same? Why was there a faint air of panic drifting up from the pages of this book, instead of warmth and comfort and love? It just didn't make sense.

She closed the book and stared straight ahead, forgetting all about the film playing on the TV.

Juliet didn't just want Christmas to be perfect; she *needed* it to be perfect.

The only problem was that Gemma had no idea why.

&

CHAPTER NINETEEN

'See? That was not so bad,' Marco said, his arm coming around her shoulder.

Juliet shrugged it off and spun around to face him. 'Are you freaking kidding me? It was the worst ten seconds of my life!'

She hadn't even opened her eyes. The sense of hurtling through the air, twisting slightly in her harness, hearing the ground rush somewhere beneath her feet … And people did this for *fun*? Her legs were shaking so badly she could hardly climb down the steps from the platform to the forest floor. 'How many more lines did they say there were?' she asked Marco weakly.

He heaved out a sigh. 'Sixteen.'

Sixteen. The number echoed through her head as they made the short trek through the rain forest on a well-trodden route to the platform for the first proper zip line. Juliet couldn't help but notice that the ground dipped away more steeply here. Somewhere in front of them she could hear the screams of another party as they navigated the course, mingling with the calls of the birds and insects.

Juliet and Marco were the last to go. The other six in their party had followed the first guide across the short wire.

Not many had whooped as Davidson had, concentrating instead on using a gloved hand to slow their progress on the approach to the next station. Marco offered to go last so Juliet wouldn't have to be the only one left with the other guide, but she clutched onto the rails at the back of the treetop platform and shook her head.

'I can't do it,' she said through clenched teeth.

Marco laid a hand on her arm. 'You can. You've seen all the others do it and not one of them was hurt.'

There was that. Even Amy had done it, holding tightly onto her harness, but with a tentative smile on her face. But somehow it didn't calm the rolling feeling in Juliet's stomach.

'What is it that you fear?' Marco asked, smiling softly at her.

She squeezed her eyes shut. She'd always hated the feeling of being totally at the mercy of something beyond her control, even if it was the usually helpful force of gravity. 'It's the thought of stepping off the edge into nothing and, that once I've started there's no going back, nothing I can do to stop it.' She gripped the rail even harder.

Marco gently peeled her fingers from the wood and walked to the front edge of the platform, stopping a shoe length before the edge, then he leaned in and whispered in her ear. 'You don't have to *do* anything, Juliet. You just have to let go.'

As his words snaked their way into her brain she went very still.

Let go.

That was what she needed to do, wasn't it? Of the idea of

her old life – because it wasn't coming back. Of hurts so old she hardly remembered the wounding, even though the scars pulled every day. Most of all, she wanted to let go of the person she'd become, the woman that was so neurotic, her kids *begged* her to run away for Christmas. She didn't like that woman at all.

But she didn't know how. She'd already banged her head against those emotional walls and come away with nothing more than a headache.

She looked across at the next platform. It was maybe a hundred feet away and fifty feet up the tree. She might not know how to do those things, but she knew how to do this, had already done it once, although she hadn't exactly 'let go' that time. Every muscle in her body had been clenched.

Slowly, she shuffled right to the edge of the platform, careful not to look down. On the other platform, Davidson grinned and waved, beckoning her forward. Juliet wasn't ready to let go of the railing either side of the gap she now stood in, but she smiled weakly back, even though at that distance he would hardly be able to see it.

Don't *do* …

She drew in a shaky breath, sat back in the harness the way Davidson had shown her, feeling the weight of her body pressed against the straps circling her thighs and bottom.

She couldn't do this bit by bit, she realised. Letting go was a black or white situation. All or nothing. Either she was full of tension, stopping her forward momentum, or she was giving in to it.

It seemed that she hung there for an age, suspended

between fear and courage. In her head she kept telling herself she just had to lift her foot, remove that last piece of resistance, but somehow the message never travelled down her leg.

Do it. Do it now. Let go.

In the end it was the tiniest movement that set her free. Just the infinitesimal lifting of her trainer. And then she was sailing towards the next platform, heart thudding, muscles tensed, hands gripping the piece of the harness that held her to the wire so hard her fingers went numb, but she kept her eyes open and when she touched down on the other platform the rest of the party cheered.

She looked from one face to another in surprise, and hardly noticed Davidson unhooking her harness from the wire and attaching her to a safety cable fixed to the giant tree trunk.

She'd done it. She'd actually done it.

And she would probably have felt more jubilant about it if there hadn't still been another fifteen lines to go.

Juliet didn't have time to recover herself properly, because after that it was line after line. The terror subsided a little as the afternoon progressed, even though the platforms got higher and some of the inclines of the wires steeper. Juliet just kept her eyes on Davidson waiting for her on the platform in front and prayed. She lost count of how many lines they'd tackled until Davidson grinned at her and said, 'This is it now. Last one. Make it count!'

She gave him a wry look. 'You mean the other ones were just practice runs for this one?'

He shook his head. 'I mean that you haven't taken your

eye off the wire or your hands off your harness the whole time.'

Juliet looked at him. That had been the plan, even though some of the others had grown more adventurous, flinging their arms wide or leaning back. Davidson had done one run upside down with his feet sticking above the wire. She took a look at the last line. It was the longest run by far, but although it started high up on a tree, they were heading for a small hillock, meaning that, although the wire slanted gently downward, the bottom of the wire met the ground instead of another treetop platform. He was right. When would she ever get the chance to do something like this again?

She surprised the group by volunteering to go first. Davidson clipped her on to the wire, and she sat down into her harness and let herself fall off the platform and into the jungle below. A split second after she was airborne she flung her arms wide. Without a hand to steady herself on the wire, she started to spin. Trees and ferns sped past, their fronds almost touching her, and she caught a glimpse of the others standing on the platform watching her as she swung round. The urge to grab her harness and tuck back into it was almost irresistible, but she forced herself to stay open. As she sped along the last section of the wire, her feet close to the ground, she let out a scream. Whether it was joy or relief she wasn't sure.

The rest of the group whizzed down behind her, Marco going last, and when he arrived he took her face in his hands and kissed her quickly and sweetly. '*Brava*! I knew you could do it.' The other women in the party sighed.

She hardly remembered the trek back down the rest of

the slope to the main reception area, or climbing out of her harness or handing her helmet back. The kids would never believe she'd done it! The inner glow at her accomplishment lasted the whole ride to the plantation where they ate lunch and had a tour all the way round the Botanical Gardens. It was still warming her as they boarded the catamaran and cast off to travel, back up the western side of the island.

Juliet wandered back to the metal railings at the bow as the sun started to turn the sky pink and the clouds blue, and Marco came to join her. He didn't say anything this time. No dry comments, no amusing stories. He just reached over and placed his fingers over hers.

Juliet held her breath.

This was something. Something concrete. Something to say that Marco was being more than friendly. Right? Or was she misinterpreting this in some way? It hardly seemed possible that she would be his first choice above all the other women at Pelican's Reach.

But then Marco brushed his fingers over hers, picked her hand up off the railing and encased it in his own.

Juliet could hardly believe it. It was a dream. That was it. She was still asleep in her bed and the alarm would go off in five minutes and she'd have to run to catch the boat.

But the alarm didn't go off. Marco's hand stayed joined with hers as the catamaran rounded the headland and motored into the thin strip of Marigot Bay for its final port of call before the return to Pelican's Reach.

They broke contact for a moment as he jumped ahead of her onto the dock, but then he turned and held his hand out again for support.

They were led to a viewing terrace at one of the fancy hotels there and were served cocktails while they waited for the sun to dip into the water. She stood shoulder to shoulder with Marco, their bare arms touching and she drank him in as much as she did the yellows and golds of the setting sun. As the last piece slipped beneath the surface of the ocean, Marco turned to her, took her cocktail glass out of her hand, laid it on the railing of the terrace and looked her in the eyes.

Juliet almost felt dizzy. She hadn't believed moments like this were real. Not proper romantic moments that felt that way when you were actually experiencing them, rather than viewed that way with the smudging of time, allowing you to ascribe things to the memory that hadn't really been there in the moment.

Marco's pupils were large and black and he stared at her, his eyes resting on one feature and then the next, as if he was trying to memorise her. As if he was trying to see inside her.

When had Greg last looked at her like that, as if he wanted to know all there was inside her and more? In the final years of her marriage she'd often wondered if he'd ever really seen her at all. She could have been a cardboard cut-out of a woman and he'd still have given her a perfunctory kiss on the cheek when he'd headed off to work in the morning, or patted her bum as his way of saying thanks for a home-cooked meal.

'Marco …' she whispered.

He shushed her, pressing a finger to her lips, smiling so softly. 'No talking, *Giulietta*,' he whispered. 'Just this …'

And then he leaned forward, touched his lips to hers and gave her the best kiss of her life.

*

The clock on the mantelpiece said twenty-two minutes past ten. One minute later than when Gemma had checked it the last time. Violet was supposed to have been home by now. Gemma dialled her niece's number again and waited, not even bothering to put the phone to her ear.

'This is the voicemail for number oh-seven-nine—'

Gemma shut the smug-sounding recording off mid-sentence.

She growled in frustration and pressed the button to send a text. It was only when she was halfway through jabbing a caustic-sounding message in with her thumbs that she looked up and screamed silently inside her head.

Flipping heck. Six and a half days. That was it all it had taken. She was turning into Juliet.

Hadn't she been on the receiving end of just such a text only a week or two ago? And it hadn't made her any more inclined to cooperate. Quite the opposite. Maybe this wasn't the way to handle the situation. She backspaced with a rhythmic tapping of her thumb and started again. Something less confrontational this time. After all, Violet was fifteen. She'd probably lost track of time and the music might be thumping so loud she couldn't hear her phone.

Still, Gemma couldn't help tapping her foot as she tried to watch the TV, and the mantelpiece clock kept drawing her gaze like a magnet. It was only twenty minutes.

Well, twenty-five now. She shouldn't be getting worried yet, should she?

Or should she?

It didn't matter. She was starting to panic anyway, so she might as well just go with the flow. Suddenly, sending the first text – the one she'd deleted – didn't seem like such a bad idea after all. She got up off the sofa and started to pace.

She felt so helpless. She couldn't go further than the street outside, because Polly and the boys were asleep upstairs, and she was totally at the mercy of a teenager in possession of a possibly out-of-battery mobile phone. She'd done all the right things, too! She'd made sure Violet had taken her phone with her, and she'd made sure she'd organised a lift home.

Thirty minutes.

Was it too early to be calling the police?

She ran out of the front door, up the short drive and stood at the end, watching the traffic zoom past, her heart thudding.

Calm down, she told herself. It's half an hour. Practically nothing in teenage time-keeping. And wasn't Juliet always saying Vi was late for everything. She'd probably mislaid her handbag and Kiera and her mother were helping her look for it.

With that rational explanation in mind, she forced herself to go back inside, sit down on the sofa and pick up on the storyline of *The Holiday* again.

*

When Juliet had imagined the perfect Christmas all those months ago at her bank holiday barbecue, this had definitely *not* been on her mental list. However, she quickly decided that kissing a hot Italian man at sunset on a tropical island may well become a must-have for all future Christmases.

This was how a kiss should be, she mused, as his lips teased hers yet again, but the real thing never quite lived up to it. Marco knew just when to take control and when to ease off, when to sweep her away and when to let her lead. When he finally pulled away she closed her eyes and rested her forehead against his chin. She needed a moment to compose herself.

Finally she gathered the courage to tip her head up and look him in the eye. His expression was serious, but there was a warmth in his eyes. She couldn't tell what he was thinking.

'Why did you do that?'

The tiniest of smiles hitched one corner of his mouth. 'Because I wanted to.' He must have read the following question in her eyes, because before she'd even parted her lips to ask it, he added, 'Because I was enjoying a beautiful moment with a beautiful woman and it seemed the only possible way to celebrate it.'

Juliet let out a shaky breath. Good answer. Did they train men in that kind of thing in Italy?

She wanted to ask more, but at that moment their tour guide called and said it was time to get back on board the boat. Now the sun had set they would travel back to Pelican's Reach. The moment was over.

But then Marco took her hand and led her back down to the jetty, and something warm and feathery flared inside her.

Hope.

Not just for another kiss, but for herself, for her life.

Why should she be so scared to hope? And why did she fill her life to the brim to stop herself from mourning the lack of it?

'Ready to go?' Marco asked, as he jumped down into the boat and held out his hand for her.

Juliet looked at him. Was she?

Didn't she always moan that she wanted to be that free-spirited woman, who could *go with the flow* and enjoy the unexpected treasure that life gave her? Didn't she want to be the kind of woman who wasn't afraid to reach for perfection instead of just plan for it?

She smiled as she placed her hand in his.

'Yes,' she said. 'I think I'm ready.'

&

CHAPTER TWENTY

At just after eleven UK time, Gemma was back out at the edge of the drive, scanning every passenger in every car. A silver-grey one slowed as it approached, and her heart lifted, but it turned too early, pulling in to the drive next door.

But instead of going all the way, the car paused at the entrance. Gemma's shoulders sagged as the window rolled down. That was all she needed – a witness to tonight's drama. Especially someone who might report back to Juliet. She didn't exactly see Will as the enemy any more, but she wasn't sure he was an ally, either.

She walked over to his car, arms folded tightly over her middle.

'What *are* you doing?' he asked when she got close enough.

Normally, Gemma would have told him to mind his own beeswax, but this was more important than that. 'It's Violet. She was supposed to have been home forty-five minutes ago, and she's not answering her phone.'

Will squinted at her and checked his watch. Gemma knew what time it would say – three minutes past eleven. Forget about blood, pure adrenalin was racing through her veins and she could feel the passing of each new second like a canon shot.

'Where did she go?' he said, frowning.

'Look, I didn't just let her go wandering off into the night on her own,' she said. 'Juliet knew about the party. It was all properly arranged with a lift home from a parent and everything!'

Will frowned harder. 'Give me a second,' he said, and pulled his car fully into his drive. A few moments later he was rounding the hedge, looking grim.

Gemma pressed the redial button on her mobile, all the while listening for any sign of movement upstairs. Even as she prayed silently Violet would pick up, another part of her brain worried that Vi's phone had been going off in her bag unheard all this time and that the repeated triggering of the ring tone had depleted the battery.

'Do you know where the party is?' Will asked.

'Of course I know where the party is!' She pulled the slip of paper on which Violet had written her friend's name and address out of her pocket and handed it to him.

'Do you want me to drive over there and look for her?'

He'd do that for her?

No. Not for her. For Juliet.

But, to be honest, she didn't care why. She was just glad someone else was there. This was one occasion when charm and 'winging it' were no asset whatsoever.

Then something struck her. 'You can't go. Abby's mother is never going to let Violet go off into the night with a strange man,' she explained. At least, she presumed the woman wouldn't. There was no way Juliet would do that if she were the one hosting the party. 'But I could go, if you'd stay and watch the kids.'

Will glanced nervously at the house. 'Are they likely to wake up?'

Gemma shrugged.

'And do you know your way round the housing estate? It's bit of a rabbit warren. Lots of cul-de-sacs and roads that never go where you think they're going to.'

She shook her head, suddenly feeling very weary. 'No ...' And hadn't she already got lost three times driving around Tunbridge Wells? And two of those instances had been in broad daylight. 'And ... oh, crap ... I've had a large glass of wine. I really shouldn't be driving.'

They stared at each other. 'Leave it to me,' he said, then rushed away.

Gemma stood there shivering for a few moments – she hadn't put a coat on when she'd come outside and now the night air was starting to seep past the goosebumps peppering her skin and into her muscles and bones. She darted back inside and reached for one of her sister's warm coats. Juliet was taller than her, so the sleeves hung down over her finger-tips a bit, but it shooed the chill away nicely.

While she waited for Will to come back, she tried Violet again. He turned up after her fourth attempt, a middle-aged woman in tow.

'This is Linda,' he said, and Gemma nodded and smiled, even though she thought it was a bit of a weird time for intro-ductions.

'Three doors down,' the other woman explained. 'I'll sit with the little ones, if you like. I can't count the number of times Juliet has come to my rescue in the past. I'll be glad to do it.'

So there was an upside to having a sister who was on the cusp of sainthood after all!

'Thank you,' Gemma said, grabbing the woman's hands and smiling warmly at her, and she wasn't even putting it on.

She and Will didn't waste any more time, but headed next door to Will's car. The drive to Abby's house took a torturous ten minutes and Gemma's heart pumped harder with every junction they encountered. She was starting to feel a little sick.

'Are you okay?' Will said.

She'd been so lost in her thoughts, she'd almost forgotten he was sitting there, and his voice made her jump. It sounded low and rich in the darkness, not at all the bland geography-teacher-type tone she'd ascribed him in her memory.

'Yes,' she said firmly. 'Fine.'

And then she realised that was Juliet's motto, and that it was Juliet's handy little lie she was spouting, sitting in Juliet's coat in Juliet's next-door neighbour's car.

'No,' she added quickly, correcting herself. 'I'm pooping myself.'

That was better, even if it did make her feel weaker and smaller, something she suddenly realised she'd never wanted to feel around this man.

'I'm sure she's okay. You know what teenagers are like ...'

'Yes, I know ...' she said wearily, remembering her own lack of punctuality, her own 'without a trace' moments that had driven her parents crazy. It should have been a comforting thought, but then she remembered some of the things she'd got up to at that age, a time when she'd been testing her parents, pushing them to see just how far she could go before they'd stop being so understanding and forgiving, seeing if there really was a limit to their adoration.

She turned to face Will and laid a hand on his arm. 'Can you go any faster?'

Will just gave her the hint of a nod and pushed his foot harder on the accelerator.

Gemma sunk back into the passenger seat, frowning. She didn't want Vi to be pushing the boundaries like she had. Even though, if there had been a point at which she could have stretched their parents' love to snapping point, she'd never found it. Sometimes she'd done it so they'd tell her off and ease up on Juliet a bit, but it had never seemed to work that way.

Of course, that had only made things worse with Juliet, the good girl who by then had a job and a nice boyfriend and who always came home on time. It must have looked as if Gemma had been taking all their parents' love and throwing it back in their faces. She'd never thought about how it must have seemed to her sister back then, had only seen her as a sourpuss who liked to tell her just how badly she was getting things wrong. She hid her face in her hands and wished the car there faster.

'My driving that bad?' There was an edge of humour in his voice.

She shook her head and looked up and out of the windscreen. 'It's not that. It's just …' She let out a sigh so huge that her torso deflated, leaving her feeling floppy and empty. 'Juliet has a lot of reasons to hate me at the moment, and I really don't want to add losing one of her kids to the list.'

'Right.'

The warmth that had been in his tone, just for a moment, vanished. But he didn't just sound serious and focused now. He sounded … angry.

'What did I say?'

He shook his head. 'There was I … thinking you were actually worried about your fifteen-year-old niece, but all you're really concerned about is yourself, whether everyone hates you or not.'

She twisted round to look at him. 'That's not what I said at all!'

In the dull glow from the dashboard, she saw his jaw clench.

Gemma folded her arms. 'Of course I'm worried about Violet! Do you think I'd be racing across Tunbridge Wells at this time of night – with you of all people – if I wasn't? And don't you dare accuse me of not caring about my family. It's exactly because I *do* care that I said what I said.'

She took a moment to steady her breathing.

'Juliet and I haven't had the smoothest of relationships in recent years, and I'd finally thought we'd made some progress. I know you don't believe it, that you've got some weird, twisted picture of who I am in that tiny little head of yours, but I love Juliet, and I've *never* wanted things to be the way they are between us!'

The fact Will didn't reply straight away and shifted uncomfortably in his seat gave her a small sense of triumph.

'Okay,' he said slowly. 'Maybe I have built up some pre-conceptions about you … But if what you say is true, why have you let things continue the way they have been for so long?'

Gemma stared out of the windscreen at the blanched tree branches, lit up for a second by the headlights, then gone again. 'I suppose, when it all boiled down to it, I didn't think she really needed me. Everything's so ordered, so under control. Even if I try to find a space in Juliet's life, she never has room for me. It makes no difference to her whether I'm there at all.' She exhaled. 'I don't know if you've noticed this, but my sister is not the easiest person to get close to.'

Will let out a humph that told her he knew exactly what she was talking about.

'I want to make things better between us,' she continued, her brows bunching together. 'I realise I've been taking her for granted. That's why I suggested she have my holiday. I want to change things, but I don't know if she'll let me – especially if one of her kids has gone AWOL on my watch.'

'I see.' His words were non-committal, but she could sense a change in his demeanour. The atmosphere in the car thawed a little.

'And Violet is a good kid,' she added. 'She often helps out with the little ones and I thought that maybe she deserved a chance to be fifteen and have some fun.'

Will nodded. 'Let's hope that's all it is.' He turned into a cul-de-sac and Gemma recognised the name on the road sign from the address Vi had given her. Before the car had even stopped she unclipped her seatbelt and had her fingers on the door lever.

It wasn't hard to tell which house was Abby's. Every single light was on and the front door was open. The steady thump of a bass beat spilled from it, along with a motley collection of teenage girls and boys, who were shouting their excited conversations at each other, even though they were only inches apart.

Will caught up with Gemma as she got to the front door. 'Anyone seen Violet Taylor?' she asked, looking from face to face.

A couple of people shrugged. One girl shook her head.

'Last time I saw her she was with Callum Brady,' said a girl with a thick blonde fringe covering half her face, and the chorus of surreptitious giggles that followed made Gemma and Will look at each other. Without interrogating the girl further, Gemma pushed past the couple of kids standing in the open doorway and into the house.

She didn't know what Vi had told Juliet about this party, but the whole thing screamed: *Parents not in*. And from the amount of squashed crisps, spilled drinks and the coat rack half-hanging off the wall, she didn't reckon they'd be happy when they *did* get back in. So what had the story that Vi had strung her about it being a supervised bash all been about?

She squeezed past some lanky teenage boys in the hall and carried on down a corridor to the kitchen, aware of a tall male presence behind her. Pleasantly aware, she realised. Much to her surprise, when she got to the kitchen, she found two women in their thirties sitting around a small table, smoking and drinking sparkling rosé out of tumblers.

'Are you Abby's mum?' she asked.

One of the women flicked the ash off her cigarette slowly then looked up at Gemma. 'Yep.'

'And you're … you're letting a bunch of fifteen-year-olds run riot round your house, drinking and smoking and…' from the glimpse she'd got of the lounge as she'd walked past '…*groping*?'

The woman just stared at her. 'They're teenagers. That's what they do.'

'Not Violet,' Gemma said. 'She's not that kind of girl.'

The two women traded a conspiratorial look.

'Where is she?' Gemma asked.

The woman that wasn't Abby's mother looked briefly at the ceiling and smirked. That was all Gemma needed. She was pushing back past the bodies lining the hall and heading for the staircase. Unfortunately, she knew just what teenagers got up to in dimly lit bedrooms at parties. From the way Will was keeping close behind her, almost propelling her forward, she guessed he was having similar thoughts. Which was odd, because she couldn't imagine him as a gawky teenage youth, feeling up a girl under the pile of coats in somebody's parents' bedroom. He just didn't seem the sort.

She put her foot on the bottom step and turned to face Will. 'Maybe you'd better stay down here?'

'No. I'm coming with you.'

'Think about it,' she said, lowering her voice a little. 'We don't know what she's getting up to with this Callum Brady. Barging in might be a little embarrassing for all involved.'

He opened his mouth and she held up a hand.

'Don't get me wrong, I'm all for barging in. It's just that

Violet might find it a little less mortifying if it's another woman catching her in a compromising position.'

Will's expression didn't change, but he nodded. 'Point taken. But if you're not back down here in five minutes, I'm coming up to find you.'

Gemma gave him a weak smile. 'If I'm not back down here in five minutes, I might be grateful for that.'

She hauled in a breath and started walking up the stairs, searching for Violet's long, dark-blonde hair amongst the tangle of teenagers. There was a whole gang, lined up on the landing drinking cans of cheap supermarket lager, and she had to step through their legs like the logs on one of those army assault courses.

'Ow!' one of them said as she passed.

'Sorry!' she said cheerily, fairly confident that the kid was numb enough not to feel the pain for longer than a few more seconds. She poked her head in one door. There were two couples, and a lot of slurpy kissing sounds going on – what was it at that age? Did the hormone levels mean you produced more saliva or what? – but no sign of Violet. She carried on down to the next room. The door was closed and she gripped the handle and shoved it open.

It was dark inside, only the glow from the streetlamp across the road illuminating the room. She could hear movement, though. Gemma squinted, trying to make out what the dark shape was on top of the bed. She grimaced, reached out with one hand and gingerly patted the mattress . Her hand met fabric of different types: silky with padding, scratchy wool, a chunky knit … She sighed with relief. She'd found the coat mountain. That was all.

There was rustle from the far side of the bed. Gemma went still.

'Hello?' she said softly.

There was a pathetic little groan.

'Violet? Is that you?'

Without waiting for an answer, she shuffled round to where the noise was coming from. Her eyes were adjusting to the light now, and she could make out a figure on all fours, breathing heavily.

Thankfully, the girl was alone.

'Vi?'

The girl turned her head and looked blearily at Gemma. 'I can't find my coat,' she slurred. 'Fink I need to find my coat.' And she patted the floor ineffectually. 'Hey! Who moved the bed?'

Everything inside Gemma that had been fearing the worst unclenched a little. Violet was here: safe, alone and, most importantly, clothed. She gently hooked her forearms under Violet's armpits and pulled her to her feet.

'Hey!'

'I'm here to take you home, sweetie.'

Violet twisted the top of her body so she could squint at her. 'Hi, Auntie Gemma. I don't feel brilliant.'

Gemma resisted the urge to laugh, mostly out of relief, but partly because Violet was kind of sweet when she was tipsy. She shifted position so her shoulder was under Vi's left armpit and gripped her round the waist. They managed to shuffle towards the door like that, before Violet began to wriggle. 'I need to find my coat! Mum'll kill me if I lose another one ...'

Gemma was about to say that Juliet probably wouldn't

care about a coat, given the circumstances, but then maybe it'd be better not to go into details about the party with her sister. No need to worry her unnecessarily. In which case, finding Vi's coat might be a really good idea – otherwise they were going to have to explain how she lost it.

She let Violet slump on the end of the bed and reached for the lamp on a nearby desk. Violet squealed and shrank away from the bright light, flipping over and burying her face in the edge of the pile of coats.

'What colour is it?' Gemma asked her niece.

'Red,' Violet mumbled against a silver ski jacket.

Gemma frowned. She was sure Violet hadn't been wearing a red coat when she'd left that evening, but black or navy. 'No, it isn't. Vi, what does your coat look like?'

'I wanted red but Mum wouldn't let me …' Violet said dreamily.

Gemma shook her head. She started rummaging through the pile, trying to see if there was anything in there she recognised. She found a dark duffel coat that looked familiar. She tapped Violet on the shoulder. 'Is this yours?'

Violet lifted her head, but her eyes were closed. 'No.'

Gemma was just about to shake her awake, when she saw a scarf poking out of the left pocket. Now *that* she recognised – she'd bought it for Vi when they'd been in town the other day. A rummage in the other pocket produced a bus pass with Violet's name and photo on it and her mobile phone.

She was just in the process of trying to manhandle a rather drunk and drowsy teenager into the coat when there was a soft rap at the door. She froze. 'Who is it?'

'The cavalry. Your five minutes are up.'

She smiled. She'd bet it was five minutes on the dot, as well.

He sounded a little nervous when he spoke again. 'Is it, um, safe … to come in?'

'It's fine,' she said.

The door nudged open and Will's head appeared.

'She's just a little unsteady on her feet,' Gemma explained. 'Not used to the hard stuff, I reckon. And by "hard stuff" I mean the watered-down syrup they're calling cider in the supermarkets these days.'

He pushed the door open and walked in while Gemma went back to shoving Violet's arms in her coat. It kind of helped that she'd collapsed onto her front, because she really only had to drape it over the semi-conscious teenager then try to work her arms into the holes without breaking any bones – not that she was sure Violet would feel it if she did. Once her mission was accomplished she stood up. Will moved to stand beside her and they both regarded the softly snoring form on the bed.

'I don't envy the way she's going to feel in the morning,' Gemma said, chuckling softly. And then she sneaked a look at Will, just in case he was all stern-faced and disapproving. Much to her surprise, he was smiling too.

'It's a rite of passage, isn't it? She'll learn.'

Gemma nudged his arm with her elbow. 'Don't tell me you were comatose on a pile on coats in your teenage years.'

He turned to look at her. 'Everyone always says people end up in the kitchen at parties, but I always ended up right there.' And he pointed at the rapidly disintegrating pile. At least a third of the coats were in various stages of making their way to the floor now.

There was a little glint in his eye that made Gemma wonder if he'd been as familiar with the delights of *under* the coat pile as she'd been, and she found herself wondering how many girls he's kissed under there.

And then she was wondering why on earth she was wondering those sorts of things about Will Truman. She felt her cheeks heat a little and broke eye contact, turning back to look at her niece.

'Are you going to help me get her out of here, or are you just going to laugh while I try to get her down the stairs?' she said, a bit more snappily than she'd meant to.

Will gave her a *what the hell* kind of look and scooped the teenager up in his arms. Violet lolled against him, but tried to push a strand of wayward hair from her face, and missed. Three times. Gemma motioned for Will to pause and stepped in and tucked the tickly bit out of the way behind Violet's ear. But that brought her closer to him, and she got a whiff of that familiar aftershave, all woodsy and male.

She stood back and shook her head.

Seriously, the teenage pheromones must be saturating the air or something. It was time to get out of here. She led the way, beaming at the line of half-drunk teenagers on the landing and breezing her way through in a jolly way that made them both confused but compliant. Then it was down the stairs, out the door and off to Will's car.

Violet lifted her head as the cold air hit her and looked back towards the house. 'Callum …' she whispered.

Gemma, who was walking next to Will, level with Violet's head, asked, 'Which one's Callum?'

She might have to break out her interrogation techniques after all, just to make sure he'd behaved himself.

Violet let out a low moan and pointed to a couple busy devouring each other leaning up against a tree looped with gaudy Christmas lights.

Ah. So that explained Violet's condition. The flirt had got there first.

No – hang on! That was Vi's friend Abby! Gemma recognised her from the photos on her niece's Facebook page.

Poor Violet.

It probably wouldn't help if Gemma told her she was better off without him, and this wouldn't be the first time a male of the species would drive her to doing something stupid – usually involving alcohol – although she might find herself graduating from cider to tequila at some point.

Now wasn't the time. And some lessons you just had to learn on your own. Gemma sighed and helped Will bundle her niece into the back of his car.

&

CHAPTER TWENTY-ONE

Gemma walked back down Juliet's stairs to find Will still in the hallway. He'd helped her get Violet up there, but had gallantly withdrawn as soon as they'd got to Vi's bedroom door.

'I didn't do much but take off her shoes and coat and cover her up with the duvet,' she confessed. 'And put a glass of water on the bedside table and a bowl on the floor. Sleeping in your clothes after a night out – that's another rite of passage, isn't it?' Vi certainly was clocking them up tonight. 'I would have said it was quite unlike her. Do you have any idea why she did it?'

He shook his head. 'Love, especially young love … Is there any rhyme or reason to it?'

That was a very wistful thing for such a practical man to say. Gemma glanced upstairs. 'I think it's more than that. Do you think …?' She trailed off, and frowned harder.

'Do I think what?'

She pulled a face, not quite comfortable with what she was about to say next. 'I just got the impression that recently … Well, maybe that Juliet has been a bit hard on her, expected too much of her.'

Will bristled a little. An instinctive reaction, she could tell.

She was criticising Juliet and he didn't like that, but then she could see him churning her question over in her head.

'Maybe,' he said. 'It's been a tough couple of years for Juliet and I think she's been relying on Violet to help. I didn't think she'd overdone it, but maybe that's not how Violet feels.'

'If Violet has felt a little overburdened, it would explain why she did something stupid and rebellious the first time she got the chance.' She let out a self-deprecating laugh. 'Believe me, I know all about that.'

She shook her head and looked directly into his eyes. 'I seem to keep having to say thank-you to you today.'

His expression didn't warm up an ounce. 'No problem. Anything to help your sister.'

Of course. For a moment she'd thought they'd been a team, worked together to get Violet back, but now she remembered she was just here by proxy. She was standing in for Juliet. But that didn't mean he didn't deserve her thanks. And maybe, as painful as it might be, an apology. She cleared her throat. 'And I'm sorry ... about what I said ...'

He raised his eyebrows. 'On which occasion?'

She ran a hand across her forehead. 'Most of them, probably. But I was referring to what I said in the summer, about the giant stick and your ... posterior.'

That hadn't been the word she'd used at the time, of course. His lips twitched. 'Thank you. I didn't know you've been paying it enough attention to reconsider the matter.'

Gemma blinked. That hadn't just been an acceptance of an apology. That had sounded suspiciously like flirting.

Her cheeks reddened, even though she was a champion flirt, and hadn't got tongue-tied around men for over thirty years. 'Neither did I. But obviously I must have.'

Alrighty, then ... And that sounded suspiciously like flirting back. Not what she'd planned to say at all. She should probably just usher him out the door and close it behind him. Firmly.

But instead she said, 'Listen, there's a bottle of wine in the fridge and I think if any evening qualified a calming drink, it's this one. Would you –' she gestured towards the kitchen '– care to join me?'

*

She poured a generous amount of wine into Will's glass, then her own, and sat down at the kitchen table. Just the lights under the cabinets were on. Juliet had hung little hand-made tree ornaments from the cupboard handles – little gingham hearts and felt stars – and it all looked very cosy and Christmassy. She wished she had some mulled wine to sip or a mince pie to eat, but she had only managed to find two boxes at the local supermarket and she was saving them for tomorrow.

Or today, she realised, as the hand on the kitchen clock swept towards one.

'Merry Christmas,' she said to Will, raising her glass. 'What shall we drink to?'

He looked steadily at her. 'A truce?'

Gemma laughed. 'I suppose so ... seeing as it's already crept up on us.'

Will just smiled. 'How have the Christmas preparations been going?'

'It's been a nightmare,' she said, taking a slurp of her drink. 'After going to the supermarket this morning I tidied up the house – up to "Juliet" standards, mind you! – and then I realised I didn't know where she'd hidden the kids' Christmas presents. It took me two hours to find where she'd stashed them, and when I'd finished tearing the place apart I had to tidy the whole house a second time.'

'And what about the food? Did you come up with any more solutions?'

Gemma sighed. 'Yes, sort of.' It had put her full set of improvisational and creative skills to use. Catering for crowds was not something she was used to, especially not when the whole menu had gone out the window. 'I had to phone the two au pairs from Juliet's church and put them off, but I couldn't do that to Mrs Waterman or Uncle Tony and his girlfriend, so they'll just have to eat what they're given. We'll have food, but it won't be Juliet's planned-to-perfection menu. It'll be a little more ...'

'Ad hoc?' Will suggested.

Gemma chuckled. 'I was going to go with *inedible*, but your word is definitely better.'

She was aware that his feet were now much closer to hers and tucked hers back under her chair. 'I tried at the green-grocer's but I couldn't find the other veggies I wanted for love nor money. It's a pity about the parsnips, but I don't really mind about the Brussels sprouts, seeing as everyone hates them.'

Will just grimaced.

Gemma looked at him in horror. 'You like them, don't you?'

'Fraid so,' he replied, shrugging one shoulder. 'Don't know what all the fuss is about.'

'Weirdo,' she said.

'Freak,' he countered.

She picked up a satsuma from the fruit bowl in the centre of the table and lobbed it half-heartedly at him. He didn't even need to dodge it, because it flew right past him and rolled along the kitchen floor until it hit the skirting board.

'I thought we'd declared a truce,' he said, looking totally unconcerned.

'We have. But that doesn't mean I won't keep you on your toes,' she said airily. 'Anyway … Aside from the chicken, I'm going to cook one dish from scratch, but it's going to have to be the bread sauce, because that's all I've got the ingredients for.'

'Christmas isn't Christmas without bread sauce,' Will said very seriously.

Gemma gave him a look.

'What? You think I'm a freak for liking bread sauce too?'

She shook her head. 'No,' she said softly. 'I *love* bread sauce. I was just taken aback by the fact we've finally found something we agree on.'

He didn't reply and he didn't smile, but that rusty warmth came back into his brown eyes. Gemma suddenly found the inside of her wine glass very fascinating. And while she was looking at the Chardonnay, a thought crept up on her. One that she hadn't entertained before, because – frankly – she hadn't wanted to.

'Will…?' she said, looking up at him from under her lashes. 'Do you have plans for tomorrow?'

She knew the answer, of course.

He shrugged. 'I do.'

'Spending the day in front of the TV with a Chinese feast for one and a bottle of red wine doesn't count,' she told him.

He looked away. 'It would be a very peaceful way to spend the day after all the blown fuse boxes, missing turkeys, kamikaze shopping trips and runaway teenagers.'

'I know Juliet invited you,' she said, tapping the notebook, which was lying in the middle of the kitchen table. 'But you never mentioned it.'

'Ah.'

She didn't press for a more verbose answer. She knew what he'd been doing. He'd been being gallant and keeping out of her way. She'd assumed they'd come to a silent agreement that it just wouldn't be a good idea, but now it seemed mean. And petty.

'Please come,' she said, lifting her head and looking at him properly now, asking him with her eyes long after her mouth had stopped moving. 'Juliet wanted it that way, and without your help we'd all be eating in the dark after cooking the chicken by candlelight, or trawling the local woods for a lost teenager. You deserve to come.'

He shook his head. 'I don't want the pity invite because you think I've earned it.'

Gemma's shoulders sagged and she looked heavenward. Okay, a truce meant no outright warfare, but obviously the pair of them still had issues. 'That's not what I meant.'

He raised just one eyebrow, a trick she'd always wanted to be able to pull off and had never been able to. 'Then what did you mean?'

'I meant …' She took a deep breath. There was no point being slick or clever with this man; he spotted all her tricks a mile off. So she decided the simple truth would just have to do. 'I meant that I want you to come.'

There. She'd said it. Admitted it out loud. To both him and herself.

The eyebrow sank down into its normal position. 'Then I would be delighted to join you. And I have a chicken in my freezer I could defrost overnight. Two birds have to be better than one. We could cook them together …'

For some reason Gemma flushed. 'No, it's okay. I told Juliet I'd handle the cooking and I will.' For some reason that was very important now.

His mouth curved up on one side. 'I meant in the same oven.'

'Oh.' Great. Now she was sounding like a flustered schoolgirl. 'Oh, okay. Marvellous idea.' She searched the room, looking for something to hang the next thread of conversation on, and her eyes fell on the bottle of wine on the counter. 'Top up?'

She didn't wait for his answer, but jumped up and filled both their glasses anyway. Neither of them spoke for a few moments; they just sipped their wine, and although Gemma tried to avoid eye contact she found she couldn't help glancing his way every few seconds.

Will put his glass down and looked intently at her. 'I had the wrong idea about you, didn't I?'

'A lot of people do,' she replied grudgingly. 'And I know where they get it from – my sister.' Gemma pushed her chair back and stood up, taking her wine glass with her. For some reason she needed to walk, to pace, as she thought this one out. 'I know I deserve some of the stuff she says about me, but I'm not as bad as she thinks I am.'

'It's a sibling thing,' Will said sympathetically.

She stopped walking and looked at him. 'Have you got brothers and sisters?'

He nodded. 'One of each, but it's my sister who's the worst. She's younger than me, but she's a psychologist, so not only is she always analysing me, she's always trying to fix me too.'

Gemma smiled. 'Welcome to the club.' And they both grinned at each other.

'Juliet thinks I was the favourite,' she told him sadly. 'And I suppose it must have looked that way, because Mum and Dad did dote on me, but I *know* my parents loved her.' She frowned. 'For some reason, Mum was always harder on her than me, but I never understood why. She would get told off over the slightest things and I got away with blue murder. Looking back, I can see how unfair it was. But they were unfair to me too …'

Will stood up and leaned against the kitchen counter across from her. 'Really?'

'They kept secrets from me,' she said, the corners of her mouth pulling down. 'Juliet told me as much, and it makes sense of why, even though my parents were wonderful, sometimes I felt a bit … removed … from everything, like I was an outsider.'

He didn't say anything, but his expression told her he was ready to hear what she wanted to say. That struck a chord deep down inside. When did Juliet ever *really* listen to her? She always filtered everything Gemma did through her own perceptions, hearing what she wanted to hear, seeing what she wanted to see.

'I know why they did it,' she said quietly and looked away. 'They didn't think I was strong enough or capable enough to deal with them.' That had always been Juliet's assigned role. She glanced back over at him. 'And I am, you know. Look at the job I do! It's really demanding and I'm really good at it, but my family could never see that. To them I've always been little Gemma – all fluff and no substance …'

She shook her head and turned away, reaching for the wine bottle and topping herself up a bit to give herself something to do, then she let out a long sigh. 'Whatever … I'm used to it now. I don't care.'

When she turned round, rested her bum against the counter and mirrored Will's pose, he was watching her. *Yes, you do,* his eyes seemed to say. 'Have you ever told Juliet any of this?'

She shook her head. 'I tried to before Christmas, but you know what it's like with families, you get so used to a certain dynamic, especially when you grow up with it, that you forget that maybe it doesn't have to be that way.' She sighed. 'We ended up having a huge row about the same old things and not resolving anything.'

She stared into her wine glass. 'I don't know if it's ever going to get better. I am who I am, Will. No matter how hard

I try, I don't think I'm ever going to be able to live up to Juliet's high standards. She won't even relax them for herself, so what chance do I have? It's easier to just …'

'Run away?' he said. His tone was light, but the warmth had left his eyes. 'You sound like someone else I used to know.'

'I don't run away,' she said, her voice dropping lower. Not unless she was pushed, anyway.

'No? Then how many relationships have you had that lasted more than six months?' Gone was the receptive silence. He was starting to sound like Juliet again.

'Not many.' But that didn't mean anything. 'What are you trying to say?'

She could feel his eyes boring into her. 'That you're one of those people.'

Gemma stopped resting on the counter and stood up taller. 'What kind of people?'

He shook his head slightly. 'The kind who never lets anyone close.'

Gemma opened her mouth to disagree, to say that was Juliet's problem, not hers, but never made it to the words and syllables stage. Wasn't that exactly what Michael had said to her, that she held part of herself back from him? It had been such a shock at the time and she'd instantly dismissed the comment as untrue.

Will must have seen a flicker of agreement in her expression, because he carried on. 'The kind who runs if anyone even tries to get close.'

She shook her head. 'That's not true. Yes, I've had a lot of relationships that fizzled out after a few months, but it wasn't all me. In fact, most of the time, they bailed before I did.'

Before I did.

The words hung between them in the air.

Those flaky men she always seemed to conveniently pick …The ones who were guaranteed to give up quickly, who'd never ask too much of her.

Gemma ignored the little nugget of truth she'd stumbled onto and barrelled on. 'For your information, I thought the last serious boyfriend I had was The One, but he dumped me, so your little theory is wrong, okay?' And she turned away and drank her wine so he couldn't see the sheen on her eyeballs.

And what was so wrong with not letting people get close too quickly? She thought it was a pretty sensible reaction when the people closest to you were always judging you and finding you wanting.

She put her wine glass down on the counter and glared at him. 'With Michael I tried and he still left. I wouldn't have run from him, not if he'd give me the chance not to.' Her voice cracked at the end of the sentence and she filled with shame.

She'd expected to see that same condemning frown Will often wore, but instead the stiffness had gone from his features. He was looking at her like he understood every word she was saying.

Ah.

'Who was she?' she asked quietly, and watched him flinch in surprise.

'Who was who?' He said it so lightly, so nonchalantly. It

seemed she wasn't the only one who could gloss over the truth and pretend she didn't care.

'The woman who ran from you?'

Will went very still. He didn't say anything and his expression glazed over.

'Come on,' Gemma said. 'I've spilled my guts, now it's your turn.'

He stayed that way for a long time, but then he inhaled sharply and his eyes focused on her once again. 'Her name was Samantha. We were together for three years, and when I asked her to marry me, she disappeared in the middle of the night and never came back.'

Ouch.

Gemma found she didn't have a glib retort. Not when she could see the bleakness in his eyes. 'Sorry,' she said, meaning it, even though it sounded like the sort of throw-away comment people said when they didn't know how to respond.

'Don't be,' he said. 'It wasn't you.'

And that wasn't a throwaway response, either. The way he was looking at her told her he understood that she'd done some stupid – and some downright insensitive – things in her time, but she'd never done that. Never would.

It made her feel warm all over.

She blamed it on the wine.

Things were getting too serious here. Too uncomfortable.

Too close.

She deliberately looked at the clock. Christmas Day was well underway. 'I'd better call it a night,' she said, draining her glass. 'I've got an insane amount of things to get done in the morning.'

Will nodded, accepting the out she'd offered him, even though he didn't take his eyes from her as he put down his glass and walked across the kitchen. She followed him to the front door. As he turned to go, she realised she had one more thing she needed from this evening, one more truth, and Will seemed to be the only person who was willing to give that to her.

She took a deep breath and asked, 'Does it seem like I "hold back" to you?'

Much to her surprise Will started to laugh. 'If this is you holding back, I think *I* ought to start running now.'

&

CHAPTER TWENTY-TWO

Barely a few hours after she'd said goodbye to Will, Gemma was in a deep sleep. Her dreams were filled with all the Christmas preparations of the last week – coloured Christmas lights that slithered around the house like snakes, Brussels sprouts falling from the sky like snow, and a turkey she was chasing round an empty supermarket, but every time she dived for it, it scooted away on its plump little plucked drumsticks, laughing.

She heard a pounding noise behind her and turned. It was getting louder, coming closer, and it sounded very much like … reindeer hooves?

Then she was back in bed, the fluorescent lights of the supermarket gone and something akin to a large sack landed on her chest. Then a second sack dropped, almost winding her.

Santa?

But now the sacks had knees and elbows and they were giggling and whispering at a level that was closer to shouting. Gemma opened her eyes and lifted her head. The bedroom door was half open, and in the gloom she could see two identical smiles, Cheshire Cat-like in their brilliance, and two pairs of beady, glittering eyes.

'Merry Christmas, boys,' she croaked, and flopped her head back down onto the pillow, letting her eyelids slide closed.

'Santa's been! Santa's been!' they chorused, and the mattress began to reverberate with their barely contained excitement.

'No bouncing!' She still had the bruises from last time.

The twins stop moving up and down, but they started poking her instead. Her eyelids sprung open.

'Can we open our stockings, Auntie Gemma?' Josh said.

She propped herself up on one elbow and twisted to look at the alarm clock. Ugh. Five thirty. Still, she supposed she was lucky they lasted this long. An instinct told her there was no point sending these two back to bed to get more sleep.

'We always open our stockings on Mummy's bed,' Jake explained. 'She likes to see what Santa brought us.'

Gemma smiled. She already knew exactly what was in each parcel, as Juliet must have done in previous years. It wasn't the presents she'd wanted to see, but the delight on her children's faces, and since Gemma had been responsible for buying at least half the contents, she discovered she was looking forward to that too, despite the fact dawn was still hours away.

'Why don't you go and see if Polly is awake, Josh?'

Josh immediately leapt off the bed and raced out the door. Jake made a move to follow him. 'Shall I get Violet?'

'No,' Gemma said slowly. 'I don't think Violet wants to be woken up just yet.'

'Why?' Jake asked.

Gemma coughed and looked towards the door, thinking of Violet, and the fact she'd probably wish it was the end of the world rather than Christmas Day when she finally prised her eyelids apart. 'Because she …Well, she had a late night.'

'And you know what teenagers are like,' a superior little voice said. Polly followed her brother back into Gemma's bedroom, hefting her stocking with her, and sat primly on the edge of the bed while her brothers sprawled and crawled and generally fidgeted. 'Violet's practically nocturnal these days.'

'But we always open our stockings together!' Jake whined. 'She'll be cross with us. Violet is always cross with us at the moment and I don't like it.'

'I think she'll understand,' Gemma said. 'And if she doesn't, you can blame it all on me.'

The boys brightened at that prospect, and the lure of tiny toys and chocolate was too great. They dived into their stockings and started ripping the paper off the top presents. After a few seconds Jake paused.

'Auntie Gemma, why are our presents all slippy and sticky?'

Ah. The Pritt stick. It still hadn't dried.

'Well, Santa has a lot of presents to wrap this year and he ran out of sticky tape,' she told them. 'And it's greener to use glue.' She wasn't sure if that was true or not, but the way they pushed environmental stuff in the primary schools these days, she reckoned she could get the kids to do anything if she told them it was eco-friendly.

Polly humphed. 'You'd think a man of his age and experience would be a little more organised,' she muttered as she gingerly pulled the paper on her first present apart.

Gemma propped one of her pillows behind her back and sank back into it, smiling. She enthused with the children over each new discovery as the wrapping paper came off, even tried to cadge a chocolate coin or two. She was dog-tired, but happy. And now she could understand why Juliet rushed around buying all these little things. The reward far outweighed the effort.

When the kids were halfway down their stockings, Josh looked up at her. 'Aren't you going to open up your stocking, Auntie Gemma?'

She just smiled at him. 'I haven't got a stocking, sweetie, and I'm just enjoying seeing you open yours.'

'Yes, you have!' Jake exclaimed and pointed to the foot of the bed.

Gemma looked where he was pointing and, much to her surprise, there sat a handmade Christmas stocking with a large bow on the top. 'How ...? What ...?' She narrowed her eyes and looked at Polly and the boys. 'Did you put this here?'

All three shook their heads.

'How could we?' Josh asked. 'That's Santa's job.'

Gemma just stared back at them, and when Polly passed her the stocking, full of gifts in a wrapping paper she didn't recognise, her throat grew thick. She hugged it to her chest, relishing the crackle of the paper and sense of giddy anticipation.

'Aren't you going to open the presents?' Polly asked.

Gemma grinned. 'Yes,' she said. 'Yes I am!' And then she

dived in, picked the top present from the pile and started ripping.

*

Gemma was staring at the bread sauce recipe in Juliet's notebook when she heard shuffling footsteps behind her. Since the little ones were in their bedrooms, playing with the toys they'd got for Christmas, it wasn't hard to guess who it was.

They'd had breakfast and waited for Violet to surface, originally intending to include her in the main present-opening session, but by half past seven the twins had worked themselves up into a whirlwind and Gemma had cracked. Besides, like Juliet was always saying: people needed to deal with the consequences of their actions.

She put down the measuring jug that she was holding and turned to face Violet. 'Merry Christmas,' she said brightly. 'How are you this morning?' Violet winced at the sound of her voice and Gemma felt a twinge of sympathy. 'That good, huh?'

Violet, who was looking a little grey and dishevelled, shrugged.

Gemma turned back to the recipe. Half a pint of milk … She tipped the bottle up and measured out the required amount, then tipped the milk into a saucepan and put it on the hotplate on the Aga. While she returned the milk bottle to the fridge she said to Violet, 'I think you owe Will a big thank-you when he comes round later.'

Violet's eyelids lowered slightly. 'Whatever.'

That one little word got right under Gemma's skin. She'd been prepared to be jovial and understanding, but the very least she expected from Violet was an apology, and maybe a little gratitude for rescuing her sorry hide.

'You gave me a real panic last night, you know,' she said, trying to keep her tone light and finding she was struggling. 'You put a lot of people out with your reckless behaviour. Why didn't you answer your phone?'

Violet shrugged again. 'Left it in my coat pocket.'

'And you were supposed to be home at ten fifteen. What happened about that lift we organised?'

'Keira's mum decided to stay and have a chat with Abby's mum before we came back,' Violet said. 'She sent me upstairs to find my coat.'

Ah. So that had been the other woman in the kitchen. Gemma remembered the size of the drink she'd had in front of her, and was suddenly very glad Violet hadn't had a lift home with her.

'Were you sick in the night?' Gemma asked.

Violet shook her head.

Lucky girl. Gemma folded her arms and waited. This was supposed to be the bit where Violet said 'Thank you, Auntie Gemma, for dashing out at almost midnight to come and get me. Thank you for not bawling me out, and making sure I was safe from physical harm, from boys who'd have taken advantage and a possible teenage pregnancy', but Violet just scuffed the kitchen floor with her sock, then looked up, eyes blank, totally unconcerned.

'Well …?'

'Well, what?' Violet replied. 'I'm hardly the first teenager in the world to get drunk at a party. Lighten up, will you?'

The milk was starting to bubble and spit on the Aga behind her, and Gemma discovered she was feeling much the same. Here she was, running around like a headless chicken, trying to make Christmas perfect for Vi and the other kids, and the girl was taking the whole thing for granted.

'I can't believe you're being so selfish,' she said in a tight voice, and at exactly the same time she heard Juliet saying the words inside her head. It was a rather bizarre kind of déjà vu, where she'd had this conversation before, but now she was standing in the other person's shoes.

Violet shrugged again, but this time Gemma looked more closely, saw the shame and guilt in her expression before she looked away.

It hit her like a slap in the face. This was exactly how Juliet felt every time Gemma downplayed one of her own slip-ups, every time she pretended it was no big deal and that Juliet was just blowing it all out of proportion.

No wonder it made the veins on the side of Juliet's temple throb.

She drew in a steadying breath and decided to try another approach. She hated it when Juliet came out with all guns blazing. It always put her on the defensive, which made her do things to drive her sister even crazier. And here was Juliet's eldest daughter, similar to her aunt in so many ways, and obviously developing the same kind of conflict-handling skills. As much as she wanted to rant and yell or make sharp little comments, she forced herself not to.

'Listen,' she said softly. 'I know you're feeling bad about it, and I know it seems easier to pretend that it's no biggie, but sometimes you need to be honest about your mistakes. Sometimes you need to own up and say you're sorry when you mess up. That way everyone can move on peacefully instead of letting all the resentment fester deep inside.'

Violet bowed her head and nodded. 'Sorry, Auntie Gemma. For being rude … and for last night.'

Gemma felt most of her anger whoosh out of her on her next breath. 'That's okay. We'll talk about it more later, but now I think you need to go and get…' she'd been going to say *dressed* but Violet was still in her jeans and T-shirt from the night before '…changed, and then come down and have some breakfast.'

Violet started to pull a face, but Gemma quickly added, 'It'll make you feel better to have something stodgy. Believe me, I know what I'm talking about.'

*

When Juliet woke the sun was slanting through the sheer curtains. She smiled. It was Christmas Day.

That hardly seemed possible. To Juliet, Christmas morning had always been about dark skies, a chilly house, the sense of comfort from wrapping up warm in a fluffy dressing gown and having her kids crowded round her, as they all dragged their home-made stockings onto her bed and shredded the wrapping paper off the tiny gifts she'd anonymously placed there.

She stopped smiling and reached over to the bedside table for her phone. She missed them so much! They'd agreed she wouldn't phone, realising it would probably just make the separation harder on all of them, but this morning she couldn't escape it. She tried to ignore the tight sensation in her chest and blinked a couple of times as she picked up her mobile.

The phone rang a couple of times then Violet picked up. 'Hi, Mum!'

She sounded happy. That was good, right?

'Happy Christmas, darling,' she said softly. 'Are you having a good day?' It must be late morning there already.

Violet chuckled. 'It's been eventful, that's for sure!'

Juliet tried not to panic. 'What does that mean?'

Her daughter sighed. 'Don't get your knickers in a twist, Mum. Everything's fine. We're all up and dressed and Auntie Gemma is cooking the dinner ...' she paused to guffaw and Juliet closed her eyes and prayed.

'Are Polly and the boys there?'

'Sure,' Violet said, and Juliet could hear thumping, like she was running downstairs.

A moment later squabbling could be heard and shouts of *Me first!* and *My turn!* When the commotion abated a bit it was Polly's voice she heard.

'Hello, Mother. How are the tropics? Do you have malaria yet?'

Juliet had to smother a laugh with her hand. Polly would get very upset if she knew she was giggling so hard her stomach was shaking. 'Merry Christmas, sweetie,' she said, hauling in a breath and steadying herself. 'The tropics are wonderful and, no, I haven't got malaria. It's not something you have to worry about in St Lucia.'

'Humph. Well, I've been looking it up so I knew how to take care of you when you came home. Are you *sure* you don't have malaria?' She almost sounded disappointed, but Juliet couldn't be upset. Polly just liked to do stuff for other people, be properly prepared.

'Quite sure,' she said. 'But I may be jet-lagged when I get back. Do you know anything that could help with that?'

'Not yet,' Polly said, but the tone of her voice said she'd perked up considerably. 'Why don't you talk to the boys while I go and check my research folder?'

And then she was gone, and the boys were fighting for the phone, and Violet had to intervene and put it on speaker so they could both talk at once. Juliet thought she heard something in there about presents and even more about chocolate and something funny Auntie Gemma had done. Jake was about to say more, but then Violet shushed them loudly and they just started giggling. She eventually told Violet to take her off speaker and prepared to say her goodbyes. She didn't care if this call had cost her a thousand pounds, it had been worth it.

'Are you sure you're all okay?' she asked Violet. 'Has Auntie Gemma been …? I mean, has everything been…?' She searched for the words to ask (without actually asking) if the house had burnt to the ground, or any of her offspring were missing limbs or whether Aunt Sylvia had to be retrieved from the top of the Christmas tree in the town centre, but came up empty '…okay,' she finished lamely.

Violet just laughed. 'Everything's *fine*, Mum.'

'Good,' she said quietly. 'I'm glad. I love you, Vi, and tell Polly and the boys I love them too.'

'We love you too, Mum. Have a great Christmas Day. I hope it's perfect for you.'

Juliet nodded. She couldn't speak for the tears flowing down her face. She heard a sniff on the other end of the line too, and both she and Violet let out a chuckle in unison. 'Bye, darling ...'

Juliet didn't hang up, Violet did. Juliet just pulled her phone away from her ear and stared at it, listened to the annoying buzz of the dialling tone. Eventually she hit the button, placed the phone back on the bedside table and sighed.

Looking at the bedside table reminded her of what was sitting inside the drawer – Gemma's present. Probably a little trinket from her travels. Gemma was good at finding little things Juliet would like from all around the world and bringing them back to her. Previously, Juliet had always been a little bit irritated by them, thinking they were just guilt presents to make up for the lack of visits, but now she thought about it, she realised how well Gemma always chose. And Juliet knew how much thought and effort went in to selecting the perfect gift. So why had she never realised that Gemma had done that?

Because you didn't want to let yourself realise the situation wasn't black and white ...

Juliet drew in a breath, acknowledging the truth of that thought. She was really tough on Gemma, wasn't she? Always had been. Why? When had sisterly love solidified into something much more ugly? She had a feeling she half knew, but that she wasn't quite prepared to look under that rock deep inside herself, probably because she knew wasn't going to find anything pretty there.

She pulled open the drawer of the bedside table and removed the little package. Even though the gift inside was probably perfect, the wrapping was all Gemma. However, the cheap paper and hastily stuck scraps of Sellotape didn't bother Juliet as they usually did. She carefully peeled off the bits of tape and unfolded the paper to reveal a small square, flat box. It looked as if it might hold a bracelet or a keyring, but when Juliet eased off the lid her mouth dropped open. This was no pretty beaded ethnic jewellery or hand-carved trinket.

Sitting on a nest of cotton wool was her grandmother's engagement ring.

She pressed her palm to her chest and stared at it. Once again, Gemma had chosen perfectly.

&

CHAPTER TWENTY-THREE

Will knocked on the door just after ten. He handed Gemma a roasting tray, covered in cling film. 'Merry Christmas.'

She accepted it from him with a dry laugh. 'No one has ever given me a raw chicken for Christmas before.'

He looked round the kitchen, now resemble the site of a small controlled explosion. 'Do you need help?'

Gemma really wanted to say yes, but she had a feeling this was something she needed to do herself. Not just to prove Juliet wrong about her, or to keep herself out of trouble, but because she wanted to.

'It's okay. I've got a list, detailing exactly what we've got to cook and when it needs to go in the oven.' She turned and smiled weakly. 'Juliet would be proud of me.'

He gave her one of those no-mouth, all-eyes smiles and she felt it right down in her knees. 'Yes, she would.'

She bustled away, ignoring the warmth, bracing her knees and telling herself this was no time to be developing inappropriate crushes on men that really weren't her type at all. And inappropriate it was – he liked Juliet. And she had a sneaking suspicion Juliet liked him back. Nothing could happen.

'I'll see you when you come back at twelve thirty with Mrs Waterman,' she said and gently closed the door.

She turned round and put her hands on her hips. 'Kids!' she yelled.

Silence. They were all too busy messing around with their Christmas presents, which was all well and good, but they had a Christmas lunch to cook. She had a feeling she wasn't the only one in the family who'd got into the habit of taking Juliet for granted, and she could definitely do with the extra pairs of hands today.

She tried again. 'Chocolate!' she yelled up the stairs.

Four eager faces appeared on the landing within seconds. Gemma smiled at them. There would be chocolate, but not just yet. First they were going to have to earn it.

She set the twins the task of clearing up the wrapping paper in the living room and showed Violet how to wind the streaky bacon round the chipolatas. She utilised Polly's maths skills by getting her to work out how long each of the packs of party bites needed in the oven and at what temperature so they'd have a steady stream of canapés once the guests arrived.

By the time noon rolled around, everything was ready to go. Carrots were peeled, potatoes boiled, and the table was laid and ready, even if the twins had a rather haphazard approach to which side the knives and forks went. She was starting to feel they might actually be able to put something edible on the table. And it wasn't just the bread sauce she'd made from scratch, either. She'd done her mother's famous stuffing and was planning on glazing the carrots, something Juliet didn't usually do, but she'd spotted a recipe when she'd been looking for something else and it hadn't seemed that hard.

She was just giving the kids a high-five and their chocolate reward when Uncle Tony and his girlfriend arrived.

He was a tall man in his fifties, with thick brown hair and a wide bright smile. For some reason she could imagine him as a dashing airline pilot when he was younger, even though Juliet had told her he'd run a sewage company. He had the right charm and swagger to be flying jets, and the air of quiet superiority that went with it.

Gemma gave him a hug as he stepped inside, even though she still wasn't sure when, or if, she'd met him before. He wasn't really her uncle, but the widower of her father's sister. However, when his hand slid down her back just a little too far and crested the curve of her buttock, she had a sudden flash of memory.

Oh, he was *that* Uncle Tony. She smiled thinly at him and untangled herself from his grasp. Now she understood why the rest of the family steered clear. She had no idea why Juliet had taken pity on him.

His girlfriend was a strange creature. She was a thin woman with a beakish nose and dyed black hair that was far too severe for both her colouring and her age. From the neck up, she looked like an unhappy vicar's wife – pinched, sombre and slightly disapproving – but from the neck down she dressed like a hooker. The leopard-print dress she wore was unforgiving in its tightness, and the skirt so short, Gemma was sure she was going to have to keep telling the boys off for whispering 'I see London …' to each other and giggling.

'Lovely to meet you, Wanda,' she said. She didn't hug.

For some reason she didn't think Wanda was much of a hugger. Wanda just nodded and followed Tony inside. Gemma took their coats and herded them into the living room, where the kids had been tasked with entertaining them.

She checked the clock. Juliet had planned to serve lunch at one thirty, so there was just over an hour to go. The chickens were cooking nicely now—thanks to Juliet's massive Aga—and the potatoes were about to go in.

She stood up and sighed. She'd worked like a dog for the last twenty-four hours, but she'd finally got there. It wouldn't be the fanciest Christmas dinner she'd ever had, but it wouldn't be the worst either. She hoped Juliet would be proud of her. She was feeling proud of herself.

She called Polly and told her she was in charge of crisps and nuts, a task which her niece immediately rose to, and after setting her off with bowls full of tortilla chips and pretzels, Gemma told her to keep them topped up and to ask Tony and Wanda what they'd both like to drink.

Polly hadn't yet returned when the doorbell rang again. Gemma frowned. Who on earth was that? It was a bit early for Will to be bringing Mrs Waterman, and he was always so punctual. She walked to the front door, wiping her hands on a tea towel and frowning.

She opened the door to find three people standing on the doorstep. Mrs Waterman and two young women she didn't recognise. Will was standing behind them.

'Merry Christmas!' Doris Waterman said loudly and beamed at her. 'This is Birgit, she's from Germany, and this is Trine, from Denmark.'

Gemma's mouth dropped open. 'But I thought I

explained! We had a bit of a disaster, and there's no way I can manage Christmas dinner for so many people.'

'You did explain,' Doris said, still smiling. 'You said *you* couldn't manage; you didn't say anything about us managing together.'

It was then Gemma noticed all three of them were carrying covered dishes and Tupperware containers. She swept past Gemma and headed to the kitchen, Birgit and Trine in her wake. Will stepped inside behind them. 'Sorry,' he said. 'She swore me to secrecy.'

Gemma blinked, then closed the door and ran after them. By the time she reached the kitchen the three women were unloading multiple dishes onto the kitchen table.

'But why ...? How ...?' Gemma stuttered.

Doris just handed her a platter full of sausage rolls and a tub of brandy butter. 'Your sister has done plenty for us, hasn't she, girls?' She looked over her shoulder at Trine and Birgit and they both nodded emphatically.

'She talked to us when we didn't know anyone and were feeling homesick,' Trine said.

'And she asked us over for tea and sometimes Sunday lunch,' Birgit added.

'That girl deserved a holiday, and the least we could do is take care of her family for her while she is away,' Doris added, and handed her a bag of vegetables. 'I have a gentleman friend who likes to garden,' she explained.

Besides that, Doris had brought a honey-glazed ham, and a proper home-made Christmas pudding, which smelled five times better than Gemma's sorry-looking shop-bought one. Birgit had brought *stollen* and Trine contributed braised red cabbage and a rich-looking rice pudding with warm cherry sauce. Traditional Danish fare, she promised.

Even Uncle Tony came up trumps, disappearing off to his car and returning with six bottles of champagne. They cracked a couple open and poured everyone a glass – except the children, who had sparkling apple juice – and then they toasted and wished each other a Merry Christmas.

Gemma looked around the room, and all the happy smiling faces, some of which belonged to people she didn't even know. It had been a mad week, and since Christmas dinner wasn't yet on the table, she was sure more madness was to come, but she had to admit that this moment was far better than spending Christmas on her own, no matter how hot and sunny the location.

She'd missed this, a sense of family, of connection, and the sad thing was she'd been so busy running away from that same family that she hadn't even realised it.

As she sipped champagne, she caught Will's eye. She'd thought of him as Juliet's stand-in while she was away, there to check up on her, judge her, and he'd been a first-hand observer to most of her cock-ups and disasters over the last week, but here he was raising his glass to her. She felt another flush, deep down inside, one that had nothing to do with warm and fuzzy Christmas feelings. It wasn't good news.

She swallowed her mouthful of champagne. 'Okay,' she said, briskly. 'Time to get back to the kitchen.' And she disappeared back there, taking her glass with her.

If she cooked Juliet's Christmas lunch in Juliet's kitchen, laying it all out on Juliet's best dishes, she might be able to lose herself in the busyness and forget about the way Juliet's man was starting to make her feel.

*

Marco found Juliet on the beach, staring out to sea. She turned as she heard him coming up behind her and smiled at him.

He smiled back. '*Buon Natale.*'

'Merry Christmas,' she said softly, and because he was standing there, looking very kissable, she kissed him.

He slid his hands down her sides and around her back, pulling her to him. 'It is a very good Christmas now …' he whispered, then he kissed her again before taking her hand and leading her up the wooden steps to his villa. 'I hope you don't mind, but when I saw you walking on the beach, I ordered some breakfast.'

She smiled and shook her head.

And as they sat and ate from a platter of fresh fruit, dolloped with creamy yogurt and finished off with crumbly melt-in-the-mouth croissants that were as buttery and light as any she'd ever had in a Paris cafe, they talked a little, but mostly they ate in companionable silence. When Juliet looked up after finishing her pastry, she found Marco looking at her.

'What?' she said, brushing non-existent croissant crumbs from her lips.

He shook his head. 'Nothing … Just that you seem different today.'

'I feel different today,' she said, frowning slightly. 'Like this is the real me. Not the person I was trying to be, but the one that was here all along.'

His brow crumpled slightly. 'I'm not sure I understand …'

She shrugged. 'Neither do I.' She laughed, and she kept laughing, because it felt good, because she wanted to.

Marco just shook his head and smiled. 'As I have said before, you are an intriguing woman.'

She poured herself some more guava juice. 'I think that's what we call "eccentric" where I come from.' But she could live with eccentric. It was one step closer to 'free-spirited and impulsive' than 'neurotic and controlling', so she was making progress.

'What do you want to do today?' he asked her.

She looked at him and smiled, very tempted to just say *you*, but she discovered she wasn't quite that brave yet. Besides, did she really need to rush?

She turned to look at the bright blue sky beyond the edge of Marco's terrace. 'I want to get on a boat and just sail,' she told him. 'I want to eat fish caught fresh from the ocean and I *don't* want to see anything resembling a turkey or a roast potato or a stuffing ball.'

Marco, as always, was ready to go with the adventure of the moment. He pushed back from the table and stood up. 'Then let's go.'

And that's what they spent the day doing. Pelican's Reach had boats for hire and Marco's lakeside upbringing meant he knew how to skipper anything with a sail on it. They snorkelled and swam in little coves and bays along the way then dropped anchor off a deserted beach and used the inflatable dinghy to reach the shore. Christmas lunch was eaten under a palm tree: salads and bread they'd picked up from the hotel before they'd left, fresh fish that they roasted themselves on a fire that Marco built.

While they'd been feasting, an old man had appeared, almost out of nowhere, selling every kind of tropical fruit imaginable. He'd reminded Juliet of a Caribbean Father Christmas, with his white beard and his jolly smile, but instead of a red suit he wore shorts and a vest and instead of a snowy sleigh he had a boat painted in yellow and red and green. He sold them a coconut and hacked the top off with a machete, and Juliet and Marco drank the water and scooped out the still soft flesh with a spoon. In comparison, the coconuts in the supermarkets back home seemed dry and wizened. But when she'd looked up to wave goodbye, the man and his boat had gone.

They spent the hottest part of the afternoon in the shaded area at the back of the boat, sipping wine that had been kept cool by tying a rope around the neck of the bottle and slinging it overboard. But as the stillness of the lazy afternoon crept into Juliet's bones, she couldn't stop her thoughts turning towards home, to what her children were doing now and whether they had enjoyed their Christmas Day.

Marco, who was stretched out on the opposite bench, only half awake, propped himself up and looked at her. 'You have that faraway look again. What are you sad about?'

Sometimes he seemed younger than his years, but sometimes he was scarily perceptive. 'I feel a little bit guilty for sitting here doing nothing, while everyone back home is working hard to make Christmas Day special, like I've run away and left them all to it.'

He frowned and smiled at the same time. 'Is Christmas usually hard work for you?'

She nodded. 'My ex-husband used to say I always made such a fuss about it, and I suppose I do, but it's only because I want it to be perfect for—' She shook her head.

Marco sat up, looking intrigued. 'For …?'

She looked at the canopy above their heads. She'd been going to say 'for my children'. But she couldn't tell Marco that. She was supposed to be Gemma, wasn't she? No ties. No roots. Certainly no children.

'Myself,' she finally mumbled. 'I always make it so difficult for myself. I stress about all these stupid tiny details, and now I'm here I'm starting to wonder if it's really all so important.'

Really, was there anything in her poinsettia notebook that was truly essential to a happy Christmas, rather than just loving her kids and spending quality time with them? To her shame, she didn't even think that featured on her colour-coded tick list.

Marco sat up and leaned forward, looking at her intently. 'Why does Christmas have to be perfect, Juliet? Why cannot it just be what it will be? It is a day like any other.'

Her lie about who she was meant she couldn't tell Marco the truth: that she didn't want her children feeling that horrible sense of dread every time December came around, fearing that this year might be the year when it all went horribly wrong, when nothing would ever feel the same afterwards.

The sensation she'd successfully outrun for years now crept up on her. She felt the chill of it blocking out the sunshine, making her skin pucker into gooseflesh. She didn't want to talk about this. No one in her family ever talked about this. And she'd got so good at *not* talking about it that she'd almost forgotten it in recent years. Her web of tasks and To Do lists had effectively had it trapped and camouflaged.

Once again Marco looked into her and saw her. Once again he asked her what she was afraid of, but this time the question was far more dangerous than when she'd been suspended fifty feet above the jungle strapped to a thin little wire.

Nothing, she was going to say, but then a stab of pain caught her by surprise under her ribs, so hard she sucked in some air and held it. She shook her head, but her mouth wouldn't open and his face, so close to her own, grew blurry.

She didn't want to talk about *that* Christmas. She didn't want to go back. She'd spent her whole life trying to escape it, glad that each passing year pushed it further into the past.

'Tell me …'

She began to shake her head again, but the sun was so bright, the waves so gentle, the setting so tranquil, that she started to wonder if ever there was a safe place to mention that horrible Christmas, maybe this was it.

She stared at the gently waving palm trees lining the shore. 'It was the Christmas I was nine …We got up in the morning and everything was fine, but later in the day I walked into the kitchen and my mother was crying.'

Marco came and sat next to her. 'Did something terrible happen?'

Juliet let out a dry laugh. 'No, that was the funny thing, really … She'd forgotten to put the sausagemeat in the stuffing, and she was trying to scoop it all out of the tin, half-cooked, and mix the sausagemeat in and it just wasn't working, and the more it all fell apart the more upset she got. Dad tried to tell her it was okay, but she just kept mixing and crying, and then she just sort of … exploded. She threw it all down and ran out the house.'

Juliet didn't tell him what had been the final straw; she was too ashamed. She didn't tell him that it was her who had set the fuse on that explosion. If she hadn't pulled a face and said she'd decided she didn't really want stuffing with her turkey, maybe her mother would have seen the funny side and they'd have all sat down for Christmas dinner as normal. But she had said what she'd said, and her mother had run from the house, still in her apron, and had jumped in the car and just driven away.

'She didn't come back until the day after Boxing Day,' Juliet said quietly. 'I was so relieved when I came downstairs and saw her standing in the hallway, hugging my father.'

Her father had been frantic until she'd reappeared, although he'd never shown it. Put on a brave face, had always been his motto. *Don't tell Gemma,* he'd instructed her. *She's too young. She won't understand.* And so she'd played with Gemma and watched films on the TV and had pretended with Dad that Mum had just had to go and visit someone who needed her. Gemma had looked up at them both with those big blue eyes, so trusting, and had believed every word they'd said. Every lie they'd told. Juliet didn't even know if Gemma remembered anything being wrong that Christmas, if it even figured in her memories. But then that had been the plan, hadn't it?

All of Christmas Day and Boxing Day, as she'd smiled and laughed and pretended everything was fine, deep in the pit of her stomach she'd lived with the fear that she'd spoiled Christmas, and because she'd spoiled Christmas – the most special day of all – nothing would ever be right again.

Dad had told her she'd been very brave, his big girl, and that she was being grown-up about it and protecting her sister. And she must have done a really good job of making him think she was coping with it all, because never once had her father sought to reassure her that her mother was coming back.

She supposed to him it had been obvious, but Juliet had been so relieved when she'd seen her mother again, that she'd run to her, sobbing, and thrown herself at her. Her mother had hugged her back, but after a few moments she'd peeled her eldest daughter off her and had set her back on her feet. 'Come, come, Juliet,' she'd said firmly, 'Don't make a fuss.' And Juliet had seen the look of fear and shame in her mother's eyes. She didn't want to be reminded of what she'd done. As Juliet pulled that memory of that expression into sharp focus, she realised that maybe her mother had resented her for knowing the truth.

'Years later we found out she'd had episodes of depression for years,' she said. 'It was just her way of coping when things got too much – she'd run away – and then come back and act as if nothing had happened.' She'd even done it once after Juliet's father had died, and a nineteen-year-old Juliet had spent the whole night trawling round where they used to live in Beckenham in her beaten-up first car, trying to spot her mother's purple coat. She hadn't told Gemma about that, either.

Her mother must have gone to the doctor when Christmas had been over, got some pills or something, because for a long time after that everything had been better. It was as if 'that Christmas' had just been a horrible dream that no one dared mention.

'I suppose it isn't just this Christmas that I've run away,' she told Marco. 'I think I've been running away from Christmas my whole life.'

He didn't look shocked or horrified; instead he smiled at her then kissed her gently. 'Then we are two Christmas runaways together,' he whispered.

She laughed and kissed him back, turning towards him and winding her arms round his neck. 'Today I'm happy about that. But we can't run away for ever. One day soon we will both have to go home.'

When they pulled apart Marco wasn't looking as carefree as he had been only seconds earlier.

'We've both got things to face up to,' she said, looking into those beautiful brown eyes. 'I need to learn to keep "letting go", and you need to go and make peace with your family. You need to go home and let them see the wonderful man you've grown into, remind them that you're not the naughty little boy they all remember.'

He stood up and left her sitting on the seat, walked over to the far bench and stared out over the sea.

'I'm sorry,' she said, and rose to go and lay a hand on his arm. 'I didn't mean to stick my nose in.'

He didn't turn, just kept staring at the shifting blue water beyond the boat, and she saw the muscles in the corner of his jaw tighten. 'You are too generous to me, Juliet. Maybe I deserve my family's judgement.'

That was a strange thing to say. She walked over to him, smoothed her palm across his face, made him look at her. 'I don't believe that, and neither should you.'

He'd been avoiding direct eye contact for a while, but now he stared right back at her, his warm brown eyes only inches from her own.

She smiled at him. 'So I think we should make a vow …'

His eyebrows rose. 'A vow?'

She nodded, still smiling. 'Yes, a solemn Christmas vow.'

He caught the joke and the corners of his mouth lifted. 'Which is …?'

'I will promise not to make Christmas too special next year, if you promise to go and spend it with your family.'

'Can you make Christmas too special?'

'Yes, I think you can,' she said honestly.

He smiled properly then. 'So … why don't you stop trying and let *me* make Christmas special for *you* this year?' he whispered into her ear.

That could definitely work for Juliet, especially when she thought about all the things Marco had already given her, little gifts that she'd hardly noticed at the time, but was now starting to realise the value of. He told her she was beautiful and surprising and unusual, and when she was with him she believed those things herself.

She twisted to kiss him properly, deeply. 'I think you already have,' she whispered back, as she wound her arms around his neck.

&

CHAPTER TWENTY-FOUR

The eclectic assembly of family and friends were in Juliet's dining room. Even though the table extended, it had been a bit of a squeeze for twelve, and they'd run out of chairs, but the twins were happy on garden chairs and Polly said the tapestry-covered piano stool looked like a throne, and was happy to perch regally on top of it. Nobody seemed to mind that they were all elbow to elbow with each other as they gazed with saliva-filled mouths at the array of different dishes before them.

Not quite the spread the Juliet would have put on, but Gemma was sure that none of them would ever forget it. Even Aunt Sylvia, who'd been slightly confused as to where she was when the minibus from Greenacres had dropped her off, was now smiling with a red tissue paper hat perched jauntily on her head.

'Dig in!' Gemma said, as she disappeared back into the kitchen to get one last dish. From the sounds of clinking cutlery and crockery as she left the room, no one was standing on ceremony. She liked that.

When she returned, she placed a small serving dish near Will's plate.

He stopped helping himself to roast potatoes and looked

up at her. She nodded and nudged the dish a little closer, even though the sight of the small round, green vegetables made her want to gag.

'But I thought you said you couldn't get any Brussels sprouts, not for love nor money,' he said with a teasing twinkle in his eyes.

'I was wrong about the *love* bit. It seems Doris has an admirer with an allotment.'

'And you cooked them. For me?'

She shrugged carelessly. 'It's only a little dish. Like I said, everybody else hates them. Even Doris.' She turned and headed for the other end of the table, but she could feel him smiling at her all the way back to her seat.

There was lots of noise and laughter, a few minor squabbles, and plenty of toasting and well-wishing as they got through their unconventional Christmas lunch. Halfway through, Gemma put a knife and fork down and sat back and smiled. It had been a wonderful day so far. Jake and Josh thought Uncle Tony was the funniest thing they'd ever seen. They laughed like drains at his stupid jokes and loved it when he pretended to pinch their noses and run away with them. Even Wanda couldn't help smiling watching the fun.

Doris and Polly had been thick as thieves, talking about history and books and science experiments. It turned out that the old lady had once been a primary school teacher, and Polly was using the opportunity to soak up as much knowledge as she could. And Doris was very good at letting her do it, while still giving Polly the opportunity to shine and show what a clever girl she was.

Violet, meanwhile, had perked up a little and had been

chatting to Birgit and Trine about fashion and make up and who should really have won *X-Factor* that year.

And then there was Will.

Will, who always seemed to be looking in her direction when she glanced his way. Will, who she really shouldn't have been aware of every second of the afternoon, even when she'd been trying to ignore him, trying to pretend the buzz in her veins was solely down to the champagne.

They finally waddled away from the table an hour or so later, and the adults flopped onto sofas and armchairs, while the younger kids disappeared to play with their new toys. Gemma positioned herself next to her aunt. 'Did you enjoy the dinner, Auntie Syl?'

Sylvia nodded, and then she looked around the room. 'Where's Juliet?'

Gemma started. That was the first time she'd heard her aunt utter her sister's name since last Easter. She squashed down her surprise and replied, 'She's having a bit of a holiday.' She decided not to elaborate more, thinking that Auntie Sylvia would only get confused.

Sylvia nodded. 'In Broadstairs? I really like Broadstairs.'

Gemma shook her head. 'No, not Broadstairs. She's gone to St Lucia.'

Her aunt sniffed. 'I bet they don't have that lovely pink and white rock in St Lucia.'

Gemma couldn't help smiling. 'No, I don't suppose they do.'

The boys ran into the room at that moment, apparently in some kind of epic do-or-die battle between the toy robots that Juliet had got them for Christmas. They charged around making laser-gun noises and then raced out of the room again. Aunt Sylvia didn't seem to mind. In fact, she smiled fondly after them.

'I do like boys with a bit of spirit,' she said. 'Your boys are fine young men. In fact, all your children are lovely.'

Gemma shook her head and corrected her aunt with a tinge of sadness in her voice. 'They're not my children.'

'Don't be silly!' Sylvia said, sitting up straighter. 'Of course they are!' And she frowned quite fiercely at Gemma for a few moments before her focus softened and she stared off into the distance. When she came back into the present from wherever she'd been, she leaned over and patted Gemma's hand. 'You're a good girl, so full of love.'

Gemma swallowed. Her aunt might have got the name right, but it wasn't her she was talking about. People didn't describe her as full of love. Full of fun, maybe. Full of life. Occasionally someone had told her she was full of crap. And usually that someone had been Will Truman. But she reckoned she'd forgiven him for that now.

'You just make sure you don't get things out of balance and forget to look after yourself, too,' Sylvia said, nodding to herself. 'Love is like Christmas, Juliet … You have to learn to receive as well as give.'

Gemma leaned forward and kissed her aunt and her papery cheek. 'Wise words, Auntie Syl. Wise words.'

And she sat back in her armchair and pondered them.

Juliet did give too much sometimes. And Gemma had only been too happy to take what her sister had offered, never once stopping to wonder if the scales were always tipped in her favour, if the equation was out of balance.

She'd wondered again and again as she'd gone through Juliet's notebook why her sister went to such lengths to make Christmas – to make life – perfect. And now she thought she might have her answer.

She and her sister were both capable of ingenuity and organisation, of generosity and creativity, but she did it so she could take her pay cheque home at the end of the month. But Juliet? Juliet did it for the people she loved.

*

Gemma looked at the assorted bodies lolling around Juliet's living room as the credits on a Harry Potter film rolled. The post-lunch crash had come to an end and now they were beginning to stir. Gemma was instantly on her feet.

'I promised Juliet I would try to do all the things in her Christmas notebook,' she explained to the half-dozing crowd. 'And it is very clear, here on page thirteen …' She picked up the book from a small table beside her and flicked it open '…that the after-dinner entertainment should involve games, specifically charades.'

There was an apathetic groan from those who were still awake, and a small, snuffling noise from Uncle Tony.

'No, no … Don't be like that! It'll be fun. Juliet's done all the cards with the films and TV shows and book titles on already. Falling asleep in front of the film wasn't exactly on Juliet's timetable, and some of us have had a nice long snooze …' She paused to look pointedly at the major culprits. 'So what do you say?'

Doris, who was sitting down the other end of the sofa from Uncle Tony and Wanda sat up straighter. 'I think a nice game of charades would be lovely.'

Gemma grinned back at her and removed a stack of neatly written index cards from inside her notebook. The adults seemed less than enthused, and the twins, who'd been draped over big cushions on the floor while the film had been rolling, just stuck their legs in the air and refused to move, but Gemma started working on them one by one, talking them into it, jollying them along, and soon they had two teams organised who were not only tolerating the activity but starting to look forward to it.

She split them into teams of two and three to act out titles and phrases for the others to guess. When squabbles arose, she adjudicated them. When the kids struggled, she whispered in their ears to give them ideas. And when Uncle Tony got a little too 'hands-on' with some of his acting, she deftly slipped out of reach, smiling through gritted teeth. The grope-factor had definitely increased with the amount of alcohol consumed.

They broke for refreshments halfway through the pack of index cards. She refilled the kids' glasses with lemonade, popping colourful curly straws in that she'd bought for their Christmas stockings, and looked up to find Will standing nearby.

'Are you okay with him?' he asked, nodding towards Tony, who'd sprawled back on the sofa with Wanda and was trying to worm his way back into her affections. 'I can have a word, if you'd like – man to man.'

Gemma put the glass she'd been filling down and looked

at him. 'Nah … I can handle the likes of him … hardly notice I'm doing it. In my line of work it's a bit of an occupational hazard.'

'I can believe that,' he said, looking straight at her. 'After the last few days, I'd believe you could handle anything.'

She let out a dry laugh. 'Have you had too much of the Christmas sherry? The last few days have been an unmitigated disaster!'

He did that crinkly warm thing with his eyes again. 'No, they haven't. There have been plenty of hiccups, yes, but you've dealt with every single one, and today you've done everything with a smile on your face and an encouraging word for everyone. You even put up with that old lech –' he nodded in the direction of the sofa '– without smacking him round the chops.'

Gemma bit down on her lip to stop herself smiling. 'I really *would* like to smack him round the chops,' she admitted, and Will's mouth curved into the smile his eyes had been promising. 'But he's Juliet's guest really, and after today I am making a point of never seeing him ever again.'

'I don't blame you. But what I was trying to say before we got sidetracked into talking about over-friendly uncles was that today has been amazing and that was down to you.' He stopped smiling and looked rather more serious. '*You* have been amazing.'

Gemma's heart did a double kick then settled down into an uneven rhythm. She felt her cheeks get warmer. 'Thank you,' she said quietly. And then, because she didn't really know what else to say, she just stared back at him.

Oh, hell. This was really not a good idea.

Not only was this Juliet's guy – well, not really Juliet's actual guy, but at the very least someone she'd bookmarked for later – but he didn't want a girl like her.

Thankfully, the driver of the Greenacres minibus rang the doorbell at that moment, saving her from doing anything stupid.

She very gently woke her aunt and explained it was time to go, then helped Sylvia into her coat and walked her to the front door. Sylvia kissed her cheek then patted it with a bony hand. 'Don't you forget what I said,' she said, with a twinkle in her eye.

'I won't, Auntie Syl.'

'Give and take, Gemma. Give and take.'

As she waved off her aunt, Tony also appeared in the hallway with Wanda in tow. 'We'd better make a move too,' he said. 'Long drive and all that.'

Wanda threw her arms around Gemma and squeezed hard, making Gemma's eyes widen. Will was standing in the doorway watching the proceedings and they shared a conspiratorial smile as she looked at him over Wanda's shoulder.

'It was lovely to be part of such a happy family Christmas,' Wanda said. That must have been the longest sentence she'd come out with all day, and no one would have guessed the truth of her words from her poker-straight expression.

Gemma pulled back and smiled at her. 'Yes, it has, hasn't it?' And then she hugged Wanda again, this time squeezing back.

Tony patted Wanda's bum. 'Why don't you go in get

settled in the car, honey? You can pick a CD to listen to, if you like. I'll say my goodbyes and be along in a second.'

Birgit and Trine also came to take their leave, thanking her profusely and offering to babysit for the kids if she needed them in the next week. Gemma was so busy hugging them goodbye, and agreeing that she'd visit either them or their families if her job ever took her to Denmark or Germany, that she wasn't paying any attention to Tony, who was waiting patiently for his turn.

She waved off the au pairs then turned round, ready to give him a goodbye hug, and more than ready to shove him out the door and shut it behind him, but instead of moving towards her, he just held his arms out wide and waited for her. It was only as she was walking into his embrace that she saw his eyes dart upwards and realised what he was up to.

She'd totally forgotten about the bunch of mistletoe Juliet had hung from the hall light fitting. Darn. It was going to be so much harder to slip out of this gracefully now they were actually hugging than if she'd anticipated his little manoeuvre and just steered clear. She really didn't want to punch a relation on Christmas Day, not if she could help it.

'Oh, look,' Tony said innocently, as he and Gemma pulled back from the hug.

But before he could form an observation about the bit of Christmas greenery they above their heads, Will cut in between them, sliding an arm possessively around her waist. 'Wanda's waiting for you,' he said to Tony, his tone friendly, his eyes not, and he drew Gemma a little closer. 'Besides, I think it's my turn.'

Tony frowned and started to say something, but Will just

smiled and waved goodbye. In the end, the older man mumbled his farewells and sloped off to join his girlfriend in the car.

They watched him leave together, Mrs Waterman and the children looking on from the living-room door, and all the while Gemma could feel the heat from Will's arm burning through the back of her blouse. She tried to ignore it.

She knew what had happened. Will's damsel-in-distress radar had kicked in again, and for once she'd been grateful for it. 'Thanks,' she said a little shakily. 'He almost caught me out that time.'

'No problem,' Will said, looking back down at her.

But he didn't let go, and she didn't move either.

It would look odd if they broke apart now, wouldn't it? They'd better follow through, even if it really was only for show.

It seemed the same idea had flashed across Will's mind, because instead of stepping away and releasing her, he bent forward and pressed a soft but firm kiss to her lips.

Gemma should have left it there, really. She should have let it be a quick, brief peck and then they could have returned to business as normal. She really shouldn't have leaned in and softened against him the way she had. And when he lingered just that little bit, she probably shouldn't have sighed at the back of her throat, either, but she just couldn't help herself.

Thankfully, Will had the control she lacked, because after a second or so he pulled away abruptly, muttered something under his breath and then strode off in the direction of the kitchen. She turned to find her audience still watching her.

Mrs Waterman gave her a little tilt of her head and Violet was beaming. Josh and Jake were pulling identical faces. 'Yuck,' Jake said.

'Yuck, yourself,' Gemma replied, pushing past them. 'Now, who wants another round of charades?'

&

CHAPTER TWENTY-FIVE

The most exclusive restaurant at Pelican's Reach sat on top of a steep hill, looking down over the whole resort. The large terrace jutted out over the incline and Juliet felt as if she was floating, suspended high above Pelican Bay with nothing to tether her to land or sky. Looking up from down below, the hill didn't seem that high, but from up here the beach was a tiny pale crescent against the blue of the sea and the velvet sky. The surf whispered in the distance, mostly drowned out by the chirruping of various night insects and the classical music that wove its way through the tables and out into the night air.

She felt as if she were in a wonderful dream. Marco had chosen *her*.

Oh, not for love and promises and happy-ever-after, she wasn't that foolish. Or she wasn't prepared to let herself be that foolish, not after only a few days. But being the sole focus of someone's attention, the one who shone, rather than the person in the shadows, was rather seductive. To be honest, she was a little drunk on the idea.

Or maybe that was the cocktails …

She was more than halfway through her holiday and it had been about time she tried out some of those strange names on the bar menu, rather than going for the same varieties of wine she always had back home. The one she had in her glass now was a house speciality. It was aptly named a Pelican Bite and was made of light rum, lime juice, melon liqueur and a few other things she had memorised, but now couldn't quite remember.

She crinkled her nose to help her think what … Had it been triple sec or vodka? For some reason the list of ingredients was starting to get a bit fuzzy.

She ate scallops and mahi-mahi with chillies and papaya and rice so light she was surprised it didn't float away, but her mind wasn't on the food, which was criminal, really. All she could think about was Marco – how his fingers felt against hers as he reached to touch her hand across the table-cloth, how those sculpted lips moved as he ate, how they'd curve knowingly when he found her studying them. How she knew she'd be tasting them again before the night was over.

The thought made her feel shaky and fluttery all at once. Maybe that was why she'd reached the bottom of her latest cocktail without noticing it.

'Are you ready to go?' he asked, nodding to her half-eaten coconut and lime ice cream, which was now not much more than a lumpy puddle on her plate.

'Yes,' she said, after hauling in a deep breath. 'I'm ready.'

Oh, but she so *wasn't* ready. Not for what was coming next, even though she desperately wanted to be. She wanted to be the woman she'd pretended to be with Marcus. She wanted to be impulsive and wild and passionate. But she was scared that even if she did get up the courage to take him to her bed, once they'd got there, the fog of this other, better self would evaporate, and he'd be left with boring, 'good old Juliet' in bed.

But as they left the restaurant, walked down the tiled steps and waited for a shuttle to appear to take them back to their villas, Marco pulled her to him and kissed her. Juliet's head swam and her skin tingled. She forgot to second-guess herself and just kissed him back, losing herself so much in the moment that the polite beep of the shuttle's horn when it arrived made her jump. He pulled away from her smiling and she breathed out.

Okay. So maybe she could do this after all. Maybe the chemistry had fizzled out between her and Greg at the end, but it certainly seemed to be sizzling hot between her and Marco. His kisses were perfect. Almost too perfect, as if he knew just when the most romantic moments were and took advantage of every single one, but she could hardly hold that against him, could she?

She spent the buggy ride back to their exclusive little cove tucked under his arm in the back of the shuttle. Every now and then he would press his lips to her hair or run his fingers up her bare arm, and a slow fire lit somewhere deep inside, one that he stoked with each touch, each movement.

So when the driver dropped them off outside her villa, she swallowed any remaining fear and turned to Marco. 'Would you … would you like to come in for …' her words froze in her throat. God, she was such a chicken. Or a prude. Maybe both. '… for a dip in the plunge pool?'

He leaned down and kissed her. Not fiercely. Not hungrily. But slowly, deeply, the sweet control promising more than raw passion could have done. 'Yes, *Giulietta* ... I would like that very much.'

Her fingers shook as she pulled the key card from her little handbag. Thank goodness it was one of those locks with a touchpad. If she'd had to swipe it, they might have been standing there all night.

'One moment and I will be back,' he said, then looked down at her grandmother's ring on her finger. 'Perhaps you should remove that. The chemicals in the water may not be kind to it.' And he disappeared out the door in the direction of his own villa.

'I'll see you in the pool,' she called after him, smiling. That was why she liked this man. He was thoughtful and kind. He gave. Just the confidence he'd given her had made her believe that maybe she didn't have to resign herself to either a life alone or finding Greg mark two and settling down to a life of mediocrity. Maybe she could meet the love of *her* life. Why not? She sighed. Such a pity it couldn't be Marco.

She also understood that whatever was going on between them would only stretch for the lifespan of this holiday. She'd never been one for flings. She liked the partnership, the give and take of a relationship, and one-night stands seemed so ... selfish. Just taking what you wanted instead of having the courage to give and be given to.

She'd had a few boyfriends before she met Greg, but she hadn't really been with anyone seriously before him. She'd met him when she was nineteen. He'd smiled at her at a friend's birthday party, then he'd come over to talk. He'd been confident and fairly nice-looking. Not too much of a jerk. And he'd been ambitious. She'd bought into it whole-heartedly. They'd plotted together to become one of those couples with not just a nice house, but a lovely one, with good jobs and adorable kids – the kind of life everyone else envied.

And she'd done her bit. Given everything she had to make it come true. What a shock it had been when she'd discovered it hadn't been enough after all, that Greg had decided he wanted more, and she wasn't the one capable of giving it to him.

How could she have done? She'd emptied herself for him. How on earth had he expected her to have anything left?

For the first time she realised that maybe she shouldn't have done that. Not because giving yourself totally to one person was wrong, but because Greg hadn't done the same, not towards the end. That kind of one-sided relationship wasn't very healthy, and by continuing in it, she'd enabled him to become more and more selfish until he'd taken all she had and walked away with it.

So maybe it was time for her to be totally selfish, to reach for what she desired and to hell with the consequences.

She'd always tucked her own desires away, like they were guilty secrets she shouldn't admit to, but now she catalogued all those things she'd neatly folded and stored away in her subconscious. There was nothing so scary or horrible. Nothing dirty or shameful about what she saw. Just dreams. Hopes. Wishes …

And she knew what she wanted to wish for now. If she was going to wish for one thing this Christmas, it was going to be Marco.

She took a long glance at the undisturbed bed as she slid her grandmother's ring off her finger and placed it on the bedside table. Then she took her time getting ready, slowly peeling off her sundress and putting on Gemma's red bikini – no, *her* red bikini – then she spritzed some of her perfume on and twisted her hair up into a loose bun. Then she walked back down to the terrace to meet Marco. No T-shirt this time.

He was already waiting in the plunge pool when she emerged from the doors. He didn't take his eyes off her as she walked towards him, an appreciative gleam in his eye, and she discovered she liked watching him watching her. Something bold and unafraid unfurled inside her as she walked down the steps into the cool water and dipped herself under. There was a seat running round half of the small pool and she rested her bottom on the opposite end of the ledge to Marco so she could look at him. She wanted to drink in the sight of him in.

He handed her a slim glass. That was when she noticed the champagne bucket sitting beside him. 'Where did that appear from?'

He gave her that sexy little half-shrug accompanied by an even sexier half-smile. 'What is Christmas without champagne?'

She took the flute from him and sipped the boisterously bubbling liquid, only just poured, by the looks of it. It was perfect. Crisp and dry and heady. But after only a sip she placed it down on the edge of the pool and looked at Marco. The moment she'd been waiting for was here, and she was going to tick this box good and proper.

He was looking very relaxed, leaning back against the opposite edge of the pool, arms stretched wide along the edge. His eyes widened a fraction as she stood and waded the few steps towards him, as if he hadn't quite been expecting her to do that. His mouth parted in a delighted smile as she took the glass out of his hands, stole a sip, then placed it on the tiles behind his head. But surprise warmed into something else as she placed a knee on either side of him and lowered herself onto his lap.

She ran her hands up his chest, from under the water until they broke the surface, and then she slid them up his glistening shoulders, round his neck and pulled him closer.

This felt right. She wasn't scared any more, of not being sexy enough or not being young or pretty enough, of the reality not living up to the fantasy, and she teased his lips with her own, exploring, tasting, doing whatever she felt like doing, and the heat inside her began to swell.

Marco seemed to know she needed this, to take control, to set the pace, and even though he kissed her back, softly, firmly, he left his arms splayed on the rim of the pool. She kissed him more deeply, losing her sense of time and place, only aware of the growing need inside her and relishing the slow winding journey she was taking to its completion. She felt the gradual build of tension in the muscles of his torso, she sensed when keeping his hands off her became an effort rather than a teasing game.

'Yes,' she whispered into his ear, knowing what he wanted and knowing that he would understand what she meant.

Marco's arms were around her in a second, hauling her to him and, his hands roving the bare skin of her back. Juliet broke the kiss, gasping for air, before diving back in, getting lost again. This was a new Marco too, she realised. Even though his kisses had often been passionate before, there had always been a sense of control in them, a sense that he was making tiny decisions, of what she needed next, of how to coax a response from her, almost as if he was a master choreographer, improvising a dance of limbs and hands and lips.

But this was different. She knew the exact second his control snapped. When he broke away, panting, his hair was messy from where she'd been running her hands through it and the water from them dripped down through his hair to his forehead and rolled down over his cheekbones. He looked half-drugged, just as swept up in the moment as she was, and she liked that. She liked that she could do that to him. She'd come into this fling – or whatever it was – feeling grateful that a man like him should even look at her, but not any more. She met him eye to eye as an equal.

'Are you sure you want this?' he asked her breathlessly, and the slight frown of concern on his forehead only made her decision more solid.

'Yes. I want this. I want *you*.'

In one smooth movement, Marco wrapped his arms tightly around her then lifted her from the water. She made a little noise of surprise as he carried her out of the pool, across the terrace and through the living room of her villa, leaving tiny puddles in his wake with each footstep, and then he climbed the stairs to the bedroom, where he gently lowered her onto the bed.

The old Juliet would have shrieked about getting the bedclothes wet, but this Juliet didn't care. She wanted it wild and messy and untidy. She wanted to be right in the middle of this cyclone they were creating around them.

She didn't let him move away, but pulled him down on top of her. '*Mio Dio, Giulietta* ...' he rumbled against her neck as he started to kiss her there. She inhaled sharply as he reached the bit just under her ear and twisted her head away to give him better access.

Mio Dio was about right.

But just as her eyes were closing she got a close-up view of her bedside table: the lamp, the alarm clock, earplugs, her sleep mask ...

Juliet's eyes snapped open again and she froze.

'My ring!' she said, pushing herself up on one arm, totally forgetting the hot Italian who had his teeth on her earlobe. 'Where's my ring?'

*

'Right, time to get into your PJs!' Gemma said loudly.

All three younger children started to whine.

'I didn't say you had to go to bed yet,' she told them, shooing them up the stairs. 'But it's eight o'clock and you at least ought to be ready for bed if I'm going to let you stay up and watch another movie.'

Groaning turned to cheering and Jake, Josh and Polly rushed up the stairs. Gemma let out a loud sigh once they'd gone. She went and put an arm round Vi, who was standing in the living-room doorway. 'How are you feeling this evening?'

Violet made a face. 'Stupid,' she said and looked at the floor.

Gemma squeezed her gently. 'I meant physically, but knowing you were daft is good too. You'll learn from this mistake.'

Violet looked up at her from under her fringe. 'You think so? I seem to do stupid stuff all the time and it never makes me any better.'

Gemma nodded, but all the while she was thinking, *Join the club*. What had she been doing letting Will kiss her like that?

She'd known when Tony had glanced upwards where things had been heading. She'd also known that Will's honourable genes hadn't let him stand by when a damsel needed rescuing, even if that damsel was her, but that didn't mean she'd had to lean in quite so eagerly, did it? She'd made a total fool of herself.

She kissed Violet on her head then wandered back into the living room to see what Doris was up to. Gemma found her sitting in an armchair, leafing through Juliet's notebook.

'He's quite a man, that one, isn't he?' she said, looking up.

Gemma rolled her eyes. 'He's a total plonker, that's what he is,' she replied. 'I don't even know how he managed to wangle an invite from Juliet – probably because the rest of the family is sick of "Uncle" Tony and he hasn't got anywhere else to go.'

Doris gave her a knowing look. 'I didn't mean him,' she said, watching Gemma's reaction very carefully. 'I meant the other one.'

'Oh.' Just thinking about what had just gone on under that

blasted mistletoe had Gemma's cheeks heating, even though it had been so tame it was hardly worth counting. 'Well, I suppose he's okay,' she said, looking down and suddenly reminding herself of Violet. 'Not really my type, though.'

Doris just threw back her head and let out a dry laugh. 'Who is, sweetheart? I was married to Mr Waterman for over forty years. Fool of a man! Always up to mischief. Everybody said it wouldn't last, that we were too different, but that man adored me until the day he died.' Her tone grew heavier as she finished her sentence and she glanced away before looking Gemma in the eye. 'What I'm saying is that you can't run from it for ever, pretending you'll always have another chance. Life doesn't always work that way. Sometimes you've got to be brave and grab it while it's there in front of you.'

Gemma didn't know what to say to that. No one had ever implied she wasn't brave before. Everyone saw her as madcap, impulsive, ready for anything. Except when it came to relationships, she realised. In that respect, she was just as emotionally constipated as Juliet.

'Talking of Will … he said he'd walk you back over the road.' She looked around and frowned. 'Where is he?' She hadn't seen him since the incident in the hall. In fact, she'd been deliberately *not* looking for him.

Doris shrugged. 'Don't know. But when you find him, tell him I'm ready to go when he is.'

When you find him. That meant she was going to have to go looking. And Gemma wasn't sure she was even ready for that, let alone being brave enough to grab onto love and not let go.

&

CHAPTER TWENTY-SIX

Juliet jumped off the bed and began hunting on the floor around the bedside table. 'It's got to be here somewhere! It can't have just vanished!'

Marco pushed himself up from the mattress and came to join her, watching her try the drawer and slam it closed again. 'Are you sure you left it there?'

She nodded. 'I only took it off after you'd suggested it at the door, maybe only twenty minutes ago. And I was in the room the whole time until I came down to meet you in the pool – apart from the short while I was in the bathroom.'

It wasn't hard to search the surrounding area. The furniture in the room was beautiful, but it wasn't plentiful, and the tiled floor made it easy to spot anything that might have dropped onto it or under the high mattress of the bed. After a thorough ten-minute search, they both sat back on the bed, breathing heavily.

Juliet looked across at Marco. This was so *not* how she'd imagined getting breathless this evening.

'Maybe you put it in the safe?' he said.

She shook her head. 'No … I'm sure I left it there.'

'You didn't move it afterwards? Why don't you check, just in case?'

Okay, she had been in a bit of a dreamy fuzz, and she'd had two Pelican Bites, but had she really forgotten moving it? She sighed. There was only one way to find out for sure.

She jumped up and snagged a filmy kaftan to throw over her bikini. Now the heat of the moment had been well and truly drenched, she was feeling a little exposed. Marco followed her downstairs and stood behind her, looking over her shoulder, as she crouched down and opened the door to the sideboard where the safe was housed. She punched the number in quickly – Violet's birthday – and the heavy metal door sprang open. The inside was covered in dark, fuzzy material, so those diamonds should have sparkled at her the instant the light hit them, but there was nothing. She reached inside and patted around anyway, shoving her passport and the great wad of cash aside. She hadn't needed all that money in the end, anyway, seeing as Pelican's Reach was all-inclusive, but Gemma had neglected to tell her that.

'No … nothing.'

She closed the safe and stood up. Marco came in close behind and wrapped his arms around her, pressing his cheek against hers. 'What do you want to do?'

She felt every muscle in her body sag. Of course she couldn't have the perfect night with the perfect man! What had she been thinking? She just wasn't that lucky.

'The only thing I can do,' she said sadly. 'I'm going to have to call hotel security. Someone must have come in while we were in the pool. My ring has been stolen.'

*

Gemma wandered through the ground floor looking for Will. It was very quiet now most of their guests had gone. Polly and the boys had reappeared in the nightclothes, but their early morning must have been catching up on them, because they'd now finished running round their house like maniacs and were happy to curl up on chairs and sofas in the living room, accompanied by assorted soft toys, and watch a film.

She looked in the kitchen, but all was still, no noise except the swoosh of the dishwasher. She turned to go, but a gust of cold air hit her, and she twisted to see where it had come from. The lights were on low in the conservatory, and no one was in there as far as she could see, but one of the doors at the far end was open.

She walked through the conservatory and peeked outside. 'Will?' she called softly, not quite daring to shout.

There was a noise to the left of the conservatory door, as if something had rubbed against one of the red brick walls of the house. Gemma was only wearing thick socks, but she couldn't see a thing while she was standing inside with the lights shining around her, so she stepped out onto the patio and started to walk in the direction of the noise.

It wasn't more than a couple of seconds before she found Will leaning up against the wall, one knee up, foot braced behind him. He turned his head as she came closer, but didn't say anything.

'What are you doing out here?' she asked, shivering slightly.

'I needed some fresh air,' was all he said. 'Preferably *cold* fresh air.'

Oh, hell. Him too? She'd been hoping she'd be able to convince herself the lip action had more to do with chivalry than anything else.

But that didn't mean she needed to do anything about it, right? She cleared her throat. 'Doris says …'

What Doris had said came rushing back into her mind, but it wasn't the bit about being ready for Will to take her back home. *Quite a man …*

And he was. There lay her problem, she thought, as she watched her breath puff white into the December night and disappear.

Will stood up and walked to the edge of the patio, stared out into a night where low purplish-grey clouds blocked out the moon and stars. Gemma slipped in behind him and took up his place on the wall, hoping he'd have left some residual heat.

She had a horrible feeling that this man had the ability to make her want to reach for her running shoes more than anyone she'd ever met. There was no point in trying to hide from him. He'd already seen the worst of her. Surely it was only a matter of time before he realised this was a mistake?

'Doris says what?' he asked finally, and Gemma suddenly realised she'd trailed off and had never finished her sentence.

She swallowed. 'Doris says she's ready when you are.'

He turned and looked at her. Gemma felt her insides wobble like the jelly on Doris's trifle. She'd once described Will as boring, dull. Then why was her pulse racing? Why was her breath stuck in her chest? She'd called him 'nice', damning him with faint praise, and had made fun of his mild-mannered temperament. But there was nothing mild or mannered about the way he was looking at her now. Nothing at all.

Nice, lawn-mowing, helping-with-the-dishes, taking-six-months-to-tell-a-woman-he-liked-her Will was gone. Or maybe that version of him had only been her invention. He started walking towards her. Gemma was tempted to back away, but unless she could dissolve through the red bricks pressing into her back that wasn't going to happen.

'And what about you, Gemma?' he said as he kept walking. 'Are you ready?'

Gemma opened her mouth, and quickly discovered she'd run run out of to put in it. 'I … I …'

'That's what I thought,' he said as he closed the last few steps between them. Then he pinned her up against the wall and finished what they'd started under the mistletoe.

*

It was past midnight when they finally returned to Juliet's villa. Marco walked her to the door but didn't come in much past the threshold.

They'd gone down to reception to talk to the concierge, and then hotel security had been called. She'd spent ages talking to them, explaining what the ring looked like and what she'd been doing all day, and when they revealed that there had been rumours of thefts at other high-end resorts both on Martinique and in the Grenadines, only a short plane hop away, and they'd seen no option but to call the police.

Of course, the two officers had arrived in St Lucian time,

wandering in after she and Marco had been waiting for almost two hours, and then she'd had to go through it all again with them. Right from the beginning.

Marco had been amazing, sitting with her through it all, listening intently to all the information gathered, asking questions if something hadn't been clear. She'd never seen him so businesslike and focused before. It was a whole new side to him. One that made her wish they could have a future beyond the beach and the palm trees, beyond the end of next week.

She'd told him more than once that he should go back to his villa, but he'd refused. Even now she knew he was here to take care of her, make sure she got back to her villa okay, rather than to take advantage of her – which is what she'd been planning to do to him.

He looked at her, his eyes full of sympathy instead of heat. 'Don't be sad. There will be other rings.'

She nodded, but maybe the stress of the situation and the late hour were getting to her, because a fat tear slid down her cheek. She looked at her toes. 'There won't be another one like that one,' she told him. 'It was my grandmother's – her engagement ring. And I was …' Oh, heck. Her voice had cracked and gone all scratchy. 'It had great sentimental value.'

When she glanced back up, Marco was giving her the strangest look. He reached out and smoothed her hair away from her face. 'Then I am very sorry about it. Maybe it isn't stolen. Maybe it will turn up unexpectedly someplace?'

She nodded again, but more to thank him for being so supportive than because she believed what he was saying.

'Thank you for being so wonderful this evening. I don't know what I would have done without you.'

He gave her a wry half-smile. 'You are a strong woman, Juliet. I am sure you would have managed just fine.'

She knew he was getting ready to take his leave. The moment that had been so ripe earlier had now passed. Instead of flinging her on to the bed and having his wicked way with her he was being all gentlemanly, damn him.

She might have done something about it if she hadn't been half-comatose with tiredness and had a headache knocking at her temple, waiting to be let in. Also, she didn't want her first time with him to be a half-hearted fumble before slipping into unconsciousness. If they were going to do it, it should be fabulous. Earth-shattering. Life-altering. She was just going to have to be patient.

'Goodnight, Juliet,' he said, and leaned in to kiss her softly on the lips.

She grabbed hold of his shirt and made sure he lingered a second of two longer. When they pulled apart, she sighed. 'I'm sorry,' she said, shaking her head.

He reached up and touched her face, running his thumb over her cheekbone. 'There is always tomorrow …'

She leaned in and kissed him again. He was back to normal now, back in control, and while it was still lovely she missed that sense of rawness they'd shared when he'd hauled her out of the pool and carried her up to her bed. 'See you in the morning, Marco.'

She watched him walk away. He turned as he reached the end of her path and waved, and then he was gone. Juliet let out a long, heartfelt breath then closed the door behind him.

&

CHAPTER TWENTY-SEVEN

Gemma was up at seven on Boxing Day. She knotted her dressing gown firmly, shoved her feet in her slippers and marched downstairs to the kitchen. Once there, she rummaged through Juliet's cookery books until she found a recipe for American pancakes, then set to work. Eggs, milk, flour, a little butter … It couldn't be that hard, could it?

She decided the children must have some kind of pancake radar, because one by one they appeared over the next twenty minutes, yawning, then sat themselves at the kitchen table and waited. Unfortunately, they had to wait a rather long time.

It wasn't the mixing that was the problem, Gemma decided, that was easy. It was the cooking that was the tricky bit, not helped by the fact that Juliet's Aga had no temperature controls.

The recipe said to turn the pancakes over when the batter bubbled on top, but she started off by turning them too early, so the whole thing just flopped back into the pan in a gloopy mess, and then she left them too long, so the pan started to smoke. Polly turned her nose up at the scorched little offerings Gemma plonked in the middle of the table.

By the time she'd mixed up a second batch of batter, she was starting to wish she'd never thought of it.

It was all Will Truman's fault.

What business had he of being all boring and grey and geography-teacherish one week and then morphing into some kind of knight in fricking armour, who kissed like a god, the next? No wonder she couldn't concentrate on pancakes!

Just thinking about it made her ears heat up. She scrubbed her left one with her free hand, trying to erase the sensation, and scowled. She should have run when she'd seen him walking towards her like that, not stood there blithering, secretly waiting, heart thudding and palms slick.

The memory of the actual choreography of the kiss was fuzzy – what mouths and lips had done, where arms and hands had gone, the moment she'd stopped clinging onto the wall and pulled him closer. Those things were blurred by the recollection of how her body had responded, fizzing, tingling, sighing … Those things she remembered with startling clarity.

She did, however, clearly remember springing apart when they'd heard someone come into the kitchen. She remembered the shock and guilt slamming through her, and from the look on Will's face, he'd been feeling the same way.

He'd taken Doris back down the road after that, and he hadn't come back.

Much as she quivered to admit it to herself, Gemma had to face the fact that she liked him. A lot. Possibly even more than she had liked Michael in the beginning. And if things were different, if this was a different time or a different place, she'd have followed Doris's advice and grabbed this chance. Unfortunately, she didn't have that luxury.

While nothing had actually happened between Will and Juliet, *something* had been brewing. They all knew it.

So she would have to keep out of Will's way for the next six days.

And she hoped to God she'd had her fair share of disasters this Christmas, because if anything else happened, there was no way she was roping him in to help out again. She would just have to muddle through on her own.

*

Juliet couldn't find Marco anywhere. She'd expected to see him sitting on his terrace eating breakfast, or leaning on his balcony. When she knocked on his door there was no answer. In the end she went for a swim then wandered off to the hotel's gift shop to look for presents for the kids. When she was on her way back she spotted him sitting at one of the tables that surrounded the main pool, an untouched coffee in front of him.

She walked up to him, suddenly feeling a little nervous. He was staring off into the distance and only noticed her when she was almost next to him. When he did spot her, however, he didn't jump, he just turned his head and looked at her.

She pulled out a chair and sat down, hugging her bag of souvenirs to her middle. 'Marco? What's wrong?'

He stared at his coffee cup for a while, then looked up at

her. 'I had a message from my brother. My father is very ill. I have to leave tomorrow.'

'Oh, no …' She reached over and covered her hand with his. He'd been so wonderful to her in the short time she'd known him, it was the least she could do to offer some comfort in return. But at the same time as she felt a rush of warm empathy for him, a cold little niggle started up in her stomach. This meant they only had one more day together – maybe even less than that – and she hadn't realised how much he was starting to mean to her.

'I wish I could stay here with you instead,' he mumbled, and once again she had the flash of the little boy he must have once been, looking lost and conflicted instead of supremely smooth and confident.

She leaned over and kissed his temple, closing her eyes, letting her lips soften against his skin, then pulled away. 'I wish you could stay longer too,' she whispered, 'but family is important. I understand.'

He looked at her, and sadness flashed in his eyes before he pulled her to him. 'I don't want to go, Juliet. I don't want to do this. I want to stay with you and have what we can have together, nothing to spoil it.'

She rested her forehead against his and breathed out shakily. 'I want that too, but sometimes life isn't about what we want, is it? Sometimes it's about what we need to give. The trick is knowing how to balance the two.'

That made her sound very wise, but it had taken her more than forty years and an almost-breakdown to stumble across that particular piece of wisdom.

'Maybe it's time for you to give your family another

chance? If your father is really ill then you need to go home and make peace with him while you still have time.' Her throat grew thick. 'I – I lost my father very suddenly, so I know what it's like to wish you had a chance to say good-bye.'

She waited until he looked at her properly then carried on.

'Go home, Marco – for yourself as much as them. I will miss you horribly … but I think you have to go and I think I'm going to have to stop being selfish and let you.'

A little bit of her still wanted to be selfish, the bit that was scared that if he left now she would never see him again, that all the promise this wonderful Christmas had brought would amount to nothing. She pulled in a breath through her nostrils and sat back in her chair.

He looked at her, his expression almost fierce. 'And you would give up this – us – whatever it was you were going to get from me, so that I could go home and be happy with my family?'

She frowned. That was a strange way of putting it, but the sentiment was about right. 'Of course.'

Marco swore and pushed back his chair, then he walked over to the edge of the pool and then back to the table, where he braced his arms on it, the tendons in his forearms straining against his skin.

She sat there for a few moments wondering what she'd said and what to do about his puzzling reaction. 'We have one day, Marco. Let's make the most of it. But before we do, I need to tell you something … I haven't been entirely honest with you. You see, I'm not who you think I am.'

He'd been staring intently at the table top, but now he lifted his head sharply. 'You are not Juliet Taylor from England?'

She gave him a weary look. 'Unfortunately, I am – and that's what I need to explain. I don't want our remaining time together to be sullied with lies. I'm tired of pretending, tired of making everything seem perfect on the surface when really it's messy and difficult underneath.'

'I don't understand what you are saying.'

She shook her head. 'I know, but … here goes …'

She put her bag on the table, stood up, then walked over to him and took his hands in hers. 'I don't work in the film industry – that's my sister's job – and I don't get to meet movie stars on a daily basis or fly all over the world. I'm a neurotic housewife from Tunbridge Wells who has four kids and a worrying addiction to baking, and the only reason I'm at Pelican's Reach is because my sister paid for the trip. I am a total fake, Marco, and I'm sorry I didn't tell you earlier, but I was scared I would seem dull and uninteresting to you.'

He was completely frozen to the spot. His mouth moved and his brow furrowed deeper, and then he grabbed her hand and marched off in the direction of their villas.

*

She stumbled along behind him, hardly able to keep up with his much longer legs. When they got to her villa, he told her to open the door. 'Come with me,' he said, unsmiling, and led her down the steps from her bedroom into her living room. He stopped in front of the large wooden sideboard and opened one of its doors.

'Check your safe.'

Juliet stared at him, frowning. What was wrong with the man? One minute they'd been opening up to each other, sharing things, and the next he turned silent and sullen and was making no sense at all. 'What do you mean?'

Marco just gestured towards the safe. 'I mean, open it. Check what's in there.' And then he turned and strode away to look out of the window.

Juliet crouched down in front of the safe, but her fingers hovered above the number keys. She really didn't want to play with the game Marco was playing, but it seemed the only option to find out what was going on was to do as he said. She tapped in the number and the metal door sprung open.

She squinted, trying to see what was inside, but she'd just come out of bright sunlight and the safe was lined with dark felt inside a shady cupboard. She shoved her hand in and felt around, patting. She could feel her camera, her mobile phone and her passport … But there were also some things she couldn't find.

She stood up and backed away from the safe, shaking her head. 'My wallet! Where's my wallet?' And she didn't mean the little one she kept in her beach bag, containing just a handful of dollars and a prepaid money card. She meant the cardboard one she'd got from the bank when she'd got both East Caribbean dollars and US dollars. Hundreds of them.

'I need to call security,' she said, heading for the phone. 'They came back!'

Marco caught her hand and led her to the sofas. 'Call them in a minute, if you want,' he said. 'First I need to show you something. Sit down.'

When she'd done as he'd asked, he came and sat opposite her, perching on the edge of an armchair, and then he reached inside his trouser pocket, pulled something out and placed it carefully in the centre of the glass and wicker coffee table.

A cardboard wallet, full of money, with the name of her bank printed on it. She stared at it for a few seconds, unable to process what this meant, and then things got even weirder as he carefully laid her grandmother's engagement ring on top of it.

Her gaze flicked up at him, back down to the money and back to him again. 'Why …? What have …? What are you doing with those?'

A tiny, illogical part of her brain wanted him to tell her the police had returned them, but somehow she knew that wasn't what he was going to say.

Marco stared back at her, his expression grim. 'This is what I do, Juliet. This is who I am. Do you still think my family should welcome me back with open arms?'

She shook her head, and kept shaking it, because she didn't know what else to do.

'This is my wonderful job and why my father despises me so.'

Juliet was starting to get a headache. 'Your *job*?'

He nodded. 'I travel from country to country, resort to resort, and I look for single women – usually in their thirties or forties – who are looking for a little company and I … befriend them.'

Juliet's mouth dropped open and she made a croaking noise.

Marco's face pulled into a sneer, but he wasn't looking at her – he was looking at his own reflection in the coffee table. 'I find rich, bored women who are ready to let me fulfil their fantasies. And I work very hard to be good at what I do.' He nodded at the wallet on the table. 'Surely that entitles me to a little compensation?'

Juliet wanted to stand up. She wanted to run away. But she couldn't seem to make her legs work.

He'd done that to her, hadn't he? She'd fallen for all of it, all the stupid things he'd told her – that she was wonderful and beautiful and unusual and exciting. He'd known just what to say to reel her in.

She gasped as the enormity of the deception began to sink in, bit by sickening bit. No wonder his kisses had seemed so perfect, his romantic timing so immaculate. Hadn't she felt at times that everything was too rehearsed? And the way he hadn't come on strong, but had coaxed her in slowly.

Oh, God. She felt like such a fool.

'I thought you were the most generous man I'd ever met,' she said in a hoarse whisper, 'but of course you were, because you weren't even real. The only reason you gave me anything was because you were planning to take it all away from me.'

More than the money. Much more than the money. Her pride. Her self-confidence. The new-found freedom she'd thought he'd given her. Suddenly she felt rather sick.

She knew she had to look at him, even though she didn't want to. She knew she had to look him in the eyes and tell him what a disgusting creature he was. It wouldn't accomplish much, but maybe it would claw back just a little of her dignity.

'I was going to give you everything – even my body,' she added with a little hiccup, because the truth of that statement was like a knife in her chest. 'And all you wanted was to steal from me. What kind of man does that make you?'

Finally, she met his gaze, but instead of triumph and arrogance all she saw was shame and defeat. 'Not a very good one.'

Pretty words, but they didn't change anything, and now the shock was starting to wear off Juliet's blood was starting to pump and her fingers were starting to tingle with the warmth. 'You're disgusting. You were going to sleep with me to get my money?'

Marco stared back down at the coffee table and shook his head.

That just made Juliet angrier. She shot to her feet and stared at him, commanding him to look at her by the sheer force of her will. She was good at making things happen by the sheer force of her will. 'Don't lie to me! That's all part of your job, isn't it? And you know what that makes you?'

His shoulders sagged and he turned his head away. 'No, not usually. I am all the things you accuse me of, but I'm not that.'

More lies. She gestured towards the ceiling with her right arm. 'Then what was the other night about? You carried me upstairs and threw me down on my bed!' A slimy coldness washed through her as her own words rang in her ears. She'd been so sure that a bit of steamy holiday sex would have been the answer to all her problems. How wrong could she have been? How blind?

'I don't sleep with the women I target,' he said, still refusing to look at her, 'but that night I … I got carried away. I usually find ways to avoid it. It's easier than you think.'

Another wave of shame and humiliation hit her. She bet it was. She'd bet he was good at getting women to do what he wanted them to do. He'd certainly had her dangling on a piece of string. 'Then why was I so different? Why were you going to change your personal *code of honour* –' she had to stop and snort at the phrase '– in my case? Was I really that much of a pushover?'

He gave that little half-shrug she'd always found so appealing, but now she'd really like to smack his shoulder so hard it dislocated from its socket. 'I just … wanted to.'

She couldn't speak, stunned into silence by the sheer selfishness of his admission.

Finally, he glanced up and looked at her. 'It was because you were different. I liked you.' He shook his head gently. 'Usually I can maintain a distance, keep my emotions out of it …'

She began to laugh, but it was a horrible dry sound. 'You're still doing it! Heaping on the flattery to get yourself out of trouble! I don't believe a word you're saying!'

The rolling feeling that had started in her stomach a few minutes earlier intensified and she found herself half-running, half-stumbling towards the open door. She needed to get out of here. She needed air.

She burst onto the terrace and kept going until she met the

railings at the far edge. She pushed against it, breathing hard, her eyes taking nothing of the beautiful sunny morning. This holiday was supposed to have been her chance of renewal, at salvation. Instead it just confirmed everything that was wrong with her life. She felt like a carcass that had been stripped clean by Greg, her family, even the crazy demands she put on herself, and now Marco had just picked the bones until there was nothing left.

She heard a noise behind her, but she didn't turn round. Couldn't.

She heard him walk until he came to stand maybe six feet away from her on the balcony railing. *Why me?* she wanted to ask. *Out of all women at Pelican's Reach, why did you pick me?* But she feared she knew. Predators like him knew how to spot the vulnerable, the weak, and she'd had 'sucker' stamped on her forehead since she'd been old enough to spell it.

'The ring … I understand how easy it was for you to take that, but how did you get the money? It was in the—'

Ah. Of course.

How stupid of her not to realise until now. He'd suggested she take the ring off in the first place, hadn't he? Then he'd insisted that she check the safe when it had gone missing. And he'd stood behind her as she'd punched the code in. Very clever.

'Did you get everything you wanted?' She raised her eyebrows and turned her head to look at him.

He shook his head. 'There wasn't as much in there as I thought there would be. I should have known then …'

She didn't care what he thought. There was one thing

that was puzzling her, though. 'You already have what you wanted. I presume you stole those things from me some time in the last twenty-four hours, so why are you still hanging around? Why aren't you long gone?'

'I am leaving tomorrow, and if I stopped spending time with you before then it would look suspicious.'

Juliet felt numb. All the time he'd been kissing her, he'd been planning and plotting this inside his head; all the time he'd been talking to her, getting her to reveal things about herself that she never told anyone else … Of course! That's why he was such a good listener. It was all fuel for his fire. The more he knew about a woman, the more he could tailor the fantasy to suit her and work his magic on her. And she'd made it so easy for him. She wanted to hate him, but she found she didn't have any energy left.

She stopped leaning on the railing and walked towards him, waited for him to look her in the eye. 'Why are you tel-ling me all this now? Why did you give everything back?' That was the one thing she still didn't get. He could have got away scot-free. The deception had been complete.

She studied him while he searched for an answer. He didn't look like a man in the process of constructing a lie, but then he never had. 'I want to stop doing this. It's changing me into something I don't like. But I told myself just a few more jobs and then I'd have enough. Usually the women I meet are hard. Game players, like me. I take and they take and we both come out even.'

Juliet wanted to laugh. Did he really believe that?

'When I first met you, you seemed that way too. There was a … distance … that I've learned to recognise. And then you started bragging about your job and the movie stars you'd met, and I thought you were fair game.'

She swallowed. Part of her was enjoying this brutal honesty, but another part was crumbling underneath it. 'What changed?'

'You did,' he said simply. 'Right before my eyes. You're nice, Juliet. You smile at the waiters and remember their names. Nobody else here does that. Look at how you helped that girl at the zip lining … And you wanted to help me, too, even though it meant you weren't going to get what you wanted from me. I disgust you?' He shook his head and closed his eyes. 'I disgust myself.'

Good, thought Juliet. She had no pity for him; she was saving it all for herself. Being selfish. Why not? Everyone else was.

'And what is so damn important that you have to go around stealing from people to get it?'

Marco turned round and rested against the railing, looking back towards the villa. 'I want to go back to Lake Garda and prove to my family I can be successful without them. I wanted to buy a boat and offer sailing lessons and charters. I just needed a couple of thousand more euros …'

'Then why don't you work for it, like normal people do!' Juliet shouted. 'Why do *this*?'

He looked down at the terracotta tiles beneath their feet. 'Because I can,' he said quietly.

Because it was easy for him, Juliet realised. He was one of those people who always took the path of least resistance. She looked at him, really properly looked at him, as he stood hunched, staring at his shoes, and thought that maybe, for the very first time, she was seeing him for who he really was. A young man, not a god. And not evil – even though she'd like to believe that of him – just weak. Lazy. Selfish.

She'd thought he was like Gemma, but Gemma was nothing like this.

Suddenly she'd had enough of him. She walked round the plunge pool and back towards her sitting room.

'Just go,' she told him. 'I don't want to see you again.'

'Are you …?'

Juliet turned at the threshold. 'Am I what?'

He looked even more ashamed of himself. 'Are you going to call security?'

She hadn't thought about that yet. She realised she'd quite like to, but nothing of hers was actually missing. He'd given it all back. No, Marco hadn't taken her belongings. The damage he'd done had gone much deeper.

She shook her head and then turned to go inside. 'Goodbye, Marco.'

&

CHAPTER TWENTY-EIGHT

Juliet kept to the busy parts of the resort for the rest of the day and booked a trip to Pigeon Island for the following morning, just so she could be sure she wouldn't have to see Marco again. But as she was waiting out the front of the main reception building for the minibus to take her on her excursion, she spotted him coming through the crowd towards her. Immediately she turned and headed off in the opposite direction, through reception, out the other side into the pool area. He didn't catch up with her until she was descending the short flight of steps that led to the beach.

'I don't want to talk to you,' she said loudly, without turning round.

'Please?' Marco said from behind her. She could feel his closeness now, sense him only inches away. 'I need to explain.'

Juliet kept walking. She didn't care about what he needed. Not any more.

'And I want to do what you said – make peace with my family … Do things the right way from now on.'

She made the mistake of glancing over her shoulder. He looked so much younger now she knew him for what he was, and the look on his face reminded her of the twins when they knew they'd overstepped the line. She must have slowed a little because he fell into step beside her.

She tried to ignore him, just kept walking, but she found all the frustration that had been building since she'd seen him last just wouldn't let her make things that easy.

'You could do anything with your life,' she told him, still focusing on the little waxy tree on the end of the beach. 'Why choose this?'

She heard him take a heavy breath. 'I didn't choose it so much as it chose me.'

Juliet turned to look at him. 'Don't give me any crap, Marco. I'm really not in the mood for it.'

He held her gaze for a moment then nodded. 'I got involved with an older woman who had a villa on the outskirts of our town. She came into the family restaurant when I was working as a waiter and flirted with me.'

Juliet snorted.

'I was young, and she was French and incredibly sexy. I know you might not believe it, but Charlotte was my first serious relationship. I fell completely in love with her, and I thought she felt the same. I left the family business, much to my father's disapproval, and moved in with her. She liked being with young men, liked buying them things, telling them how to better themselves by dressing right, listening to the right music and eating the right food. She liked being in control, I suppose.'

He fell silent and Juliet stole a glance in his direction. The centre of his forehead was bunched, as if he was reliving a painful memory. It could all be an act, of course, but she didn't really see what he had to gain from acting now.

'What happened?' she asked, curious in spite of herself.

'She found a new plaything,' he said bitterly. 'When I told her she was a heartless bitch, she said I was right, but that I'd been amply compensated, and she was even generous enough –' he sneered as he said the word *generous* '– to send me on a trip to Sicily to prove her point.'

Juliet's eyes widened. 'Did you go?'

He nodded sadly. 'I did. A month away from Riva, knowing I wouldn't run into her every day with her newer, younger lover, seemed like a gift. And I was angry. I knew it wouldn't hurt her to pay, but somehow I saw taking the trip as revenge.'

Juliet turned her attention back to the little tree. It was closer now, and the crowds and sunloungers around them were thinning out. She knew what that felt like – to feel replaced, surpassed. She just hadn't expected that someone like Marco would ever feel the same way.

He sighed. 'And while I was in Taormina, I met another woman like her, and she wanted me, so I thought, *Why not? But this time I will walk in with my eyes open and I will make her pay.* So I did.' When he looked at her, he didn't look very triumphant. Instead he looked bleak and empty.

'Did it make you feel better?'

He nodded. 'For a while. And I just kept going. It kept me away from my family and when I went home I had money, I seemed a success. I could look my father in the face before he found out the truth. I told myself I wasn't doing anything wrong – that it was a business transaction.'

They reached the tree and Juliet walked under its branches and turned to face him. 'Why are you here, Marco? What do you want from me?'

'To tell you I am sorry.'

Juliet looked at him. He had all that charm, like her sister, and he was clever – she never would have guessed what he'd done until it was too late, if he hadn't stepped in and told her. While Gemma used her talents to get herself a high-profile job, Marco wasted his. He could do so much more.

She didn't know if he was telling the truth about changing his ways, but she wished he was. While some of the time he'd been cynically playing her, she couldn't help but feel that occasionally she'd got a glimpse of the real Marco – a few times when he'd talked about his family, that night when he'd seemed less polished, less in control. Maybe he'd been honest about that after all.

'You could run a good sailing business if you wanted to,' she told him. 'People like you, and you know a lot about boats. You could make it work.'

Marco went grey, as if he was about to vomit. 'You really think so?'

Juliet tried to stop her heart going out to him, and failed. He looked totally taken aback by her reluctant belief in him. She nodded.

The look in his eyes was pure gratitude, but Juliet wasn't foolish enough to get caught up in his web again. She stepped away from under the shade of the tree and into the searing sunshine.

'Go home, Marco. But do more than this. *Be* more than

this.' And then she turned and walked to the end of the beach, stood on the rocky breakwater and stared out into the ocean.

She heard him leave, heard the shuffle of the sand beneath his feet. Even though she felt a strange kind of sympathy for him, she didn't turn round, didn't call after him. There was a time to give and a time to stop giving, and Juliet's time was now.

*

Juliet moved her forearm to cover her eyes and shifted position slightly on the sunlounger. She was vaguely aware of the squealing of children splashing in the shallows, the call of the seabirds circling high above the beach and the fizz of the waves against the shore. Her book lay forgotten on the sand beside her and her cocktail was going warm.

The only thing that was spoiling her blissful sunbathing session was the woman on the sunlounger next to her. She kept fidgeting and fussing, pulling things out of her bag and tucking them back in again. Why couldn't she just lie down and relax like everyone else?

Eventually, Juliet gave up trying to doze and picked up her book. She'd been on page one hundred and eighty-six the last time she'd put it down, and she stayed on page one hundred and eighty-six for the next twenty minutes.

Deep in her subconscious things started to float free and rise to the surface.

Surface.

Everything had a surface, didn't it? But it was the sum

total of the thing. Sometimes, like an iceberg, it was only the tiniest visible part.

That's why she'd been blinded by Marco – his surface. If someone could have tailor-made a man to fulfil her secret fantasy, they couldn't have come up with anything better than Marco Capello. She should have realised that he'd been too good to be true. No man was that generous in real life – except maybe Will. Good old Will. Somehow, she felt as if she had betrayed him.

She could have been more cross with Marco if she hadn't realised she was guilty of doing exactly the same. She gave good 'surface', didn't she? Always pretending everything was lovely, always pretending everything was fine, when really underneath it was all one big horrible mess. But it least in her case, the negative consequences were only for herself.

But as Juliet tried to read a long paragraph at the bottom of the page for the sixth time, she started to question the accuracy of that assumption. Didn't her constant need for perfection have all sorts of tiny consequences?

What about the distance between her and Violet? What about Polly's insistence on everything being right and just-so? If their mother hadn't been quite so uptight, maybe they'd have been better off.

And then there was Gemma.

And Greg. Maybe the downfall of their marriage wasn't entirely his fault. Maybe, if she'd admitted she was struggling, instead of just trying to be more and more perfect for him, they might have been able to reclaim some lost ground.

It was strange, now she was in St Lucia she could look back at the Juliet in Tunbridge Wells, thousands of miles away, and see her with much more clarity than she had been able to when she'd been up close and personal and living her life. No wonder she'd driven herself to the verge of a breakdown.

The woman next to her sat bolt upright and twisted round to look in the direction of the main pool. 'You don't know what time aqua aerobics is, do you?' she asked Juliet.

'Two o'clock,' Juliet replied.

'Thanks.' The woman sighed and shoved her feet into her flip-flops. 'That's another forty minutes … I think I'll go and have a wander around the shop.'

Juliet watched her go, then put down her book and stared out across the gently rippling turquoise sea.

She had finally achieved it, that perfect state of relaxation. And she had another three days to exist in this blissful Nirvana now she'd attained it. The only problem was, now that she'd slowed down enough to think properly, she knew exactly what was missing from her perfect holiday.

Her kids.

A break from them had been necessary – for them and for her – but two weeks was too long.

And she had a life waiting for her. Possibly a chance to rescue her relationship with her sister. She'd realised a lot about herself, and Gemma, since she'd been away. Surely she could put some of that new understanding to use to help them make a fresh start?

And then there was Will. The one solid figure on her horizon. Not a fantasy, but a real man. It was time to get off the fence about him and, surprisingly, even after the rather spectacular implosion of her romance with Marco, she realised she was ready to put fresh seeds into her love life too. Greg wasn't the only one who could move on.

From her position on the sunlounger she looked up at the palm fronds above her head, waving in the breeze. Everything was bright and warm and cheerful. Back in Tunbridge Wells it was still that lazy week between Christmas and New Year when everything slowed down and people stayed inside their houses with the fire on, cosy and happy. And despite the glorious warmth on her skin, Juliet wished for just a little nip of frost on her nose.

St Lucia had been wonderful – a revelation – but it was time to go home.

&

CHAPTER TWENTY-NINE

Juliet's kitchen was close to sparkling. Gemma had scrubbed and cleaned and swept. Maybe this was why Juliet filled her life the way she did. It didn't actually help, not really, but it was a hell of a lot better than just sitting and moping.

Violet sloped into the kitchen and put a glass and a plate into the dishwasher. 'Hey, Auntie Gemma. You okay?'

Gemma nodded and threw her cloth down on the work surface, sighing.

Violet tipped her head on one side and looked at her. 'Boy trouble, huh?'

'Yup.'

The worst kind.

Violet walked over and hugged her aunt loosely. 'I understand,' was all she said, and Gemma had to agree that she probably did understand. It would be easy to say she was too young, she didn't know how this felt. But heartache tasted the same at every age.

She pulled away and muttered, 'Nothing a few tequilas wouldn't solve.' And then she remembered who she was talking to and quickly added, 'I didn't say that.'

Violet laughed and walked away.

Gemma had been lying, of course. She didn't think tequila was the answer to this problem. She didn't think it would dull the throbbing ache in her chest.

She missed Will, which was totally stupid. He'd only been gone for two days. Not even that if you counted the hours. Which she had.

She'd seen his car pull out of his drive on the twenty-seventh and somehow she'd known he wasn't just popping out to get some milk from the supermarket. He was Staying Away. From her. It didn't help that she knew it was the right thing to do.

She shook her head and went back to wiping crumbs off the work surface. It was too quiet in the house this morning. The boys had gone to play at Juliet's friend's house, Polly was deep into reading her new *Guinness Book of World Records*, and Violet only wandered out of her bedroom when she had to. Gemma went back to cleaning. She had to fill the empty silence with something.

When she realised she was wiping down an already spotless kitchen counter she sighed and flopped into one of the chairs surrounding the table. This shouldn't be happening. She shouldn't be feeling like this. She'd had plenty of long-distance relationships due to the nature of her job, often had spent weeks – sometimes months – away from the man in her life, and yet she'd never felt this ... empty ... before.

It was then that she heard a noise at the far end of the conservatory. She looked up, and everything around her started to spin. The one stable point was the man standing outside the French doors, looking very much like he wanted to come in.

Will. He'd come back for her. She could tell that just by the grim intensity of his expression, the way he seemed to be pulling her towards him by the sheer force of his presence. How had she ever thought him average and boring? Had she been blind?

Slowly, she got up and walked through the kitchen, down to the double doors at the end of the conservatory and turned the key so he could come in. Instead of opening the door for him, she stepped back and let him do it himself.

'Hi,' she said, as he crossed the threshold and closed the door behind him.

'Hi.'

'You went away.' *Wow. Startling powers of observation, Gemma.*

He was looking at her intently. 'To my sister's. And now I'm back.'

Her stupid heart jumped up and down and clapped its hands.

'Why?'

They both knew this was a bad idea. That's why he'd gone in the first place.

He stepped forward, filling the space in the front of her until all she could see was him. 'To tell you I can't stay away any more, Gemma. I can't run away from this … from you. I just need to know if you feel the same way too.'

Hadn't she once thought that Will didn't know how to go after what he wanted, the woman he wanted? Boy, had been wrong. She didn't say anything, didn't move, but she her eyes must have given her away, because she saw warmth flood his, and she knew she'd agreed.

He reached for her hands and held them. His fingers were cold at the tips, but warm everywhere else. 'After Sam left me I closed down. Even before she left things weren't that good. The more "out there" she got, the more I felt I had to be her anchor, to be the steady one.' He cocked an eyebrow. 'The boring one.'

Gemma shook her head, but he carried on.

'So I decided I needed a different kind of woman. Someone safer, easier. Less challenging.'

Not words she heard the men in her life often use about her, unfortunately. Crazy, complicated, high-maintenance … Those she'd heard in abundance.

'I was wrong,' Will said. 'I need someone who's impulsive, creative … free-spirited to balance me out. I need *you*, Gemma.'

His plain, unvarnished words lit something inside her, but she shook her head and pulled her hands out of his, walked back into the kitchen as far as she could go, until she met the cabinets under the window that looked out over the drive.

Will followed her. She should have known he would. He was just as stubborn as she was. 'I know it's not going to be easy, that there are going to be obstacles …'

One huge, Juliet-sized obstacle, Gemma thought.

'But I want to take that chance,' he finished.

Large sticky tears began to roll down her cheeks as she turned to look at him. Oh, she wanted to say yes so badly, to jump into his arms and kiss him senseless, but she couldn't. And she had to make him see why.

'All my life I've unwittingly usurped my sister,' she told him. 'I came in and took the lion's share of our parents' love and attention – especially my mother's. I had the opportunities she was denied. There are so many things …'

So many ways that she hadn't even realised. Little things. Stupid things. But they all added up to make a bigger pattern.

She shook her head. 'If there is even the *slightest* chance that you and Juliet might have got together, I can't do it, Will. I can't be the selfish one again. This time I have to think of her first.' She dragged the heel of her hand across her cheek and sniffed. 'Tell me the truth. Was there? A chance?'

Will wasn't smiling any more. 'Yes.' He looked away. 'But I don't think it would have worked out in the long run. I think it would have fizzled out.'

The tears started up again. 'Then I can't do it. I won't.'

Will's control snapped. Up until now she'd sensed he'd been giving her space, keeping a few feet away because that was what she'd silently asked for, but now he stepped in and placed a hand on either side of her face, and while looking into her eyes he wiped the fresh salty tears away with his thumbs. 'She doesn't make me feel the way you do, Gemma.'

And then he was kissing her. This time it wasn't hot and frantic. It was deep and slow and tender, and she recognised it for what it was. Will understood. That only made the tears flow harder. This was the one man she really didn't want to hold back from, that she really didn't want to run from, but she had to.

So she kissed him back, savouring every touch of his lips, every fluttering sensation that his arms round her, his hands on her body produced, knowing that this very well might be the last time. She was selfish enough to want to make the most of it, to make it count. In that respect she was very much still the old Gemma.

A sudden noise from the doorway into the hall made them still. Gemma let her hands fall from where they'd been round the back of Will's head to his shoulders, but she kept her eyes closed and rested her forehead against his. 'Not now, Polly … Just give us a moment, will you?'

'It's not Polly.'

A cold, sick feeling spiked through Gemma. It was like being impaled on a giant icicle. Slowly, she pulled away from Will, felt the cold air rush in between them, and then she turned her head. When she'd gathered up enough courage, she opened her eyes.

And there, standing in the doorway, was Juliet.

*

Juliet looked at her sister wrapped around her next-door neighbour. Both were frozen in position, leaving Juliet with a tableau that set her insides on fire. That bliss-like state she'd achieved in her final days in St Lucia evaporated.

'You're b—back,' Gemma stuttered. 'You're not supposed to be here for another three days.'

'Well, it's just as well I decided to come home early. That was all very enlightening,' she said, looking from one to the other.

Gemma's hands slid off Will's chest and he stepped away. 'How long have you been standing there?' she asked shakily.

Juliet knew what Gemma was really asking: *How much did you hear?* She made a careless little gesture, pulling the corners of her mouth down. 'Oh, since about "She doesn't make me feel the way you do," I reckon that was long enough.'

Will stepped forward. 'Juliet, I—'

She raised her chin. 'I think you'd better get out of my house,' she said evenly.

But Will didn't move. He just stared back at her, jaw squared. Juliet knew that look. He was getting ready to defend her sister. Traitor. She was only just keeping a lid on her anger, but now it started to bubble dangerously high, threatening to pop the lid off her iron self-control.

Gemma laid a hand on his arm. 'Will, it's okay … I think Juliet and I need to talk … on our own.' His head snapped round and he transferred that intense gaze to Gemma. She nodded gently. 'Really.'

The silence was thick around them as he took one last long look at Gemma and then left. Juliet listened to his footsteps and waited until she'd heard the front door both open and close again before she turned to her sister.

She surprised herself with how cool and rational she sounded, especially as she dearly wanted to rip Gemma's head off.

'How could you?' she whispered.

Gemma shook her head and tears were streaming down her cheeks. Normally that would have tugged at Juliet's heartstrings, but she discovered that a bit of her was now cold and dead. She didn't feel anything but the slow, poisonous rage building inside.

Gemma swiped at her cheeks with her hands, and then her words came out in a rush. 'It's not what you think! I didn't try—'

'It doesn't matter what you did or didn't try to do, Gemma! The fact is, you did it. You've been rehashing the same excuse your whole life, *I didn't mean to ...*, *It wasn't my fault ...*, and that works until you're about the twins' age, but at thirty-five I don't think it holds much weight.'

Gemma closed her mouth. Juliet could almost see the sentences whirring round her sister's head. She also saw Gemma entertain then reject every single one. In the end all she said was, 'I'm sorry.'

That should have made Juliet happy. She'd been waiting for a straight apology from Gemma for years now, but she found she just didn't care. The last piece of whatever had connected the two of them had broken the moment she'd come into her kitchen and found Gemma poaching the man who'd liked her first, and she wasn't sure it was the kind of thing that could ever be mended. In a strange way, it was quite liberating.

'I thought that maybe we could start to repair things between us when I got home,' she told Gemma, 'but I don't think that's possible now. You obviously have no consideration for me or my feelings, and I can't do this one-sided thing any more. It's unhealthy, and I need to think of myself for a change.'

The look of horror in Gemma's eyes was almost comical. Her chest heaved and she shook her head. But before she could open that lying mouth of hers, Juliet cut in first. 'I think you'd better leave too.'

'Juliet … If you'd just let me explain!'

'You can explain all you want, but when it boils down to it, you still had your tongue down Will's throat when I came in, and nothing's going to change that.'

A momentary look of shame washed over Gemma's features, but then she set her jaw and her eyes glittered.

'So, this is it … You're finally free, Gemma. I'm cutting you loose. I don't want your obligatory visits any more. You don't have to buy the kids guilt presents or make pity calls. I don't want anything you have to give me.' And she moved out of the doorway and looked pointedly towards the hall.

'*Now*?' Gemma said. 'You want me to leave right now? We can't even—'

'Yes, now,' Juliet said, feeling stronger and more in control of her life than she had done in years. 'I'm going to go and say hi to my kids and then I'm going to take them to Pizza Express for lunch, and when I get back I would like you to be gone.'

'The boys are at Melanie's,' Gemma said.

Juliet just kept staring at her. 'Well, that'll give you an extra twenty minutes to pack up your stuff and get out of my house, won't it?'

Gemma marched up to her sister. 'Now, hang on a second! You're kicking me out?'

Juliet nodded. 'Too right I am.'

Gemma couldn't quite believe what she was hearing. She felt her jaw actually drop. 'After all I've done for you?'

Juliet walked away, uncomfortable by her proximity, Gemma supposed, but then she never liked to let anyone that close. Not even her poor ex-husband, who'd finally given up trying to live with his Stepford Wife and moved on.

When she'd created enough distance between them she turned round, arms folded lightly, and spoke in a cold, hard voice. 'All you've ever done is take what isn't yours, Gemma. And I think you proved that quite nicely just now.' She glanced back at the section of kitchen counter that Will had been pressing Gemma up against only moments before.

Gemma had felt bad about that up until now, but she found that was only a small part of what she was angry about. 'You have got to be kidding me!' she yelled at Juliet. 'I've just looked after your house and your kids for almost two fricking weeks … I've washed their clothes, wiped their noses, cooked their food … I entertained *your* guests on Christmas Day, including that sorry excuse for an octopus "Uncle" Tony, and – oh, yes! – I just gave you an all-expenses-paid five-star holiday to the Caribbean!' Her volume had been rising with each word and now her throat was starting to feel raw. 'Yes, that's right, Juliet! I never, ever do anything for you.'

Juliet looked a little taken aback at that speech. While her sister had stopped spitting accusations at her, Gemma took the chance to put a few other things to rights as well.

'And I wasn't the favourite growing up! That's a lie.'

Juliet opened her mouth, but Gemma wasn't finished yet.

'Yes, I know Mum was hard on you sometimes, always pushing you, always asking that little bit more of you, but don't you think that's because she thought you were capable of it? No one ever asked me to do *more*. I was just cute little Gemma, too lightweight to deal with any of the difficult stuff, so we'll just let her toddle along happily and hope she won't notice she's not as perfect as her wonderful older sister!'

Juliet shook her head. 'I was *never* perfect! But, yes, I tried to be. Do you know how much hard work it took to compete with you, with those curls and those adorable little dimples? I didn't have a choice but to be that way. I'd have never got a look-in otherwise.'

Suddenly Gemma felt more like crying than shouting. 'Why did it always have to be a competition?'

Juliet looked shocked at that, as if she hadn't ever considered it could be any other way, but once Juliet had decided she was right about something there was no way she was backing down. Gemma saw the exact moment her brain changed tack and she decided to come out fighting again.

'Yes, that's right! Turn the tables and make it all my fault … God, you're incredible!' She shook her head. 'You never take any responsibility for anything, Gemma! And you've always been happy to float around clueless, doing whatever makes you happy, while you left other people to deal with the hard stuff, to clear up the messes.'

Gemma's features crumpled into a look of confusion. What *was* Juliet on about? She was making no sense at all now. However, it didn't matter. One thing had become crystal clear during this conversation, and there was no way Gemma was going to stay here and go round and round in circles about the same old stuff for hours.

She folded her arms across her chest and glared at her sister. 'It doesn't matter what I say or what I do, does it? Nothing is ever going to be good enough for you. *I* am never going to be good enough for you. I get that now. And you're right, if that's the case, maybe it is time we stopped trying.'

She turned to march out the kitchen door. 'Oh, and by the way … I'm not leaving right this very second. I'm going to say a proper goodbye to the kids. They deserve that at least.' And then she walked out and left Juliet standing there, open-mouthed.

&

CHAPTER THIRTY

Juliet opened the front door thinking she was going to receive a package from the postman. There was a man on her doorstep all right, and he was holding a box, but it wasn't Reginald, her usual postie. She was tempted to close the door in his face.

'What do you want?'

Will looked back at her. He was taller than she was, but she was standing on the step and he on the driveway, it meant they were eye to eye.

'I think we need to talk.'

Juliet thought she needed to rewind time and do the last fortnight over, but not everybody got their wishes, did they?

He opened the lid of the Tupperware box and Juliet's eyes widened. 'Please?' he said. 'They're home-made.'

Brownies. Will had brought brownies. And even more astonishingly, from the sorry state of the squidgy brown squares in the tub, he'd made them himself. Three out of ten for baking, but ten out of ten for knowing what would soften her up.

She sighed. 'Five minutes.' And she turned and walked away, letting him follow and close the door behind him. She went through the kitchen, not quite able to bear having this conversation in the scene of the crime, and into the conservatory. She sat down on the edge of one of the sofas and placed her hands on her knees.

Will put the tub on the coffee table between them and sat down opposite her. 'I'm sorry,' he said. 'Walking in like that must have been awful, and I'm sorry you heard what I said.'

Juliet decided to focus on the sad-looking brownies. He might be sorry, but it had been the truth. Will wasn't like Marco. He wasn't the kind of man who'd say anything to get a woman where he wanted her.

She looked up at him. His brows were drawn together and he was wearing such an earnest expression. She exhaled and sat back in the sofa. 'I'm angry with you, Will, but I know you wouldn't deliberately try to hurt me. It's Gemma who I'm really furious with.'

She looked into his eyes, tried to read what she saw there. 'Was I wrong? Did I misread the signals?'

Will shook his head. 'No. I thought that maybe there was something starting between us too.'

There was. Not *is*. Whatever had been there once was now in the past tense. There would be no going back.

'It wasn't her fault,' he said, straightening slightly, the penitent look on his face being replaced by something else.

Juliet knew him well enough to read what was coming. 'Don't you dare defend her!' That was one of the things that hurt the most. She'd thought she could trust him to be on her side, and instead he'd defected to the other camp. 'I know you think she's wonderful – most men do – but it's different being her sister. And by doing what she did she proved she just doesn't care about me.'

'You're wrong, Juliet. All Gemma does is care about what you think of her. Why do you think she offered to swap Christmases with you in the first place?'

Juliet didn't know. 'Guilt, probably,' she said.

Will gave a confused little smile and shook his head. 'You don't see it, do you? You really don't see it?'

Juliet pursed her lips. No point in looking for something that wasn't there.

He leaned forward. 'When was the last time you took a good look at your sister, and I mean *really* looked at her, instead of just seeing what you think is there?'

She knew what he wanted. For her to see what he saw and, frankly, she didn't want to. That sounded a lot like rubbing it in.

Will sat back against the sofa cushions again, but his jaw was tight and she could see the urge to go into battle for her sister was still there. After a moment he shook his head and looked away. They sat there like that for a while, not saying anything, filling the silence with unspoken thoughts.

'I don't know what to say. What do you want from me, Will?'

He looked straight at her. 'We were friends before. I don't want to lose that.' When she didn't answer, he asked, 'Did you ever wonder why we didn't act on whatever was brewing between us? I've thought that our friendship was on the verge of becoming something more for over a year, and I thought you did too.'

'Not a whole year …' she muttered.

'But there was something there. And yet neither of us acted on it.'

Juliet was about to say that she wasn't that type, that she was old-fashioned and liked to take things slowly, but then she thought of Marco. She clearly *was* that type when the right man came along. Or the wrong man, as it had turned out. But Marco's deficiency didn't make Will's point any less valid.

She decided it was time to be brave, so she reached forward and prised a rather sticky brownie from the bottom of the Tupperware box. She lifted it carefully to her mouth and bit off the corner. It was okay for a first attempt, but it was a little bit bland, lacking something. Maybe he'd missed out a vital ingredient.

And maybe that's where their problem lay, too. She and Will were missing that vital ingredient. Because if it had been there they would have ended up together by now. It had been safe to like Will, she realised. Good old Will. It had allowed her to pretend she hadn't been running scared, that she was okay after her divorce, when really she had been anything but.

He must have seen her expression change, soften, because he leaned forward and said, 'Juliet, you know I think you're amazing, but ...'

'But I don't make you feel the way she does,' she finished for him.

The truth of the words stung, even though she understood now that he was right.

Will's expression turned hollow, and that twisted the knife in her chest even more. He liked Gemma. He really liked Gemma. And it hadn't taken him more than a year of pussyfooting around to work it out.

'I understand,' she told him. 'But I don't know if our friendship can survive this.'

He breathed out. 'I suppose that's fair, but if that's the case then I'm going to miss you.'

Damn him for always having the right answer.

To distract herself from caving in, from putting her own wishes aside and just smoothing everything over to make it okay again, she asked, 'Have you called her?' It had been two days since she'd come back from St Lucia.

He shook his head. 'Before I go I need to explain what happened that morning.'

Juliet put down the brownie and held her hands up, warding off images in her brain she didn't want to see.

'I don't want to know,' she said in a rather shirty manner.

Will ignored her. 'When you walked in, Gemma had just finished telling me that nothing could happen between us, and she said that because of you.'

Juliet snorted. 'Didn't much look as if nothing was happening between you. Quite the reverse.'

Will gave her a bleak look. 'We were saying goodbye.'

The shock of his words stopped Juliet short. Her mouth snapped closed and she stared at him. In the last couple of days, she'd had plenty of conversations with both Will and Gemma inside her head, and not once had this scenario played itself out. Now the red filter of her anger was gone, she thought back to the moment she'd stepped inside the kitchen, to what she'd seen. The kiss she'd witnessed had been full of passion and tenderness. It had had a bittersweet quality, the quiet desperation of a farewell.

How could she compete with that?

She didn't want to even try.

Even if she did get together with Will in the future, she'd always be second best. To her own sister. Again.

She rubbed her forehead with her hand, suddenly feeling tired and too overwhelmed to process everything coming her way. 'Thank you for the brownies, and for coming to explain this, but I can't give you the answer you want right now. I need more time to think.'

Will nodded and stood up. 'Thank you for listening,' he said, and then he walked out of her house, and possibly out of her life.

&

CHAPTER THIRTY-ONE

Gemma tied her running shoes, plugged her iPod earbuds in and headed for the front door of her flat. A good, hard run through Greenwich Park was just what the doctor ordered. For the past week and a half she'd been moping about indoors, the words of her argument with Juliet ringing round her head. It was time to pick herself up and move on.

It had been nine days since she'd spoken to Juliet and just as long since she'd seen Will. He'd phoned a couple of times on the landline – must have got her number from the book – but when she'd realised it was him she'd put the phone down. Rude, she knew, but if she spoke to him she was going to crumble and she couldn't do that.

She breathed in sharply to ward off threatening tears, then put her head down, her feet to the floor and charged out of her flat, ready to run. She didn't get very far, however, because she barrelled into something, something large and beige-coloured standing outside her front door. When she regained her balance enough to look up, she discovered that something was Juliet.

Gemma had thought that the overriding emotion she'd been feeling was sadness, but now she saw her sister standing there, her features all pinched, she discovered she was angry too.

'What are you doing here?'

'I came to—' Juliet broke off as she looked Gemma up and down.

'Came to what? I'm about to go running.'

'You *run*?'

If Gemma hadn't been so angry with her sister, the expression on her face would have been funny. She set off down the hallway to the lifts at a brisk march. 'Yes, I run, but you're not here to check up on my fitness regime? Or are you?' She wouldn't put it past Juliet to be that nosy or that controlling.

Juliet took off at a jog and caught up with her. 'No,' she panted.

They reached the lift and Gemma turned to face her. 'So …?'

Juliet took a deep breath. 'I need to talk to you … No, I mean, *we* need to talk … to each other. About last week. And other stuff. Family stuff.'

Well, that was a turn-up for the books. After hearing nothing from Juliet for almost two weeks, she'd thought her sister really had cut her off. However, when the lift doors dinged she went inside. She was fed up having to do everything on Juliet's terms. If Juliet wanted to talk to her, she'd have to do it her way.

When they got downstairs and out of the front door of her building she set off at a brisk walk, warming up.

'You'd better say what you want to say quickly,' she told Juliet. 'It takes five minutes to get to the park and after that

I'm running.' She glanced down at Juliet's rather nice mink suede boots. Even if she wanted to, she wouldn't be able to keep up. In fact, she was already looking a little pink and breathless.

The sadistic side of Gemma decided it was quite pleased about that.

'I wanted to say I'm sorry about the way I talked to you the other day,' she said, doing her best to keep up.

That was almost enough for Gemma to stop dead. Or maybe even faint. But she couldn't quite forget the look of contempt on Juliet's face that morning she'd arrived back from St Lucia and that helped her to keep striding. 'You are, huh?'

Juliet nodded. 'I had reason to be upset, but I totally overreacted.'

Gemma turned the corner and set off past the grand old white stone of the naval college. 'Ya think?'

Juliet swallowed and scurried to keep up. 'I met a man on holiday, you see …'

Gemma kept going, but she turned her head sharply to look at her sister. 'You met a man … A "not Will" kind of man, and then you had the gall to come back and bawl me out?'

Just when she thought Juliet had changed her spots and got all reasonable, her sister had to go and prove her wrong! Gemma picked up speed.

'Long story,' Juliet said, hobbling along beside her, but not dropping behind, which was most annoying. Gemma wondered if she could subtly increase her stride length, making it ever more torturous until Juliet gave up. She was

FIONA HARPER

so busy wondering if the feeling of triumph would be worth quashing her growing sense of curiosity that she almost missed what her sister said next.

'The short version is that I thought he was my wish come true, but it turned out he was a con man who tried to steal Grandma's ring and all my money.'

Now that was when Juliet got her full attention. Gemma screeched to a halt and faced her sister. 'You're kidding me!'

'No,' said Juliet, shaking her head, and then more sadly, 'I wish I was. So you can see why I was a little … touchy … when I arrived back from the airport. Combined with the sleepless night on the plane and the jet lag, I wasn't in the best of moods.'

Gemma wanted to laugh. She might even have let out the tiniest of giggles. Juliet always had had a talent for under-statement.

'It really isn't funny,' Juliet said, trying to scowl, but then her lips started to twitch.

Gemma set off walking again, at a gentler pace this time. 'What happened? Are you okay?' Crikey, that was the last thing she'd wanted to happen to Juliet when she'd offered her the holiday.

Juliet nodded. 'I'm okay. Or I will be. I'll tell you the whole story later, but for now I think we've got some more important things to talk about.'

Part of Gemma really didn't want to talk to Juliet. Those things she'd said at her house that morning had stung. Part of her wanted to blow her sister off and tell her she didn't care, it was too late. But another more sensible part of her knew that would just keep them circling round each other in

the same twisted dynamic for ever. For their relationship to
change, they both had to be willing to change too.

'Okay,' she finally said. They'd reached the park now, but
instead of sprinting off she led the way to a bench and they
both sat down. The grass was still frosty, glistening in the
winter sun and the park was deserted, except for a couple of
other runners and a few late-morning dog walkers.

'There's a lot I want to say, but I think for it all to make
sense, I need to start at the beginning.' Juliet heaved in a
breath then looked very earnestly at her sister. 'You know
when Mum broke down after Dad died?'

Gemma nodded.

'Well, that wasn't the first time ...'

And she began to tell a story of two sisters, two parents
and two very different childhoods. Gemma listened silently
as Juliet told her about a horrible Christmas when Mum had
left home, a Christmas she didn't even remember, save for
the doll she'd cherished for years until its head had fallen off.
She listened to other stories, too, of times when she'd been
living in the house, but had no idea of what was going on,
and it kept going ... Past childhood, into adolescence, adult-
hood. Right up until the time their mother had died.

When Juliet finished talking and waited for a response of
some kind Gemma found she couldn't speak. She felt as if
what she'd thought of as a happy, secure childhood had been
wiped from the blackboard of her memory and replaced with
someone else's. Had none of it been real? Memories were all
she had left of her parents. Now those were all shredded to
pieces, leaving her with nothing to hang onto. That wonderful, happy childhood that had made her feel so sure of her

place in the world was gone, and with it her courage and her confidence drained away.

She stood up on shaky legs and looked down at Juliet.

'I'm sorry,' she said hoarsely, 'but I need to do this.' And then she turned towards the great hill that led up towards the Royal Observatory and ran away as fast as she could.

*

Gemma found Juliet at the top of the hill about half an hour later, resting on the railing and looking out over the ancient park, the three-hundred-year-old naval college on this side of the Thames and then the glittering skyscrapers of Canary Wharf beyond. Two sides of the river, so very different. New and old. Traditional and cutting-edge. And both sides forever divided by the flowing water they had in common.

She slowed to a light jog and went to join Juliet, matching her pose, gazing without really looking at the city stretched out beneath them.

'I'm sorry,' she said, glancing in Juliet's direction. 'That was rather a lot to process all at once.'

Juliet didn't look round but she nodded. 'I understand. I've had years to fester over this stuff. It *was* a lot to take in one go.'

Gemma nodded. And how. 'I have some questions …'

Her sister straightened and turned to look at her. 'You still want to talk to me?' She looked very relieved at that. And younger. So much younger. Which was odd, because Juliet had always been the grown-up in Gemma's eyes.

'Can we walk?' she asked, and they set off along the path

that ran around the top of the hill. When they'd left the few people milling around the viewing area behind she asked, 'Why did they trust you with all of this and not me? Why was all this such a big secret?'

Juliet shrugged. 'I honestly don't know. I was so small when it started that I never questioned it myself. It was what we did.'

'Lying to Gemma,' she said bitterly.

Juliet looked at her sharply. 'No!' she said, her voice soft rather than strident. '*Protecting* Gemma. There's a big difference.'

'No wonder I sometimes felt as if I was on the outside, looking in.'

Juliet looked as if she might cry. 'I never knew you felt that way! I would have given anything not to know … It wasn't an honour, you know.' Her expression grew hard. 'It was more like a sentence.' Her voice grew quiet, barely more than a whisper. 'Sometimes I think she hated me for knowing the truth.'

Gemma swallowed. Well, that explained a lot. How there'd been tension between her and their mother, and how nothing Gemma did to try to help ever made things better.

Juliet nodded to herself. 'We both travelled the paths our parents laid down for us without even realising it. I doubt they even realised it themselves.' She stopped walking and turned to look at Gemma. 'I think they would hate to see how we've ended up. I know I do.'

Darn that stinging at the top of her nose! Gemma swiped a hand across her eyes. 'Me too,' she said, her voice wobbly.

Juliet looked back at her, her chest rising and falling

beneath the buttons of her camel-coloured coat. 'It seems so stupid now, being cross with you for not knowing things, for never being burdened with them, but I suppose I was jealous of the charmed life you had. Really, I should have been angry with Mum, but she seemed so fragile and you seemed so resilient.'

Gemma let out a long sigh. 'I wish you'd told me all this earlier.'

Juliet nodded. 'I wish I had too, but somehow I'd got sucked into the habit of not telling you things and I just couldn't stop. But I can see what you've been trying to tell me for ages now – that you're a capable, confident woman, Gemma. You don't need me to protect you from life, because you're more than capable of dealing with it on your own.'

Gemma swallowed and her eyes went pink round the rims. 'Thank you. But I fed into the problem too, by behaving like a child sometimes, by running away and pretending I didn't care rather than facing up to it. And I *do* care, Juliet. I always have, and I don't want things to end up the way they have.'

Much to her relief, Juliet smiled. 'That's why I came here today. I want us to start again. Maybe now we've blown the pieces of our sibling relationship to kingdom come, we can build something new. I still want us to be sisters, but I want us to be friends, too.' She looked down at her boots and then back up at Gemma. 'I need you, Gemma. I really do.'

Gemma just rushed forward and crushed her sister into the biggest hug ever – one that had been brewing for years and years – and once she'd started she couldn't seem to stop. It was just as well that Juliet clutched her just as tightly back.

When they finally pulled back, Juliet smiled and said, 'I wanted to say thank-you for everything you did over Christmas. Doris told me how you pulled it off on Christmas Day. The kids seem really happy and relaxed and the house was really tidy.'

Gemma gave her a questioning look.

'Okay, the house wasn't *really* tidy, but it was pretty good, seeing as I'd expected dystopian devastation on my return.'

'How are the kids?' Gemma asked. 'I miss them.'

'I think they miss you too. Especially at breakfast time. I had to go and buy a whole new stack of cake decorations.'

Gemma was about to defend herself on that front, but Juliet quickly added, 'It's fine, honestly. They told me you made them eat fruit, too … And it was Christmas. Anyway, Violet has fallen out with Abby – something to do with a boy, I think – the twins are hyper enough to *need* to go back to school and Polly is most upset I haven't returned home with a tropical disease so she can discover some ground-breaking treatment and be the youngest person ever to receive a Nobel Prize.'

Gemma chuckled, but thinking of the kids led to thinking of Juliet's house, and that led to thinking of the house next door … Since they were being so open and honest with each other, there was one other subject she really needed to prod.

She looked out across the park. 'Have you seen Will?' she asked, keeping her tone light.

When she glanced back at Juliet, her expression was a little more rigid than it had been.

'He came to see me,' she said. 'To explain.'

Gemma nodded. So her sister wasn't ready to go that

far yet. It was too new, too raw, too tacked on to all the other things that had happened that week. The warmth she'd been feeling bled away a little. Maybe Juliet would never be ready. But that was the choice she'd made, and she was going to live with it, however difficult it was. It was time to stop pushing now. They'd covered enough ground for one day.

'So … about this guy on holiday? Please tell me that at least he was very, very hot.'

Juliet blushed, something she never did, and Gemma was tempted to chuckle.

'He was Italian.'

Gemma fanned herself down. 'Nuff said.'

The tea house wasn't far away and she caught Juliet by the arm and steered her in that direction. 'Care to join me in some coffee and something naughty? They do fabulous chocolate cheesecake.'

Juliet looked over Gemma's Lycra-clad form. 'I thought you were on a health kick.'

Gemma made a 'whatever' kind of face. 'Nah. I'll start Monday.'

Juliet frowned. 'But *today's* Monday.'

'Oh, well. Next Monday, then,' Gemma said, and she and Juliet walked into the tea house laughing.

&

CHAPTER THIRTY-TWO

It was a chilly but bright day in central Paris. Gemma walked along the banks of the Seine, a walkie-talkie in her hand, and went through the security cordon onto the Pont des Arts. Crowds had gathered at either end of the steel pedestrian bridge, just downstream from the Île de la Cité, hoping to catch a glimpse of two of Hollywood's bright young things, who were filming a romantic comedy right in that spot.

The two stars, Ruby Coleman and Jared Fisher, were talking with the director in the middle of the bridge, preparing to shoot the big reunion scene at the end of the film, and Gemma waited patiently for them to finish their discussion. While she did, she looked around, making sure she could see everything was going smoothly.

As well as the public, crowded at each end of the bridge, there were two huge groups of extras. It wasn't easy to use real people as bystanders when they were filming, so they tended to use people who were paid to act natural. Thankfully, since Gemma usually worked on big-budget films these days, she didn't have to be responsible for herding them herself – she had someone to do it for her.

She held up her hand to shade her eyes from the bright

winter sunshine and squinted. Calvin, the director, seemed to be having a really in-depth chat with Ruby and Jared. Probably a variation on the old *What's my motivation?* theme. That meant they could be going a while yet. She sighed. She needed to talk to him about one of the supporting cast who needed emergency dental treatment. It was going to mess up their schedule for the next few days.

She glanced around, trying not to notice how beautiful Paris looked in the January sunshine. She didn't want to see the river rushing under her feet, or see the art nouveau architecture or the ancient spires rising behind the chimney pots. It was bad enough being in the city of love with an aching heart without having it rammed up your nose.

Thank goodness she was crazy busy. Filming in a city centre made things even more challenging, but instead of resenting it, Gemma was welcoming the extra madness. It stopped her having time to think, which was good, because every time her brain had nothing to do there was only one path it wanted to take, and that path took her right back to Will.

If only … she kept thinking. If only she'd noticed what he was really like before, when Juliet and Greg had been married. If only Juliet's Italian hadn't turned out to be such a slimeball and she could have come home loved up and ready to move to Italy. There were a thousand ways her mind could play it. Not that it did her any good.

She and Juliet were only just patching things up again, and if she wrecked it now she knew there'd never be a second chance. She was just going to have to be patient, pray hard, and hope that whatever had been fizzling between her and

Will would last past the healing period. But there was a lot to heal. It could take months, or even years. There might never be a right time for them.

She marched forward and squinted at the trio in the middle of the bridge again. Seriously? What was taking all this time? *What's your motivation?* You're crazy in love with the girl and when you see her standing alone on the bridge, you run up to her and sweep her into your arms. How hard could it be?

Finally they all moved away from each other. Calvin came back to his bank of monitors at what the crew nicknamed 'video village' and Ruby and Jared took up their places on the bridge. Gemma sidled in close to the First AD and the director, waiting for an opportune moment. While some days she was quite happy to hang out on set and watch the action, all this lovey-dovey stuff they were up to today was just depressing. She wanted to be out of here and back to the safety of her car-park base as soon as possible.

Gemma watched on the monitors as the actors did their first take. Ruby was fab, the pro that she was, but this was Jared's first rom-com. He was more used to action movies and he'd been dropped in the deep end, since time restrictions on using this particular bridge meant they were shooting the end of the film first.

One of the crew behind her chuckled. 'He's running like the Terminator,' he said, and then everyone had to cover their mouths with their hands.

Gemma quite enjoyed the moment of hilarity. She hadn't had a lot to laugh about recently. It was true, though. Jared was running more like Bourne or Bond than a man trying to sweep his woman off her feet. And when he got to Ruby it was even worse. The kiss he delivered looked wooden and uncomfortable. Poor Ruby.

Gemma had worked with Calvin a few times before and she knew him well enough to see that he was getting really stressed. Now was probably not the best time to break the news about Miranda's broken crown. Maybe she'd better tell him later.

Her base was on the opposite side of the river, and it'd be much quicker if she could cross the bridge and walk back there, rather than having to trek round to the next bridge along, which she'd done when she'd got here. So she waited for the next take to end and when Calvin got up to go and talk to Jared again she followed him, intending to nip across the wooden bridge before filming recommenced.

She'd just passed the actors and director when she heard someone calling her name. She turned, frowning, but she couldn't see who it was. Flip. It was probably Charlie, the First AD. Why he wasn't using his walkie-talkie she'd never know. Her shoulders slumped. Now she'd have to go back to the monitor bank and she'd lose her opportunity to cross the river before they started up again. Thanks, Charlie.

She turned and headed back to where he was standing, but then she heard it again.

'Gemma!'

This time it definitely came from behind her. She spun around again, trying to see what the big emergency was about.

It was at that exact moment that one of the extras broke ranks and started running. Well, that was a certain way to get fired. What the heck was the guy up to?

And she could still hear someone calling her name.

Then everything went weird for a little bit. She realised the extra's mouth was moving about the same time she saw a security guard set off after him. And then she noticed that the shouts and the man's mouth were synchronised.

That's when her legs went wobbly. That's when she realised who it was running and shouting. It wasn't a faceless extra running towards her, it was Will.

Bystanders at the edge of the bridge seemed to have noticed that something was going on, because she could hear cheering. She wanted to start running too, but her legs didn't want to work, and neither did her lungs, so she just stood where she was and helplessly watched him sprinting towards her.

He slowed when he was a short distance away and walked the last few steps. Gemma pressed a hand to her chest. She needed to sit down. Now. Before she fell down. He was looking ever so serious.

'The first thing I want to know is if anyone on this film set has been pestering you.'

She shook her head.

'Good,' Will said, still looking quite stern, and then he added, 'because if anyone is going to be feeling you up on a film set, it's going to be me. And I'm going to start right now.'

And then all she could think about was the wonderful sensation of being in his arms, feeling his lips on hers. 'What …? How …?' she mumbled in between kisses.

Will reluctantly pulled back to look at her. 'Juliet came to see me yesterday. She said she realised she was suffering more from a case of hurt pride than a broken heart.'

Gemma's insides started to flutter. 'What does that mean?' she asked him, grabbing onto his coat and sounding more than a little desperate.

He smiled, slowly, like the sun coming out. 'It means she gives us her blessing.'

She knew she'd joked about Juliet being close to sainthood before, but now she was starting to think that she was something of a prophet herself. Juliet had done that? For her? Tears welled up in her eyes.

She ran her fingers up Will's cheeks, skimming his cheekbones, hardly daring to believe she was touching him. Did her sister know what she'd given her? Did she even realise how wonderful this man was? He might not earn big bucks or run around on film sets all day, but she didn't care about that. He was strong and trustworthy, brave and honourable. That sounded pretty much like a hero to her. And he'd just proved he had it in him to be crazy and impulsive! She reckoned she'd hit the jackpot.

'How … how did you get here?'

'Eurostar,' he replied, a naughty twinkle in his eye.

She punched him lightly on his arm. 'I meant on set. Security is pretty tight.'

He grinned at her. 'Just managed to charm a few people, use my creative resources, be in the right place at the right time. I think you're rubbing off on me.'

'You're insane!' she told him, looking around and realising they were holding up filming and that every one of their kisses had probably cost thousands of dollars. 'You couldn't have just used the phone?'

He shook his head. 'No.'

'Even after I ran away from you?'

Her confidence wobbled a bit as she said that. Because run away from him she had. She hadn't tried to fight for him, hadn't tried to stay.

'You didn't run away from me because you were scared,' Will said, his eyes blazing with warmth. 'You ran away because you thought you had to. You were being selfless and generous and it only made me realise even more how amazing you are.'

Gemma tried to say something back, but she discovered her throat had swollen up and it was difficult enough to swallow, let alone form words.

'And there's only one thing to do when a woman like that runs away from you.'

'What's that?' she managed to croak.

Will gave her his most dazzling and most sexy smile yet. 'You run after her.' And then he dipped her over and delivered another one of those kisses. Gemma reckoned this one had to be worth a million at least.

A few feet away a director and his two leading actors watched the unfolding scene with interest. Ruby was smiling, but Jared was looking a little gobsmacked. 'Who are these people?' he asked, although he'd been working with Gemma for a week and really should have recognised her by now.

Calvin just walked up to his male lead and prodded him on the chest. 'Don't you worry about that. Just watch and take notes, Bucko, because *that* is what I'm talking about …'

&

EPILOGUE

Christmas Eve was cold and frosty this year, leaving a dusting of glitter on the roof of Juliet's house. Half the local woodland was festooned inside, and white lights twinkled round the porch. She heard a car approach on the gravel drive and walked, smiling, to open the front door. Gemma emerged from her car with a tangle of shopping bags and yelled her greeting.

When she was inside she dropped the bags in an untidy heap and the two sisters hugged.

'How was Finland?' Juliet asked.

'Beautiful, but very, very cold,' Gemma said. 'Thank goodness I'm taking that job with the new production company, because I think I'm getting too old for all this running around after movie stars. I used to be able to put up with it, but nowadays I find myself wanting to give them a good, hard slap and tell them to get over themselves.'

Juliet waited while Gemma shrugged off her coat and hung it on the coatrack under the stairs. The kids had obviously trained her well when she'd been here last year. 'Do you have a firm start date yet?'

Gemma nodded and followed her into the kitchen.

'Beginning of February. I can't wait. They've leased offices in Soho, so it's almost commuting distance from here.'

'That'll be handy,' she said smoothly, 'for when you move in next door.'

Gemma looked so shocked Juliet was tempted to laugh.

'Let's get used to living in the same country as each other first, Sis! One step at a time. Nobody wants the next world war to start in Tunbridge Wells.'

Juliet just smiled, then looked first at the kettle and then at the fridge. 'Tea or wine?'

Gemma leaned against the kitchen counter. 'After that comment … wine. Definitely.'

They chatted while Juliet poured them both a glass then headed off to the living room where the kids were currently sprawled over the sofa watching a movie.

'Auntie Gemma!' Josh, Jake and Polly cried and came rushing towards their aunt. Juliet only had time to relieve her of her glass of wine before they all bundled on top of their aunt and knocked her onto one of the sofas.

'Boys!' Gemma yelled. 'I have warned you about the bouncing before!'

They twins stopped. Eventually. When Gemma had kissed them all and promised she'd brought presents with her, they allowed her to disentangle herself enough to sit up. Juliet handed Gemma back her wine glass as she looked around the living room.

'What happened to games night?' she asked, frowning.

'Well, Violet is out with her friends until eight thirty and we have something less … stressful … planned this year.' She gave Gemma a sheepish look. 'Some traditions have their expiry date, you know, and the kids wanted to do something different.'

'Such as?'

'Movies and pizza.' She frowned as she picked up the takeaway leaflet from the coffee table. 'Christmas Pizza', the kids said, but I can't find it on the menu anywhere.'

'Ah,' Gemma said.

Juliet frowned harder. She knew that look. 'Spill,' she said.

Her sister put on her best angelic face. 'We made it up last year. It's just normal pepperoni pizza with some … ah … additions.'

Juliet raised her eyebrows. 'Such as …?'

'Rudolph noses?' Gemma said hopefully.

Juliet didn't think she wanted to know how they featured into the pizza. 'Please tell me they're cherry tomatoes.'

Gemma shook her head.

'We found glacé cherries worked much better!' Polly piped up.

Gemma pulled her niece into a headlock and whispered loudly in her ear. 'Thanks for that, Polls. I was trying to break it to your mum gently!' Polly just giggled and slipped out of Gemma's hold.

Juliet was still trying not to shudder. *Eww.* Just the thought of it was enough to put her off the pizza entirely. Still, it was Christmas …

'You'd better go and see if you can find any in the larder,' she told the kids, and they ran off, squealing.

Gemma took a big slug of wine and looked at her sister.

'Okay, let me have it … What time are we getting up in the morning to start cooking?'

Juliet eased herself into an armchair. 'Not too late,' she said. 'About three thirty.'

Gemma spat out her wine. 'Three thirty! The flipping turkey must be the size of a grizzly bear!'

Juliet shook her head. 'Oh, that's not for the turkey. It's the time we're going to start stuffing the peacock.'

Gemma just stared at her.

She couldn't hold back any more, Juliet had to giggle. 'Had you there, didn't I?'

Her sister shook her head. 'I ought to rescind my offer to help for that.'

'Too late … I've got you on bread sauce duty, and possibly stuffing. I was going to get you to peel the veggies, but the kids begged me to let them do—'

She broke off when the doorbell rang. 'That's not the pizza man,' Juliet told Gemma. 'He said he wouldn't be here for another fifteen minutes.'

Gemma was instantly off the sofa and rushing to the front door. Juliet smiled as she watched her go. She'd been on location for a month – her last big film – but she'd come here first instead of going next door. That said something.

She decided not to go and greet her other guest yet, knowing that Will and her sister would probably want a bit of privacy. They were still so sweet together. And good for each other. Will's smiles were no longer rare, and he'd lost that slightly stuffy edge. And Gemma? Well, Gemma was still Gemma, but she seemed happier, more grounded.

She rose to kiss Will hello when they finally came into the

living room. Gemma's cheeks were a little flushed and her eyes were sparkling. Will, too, seemed so happy he couldn't stop looking at Gemma with barely contained adoration.

Juliet sipped her wine and smiled to herself. She'd been the sister to get a ring for Christmas last year, but she had a feeling that this year it might be Gemma's turn.

And, while her mind was on that subject …

She turned to her sister. 'Actually, I've got a favour to ask you.'

Her sister smiled at her. 'Anything.'

Juliet looked down into her wine glass. 'I wondered if you had any plans for New Year's Eve? Because I might need a babysitter.'

Gemma dropped into the chair opposite her and leaned forward. 'The guy? The hunky PE teacher? He finally asked you out?'

Juliet bit one side of her lip. 'Actually, I asked *him* out.'

Gemma's eyes grew wide, and then she chuckled. 'You go, girl!' she said, approval in her tone.

Juliet just smiled.